CUSTOMER
SERVICE
EXCELLENCE
UK
The Government Standard

Kent
County
Council

D1354980

C333638301

Also by Christopher Priest from Gollancz:

Indoctrinaire
Fugue for a Darkening Island
Inverted World
The Space Machine
A Dream of Wessex
The Affirmation
The Glamour
The Quiet Woman
The Prestige
The Extremes
The Separation
The Dream Archipelago
The Islanders
The Adjacent

The Space Machine

•

Christopher Priest

This edition first published in Great Britain in 2014
by Gollancz
An imprint of the Orion Publishing Group
Orion House, 5 Upper St Martin's Lane, London WC2H 9EA
An Hachette UK Company

1 3 5 7 9 10 8 6 4 2

A CIP catalogue record for this book
is available from the British Library

ISBN 978 0 575 12122 5

Typeset by Deltatype Ltd, Birkenhead, Merseyside

Printed and bound by CPI Group (UK) Ltd, Croydon, CR0 4YY

The Orion Publishing Group's policy is to use papers that are natural, renewable and recyclable products and made from wood grown in sustainable forests. The logging and manufacturing processes are expected to conform to the environmental regulations of the country of origin.

www.christopher-priest.co.uk
www.orionbooks.co.uk
www.gollancz.co.uk

To H. G. Wells

ONE

The Lady Commercial

•

I

In the April of 1893 I was staying in the course of my business at the Devonshire Arms in Skipton, Yorkshire. I was then twenty-three years of age, and enjoying a modest and not unsuccessful career as commercial representative of the firm of Josiah Westerman & Sons, Purveyors of Leather Fancy Goods. Not much will be said in this narrative of my employment, for even at that time it was not my major preoccupation, but it was instrumental, in its inglorious fashion, in precipitating the chain of events which are the major purpose of my story.

The Devonshire was a low, grey-brick commercial hotel, threaded with draughty and ill-lit corridors, drab with ageing paint and dark-stained panelling. The only congenial place in the hotel was the commercials' lounge, for although it was small and burdened with furniture – the over-stuffed easy chairs were placed so close together it was scarcely possible to walk between them – the room was warm in winter and had the advantage of gas-mantle lighting, whereas the only sources of illumination in the bedrooms were dim and smoky oil-lamps.

During the evenings there was little for a resident commercial to do but stay within the confines of the lounge and converse with his colleagues. For me, the hour between the completion of dinner and nine p.m. was the one that made me the most impatient, for by long-observed tacit agreement no one would smoke between those times, and it was the accepted period for conversation. At nine, though, the pipes and cigars would appear, the air would slowly turn a suffocating blue, heads would lean back on the antimacassars and eyes would close. Then, unobtrusively, I would perhaps read for a while, or write a letter or two.

On the evening of which I am particularly thinking I had been for a short stroll after dinner, and had returned to the hotel before nine. I made a brief visit to my room to don my smoking-jacket, then went to the ground floor and entered the commercials' lounge.

Three men were already there, and although it was still only seven minutes before nine I noticed that Hughes, a representative from a Birmingham machine-tool manufacturer, had started his pipe.

I nodded to the others, and went to a chair in the furthest corner of the room.

At nine-fifteen, Dykes came into the lounge. Dykes was a young man of about my own age, and although I had affected no interest in him it was his wont to address me in some confidence.

He came directly to my corner and sat opposite me. I pulled down the top leaf over the letter I had been drafting.

'Will you smoke, Turnbull?' he said to me, offering his cigarette case.

'No thank you.' I had smoked a pipe for a while, but had desisted for more than a year.

He took a cigarette for himself, and made a display of lighting it. Like me, Dykes was a commercial representative, and often declared I was too conservative in my outlook. I was usually entertained by his outgoing manner, in the way one may enjoy the excesses of others.

'I hear there's a lady commercial in tonight,' he said casually now, but leaning towards me slightly to add emphasis to his words. 'What do you make of that, Turnbull?'

'You surprise me,' I admitted. 'Are you sure of that?'

'I came in late this evening,' he said, lowering his voice. 'Happened to glance at the register. Miss A. Fitzgibbon of Surrey. Interesting, wouldn't you say?'

Somewhat aloof, as I saw myself to be, from the day-to-day concerns of my fellow commercials, I was nevertheless interested by what he said. One cannot help but become aware of the lore of one's own occupation, and it had long been rumoured that women were now being employed as representatives. I had never before met one myself, but it seemed logical that sales of certain requisites – shall we say of a toilette or boudoir nature – might be better negotiated by women. Certainly, some of the stores I called at employed women buyers, so there was no precedent barring their entry into the sales aspect of a transaction.

I glanced over my shoulder, although I knew that she could not have entered the lounge unnoticed.

'I haven't seen her,' I said.

'No, and we're not likely to! Do you think that Mrs Anson would allow a young lady of gentle breeding into a commercial lounge?'

'So you have seen the lady?' I said.

Dykes shook his head. 'She dined with Mrs Anson in the coffee-room. I saw a tray being taken there.'

I said, for my interest was persisting: 'Do you suppose that what is said about lady commercials has any substance?'

'Undoubtedly!' said Dykes at once. 'No profession for a gentlewoman.'

'But you said that this Miss Fitzgibbon was a gentle—'

'A euphemism, dear chap.' He leaned back in his easy chair, and drew pleasurably on his cigarette.

I usually found Dykes an amusing companion, for his ready abandonment of social niceties often meant that he would regale me with bawdy anecdotes. These I would listen to in envious silence, as most of my time was passed in enforced solitude. Many commercials were bachelors – perhaps by nature – and the life of constant movement from one town to another led to an inability to make permanent ties. Thus, when word that some firms now employed ladies as their representatives was rumoured, the smoking-rooms and commercial lounges of hotels all over the country had been sibilant with salacious speculation. Dykes himself had been a source of much information on the subject, but as time passed it became clear that there was to be no substantial change to our way of life. Indeed, this was the very first occasion on which I had even been aware that a lady commercial was staying in the same hotel as myself.

'You know, Turnbull, I fancy I shall introduce myself to Miss Fitzgibbon before the evening is out.'

'But what will you say? Surely you would require an introduction?'

'That will be simple to arrange. I shall merely go to the door of Mrs Anson's sitting-room, knock boldly, and invite Miss Fitzgibbon to take a short stroll with me before turning in.'

'I—' My sentence was cut short, for I had suddenly realized that Dykes could not be in earnest. He knew the proprietress of this hotel as well as I, and we both understood what kind of reception such a move could expect. Miss Fitzgibbon might well be an Emancipationist, but Mrs Anson was still firmly rooted in the 1860s.

'Why should I describe my strategy to you?' Dykes said. 'We shall both be here until the weekend; I shall tell you then how I have fared.'

I said: 'Could you not somehow discover which firm she represents? Then you could contrive a chance meeting with her during the day.'

Dykes smiled at me mysteriously.

'Maybe you and I think alike, Turnbull. I have already obtained that information. Would you care to place a small wager with me, the winner being the man who first speaks to the lady?'

I felt my face reddening. 'I do not bet, Dykes. Anyway, it would be foolish for me to compete with you, since you have an advantage.'

'Then I shall tell you what I know. She is not a commercial at all, but an amanuensis. She works for no firm, but is in the personal employ of an inventor. Or so my informant tells me.'

'An inventor?' I said, disbelieving. 'You cannot be serious!'

'That is what I have been told,' Dykes said. 'Sir William Reynolds by name, and a man of great eminence. I know nothing of that, nor care, for my interests lie with his assistant.'

I sat with my writing-tablet on my knees, quite taken aback by this unexpected information. In truth I had no interest in Dykes's nefarious designs, for I tried at all times to conduct myself with propriety, but the name of Sir William Reynolds was a different matter.

I stared at Dykes thoughtfully while he finished his cigarette, then stood up.

'I think I shall retire,' I said.

'But it's still early. Let us have a glass of wine together, on my account.' He reached over and pressed the electrical bell-push. 'I want to see you place that wager with me.'

'Thank you but no, Dykes. I have this letter to finish, if you will excuse me. Perhaps tomorrow evening ...?'

I nodded to him, then worked my way towards the door. As I reached the corridor outside, Mrs Anson approached the lounge door.

'Good evening, Mr Turnbull.'

'Good night, Mrs Anson.'

By the bottom of the staircase I noticed that the door to the sitting-room was ajar, but there was no sign of the lady guest.

Once in my room, I lighted the lamps and sat on the edge of my bed, trying to order my thoughts.

II

The mention of Sir William's name had a startling effect on me, for he was at that time one of the most famous scientists in England. Moreover, I had a great personal interest in matters indirectly concerned with Sir William, and the casual information Dykes had imparted was of the greatest interest to me.

In the 1880s and 1890s there was a sudden upsurge in scientific developments, and for those with an interest in such matters it was an enthralling period. We were on the verge of the Twentieth Century, and the prospect of going into a new era surrounded by scientific wonders was stimulating the best minds in the world.

It seemed that almost every week produced a new device which promised to alter our mode of existence: electric omnibuses, horseless carriages, the kinematograph, the American talking machines ... all these were very much on my mind.

Of these, it was the horseless carriage which had most caught my imagination. About a year before I had been fortunate enough to be given a ride on one of the marvellous devices, and since then had felt that in spite of the attendant noise and inconvenience such machines held great potential for the future.

It was as a direct result of this experience that I had involved myself – in however small a way – with this burgeoning development. Having noticed a newspaper article about American motorists, I had persuaded the proprietor of the firm that employed me, Mr Westerman himself, to introduce a new line to his range of goods. This was an instrument which I had named the Visibility Protection Mask. It was made of leather and glass, and was held in place over the eyes by means of straps, thus protecting them from flying grit, insects, and so forth.

Mr Westerman, it should be added, was not himself wholly convinced of the desirability of such a Mask. Indeed, he had manufactured only three sample models, and I had been given the commission to offer them to our regular customers, on the understanding that only after I had obtained firm orders would the Mask be made a permanent part of the Westerman range.

I treasured my idea, and I was still proud of my initiative, but I had been carrying my Masks in my samples-case for six months, and so far I had awakened not the slightest interest of any customer. It seemed that other people were not so convinced as I of the future of the horseless carriage.

Sir William Reynolds, though, was a different matter. He was already one of the most famous motorists in the country. His record speed of just over seventeen miles an hour, established on the run between Richmond and Hyde Park Corner, was as yet unbeaten by any other.

If I could interest him in my Mask, then surely others would follow!

In this way it became imperative that I introduce myself to Miss Fitzgibbon. That night, though, as I lay fretfully in my hotel bed, I could have had no conception of how deeply my Visibility Protection Mask was to change my life.

III

All during the following day, I was preoccupied with the problem of how to approach Miss Fitzgibbon. Although I made my rounds to the stores in the district I could not concentrate, and returned early to the Devonshire Arms.

As Dykes had said the evening before, it was most difficult to contrive a meeting with a member of the opposite sex in this hotel. There were no social courtesies open to me, and so I should have to approach Miss Fitzgibbon directly. I could, of course, ask Mrs Anson to introduce me to her, but I felt in all sincerity that her presence at the interview would be an impediment.

Further distracting me during the day had been my curiosity about Miss Fitzgibbon herself. Mrs Anson's protective behaviour seemed to indicate that she must be quite young, and indeed her style as a single woman was further evidence of this. If this were so, my task was greater, for surely she would mistake any advance I made towards her for one of the kind Dykes had been planning?

As the reception-desk was not attended, I took the opportunity to look surreptitiously at the register of guests. Dykes's information had not been misleading, for the last entry was in a neat, clear handwriting: Miss A. Fitzgibbon, Reynolds House, Richmond Hill, Surrey.

I looked into the commercial lounge before going up to my room. Dykes was there, standing in front of the fireplace reading The Times.

I proposed that we dine together, and afterwards take a stroll down to one of the public-houses in the town.

'What a splendid notion!' he said. 'Are you celebrating a success?'

'Not quite. I'm thinking more of the future.'

'Good strategy, Turnbull. Shall we dine at six?'

This we did, and soon after dinner we were ensconced in the snug bar of a public-house called The King's Head. When we were settled with two glasses of porter, and Dykes had started a cigar, I broached the subject uppermost on my mind.

'Are you wishing I'd made a wager with you last night?' I said.

'What do you mean?'

'Surely you understand.'

'Ah!' said Dykes. 'The lady commercial!'

'Yes. I was wondering if I would owe you five shillings now, had I entered a bet with you.'

'No such luck, old chap. The mysterious lady was closeted with Mrs Anson until I retired, and I saw no sign of her this morning. She is a prize which Mrs Anson guards jealously.'

'Do you suppose she is a personal friend?'

'I think not. She is registered as a guest.'

'Of course,' I said.

'You've changed your tune since last night. I thought you had no interest in the lady.'

I said quickly: 'I was just enquiring. You seemed bent on introducing yourself to her, and I wanted to know how you had fared.'

'Let me put it this way, Turnbull. I considered the circumstances, and judged that my talents were best spent in London. I can see no way of making the lady's acquaintance without involving Mrs Anson. In other words, dear chap, I am saving my energies for the weekend.'

I smiled to myself as Dykes launched into an account of his latest conquest, because although I had learned no more about the young lady I had at least established that I would not be in a misleading and embarrassing competitive situation.

I listened to Dykes until a quarter to nine, then suggested we return to the hotel, explaining that I had a letter to write. We parted company in the hall; Dykes walked into the commercial lounge, and I went upstairs to my room. The door to the sitting-room was closed, and beyond it I could hear the sound of Mrs Anson's voice.

TWO

A Conversation in the Night

•

I

The staff of the Devonshire Arms were in the habit-presumably at Mrs Anson's instruction – of sprinkling the shades of the oil-lamps with eau de cologne. This had the effect of infusing a cloying perfume through the first floor of the hotel, one so persistent that even now I cannot smell cologne without being reminded of the place.

On this evening, though, I thought I detected a different fragrance as I climbed the stairs. It was drier, less sickly, more redolent of herbs than Mrs Anson's perfumes ... but then I could smell it no more, and I went on into my room and closed the door.

I lit the two oil-lamps in my room, then tidied my appearance in front of the mirror. I knew I had alcohol on my breath, so I brushed my teeth, then sucked a peppermint lozenge. I shaved, combed my hair and moustache, and put on a clean shirt.

When this was done I placed an easy chair beside the door, and moved a table towards it. On this I placed one of the lamps, and blew out the other. As an afterthought I took one of Mrs Anson's bath-towels, and folded it over the arm of the chair. Then I was ready.

I sat down, and opened a novel.

More than an hour passed, during which although I sat with the book on my knee, I read not one word. I could hear the gentle murmur of conversation drifting up from the downstairs rooms, but all else was still.

At last I heard a light tread on the stairs, and at once I was ready. I put aside the book, and draped the bath-towel over my arm. I waited until the footsteps had passed my door, and then I let myself out.

In the dim light of the corridor I saw a female figure, and as she heard me she turned. It was a chambermaid, carrying a hot water bottle in a dark-red cover.

'Good evening, sir,' she said, making a small sullen curtsey in my direction, then continued on her way.

I went across the corridor into the bath-room, closed the door, counted to one hundred slowly, and then returned to my room.

Once more I waited, this time in considerably greater agitation than before.

Within a few minutes I heard another tread on the stairs, this time rather heavier. Again I waited until the footsteps had passed before emerging. It was Hughes, on his way to his room. We nodded to each other as I opened the door of the bathroom.

When I returned to my own room I was growing angry with myself for having to resort to such elaborate preparations and minor deceptions. But I was determined to go through with this in the way I had planned.

On the third occasion I heard footsteps I recognized Dykes's tread, as he bounded up taking two steps at a time. I was thankful not to have to go through the charade with the bath-towel.

Another half-hour passed and I was beginning to despair, wondering if I had miscalculated. After all, Miss Fitzgibbon might well be staying in Mrs Anson's private quarters; I had no reason to suppose that she would have been allocated a room on this floor. At length, though, I was in luck. I heard a soft tread on the staircase, and this time when I looked down the corridor I saw the retreating back of a tall young woman. I tossed the towel back into my room, snatched up my samples-case, closed the door quietly and followed her.

If she was aware that I was behind her, she showed no sign of it. She walked to the very end of the corridor, to where a small staircase led upwards. She turned, and climbed the steps.

I hastened to the end of the corridor, and as I reached the bottom of the steps I saw that she was on the point of inserting a key into the door. She looked down at me.

'Excuse me, ma'am,' I said. 'Allow me to introduce myself. I am Turnbull, Edward Turnbull.'

As she regarded me I felt immensely foolish, peering up at her from the bottom of the steps. She said nothing, but nodded slightly at me.

'Do I have the pleasure of addressing Miss Fitzgibbon?' I went on. 'Miss A. Fitzgibbon?'

'That is I,' she said, in a pleasant, well modulated voice.

'Miss Fitzgibbon,! know you will think this an extraordinary request, but I have something here I think will be of interest to you. I wondered if I might show it to you?'

For a moment she said nothing, but continued to stare down at me. Then she said: 'What is it, Mr Turnbull?'

I glanced along the corridor, fearing that at any moment another of the guests would appear.

I said: 'Miss Fitzgibbon, may I come up to you?'

'No, you may not. I shall come down.'

She had a large leather hand-bag, and she placed this on the tiny landing beside her door. Then, raising her skirt slightly, she came slowly down the steps towards me.

When she stood before me in the corridor, I said: 'I will not detain you for more than a few moments. It was most fortunate that you should be staying in this hotel.'

While I spoke I had crouched down on the floor, and was fumbling with the catch of my samples-case. The lid came open, and I took out one of the Visibility Protection Masks. I stood up, holding it in my hand, and noticed that Miss Fitzgibbon was regarding me curiously. There was something about her forthright gaze that was most disconcerting.

She said: 'What do you have there, Mr Turnbull?'

'I call it the Visibility Protection Mask,' I said. She made no reply, so I went on in some confusion: 'You see, it is suited for passengers as well as the driver, and can be removed at a moment's notice.'

At this, the young lady stepped back from me, and seemed to be about to ascend the steps once more.

'Please wait!' I said. 'I am not explaining very well.'

'Indeed you are not. What is it you have in your hand, and why should it be of such interest to me that you accost me in an hotel corridor?'

Her expression was so cold and formal I did not know how to phrase my words. 'Miss Fitzgibbon, I understand that you are in the employ of Sir William Reynolds?'

She nodded to confirm this, so at once I stuttered out an account of how I felt sure he would be interested in my Mask.

'But you have still not told me what it is.'

'It keeps grit out of one's eyes when motoring,' I said, and on a sudden impulse I raised the Mask to my eyes, and held it in place with my hands. At this the young lady laughed abruptly, but I felt that it was not an unkind laughter.

'They are motoring goggles!' she said. 'Why did you not say?'

'You have seen them before?' I said in surprise.

'They are common in America.'

'Then Sir William already possesses some?' I said.

'No ... but he probably feels he does not need them.'

I crouched down again, hunting through my samples-case.

'There is a ladies' model,' I said, searching anxiously through the various products that I kept in my case. At last I found the smaller variety that Mr Westerman's factory had produced, and stood up, holding it out to her. In my haste I inadvertently knocked my case, and a pile of photograph albums, wallets and writing-cases spilled on the floor. 'You may try this on, Miss Fitzgibbon. It's made of the best kid.'

As I looked again at the young lady, I thought for a moment that her laughter was continuing, but she held her face perfectly seriously.

'I'm not sure that I need—'

'I assure you that it is comfortable to wear.'

My earnestness at last won through, for she took the leather goggles from me.

'There's an adjustable strap,' I said. 'Please try it on.'

I bent down once more, and thrust my spilled samples back into the case. As I did so, I glanced down the corridor again.

When I stood up, Miss Fitzgibbon had raised the Mask to her forehead, and was trying to connect the strap. The large, flowered hat that she was wearing made this exceptionally difficult. If I had felt foolish at the beginning of this interview, then it was nothing to what I now felt. My impulsive nature and awkwardness of manner had led me to a situation of the most embarrassing kind. Miss Fitzgibbon was clearly trying to humour me, and as she fumbled with the clasp I wished I had the strength to snatch the goggles away from her and run shamefacedly to my room. Instead, I stood lamely before her, watching her efforts with the strap. She was wearing a patient smile.

'It appears to have become caught in my hair, Mr Turnbull.'

She tugged at the strap, but frowned as the hairs were pulled. I wanted to help her in some way, but I was too nervous of her.

She tugged again at the strap, but the metal clasp was tangled in the strands of hair.

At the far end of the corridor I heard the sound of voices, and the creak of the wooden staircase. Miss Fitzgibbon heard the sounds too, for she also looked that way.

'What am I to do?' she said softly. 'I cannot be found with this in my hair.'

She pulled again, but winced.

'May I help?' I said, reaching forward.

A shadow appeared on the wall by the top of the staircase, thrown by the lamps in the hallway.

'We will be discovered at any moment!' said Miss Fitzgibbon, the goggles swinging beside her face. 'We had better step into my room for a few minutes.'

The voices were coming closer.

'Your room?' I said in astonishment. 'Do you not want a chaperone? After all—'

'Whom would you propose to chaperone me?' said Miss Fitzgibbon. 'Mrs Anson?'

Raising her skirt again, she hurried up the steps towards the door. After hesitating another second or two I took up my samples-case, holding the lid down with my hand, and followed. I waited while the young lady unlocked the door, and a moment later we were inside.

II

The room was larger than mine, and more comfortable. There were two gas-mantles against the wall, and when Miss Fitzgibbon turned them up the room was filled with a bright, warm radiance. A coal fire burned in the grate, and the windows were richly curtained with long, velvet drapes. In one corner there was a large French bedstead, with the covers turned down. Most of the space, however, was given over to furniture which would not have looked out of place in the average parlour, with a chaise longue, two easy chairs, several rugs, an immense dresser, a bookcase and a small table.

I stood nervously by the door, while Miss Fitzgibbon went to a mirror and untangled the goggles from her hair. She placed these on the table.

When she had removed her hat, she said: 'Please sit down, Mr Turnbull.'

I looked at the goggles. 'I think I should leave now.'

Miss Fitzgibbon was silent, listening to the sound of the voices as they passed the bottom of the stairs.

'Perhaps it would be as well if you stayed a little longer,' she said. 'It would not do for you to be seen leaving my room at this late hour.'

I laughed politely with her, but I must confess to being considerably taken aback by such a remark.

I sat down in one of the easy chairs beside the table and Miss Fitzgibbon went to the fireplace and poked the coals so that they flared up more brightly.

'Please excuse me for a moment,' she said. As she passed me I sensed that she had about her a trace of the herbal fragrance I had noticed earlier. She went through an inner door, and closed it.

I sat silently, cursing my impulsive nature. I was sorely embarrassed by this incident, for Miss Fitzgibbon clearly had no need for, nor interest in, my motoring Mask. The notion that she would persuade Sir William to experiment with my goggles was even more unlikely. I had annoyed and compromised her, for if Mrs Anson, or indeed anyone else in the hotel, should discover that I had been alone in her room at night, then the young lady's reputation would be permanently marked.

When Miss Fitzgibbon returned, some ten minutes later, I heard the sound of a cistern hissing in the next room, and surmised that it must be a private bath-room. This seemed to be so, for Miss Fitzgibbon had apparently renewed her *maquillage*, and her hair was arranged differently, so that the tight bun she had been wearing had been loosened to allow some strands of her hair to fall about her shoulders. As she moved past me to sit in the other chair I noticed that the herbal fragrance was more noticeable.

She sat down, and leaned back with a sigh. Her behaviour towards me was entirely without ceremony.

'Well, Mr Turnbull,' she said. 'I find I owe you an apology. I'm sorry I was stuffy to you outside,'

'It is I who should apologize,' I said at once. 'I—'

'It was a natural reaction, I'm afraid,' she went on, as if she had not heard me. 'I've just spent the last four hours with Mrs Anson, and she seems never to be at a loss for words.'

'I felt sure you were a friend of hers,' I said.

'She has appointed herself my guardian and mentor. I accept a lot of advice from her.' Miss Fitzgibbon stood up again, and went to the dresser and produced two glasses. 'I know you drink, Mr Turnbull, for I have smelled your breath. Would you care for a glass of brandy?'

'Thank you, yes,' I said, swallowing hard.

She poured some brandy from a metal flask which she took from her hand-bag, and placed the two glasses on the table between us. 'Like you, Mr Turnbull, I sometimes find the need for fortification.'

She sat down again. We raised glasses, and sipped the drink.

'You have lapsed into silence,' she said. 'I hope I have not alarmed you.'

I stared at her helplessly, wishing that I had never set out on this naive enterprise.

'Do you come to Skipton frequently?' she said.

'About two or three times a year. Miss Fitzgibbon, I think I should bid you good-night. It is not proper for me to be here with you alone.'

'But I still haven't discovered why you were so eager to show me your goggles.'

'I felt you might influence Sir William to consider trying them.'

She nodded her understanding. 'And you are a goggles salesman?'

'No, Miss Fitzgibbon. You see, the firm I am employed by is a manufacturer of . . .'

My voice had tailed away, for I had heard in the same instant the sound that now clearly distracted Miss Fitzgibbon. We had both heard, just beyond the door, a creaking of floorboards.

Miss Fitzgibbon raised a finger to her lips, and we sat in anguished silence. A few moments later there was a sharp and peremptory rapping on the door!

III

'Miss Fitzgibbon!' It was Mrs Anson's voice.

I stared desperately at my new friend.

'What shall we do?' I whispered. 'If I am found here at this hour—'

'Keep quiet . . . leave it to me.'

From outside, again: 'Miss Fitzgibbon!'

She moved quickly to the far side of the room, and stood beside the bed.

'What is it, Mrs Anson?' she called, in a faint, tired-seeming voice.

There was a short silence. Then: 'Has the maid brought a hot water bottle to your room?'

'Yes, thank you. I am already abed.'

'With the lamps still alight, Miss Fitzgibbon?'

The young lady pointed desperately at the door, and waved her hands at me. I understood immediately, and moved quickly to one side so that I could not be seen through the keyhole.

'I am doing a little reading, Mrs Anson. Good night to you.'

There was another silence from beyond the door, during which I felt I must surely shout aloud to break the tension!

'I thought I heard the sound of a man's voice,' said Mrs Anson.

'I am quite alone,' said Miss Fitzgibbon. I saw that her face was flushing red, although whether it was from embarrassment or anger I could not tell.

'I don't think I am mistaken.'

'Please wait a moment,' said Miss Fitzgibbon.

She crept over to me, and raised her mouth until it was beside my ear.

'I shall have to let her in,' she whispered. 'I know what to do. Please turn your back.'

'What?' I said in astonishment.

'Turn your back ... please!'

I stared at her in anguish for a moment longer, then did as she said. I heard her move away from me towards the wardrobe, and then there came the sound of her pulling at the clasps and buttons of her gown. I closed my eyes firmly, covering them with my hand. The enormity of my situation was without parallel.

I heard the wardrobe door close, and then felt the touch of a hand on my arm. I looked: Miss Fitzgibbon was standing beside me, a long striped flannel dressing-gown covering her. She had taken the pins from her hair so that it fell loosely about her face.

'Take these,' she whispered, thrusting the two brandy-glasses into my hands. 'Wait inside the bath-room.'

'Miss Fitzgibbon, I really must insist!' said Mrs Anson.

I stumbled towards the bath-room door. As I did so I glanced back and saw Miss Fitzgibbon throwing back the covers of the bed and crumpling the linen and bolster. She took my samples-case, and thrust it under the chaise longue. I went inside the bath-room and closed the door. In the dark I leaned back against the door frame, and felt my hands trembling.

The outer door was opened.

'Mrs Anson, what is it you want?'

I heard Mrs Anson march into the room. I could imagine her glaring suspiciously about, and I waited for the moment of her irruption into the bath-room.

'Miss Fitzgibbon, it is very late. Why are you not yet asleep?'

'I am doing some reading. Had you not knocked when you did, I dare say I should be asleep at this moment.'

'I distinctly heard a male voice.'

'But you can see... I am alone. Could it not have been from the next room?'

'It came from in here.'

'Were you listening at the door?'

'Of course not! I was passing down the lower corridor on the way to my own room.'

'Then you could easily have been mistaken. I too have heard voices.'

The tone of Mrs Anson's words changed suddenly. 'My dear Amelia, I am concerned only for your well-being. You do not know these commercial men as well as I. You are young and innocent, and I am responsible for your safety.'

'I'm twenty-two years of age, Mrs Anson and I am responsible for my safety. Now please leave me, as I wish to go to sleep.'

Again, Mrs Anson's tone changed. 'How do I know you're not deceiving me?'

'Look around, Mrs Anson!' Miss Fitzgibbon came to the bath-room door, and threw it open. It banged against my shoulder, but served to conceal me behind it. 'Look everywhere! Would you care to inspect my wardrobe? Or would you prefer to peer under my bed?'

'I here is no need for unpleasantness, Miss Fitzgibbon. I am quite prepared to take your word.'

'Then kindly leave me in peace, as I have had a long day at work, and I wish to go to sleep.'

There was a short silence. Then Mrs Anson said: 'Very well, Amelia. Good night to you.'

'Good night, Mrs Anson.'

I heard the woman walk from the room, and down the stairs outside. There was a much longer silence, and then I heard the outer door close.

Miss Fitzgibbon came to the bath-room, and leaned weakly against the door-post.

'She's gone,' she said.

IV

Miss Fitzgibbon took one of the glasses from me, and swallowed the brandy.

'Would you like some more?' she said softly.

'Yes, please.'

The flask was now nearly empty, but we shared what remained.

I looked at Miss Fitzgibbon's face, pale in the gaslight, and wondered if I looked as ashen.

'I must leave at once, of course,' I said.

She shook her head. 'You would be seen. Mrs Anson wouldn't dare come to the room again, but she will not go straight to bed.'

'Then what can I do?'

'We'll have to wait. I should think if you leave in about an hour's time she will no longer be around.'

'We are behaving as if we are guilty,' I said. 'Why can I not go now, and tell Mrs Anson the truth of the matter?'

'Because we have already resorted to deception, and she has seen me in my nightwear.'

'Yes, of course.'

'I shall have to turn off the gaslights, as if I have gone to bed. There is a small oil-lamp, and we can sit by that.' She indicated a folding dressing-screen. 'If you would move that in front of the door, Mr Turnbull, it will mask the light and help subdue our voices.'

'I'll move it at once,' I said.

Miss Fitzgibbon put another lump of coal on the fire, lit the oil-lamp, and turned off the gas-mantles.

I helped her move the two easy chairs towards the fireplace, then placed the lamp on the mantelpiece.

'Do you mind waiting a while?' she asked me.

'I should prefer to leave,' I said uncomfortably, 'but I think you are right. I should not care to face Mrs Anson at this moment.'

'Then please try to be less agitated.'

I said: 'Miss Fitzgibbon, I should feel much more relaxed if you would put on your clothes again.'

'But beneath this gown I am wearing my underclothing.'

'Even so.'

I went into the bath-room for a few minutes, and when I returned she had replaced her dress. Her hair was still loose, though, which I found pleasing, for I felt her face was better suited when framed in this way.

As I sat down, she said to me: 'Can I ask one more favour of you, without further shocking you?'

'What is that?'

'I will be more at ease during the next hour if you would stop addressing me by my surname. My name is Amelia.'

'I know,' I said. 'I heard Mrs Anson. I am Edward.'

'You are so formal, Edward.'

'I can't help it,' I said. 'It is what I am used to.'

The tension had left me, and I felt very tired. Judging by the way Miss Fitzgibbon – or Amelia – was sitting, she felt the same. The abandonment of formal address was a similar relaxation, as if Mrs Anson's abrupt intrusion had swept aside the normal courtesies. We had suffered, and survived, a potential catastrophe and it had drawn us together.

'Do you think that Mrs Anson suspected I was here, Amelia?' I said.

She glanced shrewdly at me. 'No, she knew you were here.'

'Then I have compromised you!'

'It is I who have compromised you. The deception was of my own invention.'

I said: 'You're very candid. I don't think I have ever met anyone like you.'

'Well, in spite of your stuffiness, Edward, I don't think I've ever met anyone quite like you before.'

V

Now that the worst was over, and the rest could be dealt with in good time, I found that I was able to enjoy the intimacy of the situation. Our two chairs were close together in warmth and semi-darkness, the brandy was glowing within, and the light from the oil-lamp laid subtle and pleasing highlights on Amelia's features. All this made me reflective in a way that had nothing whatsoever to do with the circumstances that had brought us together. She seemed to me to be a person of wonderful beauty and presence of mind, and the thought of leaving her when my hour's wait was over was too unwelcome to contemplate.

At first it was I who led the conversation, talking a little of myself. I explained how my parents had emigrated to America soon after I had left school, and that since then I had lived alone while working for Mr Westerman.

'You never felt any desire to go with your parents to America?' Amelia said.

'I was very tempted. They write to me frequently, and America seems to be an exciting country. But I felt that I scarcely knew England, and that I should like to live my own life here for a while, before joining them.'

'And do you know England any better now?'

'Hardly,' I said. 'Although I spend my weeks outside London, I spend most of my time in hotels like this.'

With this, I enquired politely of her own background.

She told me that her parents were dead – there had been a

sinking at sea while she was still a child – and that since then she had been under the legal guardianship of Sir William. He and her father had been friends since their own schooldays, and in her father's will this wish had been expressed.

'So you also live at Reynolds House?' I said. 'It is not merely employment?'

'I am paid a small wage for my work, but Sir William has made a suite of rooms in one of the wings available to me.'

'I should greatly like to meet Sir William,' I said, fervently.

'So that he may try your goggles in your presence?' Amelia said.

'I am regretting that I brought them to you.'

'And I am glad you did. You have inadvertently enlivened my evening. I was beginning to suspect that Mrs Anson was the only person in this hotel, so tight was her hold on me. Anyway, I'm sure Sir William will consider purchasing your goggles, even though he does not drive his horseless carriage these days.'

I looked at her in surprise. 'But I understood Sir William was a keen motorist. Why has he lost interest?'

'He is a scientist, Edward. His invention is prolific, and he is constantly turning to new devices.'

In this way we conversed for a long time, and the longer we spoke the more relaxed I became. Our subjects were inconsequential for the most part, dwelling on our past lives and experiences. I soon learnt that Amelia was much better travelled than me, having accompanied Sir William on some of his overseas journeys. She told me of her visit to New York, and to Dresden and Leipzig, and I was greatly interested.

At last the fire burned down, and we had drunk the last of the brandy.

I said, regretfully: 'Amelia, do you think I should now return to my room?'

For a moment her expression did not change, but then she smiled briefly and to my surprise laid her hand gently on my arm.

'Only if you wish to,' she said.

'Then I think I shall stay a few minutes longer.'

Immediately I said this I regretted it. In spite of her friendly gesture I felt that we had spoken enough of the matters that interested us, and that further delay was only an admission of the considerable degree of distraction her nearness to me was causing. I had no idea how long it was since Mrs Anson had left us – and to take out my watch would have been unpardonable – but I felt sure that it must be much more than the hour we had agreed. Further delay was improper.

Amelia had not removed her hand from my arm.

'We must speak again, Edward,' she said. 'Let us meet in London one evening; perhaps you would invite me to join you for dinner. Then, without having to hush our voices, we can talk to our hearts' content.'

I said: 'When are you returning to Surrey?'

'I think it will be tomorrow afternoon.'

'I shall be in town during the day. Will you join me for luncheon? There is a small inn on the Ilkley road ...'

'Yes, Edward. I shall enjoy that.'

'Now I had better return.' I took my watch from my pocket, and saw that an hour and a half had elapsed since Mrs Anson's intrusion. 'I'm very sorry to have talked for so long.'

Amelia said nothing, but simply shook her head slowly.

I took my samples-case, and walked quietly to the door. Amelia stood up too, and blew out the oil-lamp.

'I'll help you with the screen,' she said.

The only illumination in the room was from the dying embers of the fire. I saw Amelia silhouetted against the glow as she came towards me. Together we shifted the folding screen to one side, then I turned the handle of the door. All was still and silent beyond. Suddenly, in that great quietness I wondered how well the screen had muffled our voices, and whether in fact our innocent liaison had been overheard by more than one other person.

I turned back to her.

'Good night, Miss Fitzgibbon,' I said.

Her hand touched my arm again, and I felt a warmth of breath on my cheek. Her lips touched me for a fraction of a second.

'Good night, Mr Turnbull.' Her fingers tightened on my arm, then she moved back and her door closed silently.

VI

My room and bed were cold, and I could not sleep. I lay awake all night, my thoughts circling endlessly around subjects that could not be further removed from my immediate surroundings. In the morning, surprisingly alert in spite of my sleeplessness, I was first down to the breakfast-room, and as I sat at my usual table the head waiter approached me.

'Mrs Anson's compliments, sir,' he said. 'Would you kindly attend to this directly you have finished breakfast?'

I opened the slim brown envelope and found that it contained my account. When I left the breakfast-room I discovered that my luggage had been packed, and was ready for me in the entrance hall. The head waiter took my money, and conducted me to the door. None of the other guests had seen me leave; there had been no sign of Mrs Anson. I stood in the sharp cool of the morning air, still stunned by the abruptness of my enforced departure.

After a while I carried my bags to the station and deposited them at the luggage office. I stayed in the vicinity of the hotel all day, but saw no sign of Amelia. At midday I went to the inn on the Ilkley road, but she did not appear. As evening drew on I went back to the station, and caught the last train of the day to London.

THREE

The House on Richmond Hill

•

I

During the week following my premature return to Skipton, I was away on business in Nottingham. Here I applied myself to my work to such a degree that I adequately made up for the poor sales I had achieved in Skipton. By the Saturday evening, when I returned to my lodgings near Regent's Park, the incident had receded to a regrettable memory. To say this is not wholly accurate, however, for in spite of the consequences, meeting Amelia had been an uplifting experience. I felt I should not hope to see her again, but I did feel the need to apologize.

As I should have known it would, though, the next move came from Amelia, for waiting for me on that Saturday evening was a letter postmarked in Richmond.

The main part of the letter was type-written, and simply stated that Sir William had been told of the motoring aid I had demonstrated, and that he had expressed a desire to meet me. Accordingly, I was invited to the house on Sunday, 21 st May, when Sir William would be glad to speak to me over afternoon tea. It was signed: 'A. Fitzgibbon'.

Underneath this main message, Amelia had added a hand-written postscript:

> Sir William is usually busy in his laboratory during most of the daylight hours, so would you care to arrive at about 2.00 p.m.?

As the weather is now so much finer I thought you and I might enjoy bicycling through Richmond Park.

Amelia

I did not take long to make up my mind. Indeed, within minutes I had written my acceptance, and posted it within the hour. I was very glad to be invited to tea.

II

On the appointed day I left Richmond Station, and walked slowly through the town. Most of the shops were closed, but there was much traffic – mostly phaetons and broughams, carrying families on Sunday outings – and the pavements were crowded with pedestrians. I strolled along with everyone else, feeling smart and fashionable in the new clothes I had bought the day before. To celebrate the occasion I had even indulged myself in the extravagance of a new straw boater, and this I wore at a jaunty angle, reflecting the carefree mood I was in. The only reminder of my normal way of life was the samples-case I carried. This I had emptied of everything except the three pairs of goggles. Even the unwonted lightness of the case, though, emphasized the special nature of this visit.

I was far too early, of course, having left my lodgings soon after breakfast. I was determined not to be late, and so had overestimated the amount of time it would take me to reach here. I had enjoyed a leisurely walk through London to Waterloo Station, the train journey had taken only twenty minutes or so, and here I was, enjoying the mild air and warm sunshine of a May morning.

In the centre of the little town I passed the church as the congregation was leaving, walking out into the sunlight, the gentlemen calm and formal in their suits, the ladies gay in bright clothes and carrying sunshades. I walked on until I reached Richmond Bridge, and here I stepped out over the Thames, looking down at the boats plying between the wooded banks.

It was all such a contrast from the bustle and smells of London;

much as I liked to live in the metropolis, the ever-present press of people, the racket of the traffic and the dampening grey of the industrial pall that drifted over the rooftops all made for an unconscionable pressure on one's mind. It was reassuring to find a place like this, such a short journey from the centre of London, that enjoyed an elegance that too often I found easy to forget still existed.

I continued my stroll along one of the riverside walks, then turned round and headed back into the town. Here I found a restaurant open, and ordered myself a substantial lunch. With this finished, I returned to the station, having previously forgotten to find out the times of the trains returning to London in the evening.

At last it was time to set out for Richmond Hill, and I walked back through the town, following The Quadrant until I came to the junction with the road which led down to Richmond Bridge. Here I followed a smaller road which forked to the left, climbing the Hill. All along my left-hand side there were buildings; at first, near the bottom of the Hill, the houses were terraced, with one or two shops. At the end of the terrace there was a public house – The Queen Victoria, as I recall – and beyond this the style and class of house changed noticeably.

Several were set a long way back from the road, almost invisible behind the thickly growing trees. To my right there was parkland and more trees, and as I climbed higher I saw the sweeping curve of the Thames through the meadows by Twickenham. It was a most beautiful and peaceful place.

At the top of the Hill the road became a pitted cart-track, leading through Richmond Gate into the Park itself, and the pavement ceased to exist altogether. At this point there was a narrower track, leading more directly up the slope of the Hill, and I walked this way. Shortly along this track I saw a gateway with Reynolds House carved into the sandstone posts, and I knew I had come to the right place.

The driveway was short, but described a sharp S, so that the house was not visible from the gate. I followed the drive, remarking to myself on the way in which the trees and shrubbery had been allowed to grow unhindered. In several places the growths were so wild that the drive was barely wide enough to allow passage of a carriage.

In a moment the house came into sight, and I was at once impressed by its size. The main part of the house seemed, to my untrained eye, to be about one hundred years old, but two large and more modern wings had been added at each end, and a part of the courtyard so produced had been roofed over with a wooden-framed glass structure, rather like a greenhouse.

In the immediate vicinity of the house the shrubbery had been cut back, and a well-kept lawn lay to one side of the house, stretching round to the far side.

I saw that the main entrance was partially concealed behind a part of the glasshouse – at first glance I had not noticed it – and walked in that direction. There seemed to be no one about; the house and grounds were silent, and there was no movement at any of the windows.

As I walked past the windows of the conservatory-like extension, there was a sudden scream of metal upon metal, accompanied by a blaze of yellow light. For an instant I saw the shape of a man, hunched forward, and silhouetted by a blaze of sparks. Then the grinding ceased, and again all became dim within.

I pressed the electrical bell-push by the door, and after a few moments the door was opened by a plump, middle-aged woman in a black dress and white apron. I removed my hat.

'I should like to see Miss Fitzgibbon,' I said, as I stepped into the hall. 'I believe I am expected.'

'Do you have a card, sir?'

I was about to produce my regular business-card, supplied by Mr Westerman, but then recalled that this was more of a personal visit. 'No, but if you would say it is Mr Edward Turnbull.'

'Will you wait?'

She showed me into a reception-room, and closed the doors behind me.

I must have walked a little too energetically up the Hill, for I found that I was hot and flushed, and my face was damp with perspiration. I mopped my face with my kerchief as quickly as possible, then, to calm myself, I glanced around the room, hoping that an appraisal of its furniture would gain me an insight into Sir William's tastes. In fact, the room was ill-furnished to the point of bareness. A small octagonal table stood before the fireplace, and beside it were two faded easy chairs, but these, apart from the curtains and a threadbare carpet, were all that were there.

Presently, the servant returned.

'Would you please come this way, Mr Turnbull?' she said. 'You may leave your case here in the hallway.'

I followed her along a corridor, then turned to the left and came into a comfortable drawing-room, which opened on to the garden by way of a french window. The servant indicated that I should pass through, and as I did so I saw Amelia sitting at a white, wrought-iron table placed beneath two apple trees on the lawn.

'Mr Turnbull, ma'am,' said the woman, and Amelia set aside the book she had been reading.

'Edward,' she said. 'You're earlier than I expected. That's wonderful ... it's such a lovely day for a ride!'

I sat down on the opposite side of the little table. I was aware that the servant was still standing by the french window.

'Mrs Watchets, will you bring us some lemonade?' Amelia said to her, then turned to me. 'You must be thirsty from your walk up the Hill. We'll have just one glass each, then set off at once.'

It was delightful to be with her again, and such a pleasant surprise that she was as lovely as I had remembered her. She was wearing a most pleasing combination of white blouse and dark blue silk skirt, and on her head she had a flowered raffia bonnet. Her long auburn hair, finely brushed and held behind her ears with a clip, fell neatly down her back. She was sitting so that the sunlight fell across her face, and as the branches of the apple trees moved in the gentle breeze, their shadows seemed to stroke the skin of her face. Her profile was presented to me: she was beautiful in many ways, not least that her fine features were exquisitely framed by the style of hair. I admired the graceful way she sat, the delicacy of her fair skin, the candour of her eyes.

'I haven't brought a bicycle with me,' I said. 'I wasn't—'

'We have plenty here, and you may use one of those. I'm delighted you could come today, Edward. There are so many things I have to tell you.'

'I'm terribly sorry if I got you into trouble,' I said, wanting to get off my chest the one matter that had been preoccupying me. 'Mrs Anson was in no doubt as to my presence in your room.'

'I understand you were shown the door.'

'Directly after breakfast,' I said. 'I didn't see Mrs Anson ...'

At that moment Mrs Watchets reappeared, bearing a tray with a glass jug and two tumblers, and I allowed my sentence to go unfinished. While Mrs Watchets poured out the drinks, Amelia pointed out to me a rare South American shrub growing in the garden (Sir William had brought it back with him from one of his overseas journeys), and I expressed the greatest interest in it.

When we were once more alone, Amelia said: 'Let us talk of those matters while we are riding. I'm sure Mrs Watchets would be as scandalized as Mrs Anson to hear of our nocturnal liaisons.'

There was something about her use of the plural that sent a pleasurable, though not entirely guiltless, thrill through me.

The lemonade was delicious: ice-cold, and with a sharp hint of sourness that stimulated the palate. I finished mine with immoderate speed.

'Tell me a little of Sir William's work,' I said. 'You told me that he has lost interest in his horseless carriage. What is he engaged in at the moment?'

'Perhaps if you are to meet Sir William, you should ask him that yourself. But it is no secret that he has built a heavier-than-air flying machine.'

I looked at her in amazement.

'You cannot be serious!' I said. 'No machine can fly!'

'Birds fly; they are heavier than air.'

'Yes, but they have wings.'

She stared at me thoughtfully for a moment. 'You had better see it for yourself, Edward. It's just beyond those trees.'

'In which case,' I said, 'yes, let me see this impossible thing!'

We left our glasses on the table, and Amelia led me across the lawn towards a thicket of trees. We passed through these in the direction of Richmond Park – which ran right up to the boundary of the house grounds – until we came to an area which had been levelled, and the surface compacted with a hard covering. On this stood the flying machine.

It was larger than I could have imagined it would be, extending some twenty feet at its widest point. It was clearly unfinished: the framework, which was of wooden struts, was uncovered, and there appeared to be nowhere that the driver could sit. On each side of the main body there was a wing, sagging so that the tip touched the ground. The overall appearance was similar to that of a dragonfly at rest, although it had none of the beauty of that insect.

We walked over to it, and I ran my fingers along the surface of the nearer wing. There seemed to be several wooden formers under the fabric, which itself had the texture of silk. It was stretched very tightly, so that drumming one's fingers on the fabric produced a hollow sound.

'How does it work?' I said.

Amelia went over to the main body of the machine.

'The motor was fixed in this position,' she said, indicating four struts more substantial than the others. 'Then this system of pulley s carried the cables which raised and lowered the wings.'

She pointed out the hinges which allowed the wings to flap up and down, and I found by lifting one that the motion was very smooth and strong.

'Sir William should have continued with this!' I said. 'Surely to fly would be a wonderful thing!'

'He became disillusioned with it,' Amelia said. 'He was discontented with the design. One evening he told me that he needed the time to reconsider his theory of flight, because this machine simply imitates unsuccessfully the movements of a bird. He said that it needed a thorough reappraisal. Also, the reciprocating engine he was using was too heavy for the machine, and not powerful enough.'

'I should have thought that a man of Sir William's genius could have modified the motor,' I said.

'Oh, but he did. See this.' Amelia pointed out a queer assemblage, placed deep inside the structure. It seemed on first sight to be made of ivory and brass, but there was a crystalline quality to it that somehow deceived the eye, so that within its winking, multifaceted depths it was not possible to see the constituent parts.

'What is this?' I said, very interested.

'A device of Sir William's own invention. It is a substance that enhances power, and it was not without effect. But as I say, he was not content with the design and has abandoned the machine altogether.'

'Where is the engine now?' I said.

'In the house. He uses it to generate electricity for his laboratory.'

I bent down to examine the crystalline material more closely, but even near to, it was difficult to see how it was made. I was disappointed with the flying machine, and thought it would have been fun to see it in the air.

I straightened, and saw that Amelia had stepped back a little.

I said to her: 'Tell me, do you ever assist Sir William in his laboratory?'

'If I am called upon to do so.'

'So you are Sir William's confidante?'

Amelia said: 'If you mean that I could persuade him to purchase your goggles, then I suppose so.'

I said nothing to this, for the wretched affair of the goggles was not on my mind.

We had started walking slowly back towards the house, and as we came to the lawn, Amelia said: 'Shall we now go for our bicycle ride?'

'I'd like that.'

We went into the house and Amelia summoned Mrs Watchets. She told her that we would be out for the rest of the afternoon, but that tea should be served as normal at four-thirty. Then we went to an outhouse where several bicycles were stacked, selected one each, and pushed them through the grounds until we reached the edge of the Park.

III

We rested in the shade of some trees overlooking the Pen Ponds, and Amelia at last told me what had happened to her on the morning following our conversation.

'I was not called for breakfast,' she said, 'and being tired I overslept. At eight-thirty I was awakened by Mrs Anson bringing a breakfast-tray into the room. Then, as you might expect, I was given the benefit of Mrs Anson's views on morality ... at her customary length.'

'Was she angry with you? Did you try to explain?'

'Well, she wasn't angry, or at least she didn't reveal her anger. And I had no chance to explain. She was tight-lipped and solicitous. She knew what had happened, or she had made up her mind what had happened, and at first I thought that had I made any attempt to deny what was already a foregone conclusion it would have provoked her to a rage, so I sat and listened humbly to her advice. This was, in substance, that I was a young lady of education and breeding, and that what she referred to as "loose living" was not for the likes of me. It was, however, very revealing in another way. I realized that she could censure the imagined actions of others, yet at the same time display a prurient and consuming curiosity about them. For all her anger, Mrs Anson was hoping for insights into what had happened.'

'I suppose her curiosity was disappointed,' I said.

'Not at all,' said Amelia, smiling as she held a stem of grass in her hand and stripped away the outer leaves to reveal the bright-green, soft inner stalk. 'I supplied her with a few illuminating details.'

I found myself laughing in spite of the fact that I was at once very embarrassed and rather excited.

'I should like to hear one or two of those details,' I said, boldly.

'Sir, what of my modesty?' Amelia said, fluttering her eyelashes at me in an exaggerated way, then she too laughed aloud. 'With her curiosity satisfied, and with my life revealed to be on the downward path, she hastened from my room, and that was the end of that. I left the hotel as soon as I could. The delay had made me late for my appointment at the engineering works, and I wasn't able to get to our luncheon in time. I'm very sorry.'

'That's all right,' I said, feeling well pleased with myself, even if my scandalous reputation were a fiction.

We were sitting together against the bole of a huge tree, the bicycles leaning against another tree. A few yards away, two little boys in sailor suits were trying to make a toy yacht sail out across the Pond. Near by, their nanny watched without interest.

'Let's ride further,' I said. 'I'd like to see more of the Park.'

I leaped up and extended my hands to help Amelia to her feet. We ran over to the bicycles and disentangled them. We mounted and turned into the breeze, heading in the general direction of Kingston-upon-Thames.

We pedalled at a leisurely rate for a few minutes, but then, just as we were approaching a slight rise in the ground, Amelia called out: 'Let's race!'

I pedalled harder, but with the combination of the headwind and the gradient it was heavy going. Amelia kept abreast of me.

'Come on, you're not trying!' she shouted, and surged slightly ahead of me.

I pressed down harder on the pedals and managed to catch her up, but at once she pulled ahead again. I raised myself from the saddle, and used all my strength to try to make up the difference, but for all my efforts Amelia managed somehow to stay a few yards ahead. Suddenly, as if tired of playing with me, Amelia shot quickly forward and, bumping alarmingly over the uneven surface of the path, climbed quickly up the slope. I knew I could never keep up with her, and at once gave up the unequal struggle. I watched her ahead of me . . . then realized with a shock that she was still sitting upright in the saddle, and, as far as I could see, was *free-wheeling*!

Aghast, I watched her bicycle spin over the crest of the slope, at a speed that must have been well in excess of twenty miles an hour, and then vanish from my sight.

I pedalled on peevishly, sulking a little at the way my pride had been thwarted. As I came over the crest I saw Amelia a few yards further on. She had dismounted, and her bicycle was lying on its side, the front wheel spinning. She was sitting on the grass beside it, laughing at the sight of my hot and perspiring face.

I flung my bicycle down beside hers, and sat down in a mood as near displeasure as I had ever experienced in her company.

'You cheated,' I said.

'You could have done so too,' she cried, still laughing at me.

I mopped my face with my kerchief. 'That wasn't a race, it was a deliberate humiliation.'

'Oh, Edward! Don't take it so seriously. I only wanted to show you something.'

'What?' I said in a surly tone.

'My bicycle. Do you notice anything about it?'

'No.' I was still not mollified.

'What about the front wheel?'

'It's still spinning,' I said.

'Then stop it.'

I reached out and gripped the pneumatic tyre with my hand, but snatched it away as the friction burned me. The wheel continued to spin.

'What is it?' I said, my distemper immediately forgotten.

'It is one of Sir William's devices,' she said. 'Your bicycle is fitted with one too.'

'But how does it work? You were free-wheeling up the hill. That is against all the laws of physics.'

'Look, I'll show you.'

She reached over to her machine and took hold of the handlebar. She held the right-hand grip in a certain way, and the front wheel stopped its uncanny spinning. She righted the bicycle.

'Under here.' She showed me where to look, and between the rubber grip and the brake-bar I saw a tiny strip of mica. 'Move this forward with your fingers, so, and—'

The bicycle started to move forward, but she raised the front wheel from the ground and it spun effortlessly in the air.

'When you wish to stop, you simply slide the strip back, and the bicycle may be ridden normally.'

'And you say my machine is fitted with this?'

'Yes.'

'Why did you not tell me? Then we need not have expended any effort on the ride!'

Amelia was laughing again as I hastened to my own machine and righted it. Sure enough, under the right-hand grip there was a similar piece of mica.

'I must try this at once!' I shouted, and mounted my machine. As soon as I had found my balance I slid the mica strip forward, and the bicycle moved faster.

'It works!' I cried to Amelia, waving to her in delight ... and at that moment the front wheel hit a tuft of grass, and I was unseated.

Amelia ran over to me and helped me to my feet. My bicycle lay a few yards from me, the front wheel spinning merrily.

'What a marvellous invention!' I cried, full of enthusiasm for it. 'Now we shall race in style!'

'All right,' Amelia said. 'First back to the Ponds!'

I retrieved my machine, and she ran back to hers. In a few moments we were both mounted, and speeding spectacularly towards the crest of the slope. This time the race was more even, and as we rolled down the long gradient towards the distant Ponds we kept abreast of each other. The wind drummed against my face, and it was not long before I felt my boater snatched away. Amelia's bonnet was blowing backwards, but stayed around her neck because of its strap.

As we came to the Ponds we speeded past the nanny and the two little boys, who stared after us in amazement. Laughing aloud, we circled around the larger of the two Ponds, then pulled back the mica strips and pedalled towards the trees at a moderate pace.

As we dismounted, I said: 'What is it, Amelia? How does it work?'

I was feeling breathless, even though the actual physical energy expended had been negligible.

'It's in here,' she said.

With a twisting motion she slid back the moulded rubber hand-grip, so exposing the tubular steel of the handle-bar. She held the bar so that I could see into its interior ... and there, nestling inside, was some of the crystalline material I had seen on the flying machine.

'There is a wire which runs through the frame,' Amelia said, 'and that is connected to the wheel. Inside the hub is some more of that.'

'What is this crystalline material?' I said. 'What does it consist of?'

'That I don't know. I'm aware of some of the materials it comprises, for I have to order them, but I'm not sure how they are joined to produce the effect.'

She explained that the adapted bicycle had been developed by Sir William when bicycling became popular a few years before. His idea had been to assist the weak or elderly whenever they encountered a hill.

'Do you realize that this device alone would make him a fortune?'

'Sir William does not want for money.'

'No, but think of the public good it would do. A machine like this could transform the carriage industry.'

Amelia was shaking her head. 'You don't understand Sir William. I'm sure he has considered taking out a Patent on this, but I think he judged it better unknown. Bicycling is a sport, mostly enjoyed by the young, and it is done for fresh air and exercise. As you have seen, it requires no effort to ride a bicycle like this.'

'Yes, but there would be other uses.'

'Indeed, and that is why I say you do not understand Sir William, nor could you be expected to. He is a man of restless intellect, and no sooner has he developed one device than he goes on to another. The bicycles were adapted before he built his horseless cariage, and that was before his flying machine.'

I said: 'And he has abandoned his flying machine for a new project?'

'Yes.'

'May I enquire what that is to be?'

She said: 'You will be meeting Sir William shortly. Perhaps he will tell you himself.'

I thought about this for a moment. 'You say he is sometimes an uncommunicative man. Maybe he would not tell me.'

We were once more seated close together beneath the tree.

Amelia said: 'Then you may ask me about it again, Edward.'

FOUR

Sir William Expounds A Theory

•

I

Time was passing, and soon Amelia suggested that we return to the house.

'Shall we race or ride?' I said, not especially anxious to do either, for I had been finding our rest together beneath the trees an exquisite experience. It was still sunny and warm, and there was a pleasant dusty heat rolling through the Park.

'We will ride,' she said firmly. 'There is no exercise in freewheeling.'

'And we may take it more slowly,' I said. 'Shall we do this again, Amelia? I mean, shall we bicycle together on another weekend?'

'It will not be possible every weekend,' she said. 'Sometimes I am called upon to work, and occasionally I have to be away.'

I felt a pang of unreasoned jealousy at the idea of her travelling with Sir William.

'But when you are here, shall we bicycle then?'

'You will have to invite me,' she said.

'Then I will.'

When we mounted our machines we first retraced the way of our race, and retrieved my lost boater. It was undamaged, and I placed it on my head, keeping the brim well down over my eyes so as to prevent it blowing off again.

The ride back to the house was uneventful and, for the most part, conducted in silence. I was at last understanding the real reason why

I had come to Richmond this afternoon; it was not at all to meet Sir William, for although I was still fascinated by what I knew of him I would have gladly exchanged the coming interview for another hour, two hours, or the entire evening in the Park with Amelia.

We entered the grounds of the house through a small gateway by Sir William's abandoned flying machine, and wheeled the bicycles back to the outhouse.

'I am going to change my clothes,' Amelia said.

'You are delightful just as you are,' I said.

'And you? Are you going to meet Sir William with grass all over your suit?' She reached over and plucked a stem of grass that had somehow lodged itself under the collar of my jacket.

We entered the house through the French window, and Amelia pressed a bell-push. In a moment, a manservant appeared.

'Hillyer, this is Mr Turnbull. He will be staying with us to tea and dinner. Would you help him prepare?'

'Certainly, Miss Fitzgibbon.' He turned towards me. 'Would you step this way, sir?'

He indicated that I should follow him, and we moved towards the corridor. From behind, Amelia called to him.

'And Hillyer?' she said. 'Would you please tell Mrs Watchets that we shall be ready for tea in ten minutes, and that it is to be served in the smoking-room?'

'Yes, ma'am.'

Hillyer led me through the house to the first floor, where there was a small bath-room. Inside, soap and towels were laid out, and while I washed Hillyer took away my jacket to have it brushed.

The smoking-room was on the ground floor, and it was a small, well-used room, comfortably furnished. Amelia was waiting for me; perhaps my remark about her appearance had flattered her, for she had not after all changed, but had merely put on a tiny jacket over her blouse.

Crockery had been laid on a small octagonal table, and we sat down to wait for Sir William to arrive. According to the clock on the mantelpiece it was now some minutes after four-thirty, and Amelia summoned Mrs Watchets.

'Have you sounded the tea-bell?' Amelia said.

'Yes, ma'am, but Sir William is still in his laboratory.'

'Then perhaps you would remind him that he has a guest this afternoon.'

Mrs Watchets left the room, but a moment or two later a door at the far end of the room opened, and a tall, well-built man came in hurriedly. He was in his shirt and waistcoat, and carried a jacket over his arm. He was trying to roll down his shirtsleeves, and as he came in he glanced in my direction. I stood up at once.

He said to Amelia: 'Is tea here? I'm nearly finished!'

'Sir William, do you remember I mentioned Edward Turnbull to you?'

He looked at me again. 'Turnbull? Good to meet you!' He gestured impatiently at me. 'Do sit down. Amelia, help me with my cuff.'

He extended his arm to her, and she reached under it to connect the cuff-link. When this was done, he rolled down his other sleeve and Amelia connected this cuff too. Then he put on his jacket and went to the mantelpiece. He selected a pipe and filled its bowl with tobacco from a jar.

I waited apprehensively; I wondered if the fact that he had been about to finish his work indicated that this was an unfortunate moment to call on him.

'What do you think of that chair, Turnbull?' he said, without turning.

'Sit right back into it,' Amelia said. 'Not on the edge.'

I complied, and as I did so it seemed that the substance of the cushion remoulded itself beneath me to adapt to the shape of my body. The further back I leaned, the more resilient it seemed.

'That is a chair of my own design,' Sir William said, turning towards us again as he applied a lighted match to the bowl of his pipe. Then he said, seemingly irrelevantly: 'What exactly is your faculty?'

'My, er—?'

'Your field of research. You're a scientist, are you not?'

'Sir William,' said Amelia, 'Mr Turnbull is interested in motoring, if you will recall.'

At that moment I remembered that my samples-case was still where I had left it when I arrived: in the hall.

Sir William looked at me again. 'Motoring, eh? A good hobby for a young man. It was a passing phase with me, I'm afraid. I dismantled my carriage because its components were more useful to me in the laboratory.'

'But it is a growing fashion, sir,' I said. 'After all, in America—'

'Yes, yes, but I am a scientist, Turnbull. Motoring is just one aspect of a whole field of new research. We are now on the brink of the Twentieth Century, and that is to be the century of science. There is no limit to what science might achieve.'

As Sir William was speaking he did not look at me, but stared over my head. His fingers were fretting with the match he had blown out.

'I agree that it is a subject of great interest to many people, sir,' I said.

'Yes, but I think it is in the wrong way. The popular thought is to make what we already have work better. The talk is of faster railway-trains, larger ships. My belief is that all these will be obsolete soon. By the end of the Twentieth Century, Turnbull, man will travel as freely about the planets of the Solar System as he now drives about London. We will know the peoples of Mars and Venus as well as we now know the French and Germans. I dare say we will even travel further ... out to the stars of the Universe!'

At that moment Mrs Watchets came into the room bearing a silver tray loaded with teapot, milk-jug and a sugar-bowl. I was glad of the intrusion, for I found the combination of Sir William's startling ideas and his nervous manner almost more than I could bear. He too was glad to be interrupted, I think, for as the servant set the tray on the table, and began to pour the tea for us, Sir William stepped back and stood by the end of the mantel. He was relighting his pipe, and as he did so I was able to look at him for the first time without the distraction of his manner.

He was, as I have said, a tall and large man, but what was most striking about him was his head. This was high and broad, the face pale and with grey eyes. His hair was thinning at the temples, but on the crown it grew thickly and wildly, exaggerating the size of his head, and he wore a bushy beard which itself made more marked the pallor of his skin.

I wished I had found him more at his ease, for in the few moments he had been in the room he had destroyed the pleasant sense of well-being that had developed while I was with Amelia, and now I was as nervous as he.

A sudden inspiration came to me, that he himself might be a man not used to meeting strangers, that he was better accustomed to long hours of solitary work. My own occupation involved meeting many strangers, and it was a part of my job to be able to mix well, and so, paradoxical as it might sound, I suddenly realized that here I could take the lead.

As Mrs Watchets left the room, I said to him: 'Sir, you say you are nearly finished? I hope I have not disturbed you.'

The simplicity of my device had its desired effect. He went towards one of the vacant chairs and sat down, and as he replied his words were phrased more calmly.

'No, of course not,' he said. 'I can continue after tea. I needed a short rest in any event.'

'May I enquire as to the nature of your work?'

Sir William glanced at Amelia for a moment, but her expression remained neutral.

'Has Miss Fitzgibbon told you what I am currently building?'

'She has told me a little, sir. I have seen your flying machine, for instance.'

To my surprise, he laughed at that. 'Do you think I am insane to meddle with such follies, Turnbull? My scientific colleagues tell me that heavier-than-air flight is impossible. What do you say?'

'It's a novel concept, sir.' He made no response but continued to stare at me, so I went on hastily: 'It seems to me that the problem is a lack of an adequate power-supply. The design is sound.'

'No, no, the design is wrong too. I was going about it the wrong way. Already I have made machine flight obsolete, and before I even tested that contraption you saw!'

He drank some of his tea quickly, then, astounding me with

his speed, jerked out of his chair and moved across the room to a dresser. Opening a drawer he brought forth a thin package, and handed it to me.

'Have a look at those, Turnbull. Tell me what you think.'

I opened the package and inside found that there were seven photographic portraits. The first one was a head and shoulders picture of a boy, the second was a slightly older boy, the third was that of a youth, the fourth that of a very young man, and so on.

'Are they all of the same person?' I said, having recognized a recurring facial similarity.

'Yes,' said Sir William. 'The subject is a cousin of mine, and by chance he has sat for photographic portraits at regular intervals. Now then, Turnbull, do you notice anything about the *quality* of the portraits? No! How can I expect you to anticipate me? They are cross-sections of the Fourth Dimension!'

As I frowned, Amelia said: 'Sir William, this is probably a concept new to Mr Turnbull.'

'No more than that of heavier-than-air flight! You have grasped that, Turnbull, why should you not grasp the Fourth Dimension?'

'Do you mean the... concept of...?' I was floundering.

'Space and Time! Exactly, Turnbull ... Time, the great mystery!'

I glanced at Amelia for more assistance, and realized that she had been studying my face. There was a half-smile on her lips, and at once I guessed that she had heard Sir William expounding on this subject many times.

'These portraits, Turnbull, are two-dimensional representations of a three-dimensional person. Individually, they can depict his height and width, and can even offer an approximation of his *depth* ... but they can never be more than flat, two-dimensional pieces of paper. Nor can they reveal that he has been travelling all his life through Time. Placed together, they approximate the Fourth Dimension.'

He was pacing about the room now, having seized the portraits from my hands, and was waving them expansively as he spoke. He crossed to the mantel and set them up, side by side.

'Time and Space are inherently the same. I walk across this

room, and I have travelled in Space a matter of a few yards ... but at the same moment I have also moved through Time by a matter of a few seconds. Do you see what I am meaning?'

'That one motion complements the other?' I said, uncertainly.

'Exactly! And I am working now to separate the two ... to facilitate travel through Space discrete from Time, and through Time discrete from Space. Let me show you what I mean.'

Abruptly, he turned on his heel and hurried from the room. The door slammed behind him.

I was dumbfounded. I simply stared at Amelia, shaking my head.

She said: 'I should have known he would be agitated. He is not always like this, Edward. He has been alone in his laboratory all day, and working like that he often becomes animated.'

'Where has he gone?' I said. 'Should we follow him?'

'He's returned to his laboratory. I think he will be showing you something he has made.'

Exactly at that moment the door opened again and Sir William returned. He was carrying a small wooden box with great care, and he looked around for somewhere to place it.

'Help me move the table,' Amelia said to me.

We carried the table bearing the tea-things to one side, and brought forward another. Sir William placed his box in the centre of it, and sat down. As quickly as it had begun, his animation seemed to have passed.

'I want you to look at this closely,' he said, 'but I do not want you to touch it. It is very delicate.'

He opened the lid of the box. The interior was padded with a soft, velvet-like material, and resting inside was a tiny mechanism which, on first sight, I took to be the workings of a clock.

Sir William withdrew it from its case with care, and rested it on the surface of the table.

I leaned forward and peered closely at it. At once, with a start of recognition, I realized that much of it was made with that queer, crystalline substance I had seen twice before that afternoon. The resemblance to a clock was misleading, I saw now, lent to it simply by the precision with which the tiny parts had been fitted together, and some of the metals with which it had been made. Those I could recognize seemed to be some tiny rods of nickel, some highly polished pieces of brass and a cog-wheel made of shining chrome or silver. Part of it had been shaped out of a white substance which could have been ivory, and the base was made of a hard, ebony-like wood. It is difficult, though, to describe what I saw, for all about there was the quartz-like substance, deceiving the eye, presenting hundreds of tiny facets at whatever angle I viewed it from.

I stood up, and stepped back a yard or two. From there, the device once more took on the aspect of a clock-mechanism, albeit a rather extraordinary one.

'It's beautiful,' I said, and saw that Amelia's gaze was also on it.

'You, young man, are one of the first people in the world to see a mechanism that will make real to us the Fourth Dimension.'

'And this device will really work?' I said.

'Yes, it will. It has been adequately tested. This engine will, depending how I choose, travel forward or backward in Time.'

Amelia said: 'You could demonstrate, Sir William.'

He made no answer, but instead sat back in his chair. He was staring at the strange device, a thoughtful expression on his face. He maintained this posture for five minutes, and for all the awareness he showed of Amelia and me, we might not have existed. Once he leaned forward, and closely scrutinized the device. At this I made to say something, but Amelia signed to me and I subsided into silence. Sir William raised the device in his hand, and held it up against the daylight from the window. He reached forward to touch the silver cog-wheel, then hesitated and set down the device again. Once more he sat back in his chair and regarded his invention with great concentration.

This time he was still for nearly ten minutes, and I began to grow restless, fearing that Amelia and I were a disturbance to him.

Finally, he leaned forward and replaced the device in its case. He stood up.

'You must pardon me, Mr Turnbull,' he said. 'I have just been stricken with the possibility of a minor modification.'

'Do you wish me to leave, sir?'

'Not at all, not at all.'

He seized the wooden box, then hastened from the room. The door slammed behind him.

I glanced at Amelia and she smiled, immediately lifting the tension that had marked the last few minutes.

'Is he coming back?' I said.

'I shouldn't think so. The last time he acted like this, he locked himself in his laboratory, and no one except Mrs Watchets saw him for four days.'

II

Amelia summoned Hillyer, and the manservant went around the room, lighting the lamps. Although the sun was still up, it was now behind the trees that grew around the house, and shadows were creeping on. Mrs Watchets came in to clear away the tea-things. I realized that I had drunk only half of my cup, and swallowed the rest quickly. I was thirsty from the bicycling expedition.

I said, when we were alone: 'Is he mad?'

Amelia made no answer, but appeared to be listening. She signalled that I should be silent... and then about five seconds later the door burst open yet again, and Sir William was there, wearing a topcoat.

'Amelia, I am going up to London. Hillyer can take me in the carriage.'

'Will you be back in time for dinner?'

'No ... I shall be out all evening. I'll sleep at my club tonight.' He turned to me. 'Inadvertently, Turnbull, my conversation with you has generated an idea. I thank you, sir.'

He rushed out of the room as abruptly as he had entered, and soon we heard the sound of his voice in the hall. A few minutes later we heard a horse and carriage on the gravelled driveway.

Amelia went to the window, and watched as the manservant drove the carriage away, then returned to her seat.

She said: 'No, Sir William is not mad.'

'But he behaves like a madman.'

'Perhaps that is how it seems. I believe he is a genius; the two are not wholly dissimilar.'

'Do you understand his theory?'

'I can grasp most of it. The fact that you didn't follow it, Edward, is no reflection on your own intellect. Sir William is himself so familiar with it that when explaining it to others he omits much of it. Also, you are a stranger to him, and he is rarely at ease unless surrounded by those he knows. He has a group of acquaintances from the Linnaean – his club in London – and they are the only people to whom I have ever heard him speak naturally and fluently.'

'Then perhaps I should not have asked him.'

'No, it is his obsession; had you not expressed an interest, he would have volunteered his theory. Everyone about him has to bear it. Even Mrs Watchets has heard him out twice.'

'Does she understand it?'

'I think not,' said Amelia, smiling.

'Then I shall not expect clarification from her. You will have to explain.'

'There isn't much I can say. Sir William has built a Time Machine. It has been tested, and I have been present during some of the tests, and the results have been conclusive. He has not said so as yet, but I suspect that he is planning an expedition into futurity.'

I smiled a little, and covered my mouth with my hand.

Amelia said: 'Sir William is in perfect earnest.'

'Yes ... but I cannot see a man of his physique entering a device so small.'

'What you have seen is only a working model. He has a full-sized version.' Unexpectedly, she laughed. 'You don't think I meant the model he showed you?'

'Yes, I did.'

When Amelia laughed she looked most beautiful, and I did not mind having misunderstood.

'But large or small, I cannot believe such a Machine is possible!' I said.

'Then you may see it for yourself. It is only a dozen yards from where you are sitting.'

I jumped to my feet. 'Where is it?'

'In Sir William's laboratory.' Amelia seemed to have been infected with my enthusiasm, for she too had left her seat with great alacrity. 'I'll show you.'

III

We left the smoking-room by the door which Sir William had used, and walked along a passage to what was clearly a newly constructed door. This led directly into the laboratory, which was, I now realized, the glass-covered annexe which had been built between the two wings of the house.

I do not know what I had been expecting the laboratory to be like, but my first impression was that it bore a considerable resemblance to the milling-shop of an engineering works I had once visited.

Along the ceiling, to one side, was a steam-lathe which, by the means of several adjustable leather straps, provided motive power to the many pieces of engineering equipment I saw ranged along a huge bench beneath it. Several of these were metal-turning lathes, and there was also a sheet-metal stamp, a presser, some acetylene welding equipment, two massive vices and any number of assorted tools scattered about. The floor was liberally spread with the shavings and fragments of metals removed in the processes, and in many parts of the laboratory were what appeared to be long-abandoned pieces of cut or turned metal.

'Sir William does much of the engineering himself,' said Amelia, 'but occasionally he is obliged to contract out for certain items. I was in Skipton on one of these errands when I met you.'

'Where is the Time Machine?' I said.

'You are standing beside it.'

I realized with a start that what I had taken at first to be another collection of discarded metals did, in fact, have a coherent scheme to it. I saw now that it bore a certain resemblance to the model he had shown me, but whereas that had had the perfection of miniaturism, this by its very size appeared to be more crude.

In fact, however, as soon as I bent to examine it I saw that every single constituent part had been turned and polished until it shone as new.

The Time Machine was some seven or eight feet in length, and four or five feet in width. At its highest point it stood about six feet from the floor, but as its construction had been strictly functional, perhaps a description in terms of overall dimension is misleading. For much of its length the Time Machine was standing only three feet high, and in the form of a skeletal metal frame.

All its working parts were visible . . . and here my description becomes vague of necessity. What I saw was a repetition in extremis of the mysterious substances I had earlier that day seen in Sir William's bicycles and flying machine: in other words, much of what was apparently visible was rendered invisible by the eye-deceiving crystalline substance. This encased thousands of fine wires and rods, and much as I peered at the mechanism from many different angles, I was unable to learn very much.

What was more comprehensible was the arrangement of controls.

Towards one end of the frame was a leather-covered seat, rounded like a horse-saddle. Around this was a multiplicity of levers, rods and dials.

The main control appeared to be a large lever situated directly in front of the saddle. Attached to the top of this – incongruous in the context – was the handle-bar of a bicycle. This, I supposed, enabled the driver to grip the lever with both hands. To each side of this lever were dozens of subsidiary rods, all of which were attached at different swivelling joints, so that as the lever was moved, others would be simultaneously brought into play.

In my preoccupation I had temporarily forgotten Amelia's presence, but now she spoke, startling me a little.

'It looks substantial, does it not?' she said.

'How long has it taken Sir William to build this?' I said.

'Nearly two years. But touch it, Edward ... see how substantial it is.'

'I wouldn't dare,' I said. 'I would not know what I was doing.'

'Hold one of these bars. It is perfectly safe.'

She took my hand, and led it towards one of the brass rods which formed part of the frame. I laid my fingers gingerly on this rail ... then immediately snatched them away, for as my fingers closed on the rod the entire Machine had visibly and audibly shuddered, like a living being.

'What is it?' I cried.

'The Time Machine is attenuated, existing as it were in the Fourth Dimension. It is real, but it does not exist in the real world as we know it. It is, you must understand, travelling through Time even as we stand here.'

'But you cannot be serious... because if it were travelling it would not be here now!'

'On the contrary, Edward.' She indicated a huge metal flywheel directly in front of the saddle, which corresponded approximately with the silver cog-wheel I had seen on Sir William's model. 'It is turning. Can you see that?'

'Yes, yes I can,' I said, leaning as near it as I dared. The great wheel was rotating almost imperceptibly.

'If it were not turning, the Machine would be stationary in Time. To us, as Sir William explained, the Machine would then vanish into the past, for we ourselves are moving forward in Time.'

'So the Machine must always be in operation.'

While we had been there the evening had deepened, and gloom was spreading in the eerie laboratory.

Amelia stepped to one side and went to yet another infernal contraption. Attached to this was a cord wound around an external wheel, and she pulled the cord sharply. At once the device emitted a coughing, spitting sound, and as it picked up speed, light poured forth from eight incandescent globes hanging from the frame ceiling.

Amelia glanced up at a clock on the wall, which showed the time of twenty-five minutes past six.

'It will be time for dinner in half an hour,' she said. 'Do you think a stroll around the garden would be enjoyable before then?'

I tore my attention away from the wondrous machines Sir William had made.

The Time Machine might slowly move into futurity, but Amelia was, to my way of thinking, stationary in Time. She was not attenuated, and not at all a creature of past or future.

I said, for I was understanding that my time here in Richmond must soon be at an end: 'Will you take my arm?'

She slipped her hand around my elbow, and together we walked past the Time Machine, and the noisy reciprocating engine, through a door in the far corner of the laboratory, and out into the cool evening light of the garden. Only once did I glance back, seeing the pure-white radiance of the electrical lamps shining through the glass walls of the annexe.

FIVE

Into Futurity!

•

I

I had ascertained that the last train to London left Richmond at ten-thirty, and I knew that to catch it I should have to leave by ten. At eight-thirty, though, I was in no mood to think of returning to my lodgings. Furthermore, the prospect of returning to work the next day was one I greeted with the utmost despondency. This was because with the completion of dinner, which had been accompanied by a dry and intoxicating wine, and with the move from the dining-room to the semi-dark intimacy of the drawing-room, and with a glass of port inside me and another half finished, and the subtle fragrance of Amelia's perfume distracting my senses, I was subject to the most perturbing fantasies.

Amelia was no less intoxicated than I, and I fancied that she could not have mistaken the change in my manner. Until this moment I had felt awkward in her company. This was partly because I had had only the barest experience with young women, but more especially because of all young women Amelia seemed to me the most extraordinary. I had grown used to her forthright manner, and the emancipated airs she assumed, but what I had not until this moment realized was that I had, most inappropriately, fallen blindly and rashly in love with her.

In wine there is truth, and although I was able to contain my excesses, and fell short of protesting my undying amour, our conversation had touched on most remarkably personal matters.

Soon after nine-thirty, I knew I could delay no more. I had only half an hour before I had to leave, and as I had no idea of when or how I should see her again, I felt that then was the moment to state, in no uncertain terms, that to me she was already more than just a pleasant companion.

I poured myself a liberal helping of port, and then, still uncertain of how I was to phrase my words, I reached into my waistcoat pocket and consulted my watch.

'My dear Amelia,' I started to say. 'I see that it is twenty-five minutes to ten, and at ten I must leave. Before that I have something I must tell you.'

'But why must you leave?' she said, instantly destroying the thread of my thoughts.

'I have a train to catch.'

'Oh, please don't go yet!'

'But I must return to London.'

'Hillyer can take you. If you miss your train, he will take you all the way to London.'

'Hillyer is already in London,' I said.

She laughed, a little drunkenly. 'I had forgotten. Then you must walk.'

'And so I must leave at ten.'

'No ... I will have Mrs Watchets prepare a room for you.'

'Amelia, I cannot stay, much as I would wish to. I must work in the morning.'

She leaned towards me, and I saw light dancing in her eyes. 'Then I shall take you to the station myself.'

'There is another carriage?' I said.

'In a manner of speaking.' She stood up, and knocked over her empty glass. 'Come with me, Edward, and I shall convey you to the station in Sir William's Time Machine!'

She took my hand in hers, and half-dragged me towards the door. We started to laugh; it is difficult to write of this in retrospect, for intoxication, however mild, is not a state in which one acts one's finest. For me it was the gaiety of the moment that contributed to the compliance.

I shouted to her as we ran along: 'But to travel in Time will not take me to the station!'

'Yes it will!'

We reached the laboratory and went inside, closing the door behind us. The electrical lamps were still burning, and in the comparatively harsh glare our escapade took on a different aspect.

'Amelia,' I said, trying to restrain her. 'What are you doing?'

'I am doing what I said. We will travel to the station.'

I stood before her, and took her hands in mine.

'We have both had a little too much to drink,' I said. 'Please don't jest with me. You cannot seriously propose to operate Sir William's Machine.'

Her hands tightened on mine. 'I am not as intoxicated as you believe. My manner is gay, but I am in perfect earnest.'

'Then let us return to the drawing-room at once.'

She turned away from me, and walked towards the Time Machine. She gripped one of the brass rails in her hands, and immediately the Machine trembled as before.

She said: 'You heard what Sir William said. Time and Space are inseparable. There is no need for you to leave in the next few minutes. Although the Machine is designed to travel into futurity, it will also move across spatial distances. In short, although it will journey across thousands of years, it can also be used for a trip as prosaic as taking a friend to the station.'

'You are still jesting,' I said. 'Nor am I convinced that the Machine will even travel in Time.'

'But it has been proved.'

'Not to my satisfaction it hasn't,' I said.

She turned to face me, and her expression was as serious as before. 'Then allow me to demonstrate it to you!'

'No, Amelia! It would be foolhardy to drive the Machine!'

'Why, Edward? I know what to do ... I have watched Sir William's tests often enough.'

'But we do not know the craft is safe!'

'There would be no danger.'

I simply shook my head with the agony of the moment. Amelia

turned back to the Machine and reached over to one of the dials. She did something to this, then pulled back the lever with the bicycle handle-bar attached. Instantly, the Time Machine vanished!

II

'Look at the clock on the wall, Edward.'

'What have you done with the Machine?' I said.

'Never mind that... what is the time by the clock?'

I stared up. 'Eighteen minutes to ten.'

'Very well. At exactly sixteen minutes to ten the Machine will re-appear.'

'From where?' I said.

'From the past ... or, more precisely, from now. It is presently travelling through Time, to a point two minutes in the future of its departure.'

'But why has it vanished? Where is it at this moment?'

'Within the attenuated Temporal Dimension.'

Amelia stepped forward to where the Machine had been, and walked through the vacancy waving her arms. She glanced up at the clock.

'Stand well back, Edward. The Machine will re-appear exactly where it was.'

'Then you must come away too,' I said.

I pulled her by the arm, and held her close beside me a few yards from where the Machine had been. We both watched the clock. The second hand moved slowly round .. . and at exactly four seconds after sixteen minutes to ten, the Time Machine reappeared.

'There!' said Amelia, triumphantly. 'Just as I said.'

I stared dumbly at the Machine. The great fly-wheel was turning slowly as before.

Amelia took my hand again. 'Edward ... we must now mount the Machine.'

'What?' I said, appalled at the idea.

'It is absolutely imperative. You see, while Sir William has been testing the Machine he has incorporated a safety-device into it, which automatically returns the Machine to its moment of departure. That is activated exactly three minutes after its arrival here, and if we are not aboard it will be lost forever in the past.'

I frowned a little at this, but said: 'You could switch that off, though?'

'Yes ... but I'm not going to. I wish to prove that the Machine is no folly.'

'I say you are drunk.'

'And I say you are too. Come on!'

Before I could stop her, Amelia had skipped over to the Machine, squeezed under the brass rail and mounted the saddle. To do this she was obliged to raise her skirt a few inches above her ankles, and I confess that I found this sight considerably more alluring than any expedition through Time could have been.

She said: 'The Machine will return in under a minute, Edward. Are you to be left behind?'

I hesitated no more. I went to her side, and clambered on to the saddle behind her. At her instruction I put my arms around her waist, and pressed my chest against her back.

She said: 'Look at the clock, Edward.'

I stared up at it. The time was now thirteen minutes to ten. The second hand reached the minute, moved on, then reached the time of four seconds past.

It stopped moving.

Then, it began to move in reverse ... slowly at first, then faster.

'We are travelling backwards in Time,' Amelia said, a little breathlessly. 'Do you see the clock, Edward?'

'Yes,' I said, my whole attention on it. 'Yes, I do!'

The second hand moved backwards through four minutes, then began to slow down. As it approached four seconds past eighteen minutes to ten it slowed right down, then halted altogether. Presently it began to sweep forward in a normal way.

'We are back at the moment in which I pressed the lever,' said Amelia. 'Do you now believe that the Time Machine is no fraud?'

I still sat with my arms around her waist, and our bodies were pressed together in the most intimate way imaginable. Her hair lay gently against my face, and I could think of nothing but the nearness of her.

'Show me again,' I said, dreaming of an eternity of such closeness. 'Take me into futurity!'

III

'Can you see what I am doing?' Amelia said. 'These dials can be pre-set to the very second. I can choose how many hours, days or even years we can travel.'

I roused myself from my passionate imaginings, and peered over her shoulder. I saw her indicating a row of small dials, which were marked with days of the week, months of the year ... and then several others which counted tens, hundreds and then thousands of years.

'Please don't set our destination too far,' I said, looking at the last dial. 'I still have to think of my train.'

'But we will return to our moment of departure, even if we should travel a hundred years!'

'Maybe so. Let us not be rash.'

'If you are nervous, Edward, we need travel only as far as tomorrow.'

'No ... let us make a long trip. You have shown me the Time Machine is safe. Let us go to the next century!'

'As you wish. We can go to the one beyond, if you prefer.'

'It is the Twentieth Century I am interested in... let us first go forward ten years.'

'Only ten? That hardly seems adventurous.'

'We must be systematic,' I said, for although I am not faint-hearted, I am not an adventurous person. 'Let us go first to 1903, and then to 1913, and so on at ten-yearly intervals through the century. Perhaps we will see a few changes.'

'All right. Are you ready now?'

'That I am,' I said, settling my arms about her waist again.

Amelia made further adjustments to the dials. I saw her select the year 1903, but the day and month dials were too low for me to see.

She said: 'I have selected 22nd June. That is the first day of summer, so we shall probably find the weather clement.'

She placed her hands on the lever, and then straightened. I braced myself for our departure.

Then, much to my surprise, Amelia suddenly stood up and moved away from the saddle.

'Please wait for a moment, Edward,' she said.

'Where are you going?' I said, in some alarm. 'The Machine will take me with it.'

'Not until the lever is moved. It is just ... Well, if we are going such a long distance, I should like to take my handbag.'

'Whatever for?' I said, hardly believing my ears.

Amelia looked a little embarrassed. 'I don't know, Edward. It is just that I never go anywhere without my hand-bag.'

'Then bring your bonnet too,' I said, laughing at this most unlikely revelation of feminine foibles.

She hastened from the laboratory. I stared blankly at the dials for a moment, then, on an impulse, I too dismounted and went into the hallway to collect my boater. If an expedition it was to be, I too would travel in style!

On a further impulse I walked into the drawing-room, poured some more port into the two glasses, and carried them back to the laboratory.

Amelia had returned before me, and was already mounted on the saddle. She had placed her hand-bag on the floor of the Machine, directly in front of the saddle, and on her head she wore her bonnet.

I passed one of the port-glasses to her. 'Let us toast the success of our adventure.'

'And futurity,' she replied.

We each drank about half what was there, then I placed the glasses on a bench to one side. I climbed on to the saddle behind Amelia.

'We are now ready,' I said, making sure my boater was firmly seated on my head.

Amelia gripped the lever in both hands, and pulled it towards her.

IV

The whole Time Machine lurched, as if it had somehow fallen headlong into an abyss, and I shouted aloud with alarm, bracing myself against the coming impact.

'Hold on!' Amelia said, somewhat unnecessarily, for I would not have released her for anything.

'What is happening?' I cried.

'We are quite safe ... it is an effect of the attenuation.'

I opened my eyes, and glanced timorously about the laboratory, and saw to my astonishment that the Machine was still firmly situated on the floor. The clock on the wall was already spinning insanely forwards, and even as I watched the sun came up behind the house and was soon passing quickly overhead. Almost before I had registered its passing, darkness fell again like a black blanket thrown over the roof.

I sucked in my breath involuntarily, and discovered that in so doing I had inadvertently inhaled several of Amelia's long hairs. Even in the immense distractions of the journey I found a moment to rejoice at this furtive intimacy.

Amelia shouted to me: 'Are you frightened?'

This was no time for prevarication. 'Yes!' I shouted back.

'Hold tight... there is no danger.'

Our raised voices were necessary only as an expression of our excitement; in the attenuated dimension all was silent.

The sun came up, and set again almost as quickly. The next period of darkness was shorter, and the following daylight shorter still. The Time Machine was accelerating into futurity!

In what seemed to us only a few more seconds the procession of day and night was so fast as to be virtually undetectable, and our surroundings were visible only in a grey, twilight glow. About us, details of the laboratory became hazy, and the image of the sun became a path of light seemingly fixed in a deep-blue sky.

When I spoke to Amelia I had lost the strands of her hair from my mouth. About me was a spectacular sight, and yet for all its wonder it did not compare with the feel of this girl in my arms. Prompted no doubt by the new infusion of port into my blood I became emboldened, and I moved my face nearer and took several strands of her hair between my lips. I raised my head slightly, allowing the hair to slide sensuously across my tongue. Amelia made no response I could detect, and so I allowed the strands to fall and took a few more. Still she did not stop me. The third time I tipped my head to one side, so as not to dislodge my hat, and pressed my lips gently but very firmly on the smooth white skin of her neck.

I was allowed to linger there for no more than a second, but then she sat forward as if in sudden excitement, and said: 'The Machine is slowing, Edward!'

Beyond the glass roof the sun was now moving visibly slower, and the periods of dark, between the sun's passages, were distinct, if only as the briefest flickers of darkness.

Amelia started reading off the dials before her: 'We are in December, Edward! January ... January 1903. February ...'

One by one the months were called, and the pauses between her words were growing longer.

Then: 'This is June, Edward ... we are nearly there!'

I glanced up at the clock for confirmation of this, but I saw that the device had unaccountably stopped.

'Have we arrived?' I said.

'Not quite.'

'But the clock on the wall is not moving.'

Amelia looked briefly at it. 'No one has wound it, that is all.'

'Then you will have to tell me when we arrive.'

'The wheel is slowing... we are almost at rest ... now!'

And with that word the silence of attenuation was broken. Somewhere just outside the house there was a massive explosion, and some of the panes of glass cracked. Splinters fell down upon us.

Beyond the transparent walls I saw that it was daytime and the sun was shining . . . but there was smoke drifting past, and we heard the crackle of burning timber.

V

There came a second explosion, but this was further away. I felt Amelia stiffen in my arms, and she turned awkwardly in the saddle to face me.

'What have we come to?' she said.

'I cannot say.'

Some distance away somebody screamed horribly, and as if this were a signal the scream was echoed by two other voices. A third blast occurred, louder than either of the previous two. More panes cracked, and splinters tinkled down to the floor. One piece fell on to the Time Machine itself, not six inches from my foot.

Gradually, as our ears adapted to the confusion of sounds around us, one noise in particular stood out above all others: a deep-throated braying, rising like a factory siren, then howling around the upper note. It drowned temporarily the crackle of the fires and the cries of the men. The siren note fell away, but then it was repeated.

'Edward!' Amelia's face was snow-white, and her voice had become a high-pitched whisper. 'What is happening?'

'I cannot imagine. We must leave. Take the controls!'

'I don't know how. We must wait for the automatic return.'

'How long have we been here?'

Before she could answer there was another shattering explosion.

'Hold still,' I said. 'We cannot be here much longer. We have blundered into a war.'

'But the world is at peace!'

'In our time, yes.'

I wondered how long we had been waiting here in this hell of 1903, and cursed again that the clock was not working. It could not be long before the automatic return took us back through the safety of attenuation to our own blissfully peaceful time.

Amelia had turned her face so that it was now buried in my shoulder, her body twisted awkwardly on the saddle. I kept my aims around her, doing what I could to calm her in that fearful bedlam.

I looked around the laboratory, seeing how strangely it had changed from the first time I had seen it: debris was everywhere, and filth and dust overlaid everything bar the Time Machine itself.

Unexpectedly, I saw a movement beyond the walls of the laboratory, and looking that way I saw that there was someone running desperately across the lawn towards the house. As the figure came nearer I saw that it was that of a woman. She came right up to the wall, pressing her face against the glass. Behind her I saw another figure, running too.

I said: 'Amelia ... look!'

'What is it?'

'There!'

She turned to look at the two figures, but just as she did two things happened simultaneously. One was a shattering explosion accompanied by a gust of flame erupting across the lawn and consuming the woman ... and the other was a vertiginous lurch from the Time Machine. The silence of attenuation fell about us, the laboratory appeared whole once more, and overhead began the reverse procession of day and night.

Still turned uncomfortably towards me, Amelia burst into tears of relief, and I held her in my arms in silence.

When she had calmed, she said: 'What were you seeing just before we returned?'

'Nothing,' I said. 'My eyes deceived me.'

There was no way I could describe to her the woman I had seen. She had been like a wild animal: hair matted and in disarray, blood disfiguring her face, clothes torn so as to reveal the nakedness beneath. Nor did I know how to say what was for me the greatest horror of all.

I had recognized the woman and knew her to be Amelia, suffering her dying moments in the hellish war of 1903!

I could not say this, could not even believe what I myself had seen. But it was so: futurity was real, and that was Amelia's real destiny. In June 1903, on the 22nd day, she would be consumed by fire in the garden of Sir William's house.

The girl was cradled in my arms, and I felt her trembling still. I could not allow that destiny to be fulfilled!

So it was, without understanding the precipitate nature of my actions, that I moved to avert destiny. The Time Machine would now carry us further into futurity, beyond that terrible day!

VI

I was in a mad trance. I stood up abruptly and Amelia, who had been leaning against me, stared up in astonishment. Over my head, the days and nights were flickering.

There was a startling and heady rush of sensations coursing through me, caused I suppose, by the vertigo of the attenuation, but also because some instinct was preparing me for the act that followed. I stepped forward, placing my foot on the floor of the Machine in front of the saddle, and supporting myself on the brass rail, I managed to crouch down in front of Amelia.

'Edward, what are you doing?' Her voice was trembling, and she sobbed as soon as her sentence was said. I paid her no attention, peering instead at the dials which were now but a few inches from my face.

In that uncanny light of the procession of days, I saw that the Machine was speeding backwards through Time. We were now in 1902, and I saw the needle pass from August to July as I first glanced at it. The lever, centrally mounted in front of the dials, was standing almost vertically, its attached nickel rods extending forwards into the heart of the crystalline engine.

I raised myself a little, and sat on the front of the saddle, causing Amelia to move back to accommodate me.

'You must not interfere with the controls,' she said and I felt her leaning to one side to see what I was doing.

I grasped the bicycle handle in both hands, and pulled it towards me. As far as I could see, this had no effect on our journey. July slipped back to June.

Amelia's concern became more urgent.

'Edward, you must not tamper!' she said loudly.

'We must go on into futurity!' I cried, and swung the handlebar from side to side, as one does when cornering on a bicycle.

'*No*! The Machine must be allowed to return automatically!'

For all my efforts at the controls, the reverse procession continued smoothly. Amelia was now holding my arms, trying to pull my hands away from the lever. I noticed that above each of the dials was a small metal knob, and I took one of these in my hands. I saw, by turning it, that it was possible to change the setting of the destination. Evidently, this was the way to interrupt our progress, for as soon as Amelia realized what I was doing, her efforts to restrain me became violent. She was reaching, trying to take my hand, and when this failed she took a handful of my hair and snatched it painfully back.

At this, I released the controls, but my feet kicked instinctively forwards. The heel of my right boot made contact with one of the nickel rods attached to the main lever, and in that instant there was the most appalling lurch to one side, and everything went black around us.

VII

The laboratory had vanished, the procession of day and night had ceased. We were in absolute darkness and absolute silence.

Amelia's desperate hold on me eased, and we sat numbly in awe of the event that had overtaken us. Only the headlong vertigo – which had now taken on the characteristic of a sickening swoop from one side to another – told us that our journey through Time continued.

Amelia moved closer to me, wrapping her arms around my body, and pressed her face against my neck.

The swooping was growing worse, and I turned the handlebar to one side, hoping to correct it. All I achieved was to introduce a new motion: a most unsettling pitching movement, complicating the ever-worsening sideways swing.

'I can't stop it!' I cried. 'I don't know what to do!'

'What has happened to us?'

'You made me kick the lever,' I said. 'I felt something break.'

We both gasped aloud then, for the Machine seemed to turn right over. Light suddenly burst in upon us, emanating from one brilliant source. I closed my eyes, for the brilliance was dazzling, and tried again to work the lever to ease our sickening motion. The erratic movements of the Machine were causing the point of light to waltz crazily about us, casting black shadows confusingly over the dials.

The lever had a new feel to it. The breaking of the rod had made it looser, and as soon as I tried to let go it would sag to one side, thus precipitating more of the violent sideways manoeuvres.

'If only I can find that broken rod,' I said, and reached downwards with my free hand to see if I could find the pieces. As I did so, there was another swooping to one side, and I was all but unseated. Fortunately, Amelia had not relaxed her hold on me and with her help I struggled back upright.

'Do keep still, Edward,' she said, softly and reassuringly. 'So long as we are inside the Machine, we are safe. No harm can come to us while we are attenuated.'

'But we might collide with something!'

'We cannot ... we will pass through it.'

'But what has happened?'

She said: 'Those nickel rods are there to proscribe movement through Space. By dislodging one of them, you have released the Spatial Dimension, and we are now moving rapidly away from Richmond.'

I was aghast at this thought, and the dizzying effect of our passage only emphasized the terrible dangers we were facing.

'Then where will we fetch up?' I said. 'Who knows where the Machine will deposit us?'

Again, Amelia spoke in a reassuring voice: 'We are in no danger, Edward. I grant you the Machine is careering wildly, but only its controls have been affected. The field of attenuation is still around us, and so the engine itself is still working. Now we are moving through Space, we are likely to traverse many hundreds of miles ... but even if we should find ourselves a thousand miles from home, the automatic return will bear us safely back to the laboratory.'

'A thousand miles ...?' I said, horrified at the velocity at which we must be travelling.

She tightened her hold on me momentarily. 'I think it will not be as far as that. It seems to me we are spinning wildly in a circle.'

There was some substance in this, for even as we had been talking the point of light had been circling insanely around us. I was, naturally, comforted by what she said, but the sickening lurches continued, and the sooner this adventure was brought to its end the happier I would be. With this in mind, I decided to search again for the dislodged nickel rod.

I told Amelia what I was intending to do, and she reached forward to take the main lever in her hand. Thus freed from the necessity to hold on to the lever, I bent forward and groped on the floor of the Machine, dreading that the rod had been thrown to one side by our violent motion. I fumbled around in the erratic light, and felt Amelia's hand-bag where she had placed it, on the floor in front of the saddle. Thankfully, I found the rod a moment later: it had rolled and wedged itself between the front of the saddle and Amelia's bag.

'I've found it,' I said, sitting up and holding it so that she could see it. 'It is not broken.'

'Then how was it dislodged?'

I looked more closely at it, and saw that at each end were helical screw shapings, and that at the tip of these were markings of bright metal which revealed how the rod had been torn from its sockets. I showed this to Amelia.

'I remember Sir William saying that some of the nickel controls had been machined incorrectly,' she said. 'Can you replace it?'

'I shall try.'

It took several more minutes of my fumbling in the eerie light to locate both of the metal bushes from which the rod had been torn, and then it took much longer to manipulate the lever so as to bring it into a suitable position so that I could fit the rod into the bushes.

'It's still too short!' I said in some desperation. 'No matter how I try, the rod is too short.'

'But it must have come from there!'

I found a way of loosening the bush on the lever itself, and this helped to some measure. Now the connection could be made at each end, and with great patience I managed to screw the rod into each of the two sockets (fortunately, Sir William had engineered the screws so that one turn tightened both connections). It was held, but only tenuously so, for barely half a turn had been possible.

I sat up wearily in the saddle, and Amelia's arms went around my waist. The Time Machine was still lurching, but far less so than before, and the movement of the brilliant point of light was almost imperceptible. We sat in its harsh glare, hardly believing that I had succeeded in correcting the terrible motion.

Directly in front of me the fly-wheel continued to turn quickly, but there had been no return to the orderly procession of day and night.

'I think we are safe again,' I said, but I did not feel sure.

'We must soon be coming to a halt. As soon as the Machine is at rest, we must neither of us move. It will take three minutes for the automatic return to start.'

'And will we be taken back to the laboratory?' I said.

Amelia hesitated before replying, and then said: 'Yes.' I felt she was no more sure than I.

Quite unexpectedly, the Time Machine gave another lurch, and we both gasped. I saw that the fly-wheel was still ... and then I realized that air was whistling past us, chilling us instantly. I knew that we were no longer attenuated, that we were falling ... and in great desperation I reached forward to seize the lever—

'*Edward*!' Amelia screamed in my ear.

It was the last thing I heard, for at that instant there was a terrible concussion, and the Machine came to a sudden halt. Both Amelia and I were catapulted from it into the night.

VIII

I was lying in absolute darkness, seeming to be entirely covered by something leathery and wet. As I tried to stand, all I could accomplish was a futile thrashing with my arms and legs, and I slid further into the morass of slippery stuff. A sheet of something fell across my face, and I thrust it aside, gasping for breath. Suddenly I was coughing, trying to suck air into my lungs, and like a drowning man I struck instinctively upwards, feeling I should otherwise suffocate. There was nothing on which I could get a hold, as everything that surrounded me was soft, slippery and moist. It was as if I had been pitched head first into an immense bank of seaweed.

I felt myself falling, and this time allowed myself to go, despairing. I would surely drown in this dank foliage, for with each turn of my head my face was covered with the repulsive stuff. I could taste it now: a flat, iron-tainted wateriness.

Somewhere near to hand I heard a gasp.

I shouted: 'Amelia!'

My voice emerged as a wheezing croak, and at once I was coughing again.

'Edward?' Her voice was high-pitched and frightened, and then I heard her coughing too. She could not have been more than a few yards away from me, but I could not see her, hardly knew in which direction she lay.

'Are you unhurt?' I called, then coughed weakly again.

'The Time Machine, Edward. We must climb aboard ... it will be returning ...'

'Where is it?'

'I am by it. I cannot reach it, but I can feel it with my foot.'

I realized she was over to my left, and I struck out that way, floundering through the noisome weeds, reaching out, hoping to strike something solid.

'Where are you?' I shouted, trying to make more of my voice than the wretched wheeze which was all I had so far managed.

'I am here, Edward. Come towards my voice.' She was nearer now, but her words were strangely choked, as if she too were drowning. 'I've slipped ... I can't find the Time Machine ... it's somewhere here ...'

I struck desperately through the weed, and almost at once I found her. My arm fell across her chest, and as it did so she grabbed me.

'Edward ... we must find the Machine!'

'You say it is here?'

'Somewhere ... by my legs ...'

I crawled over her, thrashing my arms to and fro, desperately seeking the Machine. Behind me, Amelia had somehow righted herself, and she moved to my side. Face down, slithering and sliding, coughing and wheezing, trembling with the cold that was even now seeping into our bones, we conducted our desperate search well beyond the three minutes neither of us would admit was all the time we had ever had to find it.

SIX

Futurity's Alien Land

•

I

Our struggles had been leading us inevitably downwards, and after a few more minutes I found solid ground beneath my feet. At once, I shouted aloud and helped Amelia to her feet. We pressed forward again, trying to maintain our balance while the vegetation tangled around our legs. We were both soaked through, and the air was freezing cold.

At last we broke free of the vegetation, and found we were on rough, pebbly soil. We walked a few yards beyond the fringe of the vegetation then sank down in exhaustion. Amelia was shaking with cold, and she made no protest when I placed my arm around her and hugged her to me for warmth.

At last, I said: 'We must find cover.'

I had been glancing around, hoping to see houses, but all I could see by the light of the stars was an apparent wasteland. The only visible feature was the bank of vegetation, looming perhaps a hundred feet into the air.

Amelia had made no reply, and I could feel her shivering still, so I stood up and started to remove my jacket. 'Please put this about your shoulders.'

'But you will freeze to death.'

'You are soaked through, Amelia.'

'We are both wet. We must exercise to keep warm.'

'In a moment,' I said, and sat down beside her once more. I kept my jacket on, but I opened it so that she was partially covered by it when I placed my arm around her shoulders. 'First I must regain my breath.'

Amelia pressed herself close to me, then said: 'Edward, where have we landed?'

'I cannot say. We are somewhere in futurity.'

'But why is it so cold? Why is it so difficult to breathe?'

I could only surmise.

'We must be very high,' I said. 'We are in a mountainous region.'

'But the ground is flat.'

'Then we must be on a plateau,' I said. 'The air is thin because of the altitude.'

'I think I have reached the same conclusion,' Amelia said. 'Last summer I was mountaineering in Switzerland, and on the higher peaks we found a similar difficulty with breathing.'

'But this is obviously not Switzerland.'

'We will have to wait until morning to discover our whereabouts,' Amelia said, decisively. 'There must be people near here.'

'And suppose we are in a foreign country, which does seem probable?'

'I have four languages, Edward, and can identify several others. All we need to know is the location of the nearest town, and there we will likely find a British Consul.'

Through all this I had been remembering that moment of violence I had glimpsed through the windows of the laboratory.

'We have seen that there is a war in 1903,' I said. 'Wherever we are now, or whichever year this is, could that war still be in progress?'

'We see no sign of it. Even if a war has started, innocent travellers will be protected. There are Consuls in every major city of the world.'

She seemed remarkably optimistic under the circumstances, and I was reassured. On first realizing that we had lost the Machine I had been plunged into despair. Even so, our prospects were doubtful, to say the very least, and I wondered if Amelia appreciated the full scale of our disaster. We had very little money with us, and no knowledge of the political situation, the breakdown of which had certainly caused the war of 1903. For all we knew we could be in enemy territory, and were likely to be imprisoned as soon as we were discovered.

Our immediate problem – that of surviving the rest of the night exposed to the elements – grew worse with every moment. Fortunately, there was no wind, but that was the only clemency we were being afforded. The very soil beneath us was frozen hard, and our breath was clouding about our faces.

'We must exercise,' I said. 'Otherwise we will contract pneumonia.'

Amelia did not dissent, and we climbed to our feet. I started jogging, but I must have been weaker than I knew, for I stumbled almost at once. Amelia too was having difficulties, for in swinging her arms about her head she staggered backwards.

'I am a little light-headed,' I said, gasping unexpectedly.

'And I.'

'Then we must not exert ourselves.'

I looked around desperately; in this Stygian gloom all that could be seen was the bank of weeds silhouetted against the starlight. It seemed to me that dank and wet as they were, they offered the only hope of shelter, and I put this to Amelia. She had no better proposal, and so with our arms around one another we returned to the vegetation. We found a clump of fronds standing about two feet high, on the very edge of the growth, and I felt experimentally with my hands. The stalks seemed to be dry, and beneath them the ground was not as hard as that on which we had been sitting.

An idea came to me, and I took one of the stalks and broke it off with my hand. At once, I felt cold fluid run over my fingers.

'The plants issue sap if they are broken,' I said, holding out the stalk for Amelia to take. 'If we can climb under the leaves without snapping the branches, we should remain dry.'

I sat down on the soil and began to move forward, feet first. Crawling gently in this fashion I was soon beneath the vegetation, and in a dark, silent cocoon of plants, A moment later, Amelia followed, and when she was beside me we lay still.

To say that lying there under the fronds was pleasant would

be utterly misleading, but it was certainly preferable to being exposed on the plain. Indeed, as the minutes passed and we made no movement I felt a little more comfortable, and realized that the confinement of our bodies was warming us a little.

I reached out to Amelia, who was lying not six inches from me, and placed my hand on her side. The fabric of her jacket was still damp, but I sensed that she too was rather warmer.

'Let us hold each other,' I said. 'We must not get any colder.'

I placed my arm around her back, and pulled her towards me. She came willingly enough, and soon we were lying together, face to face in the dark. I moved my head and our noses touched; I pressed forward and kissed her full on the lips.

At once she pulled her face away from mine.

'Please don't take advantage of me, Edward.'

'How can you accuse me of that? We must stay warm.'

'Then let us do just that. I do not want you to kiss me.'

'But I thought – '

'Circumstance has thrown us together. Let us not forget that we barely know each other.'

I could hardly believe my ears. Amelia's friendly manner during the day had seemed an unmistakable confirmation of my own feelings, and in spite of our dreadful situation her very presence was enough to inflame my passions. I had expected her to allow me to kiss her, and after this rebuff I lay in silence, hurt and embarrassed.

A few minutes later Amelia moved again, and kissed me briefly on my forehead.

'I'm very fond of you, Edward,' she said. 'Is that not enough?'

'I thought ... well, I'd been feeling that you—'

'Have I said or done anything to indicate that I felt for you more than friendship?'

'Well ... no.'

'Then please, lie still.'

She placed one of her arms around me, and pressed me to her a little more tightly. We lay like that for a long time, barely moving except to ease cramped muscles, and during the rest of that long night we managed to doze for only a few short periods.

Sunrise came more suddenly than either of us had expected. One moment we had been lying in that dark, silent growth, the next there was a brilliance of light, filtering through the fronds. We moved simultaneously in response, both sensing that the day ahead was to be momentous.

We rose painfully, and walked haltingly away from the vegetation, towards the sun. It was still touching the horizon, dazzlingly white. The sky above us was a deep blue. There were no clouds.

We walked for ten yards, then turned to look back at the bank of vegetation.

Amelia, who had been holding my arm, now clutched me suddenly. I too stared in amazement, for the vegetation stretched as far as we could see to left and right of us. It stood in a line that was generally straight, but parts of it advanced and others receded. In places the weeds heaped together, forming mounds two hundred feet or more in height. This much we could have expected from our experience of it during the night, but nothing could have warned us of the profoundest surprise of all: that there was not a stem, not a leaf, not a bulbous, spreading tuber lying grotesquely across the sandy soil that was not a vivid blood-red.

II

We stared for a long time at that wall of scarlet plant-life, lacking the vocabulary to express our reactions to it.

The higher part of the weed-bank had the appearance of being smooth and rounded, especially towards its visible crest. Here it looked like a gentle, undulating hill, although by looking in more detail at its surface we could see that what appeared to be an unbroken face was in fact made up of thousands or millions of branches.

Lower down, in the part of the growth were we had laid, its appearance was quite different. Here the newer plants were growing, presumably from seeds thrown out from the main bulk of vegetation. Both Amelia and I remarked on a horrible feeling that the wall was inexorably advancing, throwing out new shoots and piling up its mass behind.

Then, even as we looked aghast at this incredible weed-bank, we saw that the impact of the sun's rays was having an effect, for from all along the wall there came a deep-throated groaning, and a thrashing, breaking sound. One branch moved, then another ... then all along that living cliff-face branches and stems moved in a semblance of unthinking animation.

Amelia clutched my arm again, and pointed directly in front of us.

'See, Edward!' she said. 'My bag is there! We must have my bag!'

I saw that about thirty feet up the wall of vegetation there was what appeared to be a broken hole in the smooth-seeming surface. As Amelia started forward towards it, I realized that that must be the place where the Time Machine had so precipitately deposited us.

A few feet away, absurd in its context, lay Amelia's handbag, caught on a stem.

I hurried forward and caught up with Amelia, just as she was preparing to push through the nearest plants, her skirt raised almost to her knees.

'You can't go in there,' I said. 'The plants are coming to life!'

As I spoke to her a long, creeper-like plant snaked silently towards us, and a seed-pod exploded with a report like a pistol. A cloud of dust-like seeds drifted away from the plant.

'Edward, it is imperative that I have my bag!'

'You can't go up there to get it!'

'I must.'

'You will have to manage without your powders and creams.'

She glared angrily at me for a moment. 'There is more in it than face-powder. Money ... and my brandy-flask. Many things.'

She plunged desperately into the vegetation, but as she did so a branch creaked into apparent life, and raised itself up. It caught the hem of her skirt, tore the fabric and spun her round. She fell, screaming.

I hurried to her, and helped her away from the plants. 'Stay here ... I'll go.'

Without further hesitation I plunged into that forest of groaning, moving stems, and scrambled towards where I had last seen her bag. It was not too difficult at first; I quickly learned which stems would, and which would not, bear my weight. As the height of the plants grew to a point where they were above my head I started to climb, slipping several times as the branch I gripped broke in my hand and released a flood of sap. All around me the plants were moving; growing and waving like the arms of a cheering crowd. Glancing up, I saw Amelia's hand-bag on one such stem, dangling some twenty feet above my head. I had managed to climb only three or four feet towards it. There was nothing here that would bear my weight.

There came a crashing noise a few yards to my right, and I ducked, imagining in my horror that some major trunk was moving into life ... but then I saw that it had been Amelia's bag, slipping from its perch.

Thankfully, I abandoned my futile attempt to climb, and thrust myself through the waving lower stems. The noise of this riotous growth was now considerable, and when another seed-pod exploded by my ear I was temporarily deafened by it. My only thought now was to retrieve Amelia's bag and get away from this nightmare vegetation. Not caring where I placed my feet, nor how many stems I broke and how much I drenched myself, I pushed wildly through the stalks, seized the bag and headed at once for the edge of the growth.

Amelia was sitting on the ground, and I threw the bag down beside her. Unreasonably, I felt angry with her, although I knew it was simply a reaction to my terror.

As she thanked me for collecting the bag, I turned away from her and stared at the wall of scarlet vegetation. It was visibly much more disordered than before, with branches and stems swinging out from every place. In the soil at the very edge of the growth I saw new, pink seedlings appearing. The plants were advancing on us, slowly but relentlessly. I watched the process for a few minutes more, seeing how sap from the adult plants dripped down on the soil, crudely irrigating the new shoots.

When I turned back to Amelia she was wiping her face and hands with a piece of flannel she had taken from her bag. Beside her on the ground was her flask. She held this out to me.

'Would you like some brandy, Edward?'

'Thank you.'

The liquor flowed over my tongue, immediately warming me. I took only one small mouthful, sensing that we should have to make last what we had.

With the rising of the sun, we both felt the benefit of its heat. We were evidently in an equatorial region, for the sun was rising steeply, and its rays were warm.

'Edward, come here.'

I squatted on the ground in front of Amelia. She looked remarkably fresh, but then I realized that in addition to having had a cursory wash with her dampened face-flannel, she had brushed her hair. Her clothes, though, were in a dreadful state: the sleeve of her jacket had been torn, and there was a long rent in her skirt where the plant had swung her round. There were dirty pink streaks and stains all over her clothes. Glancing down at myself, I saw that my new suit had become equally spoiled.

'Would you like to clean yourself?' she said, offering me the flannel.

I took it from her, and wiped my face and hands.

'How do you come to have this with you?' I said, marvelling at the unexpected pleasure of washing myself.

'I have travelled a lot,' she said. 'One grows accustomed to anticipating any contingency.'

She showed me that she had a traveller's tidy, containing as well as the face-flannel, a square of soap, a toothbrush, a mirror, a pair of folding nail-scissors and a comb.

I ran my hand over my chin, thinking I should soon need a shave, but that was one contingency she seemed not to have anticipated.

I borrowed her comb to straighten my hair, and then allowed her to tidy my moustache.

'There,' she said, giving it a final twirl. 'Now we are fit to re-enter civilization. But first, we must have some breakfast to sustain us.'

She dipped into her bag and produced a large bar of Menier's chocolate.

'May I ask what else you have concealed in there?' I said.

'Nothing that will be of use to us. Now, we will have to ration this, for it is the only food I have. We shall have two squares each now, and a little more as we need it.'

We munched the chocolate hungrily, then followed it with another mouthful of brandy.

Amelia closed her bag, and we stood up.

'We will walk in that direction,' she said, pointing parallel to the wall of vegetation.

'Why that way?' I said, curious at her apparent resolution.

'Because the sun rose over there,' she pointed across the desert, 'and so the weed-bank must run from north to south. We have seen how cold it can be at night, therefore we can do no better than move southwards.'

It was unassailable logic. We had walked several yards before an argument occurred to me.

'You assume we are still in the northern hemisphere,' I said.

'Of course. For your information, Edward, I have already deduced where we have landed. It is so high and cold that this can only be Tibet.'

'Then we are walking towards the Himalayas,' I said.

'We will deal with that problem when we encounter it.'

III

We found that walking across this terrain was not easy. Although our surroundings became quite pleasant as the sun rose higher, and there was a distinct spring in our step, lent, we assumed, by the clean cold air and the altitude, we discovered that we tired readily and were forced to make frequent halts.

For about three hours we maintained a steady pace, by walking and resting at regular periods, and we took it in turns to carry the bag. I felt invigorated by the exercise, but Amelia did not find it easy; her breathing became laboured and she complained frequently of dizziness.

What we both found dispiriting was that the landscape had not changed from the moment we set out. With minor variations in size, the wall of vegetation ran in an unbroken line across the desert.

As the sun moved higher its radiant heat increased, and our clothes were soon completely dry. Unprotected as we were (Amelia's bonnet had no brim, and I had lost my straw hat in the weeds) we soon began to suffer the first effects of sunburn, and we both complained of an unpleasant tingling on the skin of our faces.

A further effect of the hotter sunshine was yet another change in the activity of the weeds. The unsettling life-like movement lasted for about an hour after sunrise, but now such movements were rare; instead, we could see that the seedlings were growing at a prodigious pace, and sap trickled down constantly from the higher shoots.

One matter had been troubling me ever since our accident, and as we walked along I felt I should bring it up.

I said: 'Amelia, I do accept full responsibility for our predicament.'

'What do you mean?'

'I should not have interfered with the Time Machine. It was a reckless thing to do.'

'You are no more to blame than I. Please don't speak of it any more.'

'But we may now be in danger of our lives.'

'We shall have to face that together,' she said. 'Life will be intolerable if you continue blaming yourself. It was I ... who first tampered with the Machine. Our main concern ... now should be to return to ...'

I looked sharply at Amelia, and saw that her face had gone pale and her eyes were half closed. A moment later she staggered slightly, looked at me helplessly, then stumbled and fell full-length on the sandy soil, I rushed to her.

'Amelia!' I cried in alarm, but she did not move. I took her hand and felt for her pulse: it was faint, and irregular.

I had been carrying the bag, and I fumbled with the catch and threw it open. I searched frantically through the bag, knowing that what I sought would be somewhere there. After a moment I found it: a tiny bottle of smelling-salts. I unscrewed the top, and waved it under her nose.

The response was immediate. Amelia coughed violently, and tried to move away. I placed my arms around her shoulders, and helped her into a sitting position. She continued to cough, and her eyes were streaming with tears. Remembering something I had once seen I bent her over, gently pushing her head down towards her knees.

After five minutes she straightened and looked at me. Her face was still pale, and her eyes were watery.

'We have walked too long without food,' she said. 'I came over dizzy, and—'

'It must be the altitude,' I said. 'We will find some way down from this plateau as soon as possible.'

I delved into her bag, and found the chocolate. We had still eaten only a fraction of what we had, so I broke off two more squares and gave them to her.

'No, Edward.'

'Eat it,' I said. 'You are weaker than I am.'

'We have just had some. We must make it last.'

She took the broken-off squares and the rest of the chocolate, and put them firmly back inside the bag.

'What I should really like,' she said, 'is a glass of water. I'm very thirsty indeed.'

'Do you suppose the sap of the plants is drinkable?'

'If we do not find any water, we will have to try it in the end.'

I said: 'When we were first thrown into the weeds I swallowed some of the sap. It was not unlike water, but rather bitter.'

After a few more minutes Amelia stood up, a little unsteadily I thought, and declared that she was fit to continue. I made her take another sip of brandy before moving on.

But then, although we walked much more slowly, Amelia stumbled again. This time she did not lose consciousness, but said she felt as if she was about to be sick. We rested for a full thirty minutes, while the sun moved to its zenith.

'Please, Amelia, eat some more chocolate. I'm sure that all you are suffering from is lack of sustenance.'

'I'm no more hungry than you,' she said. 'It is not that.'

'Then what is it?'

'I cannot tell you.'

'You do know what is the matter?'

She nodded.

'Then please tell me, and I can do something to help.'

'You could do nothing, Edward. I shall be all right.'

I knelt on the sand before her, and placed my hands on her shoulders. 'Amelia, we do not know how much further we have to walk. We cannot go on if you are ill.'

'I am not ill.'

'It looks very much like it to me.'

'I am uncomfortable, but not ill.'

'Then please do something about it,' I said, my concern changing abruptly to irritation.

She was silent for a moment, but then, with my assistance, climbed to her feet. 'Wait here, Edward. I shall not be long.'

She took her bag, and walked slowly towards the weed-bank. She stepped carefully through the lower plants, and headed towards a growth of higher stalks. When she reached these she turned round and looked in my direction, then crouched down and moved behind them.

I turned my back, assuming she would prefer her privacy.

Several minutes passed, and she did not emerge. I waited for a quarter of an hour, then began to get worried. There had been an absolute silence since she had disappeared ... but even in my growing sense of alarm I felt I should wait and respect her privacy.

I had just consulted my watch, and discovered that more than twenty minutes had passed, when I heard her voice.

'Edward ...?'

Without further delay I ran in her direction, racing through the scarlet vegetation towards where I had last seen her. I was tormented by the vision of some momentous disaster that had befallen her, but nothing could have prepared me for what I saw.

I came to a sudden halt, and immediately averted my gaze: Amelia had removed her skirt and blouse, and was standing in her underwear!

She held her skirt protectively over her body, and was looking at me with an expression of cowed embarrassment.

'Edward, I cannot get them off ... Please help me ...'

'What are you doing?' I cried in astonishment.

'It is my stays that are too tight ... I can hardly breathe. But I cannot unlace them.' She sobbed more loudly, then went on: 'I did not want you to know, but I have not been alone since yesterday. They are so tight... please help me ...'

I cannot deny that I found her pathetic expression amusing, but I covered my smile and moved round behind her.

I said: 'What do I do?'

'There are two laces ... they should be tied at the bottom with a bow, but I've accidentally knotted them.'

I looked more closely, and saw what she had done. I worked at the knot with my fingernails, and loosened it without difficulty.

'There,' I said, turning away. 'It is free.'

'Please undo it, Edward. I can't reach it myself.'

The agonies I had been suppressing came abruptly to the surface. 'Amelia, you cannot ask me to undress you!'

'I just want these laces undone,' she said. 'That is all.'

Reluctantly I went back to her and started the laborious process of slipping the laces through the eyelets. When the task was half-completed, and part of the restraining garment was loose, I saw just how tight it had been on her body. The laces slipped out of the last two eyelets, and the corset came free. Amelia pulled it away from her, and tossed it casually to the ground. She turned towards me.

'I can't thank you enough, Edward. I think I should have died if I'd kept it on a moment longer.'

Had it not been she who had turned towards me, I should have felt my presence most improper, for she had allowed the skirt to fall away and I could see that her chemise was manufactured of the lightest material, and that her bosom was most prominent. I stepped towards her, feeling that I might make the affectionate gesture of a hug, but she moved backwards at once, and brought up the skirt to conceal herself again.

'You may leave me now,' she said. 'I can manage to dress on my own.'

IV

When, a few minutes later, Amelia emerged from the weeds, she was fully dressed and carrying the corset between the handles of her bag.

1 said: 'Are you not going to discard that? It is manifestly uncomfortable to wear.'

'Only for long periods,' she said, looking very abashed. 'I shall leave it off for the rest of the day, and wear it again tomorrow.'

'I shall look forward to helping you,' I said, sincerely.

'There is no need for that. By tomorrow we will be back in civilization, and I will hire a servant.'

Since she was still flushed, and I was not a little excited, I felt it appropriate to say: 'If my opinion is at all valuable to you I can assure you that your figure is just as trim without it.'

'That is not to the point. Shall we continue on our way?'

She stepped away from me, and I followed.

All this had been a temporary distraction from our plight, for soon the sun had moved far enough towards the west for the weed-bank to start throwing a shadow. Whenever we walked through this we felt immediately much colder.

After another half an hour's walking I was just about to propose a rest, when Amelia suddenly halted and looked towards a shallow depression in the ground. She walked briskly towards it.

I followed her, and she said: 'We shall have to bivouac again. I think we should prepare now.'

'I agree in principle. But I feel we should walk as far as possible.'

'No, this place is ideal. We shall stay the night here.'

'In the open?'

'There is no need for that. We have time to prepare a campsite before nightfall.' She was regarding the depression with a calculating manner. 'When I was in Switzerland I was shown how to build emergency shelters. We will need to make this hole rather deeper, and build up the sides. If you would do that, I will cut some of the fronds.'

We argued for a few minutes – I felt we should take advantage of the daylight and press on – but Amelia had made up her mind. In the end, she removed her jacket and walked over to the weed-bank, while I crouched down and, with my hands, started to scoop out the sandy soil.

It took approximately two hours to construct a camp-site to our mutual satisfaction. By this time I had removed most of the larger pebbles from the depression, and Amelia had broken off a huge pile of the leafiest, fern-like branches. These we had laid in the depression, making a bonfire-like mound of leaves, into the base of which we proposed to insinuate ourselves.

The sun was now almost out of sight beyond the weed-bank, and we were both feeling cold.

'I think we have done all we can,' Amelia said.

'Then shall we shelter inside?' I had now seen the wisdom of Amelia's wish for early preparation. Had we walked further we could never have made such elaborate precautions against the cold.

'Are you thirsty?'

'I'm all right,' I said, but I was lying. My throat had been parched all day.

'But you have taken no liquid.'

'I can survive the night.'

Amelia indicated one of the long, creeper-like stalks that she had also brought to our bivouac. She broke off a piece and held it out to me. 'Drink the sap, Edward. It is perfectly safe.' 'It could be poisonous.'

'No, I tried it earlier while I was removing my stays. It is quite invigorating, and I have suffered no ill-effects.'

I placed the end of the stalk to my lips and sucked tentatively. At once my mouth was filled with cold liquid, and I swallowed it quickly. After the first mouthful, the flavour did not seem so unpleasant.

I said: 'It reminds me of an iron-tonic I had as a child.' Amelia smiled. 'So you too were given Parrish's Food. I wondered if you would notice the similarity.'

'I was usually given a spoonful of honey, to take away the taste.'

'This time you will have to manage without.'

I said, boldly: 'Maybe not.'

Amelia looked sharply at me, and I saw the faint return of her earlier blush. I threw aside the creeper, then assisted Amelia as she climbed before me into our shelter for the night.

SEVEN

The Awakening of Awareness

•

I

We lay still, side by side, for a long time. Although Amelia had selected those plants she judged to be the driest of sap, we discovered that they were seeping beneath us. In addition, the slightest movement allowed the air to drift in from outside. I dozed for a while, but I cannot speak for Amelia.

Then, awakened by the insidious cold which was attacking my feet and legs, I felt Amelia stiffen beside me.

She said: 'Edward, are we to die out here?'

'I think not,' I said at once, for during the day the possibility had often occurred to me, and I had been trying to think of some reassurance to offer her. 'We cannot have much further to travel.'

'But we are going to starve!'

'We still have the chocolate,' I said, 'and as you yourself have observed, the sap of these weeds is nutritious.'

This at least was true; my body hungered for solid food, but since taking the sap I had felt somewhat stronger.

'I fear we will die of exposure. I cannot live in this cold much longer.'

I knew she was trembling, and as she spoke I heard her teeth chattering. Our bivouac was not all we had hoped.

'Please allow me,' I said, and without waiting for her dissent I moved towards her and slid my arm beneath her head and shoulders. The rebuff of the night before was still a painful memory, so I was pleased when she came willingly, resting her head on my shoulder and placing an arm across my chest. I raised my knees a few inches so that she could slide her legs beneath mine. In doing this we dislodged some of our covering foliage, and it took several more seconds to redistribute them.

We lay still again, Trying to recapture that comparative warmth we had had until we moved. Several more minutes passed in silence, and our closer contact began to bear fruit in that I felt a little warmer.

'Are you asleep, Edward?' Her voice was very soft.

'No,' I said.

'I'm still cold. Do you think we should quickly cut some more leaves?'

'I think we should stay still. Warmth will come.'

'Hold me tighter.'

What followed that apparently simple remark I could never have imagined, even in my most improper fancies. Spontaneously, I brought my other hand across and hugged her to me; in the same moment Amelia too placed her arms fully about me, and we discovered we were embracing each other with an intimacy that made me throw aside caution.

Her face was pressed directly against the side of mine, and I felt it moving sensuously to and fro. I responded in kind, fully aware that the love and passion I had been suppressing were growing in me at an uncontrollable rate. In the back of my mind I sensed a sudden despair, knowing that later I would regret this abandonment, but I thrust it aside for my emotions were clamouring for expression. Her neck was by my mouth, and without any attempt at subterfuge I pressed my lips to it and kissed her firmly and with great feeling. Her response was to hold me yet tighter, and uncaring of how we dislodged our shelter we rolled passionately from one side to another.

Then at last I pulled myself away, and Amelia turned her face and pressed her lips against mine. I was now lying almost completely atop her, and my weight was on her. We broke apart eventually, and I held my face half an inch from hers.

I simply said, with all the sincerity of absolute truth: 'I love you, Amelia.'

She made no answer other than to press my face to hers once more, and we kissed as if we had never stopped. She was everything that could ever exist for me, and for that period at least the extraordinary nature of our immediate surroundings ceased to matter. I wanted simply that we should continue kissing forever. Indeed, by the very nature of her response, I assumed that Amelia was in accord. Her hand was behind my head, her fingers spread through my hair, and she was pressing me to her as we kissed.

Then she suddenly snatched her hand away, wrenched her face from mine, and she cried out aloud.

The tension drained away, and my body slumped. I fell forward across her, my face once more buried in the hollow of her shoulder. We lay immobile for many minutes, my breathing irregular and painful, my breath hot in the confined space. Amelia was crying, and I felt her tears trickle down her cheek and against the side of my face.

II

I moved only once more, to ease a cramp in my left arm, and then I lay still again, most of my weight on Amelia.

For a long time my mind was blank; all desire to justify my actions to myself had drained as quickly as the physical passion. Drained also were the self-recriminations. I lay still, aware only of a slight bruising around my mouth, the residual flavour of Amelia's kiss and the strands of her hair which brushed my forehead.

She sobbed quietly for a few minutes more, but then became quiet. A few minutes later her breathing became regular, and I judged she had fallen asleep. Soon, I too could feel the fatigue of the day clouding my mind, and in due course I fell asleep.

I do not know how long I slept, but some time later I realized I was awake, yet still in the same position on top of Amelia. Our earlier problem of warmth was banished, for my whole body glowed with heat. I had slept in spite of the awkward angle in which I was lying, and now my back was badly cramped. I wanted to move, to rest from this position, and in addition I could feel the stiff collar of my shirt cutting into my neck and at the front the brass stud was biting into my throat, but I did not want to rouse Amelia. I decided to lie still, and hope to fall asleep again.

I found that my spirits were high, and this in spite of all that had happened. Considered objectively our chances of survival seemed slim; Amelia had also realized this. Unless we were to reach civilization within the next twenty-four hours it was likely we would perish out here on this plateau.

However, I could not forget that glimpse I had had of Amelia's future destiny.

I knew that if Amelia were to be living in Richmond in the year 1903 she would be killed in the conflagration about the house. I had not been rational at the time, but my irresponsible tampering with the Time Machine had been an instinctive response to this. That accident had precipitated our current predicament, but I was in no way sorry.

Wherever on Earth we were, and in whatever year, I had decided what we were to do. From now I would make it my business to see that Amelia would never return to England until that day had passed!

I had already declared my love for her, and she had seemed to respond; it would be no greater step to avow my love as being eternal, and propose marriage. Whether she would accept I could not say, but I was determined to be resolute and patient. As my wife, she would be subject to my will. Of course, she was clearly of gentle birth, and my own origins were more humble, but I argued to myself that this had not so far been allowed to affect our behaviour to one another; she was an emancipationist, and if our love were true it would not be marred by—

'Are you awake, Edward?'

Her voice was close by my ear.

'Yes. Did I wake you?'

'No ... I've been awake for some time. I heard your breathing change.'

'Is it daylight yet?' I said.

'I don't think so.'

'I think I should move,' I said. 'My weight must be crushing you.'

Her arms, which were still around my back, tightened momentarily.

'Please stay as you are,' she said.

'I do not wish to seem to be taking advantage of you.'

'It is I who is taking the advantage. You are an excellent substitute for blankets.'

I lifted myself slightly away from her, so that my face was directly above hers. Around us, the leaves rustled in the darkness.

I said: 'Amelia, I have something to say to you. I am passionately in love with you.'

Once again her arms tightened their hold, pulling me down so that my face was alongside hers.

'Dear Edward,' she said, hugging me affectionately.

'Do you have nothing else to say?'

'Only... only that I'm sorry for what happened.'

'Do you not love me too?'

'I'm not sure, Edward.'

'Will you marry me?'

I felt her head move: it was shaking from side to side, but beyond this she made no answer.

'Amelia?'

She maintained her silence, and I waited anxiously. She was now quite immobile, her arms resting across my back but exerting no pressure of any kind.

I said: 'I cannot conceive of life without you, Amelia. I have known you for such a short time, and yet it is as if I have been with you all my life.'

'That is how I feel,' she said, but her voice was almost inaudible, and her tone was lifeless.

'Then please marry me. When we reach civilization we will

find a British Consul or a missionary church, and we may marry at once.'

'We should not talk of these things.'

I said, for my spirits were low: 'Are you refusing me?'

'Please, Edward—'

'Are you already engaged to another?'

'No, and I am not refusing you. I say we must not talk of this because of the uncertainty of our prospects. We do not even know in which country we are. And until then . . .'

Her voice tailed away, sounding as uncertain as her argument.

'But tomorrow,' I went on, 'we will find where we are, and will you then present another excuse? I'm asking only one thing: do you love me as much as I love you?'

'I don't know, Edward.'

'I love you dearly. Can you say that to me?'

Unexpectedly, her head turned and for a moment her lips pressed gently against my cheek. Then she said: 'I am unusually fond of you, Edward dear.'

I had to be content with that. I raised my head, and brought my lips down to hers. They touched for a second, but then she turned her head away.

'We were foolish before,' she said. 'Let us not make the same mistake. We have been forced to pass a night together, and neither of us should take advantage of the other.'

'If that is how you see it.'

'My dear, we must not assume that we will not be discovered. For all we know, this might be someone's private estate.'

'You have not suggested that before.'

'No, but we may not be as alone as we think.'

'I doubt if anyone will investigate a mound of leaves!' I said.

She laughed then, and hugged me. 'We must sleep. We may have another long walk ahead of us.'

'Are you still comfortable in this position?'

'Yes. And you?'

I said: 'My collar is hurting me. Would you consider it improper if I were to remove my tie?'

'You are always so formal! Let me do it for you ... it must be choking you.'

I raised myself away from her, and with deft fingers she loosened the knot and released both front and back studs. When this was done I lowered myself, and felt her arms closing about my back. I pressed the side of my face to hers, kissed her once on the lobe of her ear, and then we lay still, waiting for sleep to return.

III

We were awakened not by the rising sun, as our covering leaves effectively filtered the light to an almost imperceptible maroon glow, but by the creaking and groaning of the near-by weed-bank. Amelia and I lay in each other's arms for a few minutes before rising, as if sensing that the warmth and intimacy of the overnight tryst should be savoured. Then at last we kicked and pushed the scarlet leaves aside, and emerged into the brilliant daylight and hard radiant heat. We stretched elaborately, each of us stiff from the enforced stillness of the night.

Our morning toilet was brief, our breakfast briefer. We wiped our faces with Amelia's flannel, and combed our hair. We each took two squares of chocolate, and followed them with a draught of sap. Then we collected our few belongings, and prepared to continue on our way. I noticed that Amelia still carried her corset between the handles of her bag.

'Shall we not leave that behind?' I said, thinking how pleasant it would be if she were never to wear it again.

'And these?' she said, producing my collar and tie from the hand-bag. 'Shall we leave these behind too?'

'Of course not,' I said. 'I must wear them when we find civilization.'

'Then we are agreed.'

'The difference is,' I said, 'that I do not need a servant. Nor have I ever had one.'

'If your intentions for me are sincere, Edward, you must prepare yourself for the prospect of hiring staff.'

Amelia's tone was as non-committal as ever, but the unmistakable reference to my proposal had the effect of quickening my heart. I took the bag from her, and held her hand in mine. She glanced at me once, and I thought I saw a trace of a smile, but then we were walking and we each kept our gaze directed ahead. The weed-bank was in the full throes of its seeming animation, and we stayed at a wary distance from it.

Knowing that most of our walking must be done before midday, we maintained a good pace, walking and resting at regular periods. As before, we found that the altitude made breathing difficult, and so we talked very little while we were walking.

During one of our rests, though, I brought up a subject which had been occupying me.

'In which year do you suppose we are?' I said.

'I have no idea. It depends on the degree to which you tampered with the controls.'

'I didn't know what I was doing. I altered the monthly presetting dial, and it was then during the summer months of 1902. But I did not move the lever before I broke the nickel rod, and so I am wondering whether the automatic return was not interrupted, and we are now in 1893.'

Amelia considered this for several moments, but then said: 'I think not. The crucial act was the breaking of that rod. It would have interrupted the automatic return, and extended the original journey. At the end of that, the automatic return would come into operation again, as we found when we lost the Machine. On the other hand, your changing of the monthly dial might have had an effect. By how much did you alter it?'

I thought about this with great concentration. 'I turned it several months forward.'

'I still cannot say for certain. It seems to me that we are in one of three possible times. Either we returned to 1893, as you suggest, and are dislocated by several thousand miles, or the accident has left us in 1902, at the date showing on the dials when the rod was broken… or we have travelled forward those few months, and are now at, say, the end of 1902 or the beginning of 1903. In any event, one matter is certain: we have been propelled a considerable distance from Richmond.'

None of these postulations was welcome, for any one of them meant that the disastrous day in June 1903 still lay ahead. I did not wish to dwell on the consequences of this, so I raised another topic that had been troubling me.

'If we were now to return to England,' I said, 'is it likely that we could meet ourselves?'

Amelia did not answer my question directly. She said: 'What do you mean, if we were to return to England? Surely we will arrange that as soon as possible?'

'Yes, of course,' I said, hastily, regretting that I had phrased my question in that way. 'So it is not a rhetorical question: are we soon to meet ourselves?'

Amelia frowned.

'I don't think it is possible,' she said at length. 'We have travelled in Time just as positively as we have travelled in Space, and if my own belief is correct, we have left the world of 1893 as far behind as we seem to have left Richmond. There is at this moment neither Amelia Fitzgibbon nor Edward Turnbull in England.'

'Then what,' I said, having anticipated this answer, 'will Sir William have made of our disappearance?'

Amelia smiled unexpectedly. 'I'm sure I do not know. Nor am I sure that he will even notice my absence until several days have passed. He is a man of great preoccupations. When he realizes I have gone, I suppose he will contact the police and I will be listed as a Missing Person. That much at least he will see as his responsibility.'

'But you talk of this with such coldness. Surely Sir William will be most concerned at your disappearance?'

'I am merely speaking the facts as I see them. I know that he was preparing his Time Machine for a journey of exploration, and had we not pre-empted him he would have been the first man to travel into futurity. When he returns to his laboratory he will find the Machine apparently untouched – for it would have returned directly from here – and he will continue with his plans without regard for the household.'

I said: 'Do you think that if Sir William were to suspect the cause of your disappearance he might use the Machine to try to find us?'

Amelia shook her head at once. 'You assume two things. First, that he would realize that we had tampered with the Machine, and second, that even if so he would know where to search for us. The first is almost impossible to suspect, for to all appearances the Machine will appear untouched, and the second is unthinkable, as the Machine has no record of its journeys when the automatic return has been in operation.'

'So we must make our own way back.'

At this, Amelia came a little closer and grasped my hand.

'Yes, my dear,' she said.

IV

The sun was past its zenith, and already the weed-bank was throwing a shadow, and we walked stoically on. Then, just as I was feeling we should stop for another rest, I caught Amelia's elbow and pointed forward.

'Look, Amelia!' I shouted. 'There... on the horizon!'

Directly in front of us was the most welcome sight either of us could have imagined. Something metallic and polished was ahead of us, for the sun's rays were being reflected off into our eyes. The steadiness of the dazzle was such that we knew it could not be coming from a natural feature, such as a sea or a lake. It was man-made, and our first sight of civilization.

We started towards it, but in a moment the glare vanished.

'What has happened?' Amelia said. 'Did we imagine it?'

'Whatever it was, it has moved,' I said. 'But it was no illusion.'

We walked as quickly as we could, but we were still suffering the effects of altitude and were forced to maintain our usual steady pace.

Within two or three minutes we saw the reflected light again, and knew we had not been mistaken. At last sense prevailed and we took a short rest, eating the remainder of our chocolate and drinking as much of the sap as we could stomach. Thus fortified, we continued towards the intermittent light, knowing that at last our long walk was nearly over.

After another hour we were close enough to see the source of the reflection, although by then the sun had moved further across the sky and it had been some time since we had seen the dazzle. There was a metal tower built in the desert, and it was the roof of this that had been catching the sunshine. In this rarefied atmosphere distances were deceptive, and although we had been able to see the tower for some time, it wasn't until we were almost on it that we were able to estimate its size. By then we were close enough to see that it was not alone, and that some distance beyond it were several more.

The overall height of the nearest tower was about sixty feet. In appearance, the nearest analogy I can draw is that of a huge, elongated pin, for the tower consisted of a thin central pillar, surmounted by a circular enclosed platform. This description is itself misleading, for there was not one central pillar, but three. These were built very closely together, though, and ran parallel to each other up to the platform they supported, so it was only as we walked beneath the tower that Amelia and I noticed this. These three pillars were firmly buried in the soil but staring up at them I noticed that the platform was capable of being raised or lowered, for the pillars were jointed in several places and made of telescopic tubes.

The platform at the top was perhaps ten feet in diameter, and about seven feet high. On one side there was what seemed to be a large oval window, but this was made of dark glass and it was impossible to see beyond it from where we stood. Beneath the platform was a mechanical mounting, rather like gimbals, and it was this that enabled the platform to rotate slowly to and fro, thus causing the sun's reflection to flash at us earlier. The platform was moving from side to side now, but apart from this there was no sign of anyone about.

'Hallo up there!' I called, then after a few seconds repeated the call. Either they could not hear me, or my voice was weaker than I had realized, but there was no reply from the occupants.

While I had been examining the tower, Amelia had moved past me and was staring towards the weed-bank. We had walked diagonally away from the vegetation to visit the tower, but now I saw that the bank here was even further away than I would have expected, and much lower. What was more, working at the base of it were many people.

Amelia turned towards me, and I could see the joy in her expression.

'Edward, we're safe!' she cried, and came towards me and we embraced warmly.

Safety indeed it was, for this was clear evidence of the habitation we had been seeking for so long. I was all for going over to the people at once, but Amelia delayed.

'We must make ourselves presentable,' she said, and fumbled inside her bag. She passed me my collar and tie, and while I put these on she sat down and fussed with her face. After this she tried to dab off some of the worst weed-stains from her clothes, using her face-flannel, and then combed her hair. I was in dire need of a shave, but there was nothing that could be done about that.

Apart from our general untidiness, there was another matter that was troubling us both. Our long hours exposed to the hot sunshine had left their mark, in the fact that we were both suffering from sunburn. Amelia's face had gone a bright pink – and she told me mine was no better – and although she had applied some cold-cream from a pot in her bag, she said she was suffering considerably.

When we were ready, she said: 'I will take your arm. We do not know who these people are, so it would be wise not to give the wrong impression. If we behave with confidence, we will be treated correctly.'

'And what about that?' I said, indicating her corset, all too evident between the handles of her bag. 'Now is the time to discard it. If we wish to appear as if we have been enjoying an afternoon stroll, that will make it clear we have not.'

Amelia frowned, evidently undecided. At last she picked it and placed it on the soil, so that it leaned against one of the pillars of the tower.

'I'll leave it here for the moment,' she said. 'I can soon find it again when we have spoken to the people.'

She came back to me, took my arm and together we walked sedately towards the nearest of the people. Once again the clear air had deceived our eyes, and we soon saw that the weeds were farther away than we had imagined. I glanced back just once, and saw that the platform at the top of the tower was still rotating to and fro.

Walking towards the people – none of whom had yet noticed us – I saw something that rather alarmed me. As I wasn't sure I said something about it to Amelia, but as we came closer there was no mistaking it: most of the people – and there were both men and women – were almost completely unclothed.

I stopped at once, and turned away.

'I had better go forward alone,' I said. 'Please wait here.'

Amelia, who had turned with me, for I had grasped her arm, stared over her shoulder at the people.

'I am not as coy as you,' she said. 'From what are you trying to protect me?'

'They are not decent,' I said, very embarrassed. 'I will speak to them on my own.'

'For Heaven's sake, Edward!' Amelia cried in exasperation. 'We are about to starve to death, and you smother me with modesty!'

She let go of my arm, and strode off alone. I followed immediately, my face burning with my embarrassment. Amelia headed directly for the nearest group: about two dozen men and women who were hacking at the scarlet weeds with long-bladed knives.

'You!' she cried, venting her anger with me on the nearest man. 'Do you speak English?'

The man turned sharply and faced her. For an instant he looked at her in surprise – and in that moment I saw that he was very tall, that his skin was burned a reddish colour, and that he was wearing nothing more than a stained loincloth – and then prostrated himself before her. In the same instant, the other people around him dropped their knives and threw themselves face down on the ground.

Amelia glanced at me, and I saw that the imperious manner had gone as quickly as it had been assumed. She looked frightened, and I went and stood by her side.

'What's the matter?' she said to me in a whisper. 'What have I done?'

I said: 'You probably scared the wits out of them.'

'Excuse me,' Amelia said to the people, in a much gentler voice. 'Does any one of you speak English? We are very hungry, and need shelter for the night.'

There was no response.

'Try another language,' I said.

'*Excusez-moi, parlez-vous français*?' Amelia said. There was still no response, so she added: '*¿Habla usted Español*?' She tried German, and then Italian. 'It's no good,' she said to me in the end. 'They don't understand.'

I went over to the man whom Amelia had first addressed, and squatted down beside him. He raised his face and looked at me, and his eyes seemed haunted with terror.

'Stand up,' I said, accompanying the words with suitable hand-gestures. 'Come on, old chap ... on your feet.'

I put out a hand to assist him, and he stared back at me. After a moment he climbed slowly to his feet and stood before me, his head hanging.

'We aren't going to hurt you,' I said, putting as much sympathy into my words as possible, but they had no effect on him. 'What are you doing here?'

With this I looked at the weed-bank in a significant way. His response was immediate: he turned to the others, shouted something incomprehensible at them, then reached down and snatched up his knife.

At this I took a step back, thinking that we were about to be attacked, but I could not have been more wrong. The other people clambered up quickly, took their knives and continued with the work we had interrupted, hacking and slashing at the vegetation like men possessed.

Amelia said quietly: 'Edward, these are just peasants. They have mistaken us for overseers.'

'Then we must find out who their real supervisors are!'

We stood and watched the peasants for a minute or so longer. The men were cutting the larger stems, and chopping them into more manageable lengths of about twelve feet. The women worked behind them, stripping the main stems of branches, and separating fruit or seed-pods as they found them. The stems were then thrown to one side, the leaves or fruit to another. With every slash of the knife quantities of sap issued forth, and trickled from the plants already cut. The area of soil directly in front of the weed-bank was flooded with the spilled sap, and the peasants were working in mud up to twelve inches deep.

Amelia and I walked on, carefully maintaining a distance from the peasants and walking on soil that was dry. Here we saw that the spilled sap was not wasted; as it oozed down from where the peasants were working it eventually trickled into a wooden trough that had been placed in the soil, and flowed along in a relatively liquid state, accumulating all the way.

'Did you recognize the language?' I said.

'They spoke too quickly. A guttural tongue. Perhaps it was Russian.'

'But not Tibetan,' I said, and Amelia frowned at me.

'I based that guess on the nature of the terrain, and our evident altitude,' she said. 'I think it is pointless continuing to speculate about our location until we find someone in authority.'

As we moved along the weed-bank we came across more and more of the peasants, all of whom seemed to be working without supervision. Their conditions of work were atrocious, as in the more crowded areas the spilled sap created large swamps, and some of the poor wretches were standing in muddy liquid above their waists. As Amelia observed, and I could not help but agree, there was much room for reform here.

We walked for about half a mile until we reached a point where the wooden trough came to a confluence with three others, which flowed from different parts of the weed-bank. Here the sap was ducted into a large pool, from which it was pumped by several women using a crude, hand-operated device into a subsidiary system of irrigation channels. From where we were standing we could see that these flowed alongside and through a large area of cultivated land. On the far side of this stood two more of the metal towers.

Further along we saw that the peasants were cutting the weed on the slant, so that as we had been walking parallel to their workings we eventually found what it was that lay beyond the bank of weeds. It was a water-course, some three hundred yards wide. Its natural width was only exposed by the cropping of weeds, for when we looked to the north, in the direction from which we had walked, we saw that the weeds so choked the waterway that in places it was entirely blocked. The total width of the weed-bank was nearly a mile, and as the opposite side of the waterway was similarly overgrown, and with another crowd of peasants cutting back the weed, we realized that if they intended to clear the entire length of the waterway by hacking manually through the weeds then the peasants were confronted with a task that would take them many generations to accomplish.

Amelia and I walked beside the water, soon leaving the peasants behind. The ground was uneven and pitted, presumably because of the roots of the weeds which had once grown here, and the water was dark-coloured and undisturbed by ripples. Whether it was a river or a canal was difficult to say; the water was flowing, but so slowly that the movement was barely perceptible, and the banks were irregular. This seemed to indicate that it was a natural watercourse, but its very straightness belied this assumption.

We passed another metal tower, which had been built at the edge of the water, and although we were now some way from where the peasants were cutting back the weed there was still much activity about us. We saw carts carrying the cut weed being manhandled along, and several times we came across groups of peasants walking towards the weed-bank. In the fields to our left were many more people tilling the crops.

Both Amelia and I were tempted to go across to the fields and beg for something to eat – for surely food must be there in abundance – but our first experience with the peasants had made us wary. We reasoned that some kind of community, even be it just a village, could not be far away. Indeed, ahead of us we had already seen two large buildings, and we were walking faster, sensing that there lay our salvation.

V

We entered the nearer of the two buildings, and immediately discovered that it was a kind of warehouse, for most of its contents were huge bales of the cut weed, neatly sorted into types. Amelia and I walked through the ground area of the building, still seeking someone to whom we could talk, but the only people there were more of the peasants. As all their fellows had done, these men and women ignored us, bending over their tasks.

We left this building by the way we had entered: a huge metal door, which was presently held open by an arrangement of pulleys and chains. Outside, we headed for the second building, which was about fifty yards from the first. Between the two stood another of the metal towers.

We were passing beneath this tower when Amelia took my hand in hers, and said: 'Edward, listen.'

There was a distant sound, one attenuated by the thin air, and for a moment we could not locate its source. Then Amelia stepped away from me, towards where there was a long metal rail, raised about three feet from the ground. As we walked towards it, the sound could be identified as a queer grating and whining sound, and looking down the rail towards the south we saw that coming along it was a kind of conveyance.

Amelia said: 'Edward, could that be a railway train?'

'On just one rail?' I said. 'And without a locomotive?'

However, as the conveyance slowed down it became clear that a railway train was exactly what it was. There were nine coaches in all, and without much noise it came to a halt with its front end just beyond where we had been standing. We stared in amazement at this sight, for it looked to all appearances as if the carriages of a normal train had broken away from their engine. But it was not this alone that startled us. The carriages seemed to be unpainted, and were left in their unfinished metal; rust showed in several places. Furthermore, the carriages themselves were not built in the way one would expect, but were tubular. Of the nine carriages, only two – the front and the rear – bore any conceivable resemblance to the sort of trains on which Amelia and I regularly travelled in England. That is to say that these had doors and a few windows, and as the train halted we saw several passengers descending. The seven central carriages, though, were like totally enclosed metal tubes, and without any apparent door or window.

I noticed that a man was stepping down from the front of the train, and seeing that there were windows placed in the very front of the carriage I guessed that it was from there he drove the train. I pointed this out to Amelia, and we watched him with great interest.

That he was not of the peasant stock was evident, for his whole manner was assured and confident, and he was neatly dressed in a plain grey outfit. This comprised an unadorned tunic or shirt, and a pair of trousers. In this he seemed no differently dressed from the passengers, who were clustering around the seven central carriages. All these people were similar in appearance to the peasants, for they were of the reddish skin coloration, and very tall. The driver went to the second carriage and turned a large metal handle on its side. As he did this, we saw that on each of the seven enclosed carriages large doors were moving slowly upwards, like metal blinds. The men who had left the train clustered expectantly around these doors.

Within a few seconds, there was a scene of considerable confusion.

We saw that the seven enclosed carriages had been packed to capacity with men and women of peasant stock, and as the doors were wound open these stumbled or clambered on the ground, spilling out all around the train.

The men in charge moved amongst the peasants, brandishing what had seemed to us on first sight to be short canes or sticks, but which now appeared to have a vicious and peremptory function. Some kind of electrical accumulator was evidently within the sticks, for as the men used them to herd the peasants into ranks, any unfortunate soul who was so much as brushed by the stick received a nasty electrical shock, accompanied by a brilliant flash of green light and a loud hissing sound. The hapless recipients of these shocks invariably fell to the ground, clutching the part of the anatomy that had been afflicted, only to be dragged to their feet again by their fellows.

Needless to say, the wielders of these devilish instruments had little difficulty in bringing order to the crowd.

'We must bring a stop to this at once!' Amelia said. 'They are treating them no better than slaves!'

I think she was all for marching forward and confronting the men in charge, but I laid my hand on her arm to restrain her.

'We must see what is happening,' I said. 'Wait a while ... this is not the moment to interfere.'

The confusion persisted for a few minutes more, while the peasants were force-marched towards the building we had not yet visited. Then I noticed that the doors of the enclosed carriages were being wound down into place again, and that the man who had driven the train was moving towards the far end.

I said: 'Quickly, Amelia, let us board this train. It is about to leave.'

'But this is the end of the line.'

'Precisely. Don't you see? It is now going to go in the opposite direction.'

We hesitated no more, but walked quickly across to the train and climbed into the passenger compartment that had been at the front. None of the men with the electrical whips paid the least bit of attention to us, and no sooner were we inside than the train moved slowly forward.

I had expected the motion to be unbalanced – for with only one rail I could not see that it would be otherwise – but once moving the train had a remarkably smooth passage. There was not even the noise of wheels, but simply a gentle whirring noise from beneath the carriage. What we were most appreciative of in those first few seconds, though, was the fact that the carriage was heated. It had been growing cold outside, for it was not long to sunset.

The seating arrangements inside were not too dissimilar from what we were accustomed to at home, although there were no compartments and no corridor. The inside of the carriage was open, so that it was possible to move about from one part to another, and the seats themselves were metal and uncushioned. Amelia and I took seats by one of the windows, looking out across the waterway. We were alone in the carriage.

During the entire journey, which took about half an hour, the scenery beyond the windows did not much change. The railway followed the bank of the waterway for most of the distance, and we saw that in places the banks had been reinforced with brick cladding, thus tending to confirm my early suspicion that the waterway was in fact a large canal. We saw a few small boats plying along it, and in several places there were bridges across it. Every few hundred yards the train would pass another of the metal towers.

The train stopped just once before reaching its destination. On our side of the train it looked as if we had halted at a place no larger than where we had boarded, but through the windows on the other side of the carriage we could see a huge industrial area, with great chimneys issuing copious clouds of smoke, and furnaces setting up an orange glow in the dark sky. The moon was already out, and the thick smoke drifted over its face.

While we were waiting for the train to re-start, and several peasants were being herded aboard, Amelia opened the door briefly and looked up the line, in the direction in which we were heading.

'Look, Edward,' she said. 'We are coming to a city.'

I leaned outside too, and saw in the light of the setting sun that a mile or two further on there were many large buildings, clustered together untidily. Like Amelia, I was relieved at this sight, for the all-apparent barbarities of life in the countryside had repelled me. Life in any city, however foreign, is by its nature familiar to other city-dwellers, and there we knew we would find the responsible authorities we were seeking. Whatever this country, and however repressive their local laws, we as travellers would receive favoured treatment, and as soon as Amelia and I had come to agreement (which was itself a matter I had still to resolve) we would be bound, by sea or rail, for England. Instinctively, I patted my breast pocket to make sure my wallet was still there. If we were to return immediately to England what little money we had with us – we had established earlier in the day that we had two pounds fifteen shillings and sixpence between us – would have to be used as a surety of our good faith with the Consul.

Such reassuring thoughts were in my mind as the train moved steadily towards the city. The sun had now set, and the night was upon us.

'See, Edward, the evening star is bright.'

Amelia pointed to it, huge and blue-white, a few degrees above the place of the sun's setting. Next to it, looking small, and in quarter-phase, was the moon.

I stared at the evening star, remembering Sir William's words about the planets which made up our solar system. There was one such, lonely and beautiful, impossibly distant and unattainable.

Then Amelia gasped, and I felt my heart tighten in the same moment.

'Edward,' she said. 'There are two moons visible!'

The mysteries of this place could no longer be ignored. Amelia and I stared at each other in horror, understanding at long last what had become of us. I thought of the riotous growth of scarlet weed, the thinness of the atmosphere, the freezing cold, the unfiltered heat of the sun, the lightness in our tread, the deep-blue sky, the red-bodied people, the very alien-ness of all that surrounded us. Now, seeing the two moons, and seeing the evening star, there was a final mystery, one which placed an intolerable burden on our ability to support our dearest belief, that we were still on our home world. Sir William's Machine had taken us to futurity, but it had also borne us unwittingly through the dimension of Space. A Time Machine it might be, but also a Space Machine, for now both Amelia and I accepted the frightful knowledge that in some incredible way we had been brought to another world, one where our own planet was the herald of night. I stared down at the canal, seeing the brilliant point of light that was Earth reflecting from the water, and knew only desperation and a terrible fear. For we had been transported through Space to Mars, the planet of war.

EIGHT

The City of Grief

•

I

I moved across to sit next to Amelia, and she took my hand.

'We should have realized,' she said, whispering. 'Both of us knew we could no longer be on Earth, but neither of us would admit it.'

'We could not have known. It is beyond all experience.'

'So is the notion of travel through Time, and yet we readily accepted that.'

The train lurched slightly, and we felt it begin to slow. I looked past Amelia's profile, across the arid desert towards that brilliant light in the sky.

'How can we be sure that that is Earth?' I said. 'After all, neither of us has ever –'

'Don't you know, Edward? Can't you feel it inside you? Doesn't everything else about this place seem foreign and hostile? Is there not something that speaks to us instinctively when we look at that light? It is a sight of home, and we both feel it.'

'But what are we to do?' The train braked again as I spoke, and looking through the windows on the opposite side of the carriage I saw that we were stopping inside a large, darkened train-shed. On our side of the train a wall came between us and our view of the sky and its ominous reminders.

Amelia said: 'We will have no option in the matter. It is not so much what we do, as what is to be done with us.'

'Are you saying that we are in danger?'

'Possibly . . . as soon as it is realized that we are not of this world. After all, what would be likely to happen to a man who came to Earth from another world?'

'I have no idea,' I said.

'Therefore we can have no idea what is in store for us. We shall have to hope for the best, and trust that in spite of their primitive society we will be well treated. I should not care to spend the rest of my days like an animal.'

'Nor I. But is that likely, or even feasible?'

'We have seen how the slaves are treated. If we were taken for two of those wretches, then we could well be put to work.'

'But we have already been taken for two of the overseers,' I reminded her. 'Some accident of clothing, or something about our appearance, has compounded in our favour.'

'We still need to be careful. There is no telling what we shall find here.'

In spite of the resolution in our words, we were in no condition to take charge of our fate, for in addition to the multitude of questions that surrounded our prospects, we were both dishevelled, tired and hungry from our ordeal in the desert. I knew that Amelia could feel no better than I, and I was exhausted. Both of us were slurring our words, and in spite of our attempts to articulate our feelings, the realization of where we had been deposited by the Time Machine had been the final blow to our morale.

Outside, I could hear the slaves being herded from the train, and the distinctive crackle of the electrical whips was an unpleasant reminder of our precarious position.

'The train will be moving off soon,' I said, pushing Amelia gently into an upright position. 'We have come to a city, and we must look for shelter there.'

'I don't want to go.'

'We will have to.'

I went to the far side of the carriage, and opened the nearest door. I took a quick glance along the length of the train; evidently the slaves were being taken from the opposite side of the train for here there was no movement, bar one man sauntering slowly away from me. I went back to Amelia, who was still sitting passively.

'In a few minutes the train will be going back to where we came from,' I said. 'Do you wish to spend another night in the desert?'

'Of course not. I'm just a little nervous at the thought of entering the city.'

I said: 'We must eat some food, Amelia, and find somewhere safe and warm to sleep. The very fact that this is a city is to our advantage: it must be large enough for us to go unnoticed. We have already survived a great ordeal, and I do not think we need fear anything further. Tomorrow we will try to establish what rights we have.'

Amelia shook her head lethargically, but to my relief she then rose wearily to her feet and followed me from the carriage. I gave her my hand to help her to the ground, and she took it. Her grasp was without pressure.

II

The sound of the whips echoed from the other side of the train as we hurried towards where a glow of light emanated from behind a protruding corner. There was no sign of the man I had seen earlier.

As we came round the corner we saw ahead of us a tall doorway, set well back into the brick wall and painted white. Over the top was a sign, illuminated in some manner from behind, and bearing a legend in a style of printing that was totally incomprehensible to me. It was this sign that drew our attention, rather than the door itself, for this was our first sight of Martian written language.

After we had stared at this for a few seconds – the lettering was black on a white background, but here the superficial similarity with Earth scripts came to an end – I led Amelia forward, anxious to find warmth and food. It was bitterly cold in the train-shed, for it was open to the night air.

There was no handle on the door, and for a moment I wondered if there would be some alien mechanism that would defy us. I pushed experimentally, and discovered that one side of the door moved slightly.

I must have been weak from our sojourn in the wilds, for beyond this I was incapable of shifting it. Amelia helped me, and in a moment we found that we could push the door open far enough for us to pass through, but as soon as we released it the heavy device swung back and closed with a slam. We had come into a short corridor, no longer than five or six yards, at the end of which was another door. The corridor was completely featureless, with the exception of one electrical incandescent lamp fixed to the ceiling. We went to the second door and pushed it open, feeling a similar weight. This door also closed quickly behind us.

Amelia said: 'My ears feel as though they are blocked.'

'Mine too,' I said. 'I think the pressure of air is greater here.'

We were in a second corridor, identical to the first. Amelia remembered something she had been taught when she was in Switzerland, and showed me how to relieve the pressure in my ears by holding my nose and blowing gently.

As we passed through the third door there was another increase in the density of the air.

'I feel I can breathe at last,' I said, wondering how we had survived for so long in the thin air outside.

'We must not over-exert ourselves,' Amelia said. 'I feel a little dizzy already.'

Even though we were anxious to continue on our way we waited in the corridor for a few minutes longer. Like Amelia, I was feeling light-headed in the richer air, and this sensation was sharpened by a barely detectable hint of ozone. My fingertips were tingling as my blood was renewed with this fresh supply of oxygen, and this coupled with the fact of the lighter Martian gravity – which, while we had been in the desert, we had attributed to some effect of high altitude – lent a spurious feeling of great energy. Spurious it surely was, for I knew we must both be near the end of the tether; Amelia's shoulders were stooped, and her eyes were still half-closed.

I placed my arm around Amelia's shoulders.

'Come along,' I said. 'We do not have much further to go.'

'I am still a little frightened.'

'There is nothing that can threaten us,' I said, but in truth I shared her fears. Neither of us was in any position to understand the full implications of our predicament. Deep inside, I was feeling the first tremblings of an instinctive dread of the alien, the strange, the exotic.

We stepped slowly forward, pushed our way through the next door, and at last found ourselves looking out across a part of the Martian city.

III

Outside the door through which we had come a street ran from left to right, and directly opposite us were two buildings. These, at first sight, loomed large and black, so used were we to the barrenness of the desert, but on a second examination we saw that they were scarcely bigger than the grander private houses of our own cities. Each one stood alone, and was intricately ornamented with moulded plaster on the outside walls; the doors were large, and there were few windows. If this lends to such buildings an aura of grace or elegance, then it should be added that both of the two buildings we then saw were in a state of advanced decay. One, indeed, had one wall partially collapsed, and a door hung open on a hinge. In the interiors we could see much rubble and litter, and it was clear that neither had been occupied for many years. The walls still standing were cracked and crumbling, and there was no visible sign that a roof still stood.

I glanced up and saw that the city was open to the sky, for I could make out the stars overhead. Curiously, though, the air was as dense here as it had been inside the corridors, and the temperature was much warmer than we had experienced in the desert.

The street we were in was lighted: at intervals along each side were several more of the towers we had seen, and now we realized a part, at least, of their function, for on the polished roof of each tower was a powerful light which swept to and fro as the platform rotated slowly. These constantly sweeping beams had a strangely sinister aspect, and they were far removed from the warm, placid gaslights to which we were both accustomed, but the very fact that the Martians illuminated their streets at night was a reassuringly human detail.

'Which way shall we go?' Amelia said.

'We must find the centre of the city,' I said. 'Clearly this is a quarter that has fallen into disuse. I suggest we strike directly away from this rail-terminus until we meet some of the people.'

'The people? You mean ... Martians?'

'Of course,' I said, taking her hand in mine with a show of confidence. 'We have already accosted several without knowing who they were. They seem very like us, so we have nothing to fear from them.'

Without waiting for a reply I pulled her forward, and we walked briskly along the street towards the right. When we came to the corner we turned with it, and found we were in a similar, though rather longer, street. Along each side of this were more buildings, styled as ornately as the first we had seen, but with sufficient subtle variations in architecture to avoid obvious repetition of shape. Here too the buildings were in decay, and we had no means of knowing for what purposes they had once been used. The ruination apart, this was not a thoroughfare which would have disgraced one of the spa-towns of England.

We walked for about ten minutes without seeing any other pedestrians, although as we passed one street-junction we briefly saw, at some distance down the intersecting road, a powered conveyance moving swiftly across our view. It had appeared too quickly for us to see it in any detail, and we were left with an impression of considerable speed and incontinent noise.

Then as we approached a cluster of buildings from which several lights issued, Amelia suddenly pointed along a smaller street to our right.

'See, Edward,' she said softly. 'There are people by that building.'

Along that street too were lighted buildings, and from one of them, as she had indicated, several people had just walked. I turned that way instantly, but Amelia held back.

'Let's not go that way,' she said. 'We don't know—'

'Are you prepared to starve?' I cried, although my bravura was a facade. 'We must see how these people live, so that we may eat and sleep.'

'Do you not think we should be more circumspect? It would be foolhardy to walk into a situation we could not escape from.'

'We are in such a situation now,' I said, then deliberately made my voice more persuasive. 'We are in desperate trouble, Amelia dear. Maybe you are right to think it would be foolish to walk straight up to these people, but I know no other way.'

Amelia said nothing for a moment, but she stood close by my side, her hand limp in mine. I wondered if she were about to faint once more, for she seemed to be swaying slightly, but after a while she looked up at me. As she did so, the sweeping beam from one of the towers fell full across her face, and I saw how tired and ill she looked.

She said: 'Of course you are right, Edward. I did not think we should survive in the desert. We must of course mingle with these Martian people, for we cannot return to that.'

I squeezed her hand to comfort her, and then we walked slowly towards the building where we had seen the people. As we approached, more appeared through the main doorway and headed up the street away from us. One man even glanced in our direction as two of the light-beams swept across us, so that he must have seen us clearly, but he showed no visible reaction and walked on with the others.

Amelia and I came to a halt in front of the doorway, and for a few seconds I stared down the street at the Martians. They all walked with a curious, easy loping motion; doubtless this was a product of the low gravity conditions, and doubtless a gait that Amelia and I would perfect as soon as we grew more accustomed to the conditions here.

'Do we go inside?' Amelia said.

'I can think of no other course,' I said, and led the way up the three low steps in front of the door. Another group of Martian people was coming out in the opposite direction, and they passed without appearing to notice us. Their faces were indistinct in the half-light, but close to we saw just how tall they were. They were all at least six inches taller than I.

Light from within was spilling down the passage beyond the door, and as we passed through we came into a huge, brightly lit room, one so large that it seemed it must occupy the whole of the building.

We stopped just inside the door, standing warily, waiting for our eyes to adjust to the brilliance.

All was at first confusing, for what furniture was there was in haphazard order, and consisted, for the most part, of what seemed to be tubular scaffolding. From this were suspended by ropes what I can best describe as hammocks: large sheets of thick fabric or rubber, hanging some two feet from the ground. On these, and standing around them, were several dozen of the Martian people.

With the exception of the peasant-slaves – whom we surmised to be of the lowest social order – these were the first Martians we had seen closely. These were the city-dwellers, the same as those men we had seen wielding the electrical whips. These were the people who ordered this society, elected its leaders, made its laws. These were from now to be our peers, and in spite of our tiredness and mental preoccupations Amelia and I regarded them with considerable interest.

IV

I have already noted that the average Martian is a tall being; what is also most noticeable, and of emphatic importance, is that the Martians are undeniably human, or human-like.

To speak of the average Martian is as misleading as to speak of the average human on Earth, for even in those first few seconds as we regarded the occupants of the building, Amelia and I noticed that there were many superficial differences. We saw some who were taller than most, some shorter; there were thinner Martians and fatter ones; there were some with great manes of hair, others were bald or balding; the predominant skin-tone was a reddish tint, but this was more evident in some than in others.

With this in mind, then, let me say that the average adult Martian male could be roughly described thus:

He would be of the order of some six feet six inches tall, with black or brown head-hair. (We saw no red-heads, and no blonds.) He would weigh, if he were to step on scales an Earth, some two hundred pounds. His chest would be broad, and apparently well-muscled. He would have facial hair, with thin eyebrows and wispy beard; some of the males we saw were clean-shaven, but this was uncommon. His eyes would be large, uncannily pale in coloration, and set wide apart in his face. His nose would be flat and broad, and his mouth would be generously fleshed.

At first sight the Martian face is a disturbing one for it seems brutal and devoid of emotion; as we later mingled with these people, however, both Amelia and I were able to detect facial nuances, even though we were never sure how to interpret them.

(My description here is of a city-Martian. The slave people were of the same racial stock, but due to the privations they suffered, most of the slaves we saw were comparatively thin and puny.)

The Martian female – for women there were in that room, and children too – is, like her Earthly counterpart, slightly the physical inferior of the male. Even so, almost every Martian female we saw was taller than Amelia, who is, as has already been said, taller than the average Earth woman. There is no woman on Mars who could ever be considered to be a beauty by Earth standards, nor, I suspect, would that concept have any meaning on Mars. At no time did we ever sense that Martian females were appreciated for their physical charms, and indeed we often had reason to believe that, as with some animals on Earth, the roles on Mars were reversed in this respect.

The children we saw were, almost without exception, charming to us in the way any youngster has charm. Their faces were round and eager, not yet rendered unpleasant by the broadness and flatness so evident in the adults. Their behaviour, like that of Earth children, was on the whole riotous and mischievous, but they never appeared to anger the adults, whose attitude was indulgent and solicitous to them. It often seemed to us that the children were the sole source of happiness on this world, for the only time we saw the adults laughing was in the company of children.

This brings me to an aspect of Martian life which did not at first strike us, but which in later times became increasingly obvious. That is to say that I cannot imagine a race of beings more universally lugubrious, downcast or plainly miserable than the Martians.

The aura of despondency was present in the room as Amelia and I first entered it, and it was probably this which was our eventual saving. The typical Martian I have described would be obsessed with his internal miseries to the virtual exclusion of all other factors. To no other reason can I attribute the fact that Amelia and I were able to move so freely about the city without attracting attention. Even in those first few moments, as we stood in anticipation of the first cry of alarm or excitement at our appearance, few Martians so much as glanced in our direction. I cannot imagine the arrival of a Martian in an Earth city eliciting the same indifference.

Perhaps allied to this overall depression was the fact that the room was almost silent. One or two of the Martians spoke quietly, but most stood or sat about glumly. A few children ran while their parents watched, but this was the only movement. The voices we heard were weird: soprano and mellifluous. Obviously we could not understand the words or even the tenor of the conversations – although the words were accompanied by intricate hand-signals – but the sight of these large and ugly people speaking in what seemed to us to be falsetto was most disconcerting.

Amelia and I waited by the door, unsure of everything. I looked at Amelia, and suddenly the sight of her face – tired, dirty, but so lovely – was a welcome reminder of all that was familiar to me. She looked back at me, the strain of the last two days still revealing itself in her expression, but she smiled and entwined her fingers through mine once more.

'They're just ordinary people, Edward.'

'Are you still frightened?' I said.

'I'm not sure . . . they seem harmless.'

'If they can live in this city, then so can we. What we must do is see how they conduct their everyday lives, and follow their example. They seem not to recognize us as strangers.'

Just then a group of the Martians moved away from the hammocks and walked in their strange, loping gait towards us. At once I led Amelia back through the door, and returned to the street with its ever-sweeping lights. We crossed to the further side, then turned back to watch what the Martians were doing.

In a moment the group appeared, and without looking once in our direction they set off down the way we had seen the others go earlier. We waited for half a minute, then followed them at a distance.

V

As soon as we returned to the street we realized that it had been warmer inside, and this was cause for further reassurance. I had been fearing that the native Martians lived habitually in coldness, but the inside of the building had been heated to an acceptable level. I was not sure that I wished to sleep in a communal dormitory – and wished such conditions even less for Amelia – but even if we did not care for it, we knew at least that we could tonight sleep warmly and comfortably.

It turned out that there was not far to walk. The Martians ahead of us crossed a street-junction, joined another, much larger, group walking from a different direction, then turned into the next building they came to. This was larger than many of the buildings we had so far seen, and from what we could see of it in the fitful illumination of the tower lights it appeared to be plainer in architectural style. There was light showing from the windows, and as we came nearer we could hear much noise from within.

Amelia made an exaggerated sniffing noise.

'I smell food,' she said. 'And I hear clattering of dishes.'

I said: 'And I detect wishful thinking.'

However, our mood was now much lighter, and feeble though such an exchange might be it was an indication that Amelia was sharing my feeling of renewed hope.

We did not hesitate as we approached the building, so emboldened had we been by our visit to the other building, and walked confidently through the main door into a vast, brightly lit hall.

It was clear at once that this was not another dormitory, for almost the entire floor-space was given over to long tables set in parallel rows. Each of these was crowded with Martian people apparently in the middle of a banquet. The tables were liberally spread with dishes of food, the air was laden with a steamy, greasy smell, and the walls echoed to the sound of the Martians' voices. At the far end was what we assumed was the kitchen, for here about a dozen of the slave-Martians were toiling with metal plates and huge dishfuls of food, which were set out along a raised platform by the entrance to the kitchen.

The group of Martians we had been following had walked to this platform, and were helping themselves to food.

I said: 'Our problem is solved, Amelia. Here is ample food for the taking.'

'Assuming we may eat it in safety.'

'Do you mean it could be poisonous?'

'How are we to know? We are not Martian, and our digestive systems might be quite different.'

'I don't intend to starve while I decide,' I said. 'And anyway we are being watched.'

This was the case, for although we had been able to stand unnoticed in the dormitory building, our evident hesitation was attracting attention. I took Amelia by the elbow and propelled her towards the platform.

My hunger had been such, earlier in the day, that I had thought I could have eaten anything. In the hours between, however, the gnawing hunger had passed to be replaced by a sensation of nausea, and the compulsion to eat was now much less than I would have anticipated. Furthermore, as we approached the platform it was clear that although there was food in abundance, there was little that looked at all appetizing, and I was stricken with a most unexpected fastidiousness. Most of the food was liquid or semi-liquid, and was laid out in tureens or bowls. The scarlet weed was obviously the staple diet of these people, in spite of the several fields of green-crop we had seen, for many of the stew-like dishes contained large quantities of the red stems and leaves. There were, though, one or two plates of what could be meat (although it was very under-cooked), and to one side there was something which, but for the fact we had seen no cattle, we could have taken for cheese. In addition, there were several glass jugs containing vividly coloured liquids, which were poured over the food as sauces by the Martians.

'Take small quantities of as many different kinds as possible,' Amelia said softly. 'Then if any of it is dangerous, the effect will be minimized.'

The plates were large, and made of a dull metallic substance, and we each took a generous amount of food. Once or twice I sniffed what I was taking, but this was unedifying, to say the least.

Carrying our plates, we went towards one of the tables at the side, away from the main group of Martians.

There was a small number of the people at one end of the table we selected, but we passed them by and sat at the other end. The seats were long low benches, one on each side. Amelia and I sat next to each other, not at all at ease in this strange place, even though the Martians continued to pay no attention to us now we had moved away from the door.

We each took a little of the food: it was not pleasant, but it was still quite hot and was certainly better than an empty stomach.

After a moment, Amelia said in a low voice: 'Edward, we cannot live like this for ever. We have simply been lucky so far.'

'Don't let us discuss it. We are both exhausted. We'll find somewhere to sleep tonight, and in the morning we will make plans.'

'Plans to do what? Spend a lifetime in hiding?'

We ate our way stoically through the food, being reminded continually of that bitter taste we had first experienced in the desert.

The meat was no better; it had a texture similar to some cuts of beef, but was sweet and bland in flavour. Even the "cheese", which we left until the end, was acidic.

On the whole our attention was distracted away from the food by the events about us.

I have already described the Martians' habitual expression as being one of great lugubriousness, and in spite of the amount of conversation there was no levity. On our table, a Martian woman leaned forward and rested her wide forehead on her arms, and we could see tears trickling from her eyes. A little later, on the far side of the hall, a Martian man jumped abruptly back from his seat and strode around the room, waving his long arms and declaiming in his queer, high-pitched voice. He came to a wall and leant against it, banging his fists and shouting. This at last attracted the attention of his fellows, and several hurried to him and stood about, apparently trying to soothe him, but he was disconsolate.

Within a few seconds of this incident there was set up, as if the misery were contagious, such a general caterwauling that Amelia was impelled to say to me: 'Do you suppose it is possible that here the responses are different? I mean, when they appear to be crying, are they actually laughing?'

'I'm not sure,' I said, cautiously watching the weeping Martian. He continued his outburst a little longer, then turned away from his friends and hurried from the hall with his hands covering his face. The others waited until he had vanished through the door, then returned to their own seats, looking morose.

We noticed that most of the Martians were taking large quantities of drink from glass jugs set on every table. As this was transparent we had assumed that it was water, but when I tasted some it was instantly clear that this was not so. Although it was refreshing to drink it was strongly alcoholic, to such an extent that within a few seconds of swallowing it I felt pleasantly dizzy.

I poured some for Amelia, but she only sipped at hers.

'It is very strong,' she said. 'We must not lose our wits.'

I had already poured myself a second draught, but she restrained me from drinking it. I suppose she was wise to do this, because as we watched the Martians it was plain that most of them were fast becoming inebriated. They were being noisier and more careless in their manners than before. We even heard laughter, although it sounded shrill and hysterical. Large quantities of the alcoholic beverage were being drunk, and kitchen-slaves brought out several more jugs of it. A bench fell backwards to the floor, tipping its sitters into a sprawling heap, and two of the young male kitchen-slaves were captured by a group of female Martians who then hemmed them into a corner; what followed we could not see in the confusion. More slaves came out of the kitchen, and most of these were young females. To our astonishment, not only were they completely unclothed but they mingled freely with their masters, embracing and enticing them.

'I think it is time we left,' I said to Amelia.

She stared at the developing situation for a few moments longer before replying. Then she said: 'Very well. This is grossly distasteful.'

We went towards the door, not pausing to look back. Another bench and a table were overturned, accompanied by a crash of breaking glasses and shouts from the Martian people. The maudlin atmosphere had been entirely banished.

Then, as we reached the door, a sound came echoing through the hall, chilling us and forcing us to look back. It was a harsh and discordant screeching sound, apparently emanating from one distant corner of the hall, but with sufficient volume to drown every other sound.

Its effect on the Martians was dramatic: all movement ceased, and the people present looked wildly from one to the other. In the silence that followed this brutal and sudden intrusion, we heard the sound of renewed sobbing.

I said: 'Come on, Amelia.'

So we hurried from the building, sobered by the incident, not understanding but more than a little frightened.

There were now even fewer people about than before, but the tower lights swept across the streets as if to pick out those who wandered in the night when all others were engaged inside.

I led Amelia away from that area of the city where the Martians gathered, and back towards the part we had first walked through, where fewer lights showed. Appearances, though, were deceptive, for the fact that a building showed no light and emitted no noise did not mean it was deserted. We walked for about half a mile, and then tried the door of a darkened building. Inside, lights were shining and we saw that another feast had taken place. We saw . . . but it is not correct that I should here record what we saw. Amelia had no more wish than I to witness such depravity, and we hastened away, still not able to reconcile this world with the one we had left.

When we next tried a building I went forward alone ... but the place was empty and dirty, and whatever had been its contents had been thoroughly destroyed by fire. The next building we explored was another dormitory-hall, well occupied by Martians. Without causing disturbance, we went away.

So it went, as we moved from one building to the next, seeking an unoccupied dormitory-hall; so long did we search that we began to think that there was none we could find. But then at last we were in luck, and came to a hall where hammocks hung unoccupied, and we went inside and slept.

NINE
Explorations

•

I

During the weeks that followed, Amelia and I explored the Martian city as thoroughly as possible. We were hindered by the fact that we had perforce to go everywhere on foot, but we saw as much as we could and were soon able to make reasonable estimates as to its size, how many people it contained, where the major buildings were situated, and so forth. At the same time we tried to make what we could of the people of Mars, and how they lived; to be honest, however, we did not find much satisfaction on this score.

After two nights in the first dormitory we found, we moved to a second building, much nearer to the centre of the city and more conveniently sited by a dining-hall. This too was unoccupied, but its previous users had left many possessions behind them, and we were able to live in some comfort. The hammocks would have been unbearably hard on Earth – for the fabric of which they were made was coarse and unyielding – but in the light Martian gravity they were perfectly adequate. For bedding we used large, pillow-like sacks filled with a soft compound, which were similar to the quilts used in some European countries.

We also found clothing that had been abandoned by the previous occupants, and we wore the drab garments over our own clothes. Naturally enough they were rather large for us, but the loose fit over our clothes made our bodies appear larger, and so we were able to pass more readily as Martians.

Amelia tied her hair back in a tight bun – approximating the style favoured by the Martian women – and I allowed my new beard to grow; every few days Amelia trimmed it with her nail-scissors to give it the wispy appearance of the Martians'.

At the time all this seemed to us a matter of priority; we were very aware that we looked different from the Martians. To this extent, our two days' sojourn in the desert had been to our unwitting advantage: our sunburned faces, uncomfortable as they were, were a credible approximation of the Martians' skin-hue. As the days passed, and our complexions began to fade, we returned one day to the desert beyond the city, and a few hours in that bitter radiant heat restored the colour temporarily.

But this is taking my narrative ahead of itself, for to convey how we survived in that city I must first describe the place itself.

II

Within a few days of our arrival, Amelia had dubbed our new home Desolation City, for reasons which should already be clear.

Desolation City was situated at the junction of two canals. One of these, the one by whose banks we had first landed, ran directly from north to south. The second approached from the north-west, and after the junction – where there was a complicated arrangements of locks – continued to the south-east. The city had been built in the obtuse angle formed by the two canals, and along its southern and western edges were several docking accesses to the waterways.

As near as we could estimate it the city covered about twelve square miles, but a comparison on this basis with Earth cities is misleading, for Desolation City was almost exactly circular. Moreover, the Martians had lighted on the ingenious notion of entirely separating the industrial life of the city from the residential, for the buildings were designed for the everyday needs of the people, while the manufacturing work was carried out in the industrial areas beyond the city's periphery.

There were two such industrial concentrations: the large one we had seen from the train, which lay to the north, and a smaller one built beside the canal to the south-east.

In terms of resident population, Desolation City was very small indeed, and it was this aspect which had most prompted Amelia to give it its unprepossessing name.

That the city had been built to accommodate many thousands of people was quite obvious, for buildings there were many and open spaces there were few; that only a fraction of the city was presently occupied was equally apparent, and large areas were laid to waste. In these parts many of the buildings were derelict, and the streets were littered with masonry and rusting girders.

We discovered that only the occupied parts of the city were lighted at night, for as we explored the city by day we frequently found areas of decay where none of the towers was present. We never ventured into these regions at night, for quite apart from being dark and threatening in their loneliness, such areas were patrolled by fast-moving vehicles which drove through the streets with a banshee howling and an ever-probing beam of light.

This sinister policing of the city was the first indication that the Martian people had inflicted on themselves a regime of Draconian suppression.

We often speculated as to the causes of the under-population. At first we surmised that the shortage of manpower was only apparent, created by the quite prodigious amount of effort poured into the industrial processes. By day we could see the industrial areas beyond the city's perimeter, belching dense smoke from hundreds of chimneys, and by night we saw the same areas brightly lit as the work continued; thus it was that we assumed most of the city's people were at work, labouring around the clock through work-shifts. However, as we grew more used to living in the city, we saw that not many of the ruling-class Martians ever left its confines, and that therefore most of the industrial workers would be of the slave class.

I have mentioned that the city was circular in shape. We discovered this by accident and over a period of several days, and were able to confirm it later by ascending one of the taller buildings in the city.

Our first realization came as follows. On our second or third full day in Desolation City, Amelia and I were walking northwards through the city, intending to see if we could cross the mile or so of desert between us and the larger of the two industrial concentrations.

We came to a street which led directly northwards, seeming to open eventually on to the desert. This was in one of the populated areas of the city, and watch-towers abounded. I noticed, as we approached, that the tower nearest to the desert had stopped rotating to and fro, and I pointed this out to Amelia. We considered for a few moments whether or not to continue, but Amelia said she saw no harm.

However, as we passed the tower it was quite obvious that the man or men inside were rotating the observation-platform to watch us, and the dark, oval window at the front mutely followed our progress past it. No action was taken against us, so we continued, but with a distinct feeling of apprehension.

So taken were we with this silent monitoring that we fetched up unexpectedly and shockingly against the true perimeter of the city; this took the form of an invisible, or nearly invisible, wall, stretching from one side of the roadway to the other. Naturally enough, we thought at first that the substance was glass, but this could not be the case. Nor was it, indeed, any other form of material that we knew. Our best notion was that it was some kind of energetic field, induced by electrical means. It was, though, completely inert, and under the gaze of the watch-tower we made a few rudimentary attempts to fathom it. All we could feel was the impermeable, invisible barrier, cold to the touch.

Chastened, we walked back the way we had come.

On a later occasion, we walked through one of the empty quarters of the city, and found that there too the wall existed. Before long we had established that the wall extended all around the city, crossing not just streets but behind buildings too.

Later, from the aspect of the roof, we saw that few if any of the buildings lay beyond this circle.

It was Amelia who first posited a solution, linking this phenomenon with the undoubted one that air-density and overall temperature in the city were higher than outside. She suggested that the invisible barrier was not merely a wall, but in fact a hemisphere which covered the entire city. Beneath this, she said, air-pressure could be maintained at an acceptable level, and the effect of the sun through it would be closely akin to that of a glasshouse.

III

Desolation City was not, however, a prison. To leave it was as easy as it had been for us to enter it initially. On our journeys of exploration we came across several places where it was possible merely to walk through some specially maintained fault in the wall and enter the rarefied atmosphere of the desert.

One such fault was the series of doors and corridors at the railway terminus; there were similar ones at the wharves built by the canals, and some of these were immense structures by which imported materials could be taken into the city. Several of the major streets, which ran towards the industrial areas, had transit buildings through which people could pass freely.

What was most interesting of all, though, was that the vehicles of the city were able to pass directly through the wall without either hesitation or detectable leakage of the pressurized atmosphere. We saw this occur many times.

I must now turn the attention of this narrative towards the nature of these vehicles, for among the many marvels Amelia and I saw on Mars these numbered among the most amazing.

The fundamental difference lay in the fact that, unlike Earth engineers, the Martian inventors had dispensed with the wheel entirely. Having seen the efficiency of the Martians' vehicles I was, indeed, forced to wonder how far Earthly developments in this field had been retarded by the obsession with the wheel! Furthermore, the only wheeled vehicles we saw on Mars were the crude handcarts used by the slaves; an indication of how lowly the Martians considered such methods!

The first Martian vehicle we saw (not counting the train in which we had arrived, although we assumed that this too was without wheels) was the one which had raced through the streets that first dismal night in Desolation City. The second we saw was during the morning of the next day; that too was moving at such a lick that we were left with a confused impression of speed and noise. Later, however, we saw one moving more slowly, and later still we saw several at rest.

To say that Martian vehicles walked would be inaccurate, although I can think of no closer verb. Beneath the main body (which, according to its use, was designed in a fashion more or less conventional to us) were rows of long or short metal legs, the length being determined by the kind of use to which the vehicle was put. These legs were mounted in groups of three, connected by a transmission device to the main body, and powered from within by some hidden power source.

The motion of these legs was at once curiously life-like and rigidly mechanical: at any one time only one of the three legs of each mounting would be in contact with the ground. In motion, the legs would ripple with a quasi-peristaltic motion, the two raised legs reaching forward to take the load, the third one lifting and reaching forward in its turn.

The largest vehicle we saw at close quarters was a goods-haulage machine, with two parallel rows of sixteen groups of these legs. The smallest machines, which were used to police the city, had two rows of three groups.

Each leg, on close examination, turned out to be made of several dozen finely-machined disks, balanced on top of each other like a pile of pennies, and yet activated in some way by an electrical current. As each of the legs was encased in a transparent integument, it was possible to see the device in operation, but how each movement was controlled was beyond us. In any event, the efficiency of these machines was in no doubt: we frequently saw the policing-vehicles driving through the streets at a velocity well in excess of anything a horse-drawn vehicle could attain.

IV

Perhaps even more puzzling to us than the design of these vehicles was the men who drove them.

That men were inside them was apparent, for on many occasions we saw ordinary Martians speaking to the driver or other occupants, with spoken replies coming through a metal grille set in the side of the machine. What was also quite clear was that the drivers were in positions of extraordinary authority, for when addressed by them the Martians in the street adopted a cowed or respectful manner, and spoke in subdued tones. However, at no time did we see the drivers, for all the vehicles were totally enclosed – at least, the driver's compartment was enclosed – with only a piece of the black glass set at the front, behind which the driver presumably stood or sat. As these windows were similar to those we saw on every watch-tower, we presumed that they were operated by the same group of people.

Nor were all the vehicles as prosaic as maybe I have made them appear.

Confronted, as we were, with a multitude of strange sights, Amelia and I were constantly trying to find Earthly parallels for what we saw. It is likely, therefore, that many of the assumptions we made at this time were incorrect. It was relatively safe to assume that the vehicles we thought of as drays were just that, for we saw them performing similar tasks to those we knew on Earth. There was no way, though, of finding an Earthly equivalent for some of the machines.

One such was a device used by the Martians in conjunction with their watch-towers.

Directly outside the dormitory building we settled in, and visible to us from our hammocks, was one of the watch-towers. After we had been in occupation for about eight days, Amelia pointed out that there appeared to be something wrong with it, for its observation platform had ceased to rotate to and fro. That night we saw that its light was not on.

The very next day one of the vehicles came to a halt beside the tower, and there took place a repair operation I can only describe as fantastic.

The vehicle in question was of a type we had occasionally seen about the city: a long, low machine which, above its drive-leg platform, was an apparent mass of glittering tubing, heaped in disorder. As the legged vehicle halted beside the watch-tower, this confusion of metal reared itself up, to reveal that it possessed five of the peristaltic legs, the remainder of the appendages being a score or more of tentacular arms.

It stepped down from the platform of the vehicle, the jointed arms clanging and ringing, then walked the short distance to the base of the tower with a movement remarkably like that of a spider. We both looked for some clue as to how the thing was being driven, but it seemed that either the monstrous machine had an intelligence of its own, or else it was controlled in some incredible way by the driver of the vehicle, for there was plainly no one anywhere near it. As it reached the base of the tower, one of its tentacles was brought into contact with a raised metal plate on one of the pillars, and in a moment we saw that the observation platform was lowering. Apparently it could lower itself only so far, for when the platform was about twenty feet from the ground the tentacular device seized the tower's legs in its horrid embrace, and began to climb slowly upwards, like a spider climbing a strand of its web.

When it reached the observation-platform it settled itself in position by clinging on with its legs, and then with several tentacles reached through a number of tiny ports, apparently searching for the parts of the mechanism which had failed.

Amelia and I watched the whole operation, unnoticed inside the building. From the arrival of the legged vehicle to its eventual departure, only twelve minutes elapsed, and by the time the iron monster had returned to its place on the rear of the vehicle, the observation-platform had been raised to its erstwhile height and was rotating to and fro in its usual way.

V

So far, I have not had much to say about our day-to-day survival in this desolate city, nor, for the moment, will I. Our internal preoccupations were many and great, and, in several ways, more important than what we were seeing about us. Before turning to this, though, I must first establish the context. We are all creatures of our environment, and in disturbingly subtle ways Amelia and I were becoming a little Martian in our outlook. The desolation about us was reaching our souls.

VI

As we moved about the city one question remained ever unanswered. That is to say: how did the ordinary Martian occupy his time?

We now understood something of the social ramifications of Mars. This was in effect that the lowest social stratum was the slave-people, who were forced to do all the manual and demeaning tasks necessary to any civilized society. Then came the Martians of the city, who had powers of supervision over the slaves. Above these were the men who drove the legged vehicles and, presumably, operated the other mechanical devices we saw.

It was the city-dwelling Martians in whom we were most interested, for it was among them that we lived. However, not all of these were occupied. For instance, it took relatively few of them to supervise the slaves (we often saw just one or two men able to control several hundred slaves, armed with only the electrical whips), and although the vehicles were many in number, there were always plenty of people in the city, apparently idle.

On our perambulations Amelia and I saw much evidence that

time hung heavy on these people. The nightly carousing was obviously a result of two factors: partly a way of appeasing the endless grief, and partly a way of expressing boredom. We frequently saw people squabbling, and there were several fights, although these were dissipated instantly at the sight of one of the vehicles. Many of the women appeared to be pregnant; another indication that there was not much to occupy either the minds or the energies of the people. At the height of the day, when the sun was overhead (we had come to the conclusion that the city must be built almost exactly on the Martian equator), the pavements of the streets were littered with the bodies of men and women relaxing in the warmth.

One possibility that would account for the apparent idleness was that some of them were employed in the near-by industrial area, and that the Martians we saw about the city were enjoying some leave.

As we were both curious to see the industrial areas and discover, if we could, what was the nature of all the furious activity that took place, one day, about fifteen days after our arrival, Amelia and I determined to leave the city and explore the smaller of the two complexes. We had already observed that a road ran to it, and that although the majority of the traffic was the haulage type of vehicle, several people – both city-dweller and slave – were to be seen walking along it. We decided, therefore, that we would not attract unwanted attention by going there ourselves.

We left the city by a system of pressurized corridors, and emerged into the open. At once our lungs were labouring in the sparse atmosphere, and we both remarked on the extreme climate: the thin coldness of the air and the harsh radiance of the sun.

We walked slowly, knowing from experience how exercise debilitated us in this climate, and so after half an hour we had not covered much more than about a quarter of the distance to the industrial site. Already, though, we could smell something of the smoke and fumes released from the factories although none of the clangour we associated with such works was audible.

During a pause for rest, Amelia laid her hand on my arm and pointed towards the south.

'What is that, Edward?' she said.

I looked in the direction she had indicated.

We had been walking almost due south-east towards the industrial site, parallel to the canal, but on the far side of the water, well away from the factories, was what appeared at first sight to be an immense pipeline. It did not, however, appear to be connected to anything, and indeed we could see an open end to it.

The continuation of the pipe was invisible to us, lying as it did beyond the industrial buildings. Such an apparatus would not normally have attracted our attention, but what was remarkable was the fact of the intense activity around the open end. The pipe lay perhaps two miles from where we stood, but in the clear air we could see distinctly that hundreds of workers were swarming about the place.

We had agreed to rest for fifteen minutes, so unaccustomed were we to the thin air, and as we moved on afterwards we could not help but glance frequently in that direction.

'Could it be some kind of irrigation duct?' I said after a while, having noticed that the pipe ran from east to west between the two diverging canals.

'With a bore of that diameter?'

I had to admit that this explanation was unlikely, because we could see how the pipe dwarfed those men nearest to it. A reasonable estimate of the internal diameter of the pipe would be about twenty feet, and in addition the metal of the tube was some eight or nine feet thick.

We agreed to take a closer look at the strange construction, and so left the road, striking due south across the broken rock and sand of the desert. There were no bridges across the canal here, so the bank was as far as we could proceed, but it was close enough to allow us an uninterrupted view.

The overall length of the pipe turned out to be approximately one mile. From this closer position we could see the further end, which was overhanging a small lake. This had apparently been artificially dug, for its banks were straight and reinforced, and the water undermined at least half of the length of the pipe.

At the very edge of the lake, two large buildings had been constructed side by side, with the pipe running between them.

We sat down by the edge of the canal to watch what was happening.

At the moment many of the men at the nearer end of the pipe were concentrating on extracting from it a huge vehicle which had emerged from the interior. This was being guided out of the pipe, and down a ramp to the desert floor. Some difficulty seemed to have arisen, for more men were being force-marched across to help.

Half an hour later the vehicle had been successfully extricated, and was moved some distance to one side. Meanwhile, the men who had been working by the end of the pipe were dispersing.

A few more minutes passed, and then I suddenly pointed.

'Look, Amelia!' I said. 'It is moving!'

The end of the pipe nearer to us was being lifted from the ground. At the same moment the further end was sinking slowly into the lake. The buildings at the edge of the lake were the instruments of this motion, for not only were they the pivot by which the pipe turned, but we also heard a great clattering and roaring from engines inside the buildings, and green smoke poured from several vents.

The raising of the pipe was the work of only a minute or so, because for all its size it moved smoothly and with precision.

When the pipe had been lifted to an angle of about forty-five degrees from horizontal, the clattering of the engines died away and the last traces of the green smoke drifted to one side. The time was near midday, and the sun was overhead.

In this new configuration the pipe had taken on the unmistakable appearance of a vast cannon, raised towards the sky!

The waters of the lake became still, the men who had been working had taken refuge in a series of buildings low on the ground. Not realizing what was about to happen, Amelia and I stayed where we were.

The first indication that the cannon was being fired was an eruption of white water boiling up to the surface of the lake. A moment later we felt a deep trembling in the very soil on which we sat, and before us the waters of the canal broke into a million tiny wavelets.

I reached over to Amelia, threw my arms around her shoulders and pushed her sideways to the ground. She fell awkwardly, but I flung myself over her, covering her face with my shoulder and wrapping my arms about her head. We could feel the concussions in the ground, as if an earthquake were about to strike, and then a noise came, like the deepest growlings in the heart of a thunder-cloud.

The violence of this event grew rapidly to a peak, and then it ended as abruptly as it had begun. In the same instant we heard a protracted, shrieking explosion, howling and screaming like a thousand whistles blown simultaneously in one's ear. This noise started at its highest frequency, dying away rapidly.

As the racket was stilled, we sat up and looked across the canal towards the cannon.

Of the projectile – if any there had been – there was no sign, but belching from the muzzle of the cannon was one of the largest clouds of vapour I have ever seen in my life. It was brilliant white, and it spread out in an almost spherical cloud above the muzzle, being constantly replenished by the quantities still pouring from the barrel. In less than a minute the vapour had occluded the sun, and at once we felt much colder. The shadow lay across most of the land we could see from our vantage point, and being almost directly beneath the cloud as we were, we had no way of estimating its depth. That this was considerable was evidenced by the darkness of its shadow.

We stood up. Already, the cannon was being lowered once more, and the engines in the pivotal buildings were roaring. The slaves and their supervisors were emerging from their shelters.

We turned back towards the city, and walked as quickly as we could towards its relative comforts. In the moment the sun had been shaded the apparent temperature around us had fallen to well below freezing point. We were not much surprised, therefore, when a few minutes later we saw the first snowflakes falling about us, and as time passed the light fall became a dense and blinding blizzard.

We looked up just once, and saw that the cloud from which the snow fell – the very cloud of vapour which had issued from the cannon! – now covered almost the entire sky.

We almost missed the entrance to the city, so deep was the snow when we reached it. Here too we saw for the first time the dome-shape of the invisible shield that protected the city, for snow lay thickly on it.

A few hours later there was another concussion, and later another. In all there were twelve, repeated at intervals of about five or six hours. The sun, when its rays could penetrate the clouds, quickly melted the snow on the city's dome, but for the most part those days were dark and frightening ones in Desolation City, and we were not alone in thinking it.

VII

So much for some of the mysteries we saw in the Martian city. In describing them I have of necessity had to portray Amelia and myself as curious, objective tourists, craning our necks in wonder as any traveller in a foreign land will do. However, although we were much exercised by what we saw, this seeming objectivity was far from the case, for we were alarmed by our predicament.

There was one matter of which we rarely spoke, except obliquely; this was not because we did not think of it, but because we both knew that if the subject were raised then there was nothing hopeful that could be said. This was the manifest impossibility that we should ever be able to return to Earth.

It was, though, at the centre of our very thoughts and actions, for we knew we could not exist like this for ever, but to plan the rest of our lives in Desolation City would be a tacit acceptance of our fate.

The nearest either of us came to confronting our problem directly was on the day we first saw how advanced was the Martians' science.

Thinking that in a society as modern as this we should have no difficulty in laying our hands on the necessary materials, I said to

Amelia: 'We must find somewhere we can set aside as a laboratory.'

She looked at me quizzically.

'Are you proposing to embark on a scientific career?' she said.

'I'm thinking we must try to build another Time Machine.'

'Do you have any notion of how the Machine worked?'

I shook my head. 'I had hoped that you, as Sir William's assistant, would know.'

'My dear,' Amelia said, and for a moment she took my hand affectionately in hers, 'I would have as little idea as you.'

There we had let it rest. It had been an extreme hope of mine until then, but I knew Amelia well enough to appreciate that her reply meant more than the words themselves. I realized she had already considered the idea herself, and had come to the conclusion that there was no chance that we could duplicate Sir William's work.

So, without further discussion of our prospects, we existed from day to day, each of us knowing that a return to Earth was impossible. One day we should have to confront our situation, but until then we were simply putting off the moment.

If we did not have peace of mind, then the physical needs of our bodies were adequately met.

Our two-day sojourn in the desert had not apparently caused lasting harm, although I had contracted a mild head-cold at some time. Neither of us kept down that first meal we ate, and during the night that followed we were both unpleasantly ill. Since then we had been taking the food in smaller quantities. There were three of the dining halls within walking distance of our dormitory, and we alternated between them.

As I have already mentioned, we slept in a dormitory to ourselves. The hammocks were large enough for two people, so, remembering what had passed between us earlier, I suggested a little wistfully to Amelia that we would be warmer if we shared a hammock.

'We are no longer in the desert, Edward,' was her reply, and from then we slept separately.

I felt a little hurt at her response, because although my designs on her were still modest and proper I had good cause to believe that we were less than strangers. But I was prepared to abide by her wishes.

During the days our behaviour together was friendly and intimate. She would often take my hand or my arm as we walked, and at night we would kiss chastely before I turned my back to allow her to undress. At such times my desires were neither modest nor proper, and often I was tempted most inappropriately to ask her again to marry me. Inappropriate it was, for where on Mars would we find a church? This too was a matter I had to put aside until we could accept our fate.

On the whole, thoughts of home predominated. For my own part I spent considerable time thinking about my parents, and the fact that I would not see them again. Trivialities occupied me too. One such was the irresistible certainty that I had left my lamp burning in my room at Mrs Tait's. I had been in such high spirits that Sunday morning I departed for Richmond that I did not recall having extinguished the flame before I left. With irritating conviction I remembered having lit it when I got out of bed ... but had I left it burning? It was no consolation to reason with myself that now, eight or nine years later, the matter was of no consequence. But still the uncertainty nagged at me, and would not leave me.

Amelia too seemed preoccupied, although she kept her thoughts to herself. She made an effort not to appear introspective, and affected a bright and lively interest in what we saw in the city, but there were long periods in which we were both silent, and this was itself significant. An indication of the degree to which she was distracted was that she sometimes talked in her sleep; much of this was incoherent, but occasionally she spoke my name, and sometimes Sir William's. Once I found a way of asking tactfully about her dreams, but she said she had no memory of them.

VIII

Within a few days of our arrival in the city, Amelia set herself the task of learning the Martian language. She had always had, she said, a facility with languages, and in spite of the fact that she had no access to either a dictionary or a grammar she was optimistic. There were, she said, basic situations she could identify, and by listening to the words spoken at the time she could establish a rudimentary vocabulary. This would be of great use to us, for we were both severely limited by the muteness imposed upon us.

Her first task was to essay an interpretation of the written language, in the form of what few signs we had seen posted about the city.

These were few in number. There were some signs at each of the city's entrances, and one or two of the legged vehicles had words inscribed upon them. Here Amelia encountered her first difficulty, because as far as she could discern no sign was ever repeated. Furthermore, there appeared to be a great number of scripts in use, and she was incapable of establishing even one or two letters of the Martian alphabet.

When she turned her attention to the spoken word her problems multiplied.

The major difficulty here was an apparent multitude of voice-tones. Quite apart from the fact that the Martians' vocal chords pitched their voices higher than would have been natural on Earth (and both Amelia and I tried in private to reproduce the sound, with comical effects), there was an apparently endless subtlety of tone variations.

Sometimes a Martian voice we heard was hard, with what we on Earth would call a sneer lending an unpleasant edge to it; another would seem musical and soft by comparison. Some Martians would speak with a complex sibilance, others with protracted vowel-sounds and pronounced plosives.

Further complicating everything was the fact that all Martians appeared to accompany their conversation with elaborate hand and head movements, and additionally would address some Martians with one voice-tone, and others in a different way.

Also, the slave-Martians appeared to have a dialect all of their own.

After several days of trying, Amelia came to the sad conclusion that the complexity of the language (or languages) was beyond her. Even so, until our last days together in Desolation City she was trying to identify individual sounds, and I was very admiring of her diligence.

There was, though, one vocal sound whose meaning was unmistakable. It was a sound common to all races on Earth, and had the same meaning on Mars. That was the scream of terror, and we were to hear much of that eventually.

IX

We had been in Desolation City for fourteen days when the epidemic struck. At first we were unaware that anything was amiss, although we noticed some early effects without realizing the cause. Specifically, this was that one evening there seemed to be far fewer Martians present in the dining hall, but so accustomed were we to odd things on this world that neither of us attributed to it anything untoward.

The day following was the one on which we witnessed the firing of the snow-cannon (for such was what we came to call it) and so our interests lay elsewhere. But by the end of those days when snow fell more or less without let over the city, there was no mistaking that something was seriously wrong. We saw several Martians dead or unconscious in the streets, a visit to one of the dormitories was confirmation enough that many of the people were ill, and even the activities of the vehicles reflected a change, for there were fewer of them about and one or two were clearly being used as ambulances.

Needless to say, as the full realization came to us, Amelia and I stayed away from the populated areas of the city. Fortunately, neither of us displayed any symptoms; the stuffiness as a result of my head-cold stayed with me rather longer than it might have done at home, but that was all.

Amelia's latent nursing instincts came to the surface, and her conscience told her she should go to help the sick, but it would have been grossly unwise to do so. We tried to cut ourselves off from the anguish, and hoped the disease would soon pass.

It seemed that the plague was not virulent. Many people had contracted it, and by the evidence of the number of bodies we saw being transported in one of the legged vehicles we knew that many had died. But after five days we noticed that life was beginning to return to normal. If anything, there was more misery about than ever before – for once we felt the Martians had good cause – and there were, regrettably, even fewer people in the underpopulated city, but the vehicles returned to their policing and haulage, and we saw no more dead in the streets.

But then, just as we were sensing the return to normal, there came the night of the green explosions.

TEN

A Terrible Invasion

•

I

I was awakened by the first concussion, but in my sleepy state I presumed that the snow-cannon had been fired once more. During those nights of its firing we had grown accustomed to the tremors and distant explosions. The bang that woke me, though, was different.

'Edward?'

'I'm awake,' I said. 'Was that the cannon again?'

'No, it was different. And there was a flash. It lighted the whole room.'

I stayed silent, for I had long since learned the futility of speculating about what we saw in this place. A few minutes passed, and the city was unmoving.

'It was nothing,' I said. 'Let's go back to sleep.'

'Listen.'

Some distance away, across the sleeping city, a policing-vehicle was driving quickly, its banshee siren howling. A moment later a second one started up, and passed within a few streets of where we lay.

Just then the room was lit for an instant with the most vivid and lurid flash of green. In its light I saw Amelia sitting up in her hammock, clutching her quilt around her. A second or two later we heard a tremendous explosion, somewhere beyond the city's limits.

Amelia climbed with the usual difficulty from the hammock, and walked to the nearest window.

'Can you see anything?'

'I think there's a fire,' she said. 'It's difficult to tell. There is something burning with a green light.'

I started to move from my hammock, for I wished to see this, but Amelia stopped me.

'Please don't come to the window,' she said. 'I am unclothed.'

'Then please put something on, for I wish to see what is happening.'

She turned and hurried towards where she placed her clothes at night, and as she did so the room was once more filled with brilliant green light. For a moment I caught an inadvertent glimpse of her, but managed to look away in time to spare her embarrassment. Two seconds later there was another loud explosion; this was either much closer or much larger, for the ground shook with the force of it.

Amelia said: 'I have my chemise on, Edward. You may come to the window with me now.'

I normally slept wearing a pair of the Martian trouser-garments, and so climbed hastily from the hammock and joined her at the window. As she had said, there was an area of green light visible away towards the east. It was neither large nor bright, but it had an intensity about the centre of the glow that would indicate a fire. It was dimming as we watched it, but then came another explosion just beside it and I pulled Amelia away from the window. The blast effect was this time the greatest yet, and we began to grow frightened.

Amelia stood up to look through the window again, but I placed my arm around her shoulder and pulled her forcibly away.

Outside, there was the sound of more sirens, and then another flash of green light followed by a concussion.

'Go back to the hammocks, Amelia,' I said. 'At least on those we will be shielded from the blast through the floor.'

To my surprise Amelia did not demur, but walked quickly towards the nearest hammock and climbed on. I took one more look in the direction of the explosions, staring past the watch-tower that stood outside our building and seeing the ever-spreading diffusion of green fire. Even as I looked there was another brilliant flare of green light, followed by the concussion, and so I hurried over to the hammocks.

Amelia was sitting up in the one I normally used.

'I think tonight I should like you to be with me,' she said, and her voice was trembling. I too felt a little shaken, for the force of those explosions was considerable, and although they were a good distance away were certainly greater than anything in my experience.

I could just make out her shape in the darkened room. I had been holding the edge of the hammock in my hand, and now Amelia reached forward and touched me. At that moment there was yet another flash, one far brighter than any of the others. This time the shock-wave, when it came, shook the very foundations of the building. With this, I threw aside my inhibitions, climbed on to the hammock, and wriggled under the quilt beside Amelia. At once her arms went around me, and for a moment I was able to forget about the mysterious explosions outside.

These continued, however, at irregular intervals for the best part of two hours, and as if they were provoked by the explosions the sound of the Martians' vehicle sirens doubled and redoubled as one after another hurtled through the streets.

So the night passed, with neither of us sleeping. My attention was divided, partly between the unseen events outside and the precious closeness of Amelia beside me. I so loved her, and even such a temporary intimacy was without parallel to me.

At long last dawn came, and the sound of the sirens faded. The sun had been up for an hour before the last one was heard, but after that all was silent, and Amelia and I climbed from the hammock and dressed.

I walked to the window, and stared towards the east . . . but there was no sign of the source of the explosions, beyond a faint smudge of smoke drifting across the horizon. I was about to turn back and report this to Amelia when I noticed that the watch-tower outside our building had vanished during the night. Looking further along the street I saw that all the others, which were now such a familiar part of the city, had also gone.

II

After the bedlam of the night the city was unnaturally quiet, and so it was with quite understandable misgivings that we left the dormitory to investigate. If the atmosphere in the city had been in the past one of dreadful anticipation, then this stillness was like the approach of expected death. Desolation City was never a noisy place, but now it was empty and silent. We saw evidence of the night's activity in the streets, in the form of heavy marks in the road-surface where one of the vehicles had taken a corner too fast, and outside one of the dormitory halls was a pile of spilled and abandoned vegetables.

Rendered uneasy by what we saw, I said to Amelia: 'Do you think we should be out? Would we not be safer inside?'

'But we must discover what is going on.'

'Not at risk to ourselves.'

'My dear, we have nowhere to hide on this world,' she said.

We came at last to the building where we had once ascended to see the extent of the city. We agreed to climb to the roof, and survey the situation from there.

From the top the view told us little more than we already knew, for there was no sign of movement anywhere in the city. Then Amelia pointed to the east.

'So that is where the watch-towers have been taken!' she said.

Beyond the city's protective dome we could just make out a cluster of the tall objects. If those were the towers then that would certainly account for their disappearance from the city. It was impossible to see how many were out there, but at a reasonable estimate it was certainly a hundred or more. They had been lined up in a defensive formation, placed between the city and where we had seen the explosions in the night.

'Edward, do you suppose there is a war going on here?'

'I think there must be. Certainly there has not been a happy atmosphere in the city.'

'But we have seen no soldiers.'

'Maybe we are to see some for the first time.'

I was in the lowest of spirits, sensing that at last we were going to be forced into accepting our plight. I saw at that moment no alternative to the prospect of becoming embroiled forever in Martian life. If a war it was for this city, then two aliens such as ourselves would soon be discovered. If we stayed in hiding we would doubtless be found, and, if so, would be taken for spies or infiltrators. We must, very soon, declare ourselves to those in authority and become as one with the inhabitants here.

Seeing no better vantage point available to us, we agreed to stay where we were until the situation became clearer. Neither of us had any wish to explore further; death and destruction were in the winds.

We did not have long to wait... for even as we first saw the line of watch-towers defending the city the invasion, unbeknown to us, had already begun. What happened out there beyond the city's dome must be a matter of conjecture, but having seen the aftermath I can say with some certainty that the first line of defence was a troop of Martians armed only with hand-weapons. These wretched men were soon overwhelmed, and those not killed fled to the temporary safety of the city. This much was happening even as we walked through the streets to our present vantage point.

The next development was twofold.

In the first place, we at last saw signs of movement; these were the fleeing defenders, returning to the city. Secondly, the watch-towers were attacked. This was over in a matter of minutes. The antagonists were armed with some kind of heat thrower which, when turned on the towers, almost immediately rendered them molten. We saw the destruction as bursts of flame, as one tower after another was struck with this heat, and exploded violently.

If by this description I seem to imply that the towers were defenceless, then I must add that this was not so. When, somewhat later, I saw the wreckage of the battle, I realized that a spirited, if ultimately ineffectual, defence had been put up, for several of the attackers' vehicles had been destroyed.

Amelia's hand crept into mine, and I squeezed it reassuringly. I was placing secret faith in the city's dome, hoping that the marauders would have no way of penetrating it.

We heard screams. There were more of the people about the streets now, both city-Martians and slaves, running with the strange, loping gait, looking frantically about, intent on finding safety in the maze of city streets.

Suddenly, flame exploded about one of the buildings by the perimeter of the city, and screams could distantly be heard. Another building burst into flames, and then another.

We heard a new sound: a deep-throated siren, rising and falling, quite unlike the noises we had grown accustomed to in the city.

I said: 'They have penetrated the dome.'

'What shall we do?' Amelia's voice was calm, but I felt that she was forcing herself not to panic. I could feel her hand trembling in mine, and our palms were damp with perspiration.

'We must stay here,' I said. 'We are as safe here as anywhere.'

Down in the streets more Martians had appeared, some running out from the buildings where they had been hiding. I saw that some of the people fleeing from the battle had been wounded, and one man was being carried by two of his fellows, his legs dragging.

One of the policing-vehicles appeared, moving quickly through the streets towards the battle. It slowed as it passed some of the Martians, and I heard the driver's voice, apparently ordering them to return to the fight. The people took no notice and continued their confused retreat, and the vehicle drove away. More sirens could be heard, and soon several more legged vehicles hurried past our building towards the fray. In the meantime, more buildings on the edge of the city had been fired.

I heard an explosion to the south of us, and I looked that way. I saw that flames and smoke were rising there, and realized that another force of invaders had broken through!

The plight of the city seemed desperate, for nowhere could I see a concerted defence, and there was certainly no resistance on the new front.

There came a grinding, roaring sound from the east, and another blast of that alien siren, immediately followed by a second. The Martians in the street near our building screamed terribly, their voices more high-pitched than ever.

Then at last we saw one of the marauders.

It was a large, ironclad vehicle, the rows of articulate legs concealed by metal plating at each side. Mounted high on its rear was a grey metal gun-barrel, some six or eight feet in length, which by the pivotal device on which it was mounted was able to point in any direction the driver of the vehicle chose. As soon as we saw the invading vehicle, this cannon rotated and a building to one side burst abruptly into flame. There was a terrible noise, like sheets of metal torn asunder.

The marauding vehicle was quite close to us, not more than two hundred yards away and in clear view. It showed no sign of halting, and as it passed a road junction it released another bolt of infernal energy, and one of the dining halls where we had often eaten exploded into flame.

'Edward! There!'

Amelia pointed down the intersecting street, along which we now saw five of the city's policing-vehicles approaching. I saw that they had been equipped with smaller versions of the invaders' heat-cannons, and as soon as they had a clear line of sight the two leading vehicles fired.

The effect was instantaneous: with a deafening explosion the invading vehicle blew apart, showering debris in all directions. I just had time to see that one of the attacking city-vehicles was blown backwards by the blast before the shock-wave hit the building we were on. Fortunately, Amelia and I were already crouching low, otherwise we should certainly have been knocked off our feet. Part of the parapet was blown inwards, narrowly missing me, and part of the roof behind us collapsed. For a few seconds the only sound we could hear was the crash of metal debris as it fell across the streets and buildings.

The four undamaged policing-vehicles continued on without hesitation, skirted around their damaged colleague and drove over the shattered remains of the enemy. A few seconds later they were lost to sight as they headed rapidly towards the scene of the main invasion.

We had only a few moments' respite.

With the sinister combination of clanking metal legs and ear-piercing sirens, four more of the marauders were coming into the centre of the city from the southern penetration. They moved with frightening speed, blasting occasionally at previously undamaged buildings. The smoke pouring out of the fired buildings was now swirling about our heads, and it was often difficult either to see or breathe.

We looked round desperately to see if any defenders were in the vicinity, but there was none. Scores of Martians still ran wildly in the streets.

Three of the marauders roared past our building, and disappeared into the smoke-filled streets to the north. The last, though, slowed as it came to the wreckage of its ally, and halted before the tangled metal. It waited there for a minute, then came slowly down the street towards us.

In a moment it stopped directly beneath our vantage point. Amelia and I stared down tremulously.

I said suddenly: 'Oh my God, Amelia! Don't look!!'

It was too late. She too had seen the incredible sight that had caught my attention. For a few seconds it was as if all the confusion of this invasion had stilled, while we stared numbly at the enemy machine.

It had clearly been specially designed and built for operations such as this. As I have said, there was mounted on its rear the destruction-dealing heat projector, and stowed just in front of this was a much larger version of the metallic spider-machine we had seen repairing the watch-tower, crouching with its uncanny mechanical life momentarily stilled.

At the front of the vehicle was the position where the driver of the craft was situated; this was shielded in front, behind and to each side with iron armour. The top, though, was open, and Amelia and I were looking straight down into it.

What we saw inside the vehicle was not a man, let that be abundantly clear from the outset. That it was organic and not mechanical was equally apparent, for it pulsed and rippled with repellent life. Its colour was a dull grey-green, and its glistening main body was bloated and roughly globular, some five feet in diameter. From our position we could see few details, bar a light-coloured patch on the back of the body, roughly comparable to the blow-hole on the head of a whale. But we could also see its tentacles ... These lay in a grotesque formation at the front of the body, writhing and slithering in a most revolting fashion. Later I was to see that there numbered sixteen of these evil extensions, but in that first moment of appalled fascination it seemed that the whole cab was filled with these creeping, winding abominations.

I turned away from the sight, and glanced at Amelia.

She had gone deathly pale, and her eyes were closing. I placed my arm about her shoulders, and she shuddered instinctively, as if it had been that disgusting monster-creature, and not I, that had touched her.

'In the name of all that is good,' she said. 'What have we come to?'

I said nothing, a deep nausea stifling all words and thoughts. I simply looked down again at the loathsome sight, and registered that in those few seconds the monster-creature had levelled its heat-cannon into the heart of the building on which we crouched.

A second later there was a massive explosion, and smoke and flame leapt about us!

III

In great terror, for in the impact more of the roof had fallen away behind us, we climbed unsteadily to our feet and headed blindly for the staircase by which we had ascended. Smoke was pouring densely from the heart of the building, and the heat was intense.

Amelia clutched my arm as more of the fabric collapsed beneath us, and a curtain of flame and sparks flared fifty feet above our heads.

The stairs were built of the same rock as the walls of the building, and still seemed sound, even as gusts of heat were billowing up them.

I wrapped my arm over my nose and mouth, and closing my eyes to slits I plunged down, dragging Amelia behind me. Two-thirds of the way to the bottom, part of the staircase had fallen away and we had to slow our flight, reaching hesitantly for footholds on the jagged parts of the slabs remaining. Here it was that the conflagration did its worst: we could not breathe, could not see, could not feel anything but the searing heat of the inferno below us. Miraculously, we found the rest of the steps undamaged, and thrust ourselves down again ... at last emerging into the street, choking and weeping.

Amelia sank to the ground, just as several Martians rushed past us, screaming and shouting in their shrill, soprano voices.

'We must run, Amelia!' I shouted over the roar and confusion around us.

Gamely, she staggered to her feet. Holding my arm with one hand, and still clutching her hand-bag with the other, she followed me as we set off in the direction taken by the Martians.

We had gone but a few yards before we came to the corner of the blazing building.

Amelia screamed, and snatched at my arm: the invading vehicle had driven up behind us, hitherto concealed by the smoke. Thought of the repulsive occupant was alone enough to spur us on, and we half-fell, half-ran around the corner ... to find a second vehicle blocking our way! It seemed to loom over us, fifteen or twenty feet high.

The Martians who had run before us were there; some were cowering on the ground, others were milling frantically about, searching for an escape.

On the back of the monstrous vehicle the glittering, spider-like machine was rearing up on its metal legs, its long articulate arms already reaching out like slow-moving whip-cord.

'*Run*!' I shouted at Amelia. 'For God's sake, we must escape!'

Amelia made no response, but her clutch on my arm loosened, the hand-bag slipped from her fingers, and in a moment she fell to the ground in a dead faint. I crouched over her, trying to revive her.

Just once I looked up, and saw the dreadful arachnoid lurching through the crowd of Martians, its legs clanking, its metal tentacles swinging wildly about. Many of the Martians had fallen to the ground beneath it, writhing in agony.

I leaned forward over Amelia's crumpled figure, and bent over her protectively. She had rolled on to her back, and her face stared vacantly upwards. I placed my head beside hers, tried to cover her body with mine.

Then one of the metal tentacles lashed against me, wrapping itself around my throat, and the most hideous bolt of electrical energy coursed through me. My body contorted in agony, and I was hurled to one side away from Amelia!

As I fell to the ground I felt the tentacle snatching away from me, ripping open part of the flesh of my neck.

I lay supine, head lolling to one side, my limbs completely paralysed.

The machine advanced, stunning and crippling with its arms. I saw one wrap itself around Amelia's waist, and the jolt of electricity broke through her faint and I saw her face convulsing. She screamed, horribly and pitiably.

I saw now that the foul machine had picked up many of those Martians it had stunned, and was carrying them in rolls of its glittering tentacles, some still conscious and struggling, others inert.

The machine was returning to its parent vehicle. I could just see the control-cab from where I was lying, and to my ultimate horror I suddenly saw the face of one of the abominable beings who had initiated this invasion, staring at us through an opening in the armour. It was a broad, wicked face, devoid of any sign of good. Two large pale eyes stared expressionlessly across the carnage it was wreaking. They were unblinking eyes, merciless eyes.

The spider-machine had remounted the vehicle, dragging in

its tentacles behind it. The Martians it had seized were wrapped in folds of jointed, tubular metal, imprisoned in this heaving cage. Amelia was among them, pinned down by three of the tentacles, held without care so that her body was twisted painfully. She was still conscious, and staring at me.

I was totally unable to respond as I saw her mouth open, and then her voice echoed shrilly across the few yards of space that separated us. She screamed my name, again and again.

I lay still, the blood pumping from the wound in my throat, and in a moment I saw the invading vehicle move away, driving with its unnatural gait through the broken masonry and swirling smoke of the devastated city.

ELEVEN

A Voyage Across the Sky

•

I

I do not know for how long I was paralysed, although it must have been several hours. I cannot remember much of the experience, for it was one of immense physical agony and mental torment, compounded by an impotence of such grossness that to dwell for even a moment on Amelia's likely fate was sufficient to send my thoughts into a maelstrom of anger and futility.

Only one memory remains clear and undimmed, and that is of a piece of wreckage that happened to lie directly within my view. I did not notice it at first, so wild and blinding were my thoughts, but later it seemed to occupy the whole of my vision. Lying in the centre of the tangle of broken metal was the body of one of the noisome monster-creatures. It had been crushed in the explosion that had wrecked the vehicle, and the part of it I could see revealed an ugly mass of contusions and blood. I could also see two or three of its tentacles, curled in death.

In spite of my mute loathing and revulsion, I was satisfied to realize that beings so powerful and ruthless were themselves mortal.

At length I felt the first sensations returning to my body; I felt them first in my fingers, and then in my toes. Later, my arms and legs began to hurt, and I knew that control over my muscles was being restored. I tried moving my head, and although I was taken with dizziness I found I could raise it from the ground.

As soon as I could move my arm, I placed my hand against my

neck and explored the extent of my throat-wound. I could feel a long and ugly cut, but the blood had stopped flowing and I knew the wound must be superficial, otherwise I should have died within seconds.

After several minutes of trying I managed to lift myself into a sitting position, and then at last I found I could stand. Painfully, I looked about me.

I was the only living thing in that street. On the ground about me were several Martians; I did not examine them all, but those I did were certainly dead. Across by the other side of the street was the damaged vehicle, and its hateful occupant. And a few yards from where I stood, poignantly abandoned, was Amelia's handbag.

I walked over to it with heavy heart, and picked it up. I glanced inside, feeling as if I were invading her privacy, but the bag contained the only material possessions we had had, and it was important to know if they were still there. Nothing appeared to have been moved, and I closed the bag quickly. There were too many things inside it that reminded me of Amelia.

The body of the monster creature was still dominating my thoughts, in spite of my dread and loathing. Almost against my own will I walked across to the wreck, carrying Amelia's bag in my hand.

I stopped a few feet away from the hideous corpse, fascinated by the grisly sight.

I stepped back, not having learnt anything, but still there was something uncannily familiar about it that detained me. I diverted my attention from the dead being to the wreck that contained it. I had assumed that the vehicle had been one of those that had invaded the city. But then, looking anew, I remembered the policing-vehicle that had been blasted in the explosion, and realized that this must be it!

With that sudden awareness, the awful implications of the anonymous and faceless drivers of those city vehicles came to me ... and I stepped back from the wreck in horror and amazement, more frightened than I had ever been in my life.

II

A few minutes later, as I walked in a dazed fashion through the streets, a vehicle suddenly appeared in front of me. The driver must have seen me, for the vehicle halted at once. I saw that it was one of the city haulage-vehicles, and that standing in the back were between twenty and thirty Martian humans.

I stared at the control-cab, trying not to imagine the being that was behind the black oval window. A voice rasped out through the metal grille.

I stood quite still, panicking inside. I had no idea what to do, no idea what was expected of me.

The voice came again, sounding to my ready ear angry and peremptory.

I realized that several of the men in the back of the vehicle were leaning over towards me, extending their arms. I took this to mean that I was expected to join them, and so I walked over to them, and without further ado was helped aboard.

As soon as I and my bag were in the open rear compartment, the vehicle moved off.

My bloodied appearance ensured that I was the centre of attention as soon as I had boarded. Several of the Martians spoke directly to me, clearly awaiting some kind of reply. For a moment I was in a renewed state of panic, thinking that at last I should have to reveal my alien origins . . .

But then a most fortunate inspiration came to me. I opened my mouth, made a gagging noise, and pointed at the heinous wound in my neck. The Martians spoke again, but I simply looked blank and continued to gag at them, hoping thereby to convince them that I had been stricken dumb.

For a few more seconds the unwanted attention continued, but then they seemed to lose interest in me. More survivors had been seen, and the vehicle had halted. Soon, three more men and a woman were being helped aboard. They had apparently not suffered at the hands of the invaders, for they were uninjured.

The vehicle moved off again, prowling the streets and occasionally letting forth an unpleasant braying sound through its metal grille. It was reassuring to be in the company of these Martian humans, but I could never quite put from my mind the grotesque presence of the monster-creature in the control-cab.

The slow journey around the city continued for another two hours, and gradually more survivors were picked up. From time to time we saw other vehicles engaged in the same operation, and I presumed from this that the invasion was over.

I found a corner at the back of the compartment, and sat down, cradling Amelia's bag in my arms.

I was wondering if what we had seen was, after all, a full-scale invasion. With the marauders departed, and the city smoking and damaged, it seemed more likely that what we had witnessed was more in the nature of a skirmish, or a reprisal mission. I recalled the firing of the snow-cannon, and wondered if those shells had been aimed at the cities of the enemy. If so, then Amelia and I had blundered into a fracas in which we had no part, and of which Amelia at least had become an unwitting victim.

I thrust this thought aside: it was unbearable to think of her at the mercy of these monster-creatures.

Somewhat later another thought occurred to me, one which gave me several unpleasant minutes. Could it be, I wondered, that I had been mistaken about the departure of the enemy? Was this truck being driven by one of the conquerors?

I pondered this for some time, but then remembered the dead monster I had seen. That was apparently of this city, and furthermore the humans I was with did not show the same symptoms of fear as I had seen during the fighting. Could it be that every city on Mars was managed by the vile monster-creatures?

There was hardly any time to consider this, for soon the compartment was filled, and the vehicle set off at a steady pace towards the edge of the city. We were deposited outside a large building, and directed inside. Here, slaves had prepared a meal, and with the others I ate what was put before me. Afterwards, we were taken to one of the undamaged dormitory buildings and allocated hammock-space. I spent that night lying in a cramped position with four Martian males on one hammock.

III

There followed a long period of time (one so painful to me that I can barely bring myself to record it here), during which I was assigned to a labour-team set to repair the damaged streets and buildings. There was much to do, and, with the reduced population, no apparent end to the time I would be forced to work in this way.

There was never the least possibility of escape. We were guarded by the monster-creatures every moment of every day, and the apparent freedoms of the city, which had allowed Amelia and I to explore it so thoroughly, were long gone. Now only a minute area of the city was occupied, and this was policed not only by the vehicles, but also overseen by the watch-towers not damaged in the raid. These were occupied by the monsters, who were apparently capable of staying immobile in their perches for hours at a time.

Large number of slaves had been drafted in to the city, and the worst and heaviest tasks were given to them. Even so, much of the work I had to do was onerous.

I was glad in one way that the work was demanding, for it helped me not to dwell too long on Amelia's plight. I found myself wishing that she were dead, for I could not contemplate the horrible perversions the obscene creatures would put her to if she remained alive in their captivity. But at the same time, I could not for one moment allow myself to think she was dead. I wanted her alive, for she was my own raison d'etre. She was always in my thoughts, however distracting the events around me, and at nights I would lie awake, tormenting myself with guilt and self-acrimony. I wanted and loved her so, that scarcely a night passed when I did not sob in my hammock.

It was no consolation that the misery of the Martians was an equal to mine, nor that at last I was understanding the causes of their eternal grief.

IV

I soon lost count of the days, but it could not have been less than six of Earth's months before there came a dramatic change in my circumstances. One day, without prior warning, I was force-marched with about a dozen men and women away from the city. A monster-vehicle followed us.

I thought at first we were being taken to one of the industrial sites, but shortly after leaving the protective dome we headed south, and crossed the canal by one of the bridges. Ahead of us I saw the barrel of the snow-cannon looming up.

It appeared to have escaped undamaged in the raid – or else had been efficiently repaired – for there was an activity about the muzzle equal to the amount Amelia and I had seen that first time. At sight of this my heart sank, for I did not relish the thought of having to work in the thin, outer atmosphere; I was not the only one breathing laboriously as we marched, but I felt the native Martians would be better suited to working in the open. The weight of Amelia's hand-bag – which I took with me everywhere – was a further encumbrance.

We marched as far as the centre of the activity: close to the muzzle itself. By this time I was on the point of collapse, so difficult was it to breathe. As we came to a halt I discovered I was not alone in my agony, for everyone sat weakly on the ground. I joined them, trying to force my heart to still its furious beating.

So occupied was I with my discomforts that I had neglected to take stock of the events around me. I was aware of the great, black muzzle twenty yards from me, and the fact that we had halted by a crowd of slaves, but that was all.

There were two city-Martians standing to one side, and they were regarding us with some interest. Once I realized this, I looked back at them and saw that in certain respects they were different from other men I had seen here. They seemed very poised, for one thing, and they wore clothes that were different from those worn by everyone else. These were black garments, cut in almost military style.

Apparently my looking back at them had drawn attention to myself, for a moment later the two Martians walked over to me and said something. Playing my role as a mute, I stared back at them. Their patience was thin: one reached down to me and pulled me to my feet. I was pushed to one side, where three male slaves were already standing apart. The two city-Martians then went to where the rest of the slaves were standing, selected a young girl, and brought her over to join us.

I was uneasily aware that I and the four slaves had become the focus of some interest. Several of the Martians were staring at us, but as the two men in black came over to us they turned away, leaving us to whatever plight was in store.

An order was issued, and the slaves turned obediently away. I followed at once, still anxious not to seem different. We were herded towards what appeared at first sight to be an immense vehicle. As we approached, however, I saw that it consisted in fact of two objects, temporarily joined together.

Both parts were cylindrical in shape. The longer of the two was really the most bizarre machine I had seen during my time on Mars. It was about sixty feet in length, and, apart from its overall conformation to a cylindrical diameter of about twenty feet, was not regularly shaped. Along its base were many groups of the mechanical legs, but on the whole its exterior was smooth. At several places around its outer skin were perforations, and I could see water dribbling from some of these. At the far end of the machine a long, flexible pipe led away. This ran right across the desert, at least as far as the canal, and was looped and coiled in several places.

The smaller of the two objects is simpler to describe, in that its shape was readily identifiable. So familiar was this shape that my heart began to beat wildly once more: this was the projectile that would be fired from the cannon!

It was itself cylindrical for most of its length, but with a curving, pointed nose. The resemblance to an artillery-shell was startling ... but there was never on Earth any shell of this size! From one end to another it must have been at least fifty feet long, and with a diameter of about twenty feet. The outer surface was finely machined so that it shone and dazzled in the bright sunlight. The smoothness of the surface was broken only in one place, and this was on the flat, rear end of the projectile. Here were four extrusions, and as we walked closer I saw that they were four of the heat-cannons we had seen the monster-creatures using. The four were placed symmetrically: one at the centre, the other three in an equilateral triangle about it.

The two Martians led us past this to where a hatchway had been opened, near the nose of the projectile. At this I hesitated, for it had suddenly become clear that we were to go inside. The slaves had hesitated too, and the Martians raised their whips in a menacing fashion. Before another move could be made, one of the slaves was touched across the shoulders. He howled with pain, and fell to the ground.

Two of the other slaves immediately bent to pick up the stricken man, and then, without further delay, we hurried up the sloping metal ramp into the projectile.

V

So it was that I began my voyage across the skies of Mars.

There were seven human beings aboard that craft: myself and the four slaves, and the two black-suited city-Martians who were in control.

The projectile itself was divided into three parts. At the very front of the craft was the small compartment where the two drivers stood during the flight. Immediately behind this, and separated from it by a metal partition, was a second compartment, and it was into this that I and the slaves were ushered. At the back of this compartment was a solid metal wall, entirely dividing this part of the craft from the main hold. It was there that the detestable monster-creatures and their deadly machines were carried. All this I discovered by a means I shall presently explain, but first I must describe the compartment in which I was placed.

I had by chance been the last to enter the craft, and so I found myself nearest to the partition. The two men in charge were shouting instructions to more men outside, and this lasted for several minutes, allowing me to take stock of where we were.

The interior of our compartment was almost bare. The walls were of unpainted metal, and because of the shape of the craft the floor where we stood curved up to become the ceiling too. Suspended from top to bottom, if my meaning is understood, were five tubes of what seemed to be a transparent fabric. Standing against the wall which separated this compartment from the main hold was what I at first took to be a large cupboard or cubicle, with two doors closed across it. I noticed that the slaves huddled away from it, and not knowing what it was for I too kept my distance.

The forward area was small and rather cramped, but what most overwhelmed me was the array of scientific equipment it contained. There was little here that I could comprehend, but there was one instrument whose function was immediately self-evident.

This was a large glass panel, placed directly in front of where the two drivers would stand. It was illuminated in some wise from behind, so that displays were projected on to it, not unlike several magic lanterns being operated at once. These displays revealed a number of views, and my attention was drawn to them.

The largest of the pictures showed the view directly forward of the projectile; that is to say, at the moment I first saw it the picture was entirely occupied by the machine presently connected to the nose of the projectile. Then there were views of what was happening to each side of the projectile, and behind. Another showed the very compartment in which I stood, and I could see my own figure standing by the partition. I waved my hand to myself for several moments, enjoying the novelty. The last showed what I presumed was the interior of the main hold of the craft, but here the image was dark and it was not possible to make out details.

Less interesting than this panel were the other instruments, the largest of which were clustered before two more of the flexible, transparent tubes which ran from top to bottom of the compartment.

At last the men at the hatch finished their instructions, and they stepped back. One of them wound a wheeled handle, and the hatch door was slowly brought up until it was flush with the rest of the hull. As it did so, our one source of daylight was sealed, and artificial lighting came on. Neither of the two men paid any attention to us, but moved across to the controls.

I looked at the slaves with me inside the compartment. The girl and one of the men were squatting on the floor, while a third spoke reassuringly to the man who had been struck with the whip. This last was in a bad way: he was trembling uncontrollably, and had lost the use of his facial muscles so that his eyes were slack, and saliva trickled from his mouth.

Returning my gaze to the displays I saw that with the turning on of the artificial lights, the main hold of the craft could now be seen. Here, in conditions which looked intolerably cramped, were the monster-creatures. I counted five of them, and each had already installed itself in a larger version of the transparent fabric tubes that I had already seen. Seeing these ghastly beings thus suspended was no less horrific for being slightly comical.

Looking at the other panels I saw that there was still considerable activity around the projectile. There seemed to be several hundred people outside, mostly slaves, and they were engaged in hauling away various pieces of heavy equipment which stood around the muzzle of the cannon.

Many minutes passed, with no apparent movement in the craft. The two men at the controls were busy checking their instruments. Then, unexpectedly, the whole projectile lurched, and looking at the various panels I saw that we were moving slowly backwards. Another panel showed the view at the rear of the craft: we were being propelled slowly up the ramp towards the muzzle of the cannon.

VI

The legged vehicle attached to the nose of the craft appeared to be in control of this operation. As the shell itself was pushed into the mouth of the barrel I noticed two things more or less simultaneously. The first was that the temperature inside the craft immediately lowered, as if the metal of the barrel were somehow artificially cooled, and thus sucking the warmth from the projectile; the second was that on the forward-looking panel I saw great fountains of water spraying from the controlling vehicle. The collar from which the spray was shot was rotating about the main body of the vehicle, for the spray was circling. This much I saw as we entered the barrel, but after a few seconds we had been advanced so far that the controlling vehicle itself entered the barrel and so blocked the daylight.

Now, although there were a few electrical lights implanted in the walls of the cannon, very little could be seen on the panels. Faintly, though, beyond the metal hull of the projectile, I could hear the hiss of the water spraying about us.

The temperature inside the projectile continued to fall. Soon it seemed as cold as it had been that first night Amelia and I had spent in the desert, and had I not been long accustomed to this frozen and hostile world I should have thought I would surely die of frostbite. My teeth were beginning to chatter when I heard a sound I had learned to dread: the harsh grating of the monster-creatures' voices, coming from a grille in the control cabin. Soon after this, I saw one of the men in charge pull a lever, and in a moment a draught of warmer air flowed through the compartment.

So our long passage down the barrel of the cannon continued. After the first moments, when the men in control were working furiously, there was not much for anyone to do but wait until the operation was completed. I passed the time by watching the monster-creatures in the hold: the one nearest me on the display-panel seemed to be staring directly at me with its cold, expressionless eyes.

The end of the operation, when it came, was without ceremony. We simply came to the deepest recess of the barrel – where there had already been placed a solid core of ice, blocking our way – and waited while the vehicle in control finished its water-spraying operation. Looking at the rearward display-panel I saw that the projectile had come to rest only inches from the core of ice.

From this moment, the remainder of the operation passed smoothly and quickly. The controlling vehicle separated from the projectile, and retreated quickly away up the barrel. Without the load of the craft the vehicle travelled much faster, and within a matter of minutes it had cleared the end of the barrel.

On the forward display-panel I could see up the entire length of the barrel, to a tiny point of daylight at the very end. The barrel between us and the daylight had been coated with a thick layer of ice.

VII

Once more came the sound of the monster-creatures' voices from the grille, and the four slaves I was with leapt to obey. They hastened towards the flexible tubes, helping the wounded man to his own. I saw that in the control cabin the other two men were climbing into the tubes that stood before the controls, and I realized that I too must obey.

Glancing round, I saw that one of the transparent tubes was placed in such a position that view of the control cabin could be maintained, but that one of the men slaves was already climbing into it. Not wishing to lose my advantageous view of the proceedings, I caught the man by his shoulder and waved my arms angrily. Without hesitation the slave cowered away from me, and moved to another tube.

I picked up Amelia's bag and climbed into the tube through a fold in the fabric, wondering what I was in for. When I was inside the fabric hung loosely about me like a curtain. Air was ducted through it from above, so in spite of the feeling of total enclosure it was not unbearable.

My view was rather more restricted, but I could still see three of the displays: the ones facing fore and aft of the projectile, and one of those facing to the side. This last, of course, was presently black, for it showed nothing but the wall of the barrel.

Quite unexpectedly there came a deep vibration in the projectile, and at the same moment I felt myself being tipped backwards. I tried to step back to maintain balance, but I was totally enclosed by the transparent fabric. Indeed, I was now understanding part of the function of this transparent tube, for as the muzzle of the cannon was being raised, the tube was tightening around me and so supporting me. The further the cannon barrel was raised the tighter the tube wrapped itself about me, to the point that as the tilting came to an end I was totally incapable of any movement at all. I was now lying with most of my weight supported by the tube, for although my feet were still touching the floor, the cannon had been raised until we were about forty-five degrees from horizontal.

No sooner had we come to rest than I saw a blaze of light shine out on the rearward-facing panel, and there was a tremendous jolt. A great and ineluctable pressure bore down on me, and the transparent tube tightened still more. Even so, the thrust of acceleration pressed against me as if with an immense hand.

After the first jolt there was no discernible sensation of motion apart from this pressure, for the ice had been laid with great precision and polished like a mirror. Looking at the rearward display I saw only darkness, stabbed with four beams of white light; ahead, the point of daylight visible at the muzzle was approaching. At first its apparent approach was almost undetectable, but within a few seconds it was rushing towards us with ever-increasing velocity.

Then we were out of the barrel, and in the same instant the pressure of acceleration was gone, and bright pictures flooded to the three displays I could see.

In the rearward panel I could see for a few seconds a receding view of the cannon, a huge cloud of steam pouring from the muzzle; on the side panel I caught erratic glimpses of land and sky whirling about; on the forward display I could see only the deep blue of the sky.

Thinking that at last it would be safe to leave the protection of the fabric I tried to step out, but discovered that I was still firmly held. There was a terrible vertiginous sensation spinning my head, as if I were falling from a great height, and at last I experienced in full the terrors of helpless confinement; I was truly trapped in this projectile, incapable of movement, tumbling through the sky.

I closed my eyes and took a deep breath. The air ducted through the tube was cool, and it reassured me to know that I was not intended to die here.

I took another deep breath, then a third, forcing myself to be calm.

At length I opened my eyes. Nothing inside the projectile had changed, as far as I could see. The scenes on the three displays were uniform: each showed the blue of the sky, but on the rearward one I could see a number of objects floating behind our craft. I wondered for a while as to what these could be, but then identified them as the four heat-projectors which had been played on the ice inside the cannon. I presumed by the fact of their being discarded that they had no further function.

That the craft was turning slowly on its axis became apparent a few seconds later, when the sideways panel unexpectedly revealed the horizon of the land, swinging up and across the picture. Soon the entire display was filled with a high view of land, but we were at such an altitude that it was almost impossible to see details. We were passing over what looked like a dry, mountainous region, but a major war had obviously taken place at some time as the ground was pock-marked with huge craters. Later, the craft rolled further so that the sky returned to fill the display.

From the forward display I learned that the craft must now have levelled off, for the horizon could be seen here. I presumed that this meant we were now in level flight, although the axial spin continued, evidenced by the fact that the forward horizon was spinning confusingly. The men controlling the craft must have had some way of correcting this, for I heard a series of hissing noises and gradually the horizon steadied.

I had thought that once we were in flight there would be no more shocks in store, so I was very alarmed a few minutes later when there was a loud explosion and a brilliant green light flooded across all the panels I could see. The flash was momentary, but another followed seconds later. Having seen those green flashes in the hours before the invasion I thought at first we must be under attack, but between each explosion the atmosphere inside the craft remained calm.

The frequency of these green explosions increased, until there was one almost every second, deafening me. Then they ceased for a while, and I saw that the projectile's trajectory had been drastically lowered. For an instant I saw in the forward panel the image of a vast city on the ground before us, then there was another burst of green fire burning continually outside the craft, and all became obscured by the blaze. In the noise of the roaring, explosive light I felt the transparent fabric tightening around me ... and my last impression was of an almost intolerable deceleration, followed by a tremendous crash.

TWELVE

What I Saw Inside the Craft

•

I

The panels had gone black, the fabric tubes had relaxed, and all was silent. The floor was tilted sharply forward, and so I fell from the supporting folds and collapsed against the partition, hardly daring to believe that once more the projectile was on solid ground. Beside me, the four slaves also fell or stepped from their tubes, and we all crouched together, trembling a little after the shocks of the flight.

We were not left alone for long. From beyond the partition I heard the sound of voices, and in a moment one of the men appeared; he too looked shaken, but he was on his feet and carrying his whip.

To my anger and surprise he raised this devilish instrument, and shouted imprecations at us in his soprano voice. Naturally, I could not understand, but the effect on the slaves was immediate. One of the men-slaves clambered to his feet and shouted back, but he was struck with the whip and fell to the floor.

Again the man in charge shouted at us. He pointed first at the slave who had been whipped as we entered the projectile, then at the man he had just stunned, then at the third male slave, then at the girl and finally at me. He shouted once more, pointed at each of us in turn, then fell silent.

As if to reinforce his authority, the villainous voice of one of the monster-creatures came braying through the grille, echoing in the tiny metal compartment.

The slave who had been pointed at first was lying nervelessly on the floor, where he had fallen from his protective tube, and the girl and the other slave bent to help him to his feet. He was still conscious, but like the other man he appeared to have lost all use of his muscles, I went forward to help them with him, but they ignored me.

Now their attention was directed towards the protruding cubicle I had noticed earlier. The doors had remained closed throughout the flight, and I had assumed that the cubicle contained some equipment. That this was not so was instantly revealed when the girl pulled the doors open.

Because of the tilting of the craft the doors swung right open, and I was able to see what was inside. The entire space was no larger than that of a cupboard, with just enough room for a man to stand within it. Attached to the metal bulkhead were five clamps, like manacles, but made with a fiendish precision that lent to them a distinctly surgical air.

The male slave was pushed awkwardly to the entrance to this cubicle, his head lolling and his legs slack. However, some awareness must have been filtering through his befuddled mind, for as soon as he saw where he was about to be put he set up as much resistance as he could muster; he was, though, no match for the other two, and after about a minute's struggle they managed to get him upright into the cubicle.

As soon as the relevant part of his body was in contact, the manacles closed of their own accord. His two arms were held first, then his legs, and finally his neck. A low moaning noise came from his mouth, and he moved his head desperately, trying to escape. The girl moved quickly to close the doors on him, and at once his feeble cries could scarcely be heard.

I looked in appalled silence at the others. They stared at the floor, avoiding everyone else's gaze. I noticed that the man in charge still stood by the partition, his whip ready for further use.

Five anguished minutes passed, then with a shocking suddenness the doors of the cubicle fell open and the man collapsed across the floor.

I bent down to examine him, as he had fallen near my feet. He was certainly unconscious, probably dead. Where the manacles had held him were rows of punctures, about one-eighth of an inch in diameter. A trace of blood flowed from each one, on his limbs and his neck. There was not much blood oozing, for his body was as white as snow; it was as if every drop of blood had been sucked away.

Even as I was examining this unfortunate, the second stunned man was being dragged towards the cubicle. His resistance was less, for the electrical shock had been administered more recently, and within a few seconds his body had been manacled in place. The doors were closed.

One of the most shocking aspects of all this was the uncomplaining acceptance by the slaves of their lot. The two remaining slaves, the man and the girl, stood passively, waiting for the wretch in the cubicle to be bled dry. I could not believe that such barbarities would be tolerated, and yet so strong was the regime of the monster-creatures that even this atrocity was implemented by the city-Martians.

I looked away from the man with the whip, hoping he would lose interest in me. When, a few moments later, the man in the cubicle was released and fell inertly across the floor, I followed the lead of the other two and calmly moved his body out of the way to make access again to the cubicle.

The remaining male slave went of his own accord to the cubicle, the manacles closed around him, and I shut the doors quickly.

The man with the whip stared at the girl and me for a few seconds longer, then, evidently satisfied that we were capable of continuing unsupervised, returned unexpectedly to the control cabin.

Sensing a minuscule chance of escape, I glanced at the girl; she seemed uninterested and had sat down with her back to the partition. Free for a moment to act and think independently, I looked desperately around the compartment. As far as I could see there was no way out except by the hatchway beyond the partition. I looked at the curving ceiling and floor, but these were unbroken except for the fittings of the flexible tubes.

I went quietly to the partition, and peered around it at the two Martians in charge. They had their backs towards me, attending to some matter at the controls of the craft. I looked at the wheel-device which opened and closed the hatch; it would be impossible for me to open it without their hearing me.

Behind me, the cubicle door burst open and the male slave fell out, his bloodless arm falling across the girl. At the sound of this, the two Martians at the controls turned round, and I ducked out of sight. The girl was looking at me, and for a moment I was mortified by the expression of stark fear which contorted her features. Then, without a sound, she stepped into the cubicle, and I was alone with the three bodies of the slaves.

I closed the doors of the cubicle without glancing inside, then went to a part of the compartment where no bodies lay, and was violently sick.

II

I could no longer stay in that hellish compartment with its sights and odours of death; blindly, I struggled over the heaped bodies and hurled myself around the partition, determined to do to death the two Martian humans who were the instruments of the torturous slaughter.

I had never in all my life been taken with such a blinding and all-consuming rage and nausea. In my hatred I threw myself across the control cabin and landed a huge blow with my arm on the back of the neck of the Martian nearer to me. He crumpled immediately, his forehead smiting a jagged edge of the instrumentation.

His electrical whip fell to the floor beside him, and I snatched it up.

The other Martian was already seated on the floor, and in the two or three seconds my first attack had taken had time only to turn his face towards me. I swung the whip viciously, catching him across his collar-bone, and at once he jerked and fell sideways. Coldly and deliberately I stood over him, pressing the end of the whip against his temple. He jerked spasmically for a few seconds, then was still. I turned my attention to the other Martian, who was now lying semi-conscious on the floor, blood pouring from the wound in his head. He too I treated with the whip, then at last I threw aside the terrible weapon, and turned away. I was taken with dizziness, and in a moment I passed out. My last memory was of hearing the sound of the slave-girl's body as it fell into the compartment behind me.

THIRTEEN

A Mighty Battle

•

I

My faint must have turned naturally to sleep, for the next few hours are unremembered.

When at last I awoke my mind was tranquil, and for several minutes I had no memory of the hideous events I had witnessed. As soon as I sat up, though, I was confronted with the bodies of the two city-Martians, and everything returned in vivid detail.

I consulted my watch. I had kept this wound, as I had discovered that the length of a Martian day was almost the same as that on Earth, and although a knowledge of the exact hour was unnecessary on Mars, it was a useful guide to elapsed time. Now I saw that I had been aboard the projectile for more than twelve hours. Every minute I stayed within its confines was reminder of what I had seen and done, so I crossed directly to the hatch and attempted to open it. I had seen it being closed, so I assumed that a simple reversal of the action would be sufficient. This was not so; after moving an inch or two the mechanism jammed. I wasted several minutes trying, before I abandoned the effort.

I looked around the cabin, sensing for the first time that I might well be trapped here. It was a terrifying thought and I began to panic, pacing up and down in the confined space, my mind anguished.

At last sense filtered through, and I set myself to a meticulous and systematic examination of the cabin.

First, I examined the controls, hoping that there might be some way I could set the display-panels working, so that I could see where the craft had landed. With no success here (the impact of landing appeared to have broken the workings), I turned my attention to the flying controls themselves.

Although at first sight there seemed to be an amazing confusion of levers and wheels, I soon noticed that certain instruments were placed inside one of the transparent pressure-tubes. It was in these that the two Martians had passed the flight, and so it was logical that they would have had to be able to control the trajectory from within.

I parted the fabric with my hands (now that the flight was over it was quite limp), and inspected these instruments.

They were solidly built – presumably to withstand the various pressures of the firing and final impact – and simple in design. A kind of podium had been built on the floor of the cabin, and it was on this that they were mounted. Although there were certain needle-dials whose function I could not even guess, the two major controls were metal levers. One of these bore a remarkable resemblance to the lever on Sir William's Time Machine: it was mounted pivotally and could be moved fore or aft, or to either side. I touched it experimentally, and moved it away from me. At once, there was a noise in another part of the hull, and the craft trembled slightly.

The other lever was surmounted by a piece of some bright-green substance. This had only one apparent movement – downwards – and at the same moment I laid my hand on it there was a tremendous explosion outside the hull, and I was thrown from my feet by a sudden, sharp movement of the entire craft.

As I clambered to my feet again I realized that I had discovered the device that triggered the green flashes which had controlled our landing.

Understanding at last that the projectile was still functioning, if momentarily at rest, I decided that it would be safer if I were instead to concentrate on escaping.

I returned to the hatch and renewed my efforts to turn the wheel. Much to my surprise it was freer, and the hatch itself actually shifted a few inches before jamming again. As it did so a quantity of gravel and dry soil poured through the crack. This was rather perplexing, until I realized that in the impact of our landing a large part of the craft, and most certainly the nose, would have been buried in the ground.

I considered this with some care, then closed the hatch thoughtfully. I returned to the controls, then, bracing myself, I depressed the green-tipped lever.

A few seconds later, slightly deafened and certainly unsteady on my feet, I returned to the hatch. It was still jammed, but there was more play than before.

It took four more attempts before the hatch opened far enough to admit a minor avalanche of soil and pebbles, and daylight showed above. I hesitated only long enough to pick up Amelia's hand-bag, then squeezed my way through the aperture to freedom.

II

After a long climb through loose soil, using the solid bulk of the hull to support myself, I reached the top of the wall of dirt.

I saw that the projectile had on landing created for itself a vast pit, in which it now rested. On every side of it had been thrown up large mounds of soil, and acrid green smoke – produced presumably as a result of my efforts – drifted about. I had no way of telling how deeply the projectile had been buried on its first impact, although I guessed I had shifted it from its original position during my escape.

I walked around to the rear end of the projectile, which was clear of the ground and overhanging unbroken soil. The monster-creatures had thrown open the huge hatch, which was the rear wall of the projectile, and the main hold – which I now saw as taking up most of the volume of the craft – was empty both of beings and their devices. The bottom lip was only a foot or two above the ground, so it was easy to enter the hold. I went inside.

It was the work of a few moments to walk through the cavernous hold and inspect the traces of the monsters' presence, and yet it was nearly an hour before I finally emerged from the craft.

I found that my earlier count had been accurate: that there was space for five of the monsters in the hold. There had also been several of the vehicles aboard, for I saw many bulkheads and clamps built into the metal hull by which they had been restrained.

In the deepest part of the hold, against the wall which separated it from the forward section, I came across a large canopy, the shape and volume of which indicated unerringly that it was for the use of the monsters. With some trepidation I peered inside ... then recoiled away.

Here was the mechanism which operated the blood-sucking cubicle in the slaves' compartment, for I saw an arrangement of blades and pipettes, joined by transparent tubes to a large glass reservoir still containing much blood.

By this device did these vampiric monsters take the lives of humans!

I went to the opened end of the hold, and cleared my lungs of the stench. I was utterly appalled by what I had found, and my whole body was trembling with revulsion.

A little later I returned to the interior of the craft. I went to examine the various pieces of equipment the monsters had left behind them, and in doing this I made a discovery that made my elaborate escape seem unnecessary. I found that the hull of the projectile was actually of double thickness, and that leading from the main hold was a network of narrow passages which traversed most of the length of the craft. By clambering through these I came eventually, through a trap-door in the floor that I had not previously noticed, into the control-cabin.

The bodies of the two Martian humans were enough reminder of what I had seen aboard the projectile, so without further delay I returned through the passages to the main hold. I was about to jump down to the floor of the desert when it occurred to me that in this dangerous world it would be as well to be armed, and so I searched the hold for something that might serve as a weapon. There was not much to choose from, for the monsters had taken all movable pieces with them ... but then I remembered the blades in the blood-letting canopy.

I filled my lungs with fresh air, then hurried to the canopy. There I found that the blades were held in place by a simple sheath, and so I selected one of about nine inches in length. I unscrewed it, wiped it clean on the fabric of one of the pressure-tubes, and placed it inside Amelia's hand-bag.

Then at last I hurried from the craft, and went out into the desert.

III

I looked about me, wondering which way I should travel to find shelter. I knew I was somewhere near another city, for I had seen it on the display as we landed, but where it was I did not know.

I glanced first at the sun, and saw that it was near meridian. At first this confused me, for the projectile had been launched at the height of the day and I had slept for only a few hours, but then I realized just how far the craft must have travelled. It had been launched in a westerly direction, so I must now be on the other side of the planet during the same day!

However, what was important was that there were still several hours to nightfall.

I walked away from the projectile towards an outcropping of rock some five hundred yards away. This was the highest point I could see, and I judged that from its peak I should be able to survey the whole region.

I was not being mindful of my surroundings: I kept my eyes directed towards the ground in front of me. I was not elated at my escape, and indeed there was a great gloom in me; a familiar emotion, for I had lived with it since that day in Desolation City when Amelia had been snatched away from me. Nothing had served to remind me of her. It was simply that now I was freed of my immediate concerns, my thoughts returned inevitably to her.

Thus it was that I was halfway to the rocks before I noticed what was going on around me.

I saw that many more projectiles had landed. There were a dozen within my view, and to one side I could see three of the legged ground vehicles standing together. Of the monsters themselves, or the humans who had brought them here, there was no sign, although I knew that most of the monsters were probably already seated inside the armoured housings of their vehicles.

My lonely presence attracted no attention as I trudged across the reddish sand. The monsters cared little for the affairs of humans, and I cared nothing for theirs. My only hope was to locate the city, and so I continued on my way to the rocks.

Here I paused for a moment, staring around. The texture of the rocks was brittle, and as I placed my weight on a low ledge, tiny chips of the alluvial rock fell away.

I climbed carefully, balancing my weight with Amelia's bag.

When I was about twenty feet above the desert floor I came to a broad shelf across the face of the rocks, and I rested for a few seconds.

I looked out across the desert, seeing the ugly craters made by the projectiles as they landed, and seeing the blunt, open ends of the projectiles themselves. I stared as far I could see in all directions, but there was no sign of the city. I picked up the bag again, and started to work my way around the face of the rocks, climbing all the way.

The outcrop was larger than I had first supposed, and it took me several minutes to reach the other side. Here the rocks were more broken, and my hold was precarious.

I came around a large rocky protuberance, feeling my way along a narrow ledge. As I cleared the obstacle, I stopped in amazement.

Directly in front of me – and, coincidentally, blocking my view across the desert – was the platform of one of the watch-towers!

I was so surprised to see one here that I felt no sense of danger. The thing was still; the black, oval window was on the further side, so even if there were a monster-creature inside I would not be noticed.

I looked across the rock-face in the direction I had been climbing towards, and saw that here there was a deep cleft. I leaned forward, supporting myself with my hand, and glanced down; I was now about fifty feet above the desert floor, and it was a sheer drop. My only way down was by the way I had come. I hesitated, debating what to do.

I felt certain that there was one of the monster-creatures inside the platform of the tower, but why it was standing here in the shelter of the rocks I could not say. I remembered the towers in the city: during normal times the towers seemed to be left to work mechanically. I wondered if this were one such. Certainly, the fact that its platform was immobile lent weight to the notion that the platform was unoccupied. Furthermore, by its very presence it was denying me the purpose of my climb. I needed to locate the city, and from where I was forced to stand by nature of the rocks' configuration, my view was blocked by the tower.

Looking again at the platform of the tower I wondered if this obstacle might be turned to my advantage.

I had never before been quite as close to one as this, and the details of its construction became of great interest to me. Around the base of the platform itself was a shelf or ledge some twenty-four inches in depth; a man could stand in comfort on it, and indeed in greater safety than in my present position on the rocks. Above this shelf was the body of the platform itself: a broad, shallow cylinder with a sloping roof, some seven feet high at the back, and about ten feet high at the front. The roof itself was domed slightly, and around part of its circumference was a rail about three feet high. On the rear wall were three metal rungs, which presumably assisted entry to and exit from the platform itself, for set into a part of the roof directly above them was a large hatch, which was presently closed.

Without further delay I gripped the rungs and hauled myself up to the roof, swinging Amelia's bag before me. I stood up and stepped gingerly towards the rail, gripping it with my free hand. Now at last my view across the desert was uninterrupted.

The sight I saw was one which no man before me had ever beheld.

I have already described how much of the Martian terrain is flat and desert-like; that there are also mountainous regions was evidenced by my view from the projectile in flight. What I did not until that moment realize was that, in certain parts of the desert, single mountains – of a height and breadth with no Earthly parallel – thrust themselves out of the plain, standing alone.

One such stood before me.

Now, lest my words should mislead, I must immediately modify my description, for my very first impression of this mountain was that its scale was quite insignificant. Indeed, my attention was drawn first to the city I had been seeking, which lay some five miles from where I stood. This I saw through the crystal-clear Martian air, and registered that it was built on a scale that vastly exceeded that of Desolation City.

Only when I had established the direction in which I should have to travel, and the distance I would have to cover to reach it, did I look beyond the city towards the mountains against whose lower slopes it had been built.

At first sight this mountain appeared to be the beginnings of a rounded plateau region; instead of the upper surface being sharply defined, however, the heights were vague and unclear. As my senses adapted, I realized that this lack of definition was caused by my looking along the very surface of the mountain's slope. So large was the mountain, in fact, that the major part of it lay beyond the horizon, so that the thrust of its height was competing with the planet's curvature! In the far distance I could just make out what must have been the mountain's peak: white and conical, with vapour drifting from the volcanic crater.

This summit seemed to be no more than a few thousand feet high; taking into account the fact of the planet's curvature, I dare say that a more accurate estimate of the height would be at least ten or fifteen miles above ground level! Such physical scale was almost beyond the comprehension of a man from Earth, and it was many minutes before I could accept what I saw.

I was preparing to climb back to the rocks, and start my descent to the ground, when I noticed a movement some distance to my left.

I saw that it was one of the legged vehicles, moving slowly across the desert in the direction of the city. It was not alone; in fact, there were several dozen of these vehicles, presumably brought in the many projectiles which lay scattered across the desert.

What was more, there were scores of the watch-towers, some standing about the vehicles, others sheltering, like the one on which I was perched, beside one or another outcropping of rock, of which there were several between here and the city.

I had long realized that the flight in which I had taken part was a military mission, retaliating against the invasion of Desolation City. I had further assumed that the target would be a minor foe, for I had seen the might of those invaders and did not think that vengeance would be sought directly against them. But this was not the case. The city against which the vehicles were ranged was immense, and when I looked towards it I could just make out the extent to which the place was defended. The outer limits of the city, for example, seemed forested with watch-towers, lining the perimeter so thickly in places that it was as if a stockade had been erected. Moreover, the ground was swarming with fighting-vehicles, and I could see orderly patterns of them, like black metal soldiers on parade.

Against this was the pitiful attacking force on whose side accident had placed me. I counted sixty of the legged ground vehicles, and about fifty of the watch-towers.

I was so fascinated by this spectacle of a coming battle that I forgot for a moment where I was standing. Indeed, I was speculating about just what kind of role the watch-towers would play, neglecting the fact that if I did not move I should surely find out! My best estimate was that the legged vehicles would move forward to attack the city, while the watch-towers would stand defence over the projectiles.

At first this seemed to be the case. The legged vehicles moved slowly and steadily towards the city, and those watch-towers unprotected by the rocks began to raise their platforms to the full height of sixty feet.

I decided that it was time I left my vantage point, and turned round to look back at the rocks, still gripping the rail in my hand.

Then something happened I could never have anticipated. I heard a slight noise to my right, and I looked round in surprise. There, emerging from behind the bluff wall of the rocks, came a watch-tower.

It was walking: the three metal shafts that were the legs of the tower were striding eerily beneath the platform!

The tower on which I stood suddenly lurched, and we fell forward. All around, the other watch-towers withdrew their legs from the gravelly soil, and strode forward in the wake of the ground-vehicles.

It was too late to jump to safety on the rock-face: already it was twenty yards away. I gripped the rail for all I was worth, as the walking watch-tower bore me out into battle!

IV

It was no good recriminating with myself for my lack of foresight; the incredible machine was already moving at about twenty miles an hour, and accelerating all the while. The air roared past my ears, and my hair flew. My eyes were streaming.

The watch-tower that had been beside mine at the rocks was a few yards ahead of us, but we were keeping pace. Because of this I was able to see how the contraption managed its ungainly gait. I saw that it was no less than a larger version of the tripodal legs that powered the ground-vehicles, but the effect here was quite startling in its total alienness. When driving forward at speed there were never more than two legs in contact with the ground at any moment, and that only for a fleeting instant. The weight was transferred constantly from one leg to the next in turn, while the other two swung up and forwards. To effect this the platform at the top was tilted slightly to the right, but the very smoothness of the motion indicated that there was a kind of transmission mounting below the platform that absorbed the minor irregularities of the ground. I felt far from secure on my precarious perch, but for the moment a firm grip on the rail was enough to ensure that I would not be easily pitched to the ground.

In the heat of the moment I cursed myself for not having realized that these towers themselves must be mobile. It was true that I had never before seen one in motion, but none of my speculations about their use had made any kind of consistent sense.

We were still increasing our speed, moving in a wide formation towards the enemy city.

In the van was a line of the vehicles. They were flanked on each side by four of the towers. Behind them, spread out in a second rank about half a mile long, were ten more of the ground-vehicles. The rest, including the tower on which I stood, holding on for dear life, followed in open formation behind. Already we were moving at such a speed that the legs were throwing up a cloud of sand and grit, and the wake from the leading vehicles was stinging my face. My own machine ran smoothly on, the engine humming powerfully.

Within about a minute we were travelling as fast as any steam-train could go, and here the speed stayed constant. There was no longer any question of escaping from this frightful situation; it was all I could do to stay upright and not be dislodged.

My downfall was nearly precipitated when, without warning, a metal flap opened beneath my legs! I hauled myself to one side away from it, thankful that the motion of the machine was steady, and watched incredulously as there unfolded from the aperture an immense metal contraption, extended on telescopic rods. As it brushed within a few inches of my face I saw to my horror that the object mounted was the barrel of one of the heat-cannons. It raised itself higher, until it was protruding above the roof of the tower by some eight feet or more.

Ahead of us I saw that the other towers had also extended their cannons, and we plunged on across the desert, headlong in this most bizarre of cavalry-charges!

I was now almost blinded by the sand being thrown up by the leading vehicles, so for the next minute or two I was unable to see more than the two hurtling towers immediately ahead of my own. The leading vehicles must have wheeled to left and right suddenly, for without warning there came a break in the cloud of grit and I was able to see directly ahead.

We had been flung, by the diversion of the leading vehicles, into the front-line of the battle!

Ahead of me now I could see the machines of the defending city coming across the desert to meet us. And what machines they were! There were few of the ground-vehicles, but the defenders strode confidently towards us on their towers. I could hardly believe what I saw. These battle-machines easily dwarfed those of my side, rising at least one hundred feet into the air.

The nearest to us were now less than half a mile away, and coming nearer with every second.

I stared in amazement at these Titans striding towards us with such effortless ease. The assemblage at the top of the three legs was no unadorned platform, but a complicated engine of tremendous size. Its walls were littered with devices of inconceivable function, and where on the smaller watch-towers was the black oval window, was a series of multi-faceted ports, winking and glittering in the sunlight. Dangling articulate arms, like those of the spiderlike handling-machines, swung menacingly as the battle-machines advanced, and at each joint of the incredible legs, bright-green flashes emanated with every movement.

They were now almost upon us! One of the towers that ran to the right of mine let fly with its heat-cannon, but ineffectually. An instant later more towers on my side fired at these mammoth defenders. There were several hits, evidenced by brilliant patches of fire that glowed momentarily against the upper platform of the enemy, but none of the battle-machines fell. They came on towards us, holding their fire but weaving from side to side, their slender metal legs stepping gracefully and nimbly over the rocky soil.

I realized that my whole body was tingling, and there was a crackling noise above my head. I glanced up, and saw a queer radiance about the muzzle of the heat-cannon, and saw that it must be firing at the defenders. In the instant it took me to so glance up, the defending battle-machines had passed our lines, still holding their fire, and the watch-tower on which I stood turned sharply to the right.

Now began a sequence of attacking manoeuvres and evasive

tactics that had me simultaneously in fear for my life and aghast with the fiendish brilliance of these machines.

I have compared our running attack to that of a cavalry-charge, but I soon saw that this had merely been the preamble to the battle proper. The tripodal legs did more than facilitate a fast forwards motion; in close combat they allowed a manoeuvrability unequalled by anything I had ever seen.

My tower, no less than any other, was in the thick of the fighting. As one with the others, the driver of my watch-tower wheeled his machine from side to side, spinning the platform, ducking, flailing the metal legs, balancing, charging.

All the while, the heat-cannon unleashed its deadly energy, and in that melee of whirling, pirouetting towers the beams seared through the air, striking home, flaring constantly against the armoured sides of the upper platforms. And now the defenders were no longer holding their fire; the battle-machines danced through the confusion, letting fly their deadly bolts with horrifying accuracy.

It was an unequal conflict. Not only were the towers of my side dwarfed by the hundred-feet high defenders, but outnumbered too. For every one of the towers on my side there seemed to be four of the giants, and already their beams of destructive heat were having a telling effect. One by one the smaller towers were struck from above; some exploded violently, others simply toppled to the ground, making ever more hazardous the upthrown soil on which the battle was pitched. Now it was that I became frightened for my own life, realizing that if the fortunes of the battle continued, it was only a matter of seconds before I was struck down.

I was, therefore, greatly relieved when the tower on which I stood abruptly wheeled round and hastened from the centre of the fighting. In all the confusion I had been able to do no more than maintain my hold, but as soon as we were away from the immediate dangers I discovered that I was shaking with fear.

I had no time to recover my poise. Instead of retreating fully, the tower hurried around the fringes of the battle, and joined two others which had similarly separated themselves. Without a pause we rejoined the fight, following what was clearly a prearranged tactical plan.

Marching as a phalanx we advanced towards the nearest of the colossal defenders. As one, our three cannons fired, the beams concentrating on the upper part of the glittering engine. Almost at once there came a minor explosion, and the battle-machine whirled uncontrollably round and crashed to the ground in a thrashing of metal limbs.

So excited was I by this demonstration of intelligent tactics that I found myself cheering aloud!

However, this battle would not be won by destroying one defender, a fact well understood by the monstrous drivers of these watch-towers. The three of us hurtled on into the fighting, heading towards our second intended victim.

Once again we were attacking from the rear, and as the heat-beams came into play the second defender was disposed of as spectacularly and efficiently as the first.

Such fortune could not last for ever. Scarcely had the second battle-machine fallen to the ground than a third stood before us. This one did not have its attention diverted by the ineffectual sniping of the other attackers – for there were few left in the fray – and as we plunged towards it the barrel of its heat-cannon was turned full on us.

What happened next was over in seconds, and yet I can recall the incident in detail, as if it had unfolded over a matter of minutes. I have said that we charged as a phalanx of three; I was mounted on the tower which was to the right and on the outside of the group. The battle-machine's heat-beam fell full across the tower in the centre, and this exploded at once. So great was the blast that only the fact that I was thrown against the telescopic mount of the cannon saved me from being dashed to the ground. My tower was damaged by the blast, a fact which became instantly clear as it lurched and staggered wildly, and as I clung to the telescopic mount I awaited our crashing to the desert floor as an already established matter of fact.

The third of the attacking towers, though, was as yet undamaged, and it marched on towards its taller antagonist, the heat-cannon playing its beam without effect across the armoured face of the defender. It was a last, desperate attack, and the monstrous creature which drove the tower must have expected its own annihilation at any moment. Although the defender responded with its own heat-cannon, the watch-tower went on unheeding, and flung itself suicidally against the very legs of the other. As they made contact there was a massive discharge of electrical energy, and both machines fell sideways to the ground, their legs still working wildly.

As this happened I was fighting for my own survival, clutching the telescopic rods of the cannon-mount as the damaged tower staggered away from the battle.

The first shock of damage had passed, and the driver – brilliant and evil – had managed to regain a semblance of control. The wildness of the tower's career was corrected, and with some unevenness of gait, which would have been enough to throw me to the ground had I not had a firm purchase on the mounting, it limped away from the fracas.

Within a minute, the battle – which still continued – was half a mile behind us, and some of the tension which had gripped me began to drain away. Only then did I realize that but for the faint humming of the engines, and the intermittent clangour of crashing machines, the entire engagement had been conducted in a deadly silence.

V

I did not know how badly damaged the ambulant tower had been, but there was an unprecedented grinding noise whenever one of the three legs bore the weight. This could not be the only damage, though, for I could tell that the motive power was failing. We had left the battle at a considerable velocity, having gained momentum during the charge, but now we were moving much slower. I had no real measure of speed, but the grinding of the damaged leg came at less frequent intervals and the air no longer roared past my ears.

The original charge across the desert had taken me much nearer to the city, a fact for which I had been thankful, but now we were heading away from it, towards one of the banks of red weed.

My immediate concern was how I could leave my perch on the tower. It seemed to me that the monster-creature which sat at the controls might well attempt a repair of his tower, and would leave the platform to do so. If that was to happen, I had no desire to be anywhere near at the time. There was, though, no chance for me to escape until the tower halted.

I became aware of a pressure in my left hand, and looking down at it for the first time since the tower had lurched into battle I found that I was still holding Amelia's hand-bag. How it had not been dropped in the excitement of the fighting I did not know, but some instinct had made me retain it. I changed my position cautiously, taking the bag into my other hand. I had suddenly remembered the blade I had placed inside it, and I took it out, thinking that at last I might need it.

The tower had virtually halted now, and was walking slowly through an area of irrigated land where green crops grew. Not two hundred yards away I could see the scarlet weed-bank, and working at its base, hacking at the stems and releasing the sap, were the slaves.

There were many more than any group I had seen in Desolation City, and the wretched people were working in the slimy soil as far along the weed-bank as I could see in either direction. Our arrival had not gone unnoticed, for I saw many of the people look in our direction before turning back hurriedly to their work.

The damaged leg was making a terrible noise, setting up a metallic screech whenever it took the weight, and I knew we could not travel much further. At last the tower came to a halt, the three legs splayed out beneath us.

I leaned over the edge of the platform roof, trying to see if it would be possible to shin down one of the legs to the ground.

Now the excitement of the battle was past, I found my thoughts were more pragmatic. I had, for a time, been aroused by the thrill of the fighting, even to the extent of admiring the plucky way the smaller force had thrown itself against the far superior defenders. But on Mars there was no element of goodness in the monster-creatures; I had no place in this war between monsters, and the fact that chance had placed me on one of two warring sides should not have beguiled me into spurious sympathies. The creature which had driven this tower into battle had earned my respect for its valour, but as I stood on the roof of the platform, planning my escape, its essential cowardice and beastliness were suddenly revealed.

I heard again the crackling noise above my head, and I realized the heat-cannon was being fired.

At first I thought that one of the defending battle-machines must have followed us, but then I saw where the deadly beam was being directed. Far away, over to the right, flame and smoke were leaping up from the weed-bank!

I saw several slaves caught by the full force of the beam, and they fell, lifeless, to the muddy ground.

The monster was not content with this atrocity, for then it started to swing the cannon to the side, sweeping the beam along the weed-bank.

The flames burst and leapt, as if spontaneously, as the invisible beam touched on vegetation and slave alike. Where the malign heat fell on the spilled sap, gouts of steam exploded outwards. I could see the slaves struggling to escape as they heard the screams of those afflicted, but in the swampy mire in which they had to work it was difficult for them to scramble away in time. Many of them threw themselves prostrate in the mud, but others were killed instantly.

This unspeakable deed had been continuing for no more than two or three seconds before I took a part in ending it.

Ever since I had understood the full monstrosity of the power these beings held, a part of my self had been overwhelmed with hatred and loathing of the monsters. I did not need to debate the rights or wrongs of this: the monster with its damaged tower, taking its unpardonable spite on the helpless humans below, with cold deliberation and serene malice.

I took a deep breath, then turned away from the awful sight. Fighting down the revulsion within me, I reached for the handle of the metal door built into the sloping roof of the tower. I turned it in vain; it seemed to be jammed.

I glanced back over my shoulder. The heat-beam was still creeping along the weed-bank, wreaking its hideous carnage ... but now some of the slaves nearest to the vindictive tower had seen me, for one or two of them were waving helplessly as they struggled through the swamp to avoid the beam.

The handle was one I had not seen or used on Mars before, but I knew that it could not be a sophisticated lock, for the monster itself, with its clumsy tentacles, must be capable of using it. Then, on an inspiration, I turned it the other way, the way that on Earth would normally close a lock.

Instantly, the handle turned and the door sprung open.

Filling most of the interior of the platform was the body of the monster; like a sickening bladder, the grey-green sac bulged and pulsed, shining moistly as if with perspiration.

In utter loathing I swung my long blade down, bringing it smartly against the very centre of the back. The blade sunk in, but as I withdrew it for a second plunge I saw that it had not penetrated the sponge-like consistency of the creature's flesh. I stabbed again, but with as little effect.

However, the creature had felt the blows even if it had not been harmed by them. A vile screech was emitted from the beak-like mouth at its front, and before I could evade it one of the tentacles slithered quickly towards me and wrapped itself about my chest.

Taken unawares, I stumbled down into the interior of the platform, pulled forward by the tentacle, and was dragged between the metal wall and the nauseous body itself!

My knife-arm was not constricted, and so in desperation I hacked again and again at the serpentine tentacle. Beside me the monster was braying hoarsely, in fear or in pain. At last, my knife was beginning to tell, for the pressure of the tentacle eased as I drew blood. A second tentacle slinked towards me, and just in time I slashed the first one away, causing blood to pump from the wound. As the second tentacle wound itself about my knife-arm, I panicked momentarily, before transferring the blade to my other hand. Now I knew the vulnerable place on the tentacle, it took only seconds to hack it away.

My exertions, and the drag of the tentacles, had taken me to the very front of the platform, so that I was before the face of the monster itself!

Here it was as if the whole interior was alive with the tentacles, for ten or a dozen were wrapping themselves around me. I cannot record how appalling was that touch! The tentacles themselves were weak, but the combined effect of several, stroking and clutching me, was as if I had fallen headlong into a nest of constrictors. Before me, the beak-like mouth opened and closed, shrieking in pain or anger; once the beak closed around my leg, but there was no strength in it and it was not able even to rip the cloth.

Above all were the eyes: those large, expressionless eyes, watching my every action.

I was now in trouble, for both my arms were pinned, and although I still held the knife I could not use it. Instead, I kicked at the soft face before me, aiming at the roots of the tentacles, the shrilling mouth, the saucer eyes ... anything that came within range. Then at last my knife-arm came free, and I slashed wildly at any part of the filthy body that presented itself.

This was the turning-point in the squalid affair, for from then on I knew I could win. The front of the creature's body was firm to the touch, and therefore vulnerable to the knife. Every blow I landed now drew forth blood, and soon the platform was a bedlam of gore, severed tentacles and the frightful screams of the dying monster.

At last I drove the blade straight in between the creature's eyes, and with one last fading scream it finally expired.

The tentacles relaxed and sagged to the floor, the beak-mouth fell open, from within the corpse there came a long eructation of noxious vapours and the great lidless eyes stared bleakly and lifelessly through the darkened oval window at the front of the platform.

I glanced through this window just once, and saw dimly that the massacre had been brought to a timely end. The weed-bank no longer shot forth flame, although steam and smoke still drifted from various places, and the surviving slaves were dragging themselves from the mire.

VI

With a shudder I flung aside the bloodied knife, and hauled myself past the sagging corpse to the door. I struggled through with some difficulty for my hands were slick with blood and ichor. At last I pulled myself back to the roof, breathing in the thin air with relief, now that I was away from the rank odours of the monster. The hand-bag was where I had left it on the roof.

I picked it up, and, because I should need free use of my hands, looped one of the long handles over my neck.

For a moment I stared down at the ground. For as far as I could see in every direction those slaves that had survived the massacre had abandoned their toils and were wading through the mud towards the tower. Some had already reached dry land, and were running across to me, waving their long spindly arms and calling out in their high, reedy voices.

The leg nearest me seemed to be the straightest of the three, bent in only one place. With the greatest difficulty I eased myself over the protruding shelf, and managed to grip the metal limb with my knees. Then I released my hold on the platform, and placed my hands around the rough metal of the leg. Much blood had spilled from the platform, and although it was drying quickly in the sunshine it made the metal perilously slippery. With great caution at first, then with more confidence as I grew accustomed to it, I shinned down the leg towards the ground, the hand-bag swinging ludicrously across my chest.

As I reached the ground and turned, I saw that a huge crowd of the slaves had watched my descent and were waiting to greet me. I took the bag from around my neck, and stepped towards them. At once they moved back nervously, and I heard their voices twittering in alarm. Glancing down at myself I saw that my clothes and skin were soaked with the blood of the monster, and in the few minutes I had been in the sunlight the radiant heat had dried the mess and an unpleasant smell was exuding.

The slaves regarded me in silence.

Then I saw that one slave in particular was struggling through the crowd towards me, pushing the others aside in her haste. I saw that she was shorter than the rest, and fairer of skin. Although she was caked in the mud of the weed-bank, and raggedly dressed, I saw that her eyes were blue, and bright with tears, and her hair tumbled around her shoulders.

Amelia, my lovely Amelia, rushed forward and embraced me with such violence that I was nearly toppled from my feet!

'Edward!' she shouted deliriously, covering my face with kisses. 'Oh, Edward! How brave you were!'

I was overcome with such excitement and emotion that I could hardly speak. Then at last I managed a sentence, choking it out through my tears of joy.

'I've still got your bag,' I said.

It was all I could think to say.

FOURTEEN

In the Slave-Camp

•

I

Amelia was safe, and I was safe! Life was to be lived again! We disregarded everything and everyone around us; ignored the malodorous condition we were both in; forgot the encircling, curious Martian slaves. The mysteries and dangers of this world were of no consequence, for we were together again!

We stood in each other's arms for many minutes, saying nothing. We wept a little, and we held each other so tight that I thought we might never separate but become fused in one single organism of undistilled joy.

We could not, of course, stand like that forever, and the interruption was approaching even as we embraced. Soon we could not ignore the warning voices of the slaves around us, and we pulled reluctantly apart, still holding each other's hand.

Glancing towards the distant city I saw that one of the huge battle-machines was striding across the desert towards us.

Amelia looked about the slaves.

'Edwina?' she called. 'Are you there?'

In a moment a young, female Martian stepped forward. She was no more than a child, roughly equivalent to about twelve Earth years old.

She said (or at least it sounded as if she said): 'Yes, Amelia?'

'Tell the others to go back to work quickly. We will return to the camp.'

The little girl turned to the other slaves, made some intricate hand and head signs (accompanied by a few of the high, sibilant words), and within seconds the crowd was dispersing.

'Come along, Edward,' said Amelia. 'The thing in that machine will want to know how the monster was killed.'

I followed her as she strode towards a long, dark building set near the weed-bank. After a moment, one of the city-Martians appeared and fell in beside us. He was carrying one of the electrical whips.

Amelia noticed the askance expression with which I registered this.

'Don't worry, Edward,' she said. 'He won't hurt us.'

'Are you sure?'

In answer, Amelia held out her hand and the Martian passed her the whip. She took it carefully, held it out for me to see, then returned it.

'We are no longer in Desolation City. I have established a new social order for the slaves.'

'So it would appear,' I said. 'Who is Edwina?'

'One of the children. She is naturally adept at languages – most young Martians are – and so I have taught her the rudiments of English.'

I was going to ask more, but the ferocious pace Amelia was setting in this thin air was making me breathless.

We came to the building, and at the doorway I paused to stare back. The battle-machine had stopped by the crippled tower on which I had ridden, and was examining it.

There were four short corridors into the building, and inside I was relieved to find that it was pressurized. The city-Martian walked away and left us, while I found myself coughing uncontrollably after the exertions of our walk. When I had recovered I embraced Amelia once more, still unable to believe the good fortune that had reunited us. She returned my embraces no less warmly, but after a moment drew away.

'My dear, we are both filthy. We can wash here.'

'I should very much like a change of clothes,' I said.

'There is no chance of that,' Amelia said. 'You will have to wash your clothes as you wash yourself.'

She led me to an area of the building where there was an arrangement of overhead pipes. At the turn of a tap, a shower of liquid – which was not water, but probably a diluted solution of the sap – issued forth. Amelia explained that all the slaves used these baths after work, then she went away to use another in private.

Although the flow of liquid was cold I drenched myself luxuriously, taking off my clothes and wringing them to free them of the last vestiges of the foul fluids they had absorbed.

When I considered neither I nor my clothes could be any further cleansed, I turned off the flow and squeezed my clothes, trying to dry them. I pulled on my trousers, but the cloth was dank and heavy and felt most uncomfortable. Dressed like this I went in search of Amelia.

There was a large metal grille set in one of the walls just beyond the bathing area. Amelia stood before it, holding out her ragged garment to dry it. At once I turned away.

'Bring your clothes here, Edward,' she said.

'When you have finished,' I said, trying not to reveal by the sound of my voice that I had noticed she was completely unclad.

She placed her garment on the floor, and walked over and stood facing me.

'Edward, we are no longer in England,' she said. 'You will contract pneumonia if you wear damp clothes.'

'They will dry in time.'

'In this climate you will be seriously ill before then. It takes only a few minutes to dry them this way.'

She went past me into the bathing area, and came back with the remainder of my clothes.

'I will dry my trousers later,' I said.

'You will dry them now,' she replied.

I stood in consternation for a moment, then reluctantly removed my trousers. Holding them before me, in such a way that I was still covered, I allowed the draught of warmth to blow over them. We stood a little apart, and although I was determined not to gaze immodestly at Amelia, the very presence of the girl who meant so much to me, and with whom I had suffered so much, made it impossible not to glance her way several times. She was so beautiful, and, unclad as she was, she bore herself with grace and propriety, rendering innocent a situation which would have scandalized the most forward-looking of our neighbours on Earth. My inhibitions waned, and after a few minutes I could contain my impulses no more.

I dropped the garment I was holding, went quickly to her, then took her in my arms and we kissed passionately for a minute or more.

II

We were virtually alone in the building. It was still two hours before sunset, and the slaves would not return before then. When our clothes had dried, and we had put them on again, Amelia took me around the building to show me how the slaves were housed. Their conditions were primitive and without convenience: the hammocks were hard and cramped, what food there was had to be eaten raw, and nowhere was there any possibility of privacy.

'And you have been living like this?' I said.

'At first,' Amelia said. 'But then I discovered I was someone rather important. Let me show you where I sleep.'

She led me to one corner of the communal sleeping-quarters. Here the hammocks were arranged no differently, or so it appeared, but when Amelia tugged on a rope attached to an overhead pulley, several of the hammocks were lifted up to form an ingenious screen.

'During the days we leave these down, in case a new overseer is sent to inspect us, but when I wish to be private ... I have a boudoir all of my own!'

She led me into her boudoir, and once again, sensing that foreign eyes could not light upon us, I kissed Amelia with passion. I knew now what I had been hungering for during that dire period of loneliness!

'You seem to have made yourself at home,' I said at length. Amelia had sprawled across her hammock, while I sat down on a step that ran across part of the floor.

'One has to make the best of what one finds.'

I said: 'Amelia, tell me what happened after you were taken by that machine.'

'I was brought here.'

'Is that all? It cannot have been as simple as that!'

'I should not wish to experience it again,' she said. 'But what about you? How is it that after all this time you appear from within a watch-tower?'

'I should prefer to hear your story first.'

So we exchanged the news of each other that we both so eagerly sought. The prime concern was that neither of us was the worse for our adventures, and we had each satisfied the other as to that. Amelia spoke first, describing the journey across land to this slave-camp.

She kept her account brief and seemed to omit much detail. Whether this was to spare me the more unpleasant aspects, or because she did not wish to remind herself of them, I do not know. The journey had taken many days, most of it inside covered vehicles. There was no sanitation, and food was supplied only once a day. During the journey Amelia had seen, as I had seen aboard the projectile, how the monsters themselves took food. Finally, in a wretched state, she and the other survivors of the journey – some three hundred people in all, for the spiderlike machines had been busy that day in Desolation City – had been brought to this weed-bank, and under supervision of Martians from the near-by city had been put to work on the red weed.

I assumed at this point that Amelia had finished her story, for I then launched into a detailed account of my own adventures. I felt I had much to tell her, and spared few details. When I came to describe the use of the killing-cubicle aboard the projectile I felt no need to expurgate my account, for she too had seen the device in operation. However, as I described what I had seen, she paled a little.

'Please do not dwell on this,' she said.

'But is it not familiar to you?'

'Of course it is. But you need not colour your account with such relish. The barbaric instrument you describe is everywhere used. There is one in this building.'

That revelation took me by surprise, and I regretted having mentioned it. Amelia told me that each evening six or more of the slaves were sacrificed to the cubicle.

'But this is outrageous!' I said.

'Why do you think the oppressed people of this world are so few in number?' Amelia cried. 'It is because the very best of the people are drained of life to keep the monsters alive!'

'I shall not mention it again,' I said, and passed on to relate the rest of my story.

I described how I escaped from the projectile, then the battle I had witnessed, and finally, with not inconsiderable pride, I described how I had tackled and slain the monster in the tower.

At this Amelia seemed pleased, and so once more I garnished my narrative with adjectives. This time my authentic details were not disapproved of, and indeed as I described how the creature had finally expired she clapped her hands together and laughed.

'You must tell your story again tonight,' she said. 'My people will be very encouraged.'

I said: 'Your people?'

'My dear, you must understand that I do not survive here by good fortune. I have discovered that I am their promised leader, the one who in folklore is said to deliver them from oppression.'

III

A little later we were disturbed by the slaves returning from their labours, and for the moment our accounts were put aside.

As the slaves entered the building through the two main pressurizing corridors, the overseeing Martians, who apparently had quarters of their own within the building, came in with them.

Several were carrying the electrical whips, but once inside they tossed them casually to one side.

I have recorded before that the habitual expression of a Martian is one of extreme despair, and these wretched slaves were no exception. Knowing what I did, and having seen the massacre that afternoon, my reaction was more sympathetic than before.

With the return of the slaves there was a period of activity, during which the dirt of the day's work was washed away, and food was brought out. It had been some time since I had eaten, and although in its uncooked state the weed was almost inedible I took as much as I could manage.

We were joined during the meal by the slave-child Amelia called Edwina. I was amazed at the apparent grasp she had of English, and, what is more, rather amused by the fact that although the girl could not manage some of the more sophisticated English consonants, Amelia had vested her with distinct echoes of her own cultured voice. (In rendering Edwina's words in this narrative I shall make no attempt to phoneticize her unique accent, but state her words in plain English; however, at first I had difficulty in understanding what she said.)

I noticed that while we ate (there were no tables here; we all squatted on the floor) the slaves kept a distance from Amelia and me. Many covert glances came our way and only Edwina, who sat with us, seemed at ease in our company.

'Surely they are used to you by now?' I said to Amelia.

'It is of you they are nervous. You too have fulfilled a legendary role.'

At this, Edwina, who had heard and understood my question, said: 'You are the pale dwarf.'

I frowned at this, and looked to see if Amelia knew what she meant.

Edwina went on: 'Our wise men tell of the pale dwarf who walks from the battle-machine.'

'I see,' I said, and nodded to her with a polite smile.

Somewhat later, when Edwina was no longer within hearing, I

said: 'If you are the messiah to these people, why do you have to work at the weed-bank?'

'It is not my choice. Most of the overseers are used to me now, but if any new ones came from the city I might be singled out if I were not with the others. Also, it is said in the myths that the one who leads the people will be one of them. In other words, a slave.'

'I think I should hear these myths,' I said.

'Edwina will recite them for you.'

I said: 'You talk about the overseers. How is it that no one seems to fear them now?'

'Because I have persuaded them that all humans have a common enemy. I am more than playing a role, Edward. I am convinced that there must be a revolution. The monsters rule the people by dividing them: they have set one group of humans against the other. The slaves fear the overseers because it seems the overseers have the authority of the monsters behind them. The city-Martians are content to support the system, for they enjoy certain privileges. But as you and I have seen, this is merely an expedient to the monsters. Human blood is their only demand, and the slave-system is a means to an end. All I have done here is to persuade the overseers – who also know the folklore – that the monsters are an enemy common to all.'

While we were talking, the slave people were carrying away the remains of the meal, but suddenly all activities were halted by an outburst of sound: the most horrible, high-pitched siren, echoing around the inside of the hall.

Amelia had gone very pale, and she turned away and walked into her private area. I followed her inside, and found her in tears.

'That call,' I said. 'Does it mean what I think?'

'They have come for their food,' Amelia said, and her sobs were renewed.

IV

I will not recount the ghastliness of the scene that followed, but it should be said that the slaves had devised a system of lots, and the six hapless losers went to the killing-cubicle in silence.

Amelia explained that she had not expected the monsters to visit the slave-camps tonight. There were many dead scattered about the weed-bank, and she had hoped that the monsters would have drained these bodies for their nightly repast.

V

Edwina came to see Amelia and me.

'We would like to hear the adventures of the pale dwarf,' she said to Amelia. 'It would make us happy.'

'Does she mean I have to address them?' I said. 'I should not know what to say. And how would they understand me?'

'It is expected of you. Your arrival was spectacular, and they want to hear it in your own words. Edwina will interpret for you.'

'Have you done this?'

She nodded. 'I was told about this ritual when I was teaching Edwina to speak English. When she had mastered enough vocabulary, we rehearsed a little speech and from that day I was accepted as their leader. You will not be fully acknowledged by them until you have done it too.'

I said: 'But how much should I tell them? Have you told them we are from Earth?'

'I felt they would not understand, and so I have not. Earth is mentioned in their legends – they call it the "warm world" – but only as a celestial body. So I have not revealed my origins. Incidentally, Edward, I think it is time you and I recognized that we shall never again see Earth. There is no means of return. Since I have been here I have been reconciled to that. We are both Martians now.'

I pondered this in silence. It was not a notion I cared for, but I understood what Amelia meant. While we clung to a false hope we should never settle.

Finally, I said: 'Then I will tell them how I flew in the projectile, how I mounted the watch-tower and how I disposed of the monster.'

'I think, Edward, that as you are fulfilling a mythic prophecy, you should find a stronger verb than "dispose".'

'Would Edwina understand?'

'If you accompany your words with the appropriate actions.'

'But they have already seen me leave the tower covered in blood!'

'It is the telling of the tale that is important. Just repeat to them what you told me.'

Edwina was looking as happy as any Martian I had ever seen.

'We will hear the adventures now?' she said.

'I suppose so,' I said. We stood up and followed Edwina into the main part of the hall. Several of the hammocks had been moved away, and all the slaves were sitting on the floor. As we appeared they climbed to their feet, and started to jump up and down. It was a rather comical action – and one not wholly reassuring – but Amelia whispered to me that this was their sign of enthusiasm.

I noticed that there were about half a dozen of the city-Martians present, standing at the back of the hall. They were clearly not yet at one with the slaves, but at least the sense of intimidation we had seen in Desolation City was absent.

Amelia quietened the crowd by raising her hand and spreading her fingers. When they were silent, she said: 'My people. Today we saw the killing of one of the tyrants by this man. He is here now to describe his adventures in his own words.'

As she spoke, Edwina translated simultaneously by uttering a few syllables, and accompanying them with elaborate hand-signs. As they both finished, the slaves jumped up and down again, emitting a high-pitched whining noise. It was most disconcerting, and appeared to have no end.

Amelia whispered to me: 'Raise your hand.'

I was regretting having agreed to this, but I raised my hand and to my surprise silence fell at once. I regarded these queer folk – these tall, hot-coloured alien beings amongst whom fate had cast our lot, and with whom our future now lay – and tried to find the words with which to begin. The silence persisted, and with some diffidence I described how I had been put aboard the projectile. Immediately, Edwina accompanied my words with her weird interpretation.

I began hesitantly, not sure of how much I should say. The audience remained silent. As I warmed to my story, and found opportunities for description, Edwina's interpretation became more florid, and thus encouraged I indulged myself in a little exaggeration.

My description of the battle became a clashing of metallic giants, a pandemonium of hideous screams and a veritable storm of blazing heat-beams. At this, I saw that several of the slaves had risen, and were jumping up and down enthusiastically. As I came to the point in the story where I realized that the monster was turning its heat-beam on to the people, the whole audience was on its feet and Edwina was signing most dramatically.

Perhaps in this telling rather more tentacles were hacked away than there had been in actuality, and perhaps it seemed more difficult to kill the beast than had been my experience, but I felt obliged to remain true to the spirit of the occasion rather than satisfy the demands of scrupulous authenticity.

I finished my story to a splendid cheer from the audience, and a most remarkable display of leaping. I glanced at Amelia to see her reaction, but before we had a chance to speak we were both mobbed by the crowd. The Martians surrounded us, jostling and thumping us gently, in what I interpreted as further enthusiasms. We were being propelled steadily and firmly towards Amelia's private quarters, and as we came to where the hammocks had been slung to form the partition, the noise reached its climax. After a little more genial pummelling, we were thrust together through the partition.

At once, the noise outside subsided.

I was still buoyed up by the reception I had been given, and swept Amelia into my arms. She was as excited as I, and responded to my kisses with great warmth and affection.

As our kissing became prolonged I found rising in me those natural desires I had had to suppress for so long, and so, reluctantly, I turned my face away from hers and loosened my hold, expecting her to draw away. Instead, she held me tightly, pressing her face into the hollow of my neck.

Beyond the partition I could hear the slaves. They seemed to be singing now, a high, tuneless crooning noise. It was very restful and strangely pleasant.

'What do we do next?' I said after several minutes had passed.

Amelia did not reply at once.

Then she held me more tightly, and said: 'Do you need to be told, Edward?'

I felt myself blushing.

'I meant, is there any more ceremonial we must observe?' I said.

'Only what is expected of us in legend. On the night the pale dwarf descends from the tower ...' She whispered the rest in my ear.

She could not see my face, so I clenched my eyes tightly closed, almost breathless with excitement!

'Amelia, we cannot. We are not married.'

It was my last concession to the conventions that had ruled my life.

'We are Martians now,' Amelia said. 'We do not observe marriage.'

And so, as the Martian slaves sang in their high, melancholy voices beyond the hanging partition, we abandoned all that remained within us of our Englishness and Earthliness, and became, through that night, committed to our new roles and lives as leaders of the oppressed Martian peoples.

FIFTEEN

A Revolution is Planned

•

I

From the moment of our waking the following morning, Amelia and I were treated with deference and humility. Even so, the legends that were now directing our lives seemed quite emphatic that we were to work with the others on the weed-bank, and so much of our day was spent in cold mud up to our knees. Edwina worked with us, and although there was something about her bland stare that made me uneasy, she was undoubtedly useful to us.

Neither Amelia nor I did much actual weed-cutting. As soon as we were established at the bank we received many different visitors: some of them slaves, others overseers, all of them evidently anxious to meet those who would lead the revolt. Hearing what was said – translated earnestly, if not always entirely comprehensibly, by Edwina – I realized that Amelia's talk of revolution had not been made lightly. Several of the overseers had come from the city itself, and we learnt that there elaborate plans were being made to overthrow the monsters.

It was an enthralling day, realizing that we might at last have provided the stimulus to these people to take revenge on their abhorrent masters. Indeed, Amelia reminded our visitors many times of my heroic deed the day before. The phrase was repeated often: *the monsters are mortal.*

However, mortal or not, the monsters were still in evidence, and presented a constant threat. Often during the day the weed-bank was patrolled by one of the immense tripodal battle-machines, and at those times all revolutionary activities were suspended while we attended to the cutting.

During one period when we were left alone, I asked Amelia why the weed-cutting continued if the revolution was so far advanced. She explained that the vast majority of the slaves were employed in this work, and that if it was stopped before the revolution was under way the monsters would instantly realize something was afoot. In any event, the main benefactors were the humans themselves, as the weed was the staple diet.

And the blood-letting? I asked her. Could that not then be stopped?

She replied that refusal to give any more blood was the only sure way the humans had of conquering the monsters, and there had been frequent attempts to disobey the most dreaded injunction on this world. On those occasions, the monsters' reprisals had been summary and widespread. In the most recent incident, which had occurred some sixty days before, over one thousand slaves had been massacred. The terror of the monsters was constant, and even while the insurgency was planned, the daily sacrifices had to be made.

In the city, though, the established order was in imminent danger of being overthrown. Slaves and city-people were uniting at last, and throughout the city there were organized cells of volunteers; men and women who, when the command was given, would attack specified targets. It was the battle-machines which presented the greatest threat: unless several heat-cannons could be commandeered by the humans, there could be no defence against them.

I said: 'Should we not be in the city? If you are controlling the revolution, surely it should be done from there?'

'Of course. I was intending to visit the city again tomorrow. You will see for yourself just how advanced we are.'

Then more visitors arrived: this time, a delegation of overseers who worked in one of the industrial areas. They told us, through Edwina, that small acts of sabotage were already taking place, and output had been temporarily halved.

So the day passed, and by the time we returned to the building I was exhausted and exhilarated. I had had no conception of the good use to which Amelia had put her time with the slaves. There was an air of vibrancy and purpose ... and great urgency. Several times I heard her exhorting the Martians to bring forward their preparations, so that the revolution itself might begin a little earlier.

After we had washed and eaten, Amelia and I returned to what were now our shared quarters. Once in there, and alone with her, I asked her why there was such need for urgency. After all, I argued, surely the revolution would be more assured of success if it was prepared more carefully?

'It is a question of timing, Edward,' she said. 'We must attack when the monsters are unprepared and weak. This is such a time.'

'But they are at the height of their power!' I said in surprise. 'You cannot be blind to that.'

'My dear,' said Amelia, 'if we do not strike against the monsters within the next few days, then the cause of humanity on this world will be lost forever.'

'I cannot see why. The monsters have held their sway until now. Why should they be any less prepared for an uprising?'

This was the answer that Amelia gave me, gleaned from the legends of the Martians amongst whom she had been living for so long:

II

Mars is a world much older than Earth, and the ancient Martians had achieved a stable scientific civilization many thousands of years ago. Like Earth, Mars had had its empires and wars, and like Earthmen the Martians were ambitious and forward-looking. Unfortunately, Mars is unlike Earth in one crucial way, which is to say that it is physically much smaller. As a consequence, the two substances essential to intelligent human life – air and water – were gradually leaking away into space, in such a way that the ancient

Martians knew that their existence could not be expected to survive for more than another thousand of their years.

There was no conceivable method that the Martians had at their command to combat the insidious dying of their planet.

Unable to solve the problem directly, the ancient Martians essayed an indirect solution. Their plan was to breed a new race – using human cells selected from the brains of the ancient scientists themselves – which would have no other function than to contain a vast intellect. In time, and Amelia said that it must have taken many hundreds of years, the first monster-creatures were evolved.

The first successful monsters were completely dependent on mankind, for they were incapable of movement, could survive only by being given transfusions of blood from domestic animals, and were subject to the slightest infection. They had, however, been given the means to reproduce themselves, and as the generations of monster-creatures proceeded, so the beings developed more resistance and an ability to move, albeit with great difficulty. Once the beings were relatively independent, they were set the task of confronting the problem which threatened all existence on Mars.

What those ancient scientists could not have foreseen was that as well as being of immense intellect, the monster-creatures were wholly ruthless, and once set to this task would allow no impediment to their science. The very interests of mankind, for which they were ultimately working, were of necessity subordinated to the pursuit of a solution! In this way, mankind on Mars eventually became enslaved to the creatures.

As the centuries passed the demands for blood increased, until the inferior blood of animals was not enough; so began the terrible blood-letting that we had witnessed.

In the initial stages of their work the monster-creatures, for all their ruthlessness, had not been entirely evil, and had indeed brought much good to the world. They had conceived and supervised the digging of the canals that irrigated the dry equatorial regions, and, to prevent as much water as possible from evaporating into space, they had developed plants of high water-content which could be grown as a staple crop alongside the canals.

In addition, they had devised a highly efficient heat-source which was used to provide power for the cities (and which, latterly, had been adapted to become the heat-cannon), as well as the domes of electrical force which contained the atmosphere around the cities.

As time passed, however, some of the monster-creatures had despaired of finding a solution to the central problem. Others of their kind disagreed that the task was insurmountable, and maintained that however much the role of humans may have changed, their primary task was to continue.

After centuries of squabbling, the monster-creatures had started fighting amongst themselves, and the skirmishes continued until today. The wars were worsening, for now the humans themselves were an issue: as their numbers were being steadily depleted, so the monsters were becoming concerned about shortages of their own food.

The situation had resolved into two groups: the monsters who controlled this city – which was the largest on Mars – and who had convinced themselves that no solution to the eventual death of Mars was possible, and those of the other three cities – of which Desolation City was one – who were prepared to continue the quest. From the humans' viewpoint, neither side had anything to commend it, for the slavery would continue whatever the outcome.

But at the present moment the monster-creatures of this city were vulnerable. They were preparing a migration to another planet, and in their preoccupation with this the rule of slavery was the weakest the Martian humans could remember. The migration was due to start within a few days, and as many of the monster-creatures would remain on Mars, the revolution must take place during the migration itself if it was to have any chance of success.

III

As Amelia finished her account I found that my hands had started to tremble, and even in the customary coldness of the building I found that my face and hands were damp with perspiration. For many moments I could not say anything, as I tried to find a way of expressing the turbulence of my emotions.

In the end my words were plain.

I said: 'Amelia, do you have any notion which planet it is these beings are intending to colonize?'

She gestured impatiently.

'What does it matter?' she said. 'While they are occupied with this, they are vulnerable to attack. If we miss this chance, we may never have another.'

I suddenly saw an aspect of Amelia I had not seen before. She, in her own way, had become a little ruthless. Then I thought again, and realized she seemed ruthless only because our own acceptance of our fate had destroyed her sense of perspective.

It was with love, then, that I said: 'Amelia ... are you now wholly Martian? Or do you fear what might happen if these monsters were to invade Earth?'

The perspective returned to her with the same shock as I myself had experienced. Her face became ashen and her eyes suddenly filled with tears. She gasped, and her fingers went to her lips. Abruptly, she pushed past me, went through the partition and ran across the main hall. As she reached the further wall, she covered her face with her hands and her shoulders shook as she wept.

IV

We passed a restless night, and in the morning set off, as planned, for the city.

Three Martians travelled with us: one was Edwina, for we still required an interpreter, and the other two were city-Martians, each brandishing an electrical whip. We had said nothing of our conversation to any of the Martians, and our plan was still ostensibly to visit several of the insurgents' cells in the city.

In fact, I was much preoccupied with my own thoughts, and I knew Amelia was suffering a torment of conflicting loyalties. Our silence as the train moved steadily towards the city must have intrigued the Martians, because normally we both had much to say. Occasionally, Edwina would point out landmarks to us, but I at least could not summon much interest.

Before we had left the slave-camp, I had managed a few more words with Amelia in private.

'We must get back to Earth,' I said. 'If these monsters land there is no telling what damage they might cause.'

'But what could we do to stop that?'

'You agree, though, that we must find a way to Earth?'

'Yes, of course. But how?'

'If they are travelling by projectile,' I had said, 'then we must somehow stow away. The journey will not take more than a day or two, and we could survive that long. Once we are on Earth we can alert the authorities.'

For a makeshift plan this was good enough, and Amelia had agreed with it in principle. Her main doubts, though, were elsewhere.

'Edward, I cannot just abandon these people now. I have encouraged them to revolt, and now I propose to leave them at the crucial moment.'

'I could leave you here with them,' I had said, with deliberate coldness.

'Oh no.' She had taken my hand then. 'My loyalties are with Earth. It is simply that I have a responsibility here for what I have started.'

'Isn't that at the centre of your dilemma?' I said. 'You have *started* the revolution. You have been the necessary stimulus for the people. But it is their fight for freedom, not yours. In any event, you cannot direct an entire revolution alone, with an alien race you barely understand, in a language you do not speak. If the preparations are being made, and you have not yet seen most of them, already you have become little more than a figurehead.'

'I suppose so.'

She was still absorbed in thought, though, as we sat in the train, and I knew it was a decision she would have to make for herself.

The two Martian overseers were pointing proudly towards one of the industrial sites the train was passing. There seemed to be little activity here, for no smoke came from any of the chimneys. There were several of the battle-machines standing about, and we saw many legged vehicles. Edwina explained that it was here that sabotage had already been committed. There had been no reprisals, for the various acts had been made to appear accidental.

For my part, I had been taken by an enthralling notion, and was presently considering every aspect of it.

The revolution that meant so much to Amelia was of less concern to me, for it had been conceived and planned in my absence. I think, had I not heard of the monsters' planned migration from Mars, that I too would have thrown myself into the cause and fought for it, and risked my life for it. But in all the weeks and months I had been on Mars, I had never lost an inner ache: the feeling of isolation, the sense of homesickness. I wanted desperately to return to my own world, or that part of it I knew as home.

I had been missing London – for all its crowds and noises and rank odours – and I had been hungering for the sight of greenery. There is nothing so beautiful as the English countryside in spring, and if, in the past, I had taken it for granted, I knew that I could never do so again. This was a world of foreign colours: grey cities, rufous soil, scarlet vegetation. If there had been so much as one oak-tree, or one bumpy meadow, or one bank of wild flowers, I might at last have learned to live on Mars, but none of these existed.

That the monster-creatures had the means of reaching Earth was therefore of intense importance to me, for it provided a way back to our home.

I had proposed to Amelia that we stow away on one of their deadly projectiles, but this was a dangerous idea.

Quite apart from the fact that we might be discovered during the voyage, or that some other danger might appear, we would be arriving on Earth in the company of the most hostile and ruthless enemy mankind would have ever had to face!

We did not know the monsters' plans, but we had no reason to suppose that their mission was one of peace. Neither Amelia nor I had the right to participate in an invasion of Earth, however passive the part we played. Moreover, we had a bounden duty to warn the world of the Martians' plans.

There was a solution to this, and from the moment it occurred to me the simple audacity of it made it irresistible.

I had been aboard one of the projectiles; I had seen it in flight; I had examined its controls.

Amelia and I would steal one of the projectiles, and fly it ourselves to Earth!

V

We arrived in the city without being challenged, and were led through the streets by our Martian accomplices.

The sparseness of the population was not as evident here as it had been in Desolation City. There were fewer empty buildings, and the obvious military strength of the monster-creatures had averted any invasions. Another difference was that there were factories within the city itself – as well as in separate areas outside – for there was a smoky industrial pall that served to heighten my feelings of homesickness for London.

We had no time to see much of the city, for we were taken immediately to one of the dormitories. Here, in a small room at the rear, we met one of the main cells of the revolution.

As we entered, the Martians showed their enthusiasm by leaping up and down as before. I could not help but warm to these poor, enslaved people, and share their excitement as the overthrow of the monsters became ever a more realistic proposition.

We were treated as royalty is treated in England, and I realized that Amelia and I were acting regally. Our every response was eagerly awaited, and mute as we had to be, we smiled and nodded as one Martian after another explained to us, through Edwina, what his assigned task was to be.

From here we were taken to another place, and more of the same happened. It was almost exactly as I had described it to Amelia: she had provoked the Martians to action, and set in motion a sequence of events she could no longer control.

I was becoming tired and impatient, and as we walked to inspect a third cell, I said to Amelia: 'We are not spending our time well.'

'We must do as they wish. We owe them at least this.'

'I would like to see more of the city. We do not even know where the snow-cannon is to be found.'

In spite of the fact that we were with six Martians, each of whom was trying to speak to her through Edwina, Amelia expressed her feelings with a tired shrug.

'I cannot leave them now,' she said. 'Perhaps you could go alone.'

'Then who would interpret for me?'

Edwina was tugging at Amelia's hand, trying to show her the building to which we were presently walking and where, presumably, the next cell was concealed. Amelia dutifully smiled and nodded.

'We had best not separate,' she said. 'But if you ask Edwina, she could find out what you want to know.'

A few moments later we entered the building, and in the darkened basement we were greeted by some forty enthusiastic Martians.

A little later I managed to take Edwina away from Amelia long enough to convey to her what I wanted. She seemed not interested, but passed on the message to one of the city-Martians present. He left the basement soon after, while we continued the inspection of our revolutionary troops.

VI

Just as we were readying ourselves to leave for the next port of call, my emissary returned, bringing with him two young Martian men dressed in the black uniforms of the men who drove the projectiles.

At the sight of them I was a little taken aback. Of all the humans I had met here, the men trained to fly the projectiles had seemed the closest to the monster-creatures, and were therefore the ones I had least expected to be trusted now the old order was about to be overthrown. But here the two men were, admitted to one of the revolutionary nerve-centres.

Suddenly, my idea became easier to put into effect. I had intended to gain entry to the snow-cannon, while Amelia and I were disguised, and attempt to work out the controls for myself. However, if I could communicate to these two what I wanted they could show me themselves how to operate the craft, or even come with us to Earth.

I said to Edwina: 'I want you to ask these two men to take me to their flying war-machine, and show me how it is operated.'

She repeated my sentence to me, and when I had made sure she understood me correctly, she passed it on. One of the Martians replied.

'He wants to know where you are taking the craft,' said Edwina.

'Tell them that I wish to steal it from the monsters, and take it to the warm world.'

Edwina replied immediately: 'Will you go alone, pale dwarf, or will Amelia go with you?'

'We will go together.'

Edwina's response to this was not what I would have wished. She turned towards the revolutionaries, and embarked on a long speech, with much sibilance and waving arms. Before she had finished, about a dozen Martian men hurried towards me, took me by the arms and held me with my face pressing against the wall.

From the far side of the room, Amelia called: 'What have you said now, Edward?'

VII

It took Amelia ten minutes to secure my release. In the meantime I suffered considerable discomfort, with both my arms twisted painfully behind my back. For all their frail appearance, the Martians were very strong.

When I was freed, Amelia and I went into a small room at the back, accompanied by two of the Martian men. In this they played unwittingly into our hands, for without Edwina they could not understand us, and it was to talk to Amelia that I wanted.

'Now please tell me what that was all about,' she said.

'I have worked out a new idea for our return to Earth. I was trying to put it into effect, and the Martians misunderstood my motives.'

'Then what did you say?'

I outlined for her the essence of my plan to steal a projectile in advance of the monsters' invasion.

'Could you drive such a machine?' she said when I had finished.

'I shouldn't imagine there would be any difficulty. I have examined the controls. It would be a matter of a few minutes to familiarize myself.'

Amelia looked doubtful, but she said: 'Even so, you have seen how the people react. They will not let me go with you. Does your plan allow for that?'

'You have already said that you will not stay here.'

'Of my own free will I would not.'

'Then we must somehow persuade them,' I said.

The two Martians guarding us were shifting restlessly. As I had been speaking I had laid my hand on Amelia's arm, and at this they had started forward protectively.

'We had better return to the others,' Amelia said. 'They do not trust you as it is.'

'We have resolved nothing,' I said.

'At this moment we have not. But if I intervene I think we may persuade them.'

I was learning at last to interpret the expressions of the Martians, and when we returned to the basement I sensed that the feeling had moved even further against me. Several people went forward to Amelia with their hands raised, and I was thrust aside. The two men who had been guarding us stayed with me, and I was forced to stand apart while Amelia was acclaimed possessively. Edwina was with her, and hasty words were exchanged for several minutes. In the uproar I could not hear what was being said.

I watched Amelia.

In the midst of the confusion she stayed placid and in control of her emotions, listening to Edwina's translations, then waiting while more voices harangued her in that foreign sibilance. It was, in spite of the tension, a wonderful moment, because in that enforced objectivity I was able to see her from a standpoint that was at once more intimate and more distanced than I cared. We had been thrust into each other's company by our adventures, and yet now we were being torn away from each other as a consequence. The fundamental alienness of these Martian people never seemed more affecting to me than at that moment.

I knew that if Amelia was prevented from flying with me in the projectile, then I would stay with her on Mars.

At last order was restored, and Amelia moved to the end of the room. With Edwina by her side she turned to face the crowd. I was still kept to one side, hemmed in by my two guards.

Amelia raised her right hand, spreading her fingers, and silence fell.

'My people, what has happened has forced me to reveal to you my origins.' She was speaking slowly and softly, allowing Edwina to interpret for her. 'I have not done so before, because your legends spoke of your freedom being delivered by one who was enslaved from birth. I have suffered with you and worked with you, and although you have accepted me as your leader I was not born to slavery.'

There was an instant reaction to this, but Amelia went on: 'Now I have learned that the race of beings which has enslaved you, and which will shortly be overthrown by your valour, is intending to spread its dominance to another world ... the one you know as the warm world. What I have not told you before is that I am myself from the warm world, and I travelled across the sky in a craft similar to the one your masters use.'

She was interrupted here by much noise from the Martians.

'Our revolution here cannot fail, for our determination is as great as our bravery. But if some of these creatures are allowed to escape to another world, who could say that they would never return at a later time? But then, the passions of revolution would be spent, and the creatures would easily enslave you once more.

'For the revolution to succeed, we must ensure that every one of the creatures is killed!

'Therefore it is essential that I return to my own world to warn my people of what is being planned here. The man you call the pale dwarf, and I, must carry this warning, and unite the people of the warm world as we have united you here to fight this menace. Then, when we are able, I will return to share with you the glories of freedom!'

I knew that Amelia had already allayed the worst of the Martians' suspicions, for several were leaping enthusiastically.

She had more to say, though: 'Finally, you must no longer distrust the man you call the pale dwarf. It is his heroic deed which must become your example. He, and only he, has shown that the monsters are mortal. Let his brave act be the first blow for freedom!'

All the Martians were leaping and shrilling, and in the noise I doubted if any could hear her. But she looked at me and spoke softly, and her words carried to me as clearly as if the room were silent.

She said: 'You must trust and love him, just as I trust and love him.'

Then I rushed across the room towards her and took her in my arms, oblivious of the demonstrative approval of the Martians.

SIXTEEN
Escape From Oppression!

•

I

With our plan of action finally understood and approved by the Martians, Amelia and I separated for the rest of the day. She continued with her tour of the revolutionary units, while I went with the two Martians to inspect the snow-cannon and projectile. Edwina came with us, for there was much that would have to be explained.

The cannon-site was outside the main part of the city, but to reach it we did not have to cross open territory. By a clever device, the monster-creatures had extended their electrical force-screen into a tunnel shape, through which it was possible to walk in warm and breathable air. This tunnel led directly towards the mountain, and although from this level not much of the mountain could be seen, ahead of us I noticed the immense buildings of the cannon-site.

There was much traffic in this extension, both pedestrian and vehicular, and I found the activity reassuring. I had been given a suit of the black clothes, but the "dwarf" sobriquet was a reminder of my abnormal appearance.

As the extension reached the place where the protective screen opened out again, by the entrance to the cannon-site itself, we came under the direct scrutiny of several of the monsters. These were mounted inside permanent guard-positions, and the monsters themselves sat behind faintly tinted glass screens, observing all who passed with their broad, expressionless eyes.

To pass this point we adopted a previously agreed deception. I and the two men pushed Edwina before us, as if she were being taken for some inhuman treatment. One of the Martians was holding an electrical whip, and he brandished it with great conviction.

Inside the area itself there were more monsters in evidence than I had ever seen anywhere on Mars, but once past the guard-post we were ignored. Most of the odious creatures had legged vehicles in which to move about, but I saw several who were dragging themselves slowly along the ground. This was the first time I had seen this; until now I had assumed that without their mechanical aids the monsters were helpless. Indeed, in face-to-face combat with a human a monster would be totally vulnerable, for the motion was slow and painful, four of the tentacles being used as clumsy, crab-like legs.

The presence of the monsters was not, however, the most intimidating aspect of this area.

Having noticed the cannon-site buildings while walking towards them from the city, I had registered that they were of great size, but now we were among them I realized just how enormous were the engines of science on this world. Walking between the buildings, it was as if we were ants in a city street.

My guides attempted to explain the purpose of each building as we passed it. Edwina's vocabulary was limited, and I obtained only the vaguest idea of the overall plan. As far as I could understand, the various components of the battle-machines were manufactured in the outlying factories, then brought to this place where they were assembled and primed. In one building – which must have been at least three hundred feet high – I could see through immense open doors that several of the tripodal battle-machines were in the process of being built: the one furthest from us was no more than a skeletal framework suspended from pulleys, while beneath it one of the three legs was being attached, but the battle-machine nearest us seemed to be complete, for its platform was being rotated while around it many supplementary instruments scanned and tested.

Both men and monsters worked in these mighty sheds, and to my eyes it seemed that the co-existence was unforced. There were no obvious signs of the slave-rule, and it occurred to me that perhaps not every human on Mars would welcome the revolution.

After we had passed some twenty or so of these sheds, we came to a vast stretch of open land, and I stopped dead in my tracks, speechless at what I saw.

Here were the fruits of such prodigious industry. Lined up, in one rank after another, were the projectiles. Each one was identical to the next, as if each had been turned on the same lathe by the same craftsman. Each one was machined and polished to a gleaming, golden shine; there were no extrusions to mar the cleanness of the line. Each one was nearly three hundred feet in length; sharply pointed at the nose, curving up so that the craft had a cylindrical body for most of its length, and its rear was circular, revealing the huge diameter. I had stood amazed at the size of the craft fired by the monsters of Desolation City, but they were mere playthings compared to these. I could hardly credit what I saw, but as I walked past the nearest of the projectiles I realized that it must have an overall diameter of around ninety feet!

My guides walked on unconcerned, and after a moment I followed them, craning my neck and marvelling.

I tried to estimate how many projectiles there were, but the area on which they were laid was so vast that I was not even sure I could see all the craft. Perhaps each rank had upwards of a hundred such waiting projectiles, and I passed through eight ranks of them.

Then, as we emerged from between the projectiles in the front rank, I was confronted with the most astonishing sight of all.

Here is was that the ascending slope of the volcano became pronounced, rising before us. Here it was that the monster-creatures of this hateful city had laid their snow-cannons.

There were five in all. Four of them were of the same order as the one at Desolation City, but there was no complication here with pivotal buildings and a lake to absorb the heat, for the barrels of the cannon were laid along the slope of the mountain itself! Nor was there any need for the elaborate process of inserting the projectile through the muzzle, for by a cunning arrangement of railway lines, and a stout entrance at the breech of the barrel, the projectiles could be loaded here.

But my attention was not drawn towards these pieces of ordnance, for, mighty as they were, their presence was overshadowed by the fifth snow-cannon.

Whereas the lesser snow-cannons had barrels a mile or so long, with bores of about twenty feet, this central cannon had a barrel with an external diameter well in excess of one hundred feet. As for its length ... well, it extended further than the eye could see, running straight and true up the side of the mountain, sometimes resting on the soil, sometimes carried by huge viaducts where the slope was less pronounced, sometimes running through canyons blasted from the rock itself. At its base, the very breech was like a metal mountain of its own: a great, bulbous piece of black armour, thick enough and mighty enough to support the ferocious blast of the vaporizing ice which powered the projectiles. It loomed over everything, a stark reminder of the terrible skills and sciences these accursed monster-creatures commanded.

It was with this cannon, and with these hundreds of gleaming projectiles, that the monster-creatures plotted their invasion of Earth!

II

A projectile had been placed already in the breech, and my guides led me up a metal companionway that attached to the bulk of the cannon like a flying buttress against the wall of a cathedral. From its dizzying height I looked down across the massed machines of the monsters, and beyond them, across the dividing strip of land to the near-by city.

The companionway ended at one of the access-points to the barrel itself, and we entered through a narrow tunnel. At once the temperature fell sharply. Interpreting for one of the men, Edwina explained that the barrel was already lined with ice, and that its entire length could be relined and frozen in just over half a day.

The tunnel led directly to a hatch into the craft itself. I suppose I had been expecting a larger version of the projectile in which I had already flown, but this was so only in its overall design.

We stepped out of the hatch into the forward control-area, and from here explored the entire craft.

As with the smaller projectiles, this one was divided into three main areas: the control section, a hold in which the slaves would be carried and the main hold in which the monsters and their terrible battle-machines were to ride. These last two compartments were linked by one of the blood-letting devices. That at least was no different, but one of the men explained that during the flight the monsters would be sedated with a sleeping-draught, and that their food requirements would be minimal.

I had no desire to dwell on this aspect of the monsters' arrangements, and so we passed on into the main hold itself.

Here I saw the full scale of the monsters' arsenal. Five of the tripodal battle-machines were stored here, their legs detached and neatly folded, the platforms collapsed to occupy as little space as possible. Also aboard were several of the small, legged vehicles, a score or more of the heat-cannons, and innumerable quantities of different substances, packaged away in dozens of huge containers. Neither I nor my guides could hazard a guess as to what these might be.

At various parts of the hold hung the tubes of transparent material which absorbed the shocks of launch and landing.

We did not stay long in this hold, but I saw enough to realize that what was here was in itself reason enough to fly to Earth. What a prize this would be for our scientists!

The control-area, in the prow of the ship, was a huge room with the overall shape of the pointed nose of the craft. The projectile had been set in the barrel in such a way that the controls were on what was presently the floor, but it was explained to me that in flight the craft would be rotated so as to produce weight. (This was a concept lost on me, and I decided that Edwina's translation was inadequate.) After the cramped quarters of the other projectile the control-area was palatial indeed, and the builders had gone to some pains to make the drivers comfortable. There was much dried food available, a tiny commode, and in one part of the wall was a shower-system, rather like the one we had used at the slave-camp. The siting of this, and the hammocks on which we would sleep, was rather puzzling, for they had been hung from the ceiling, some eighty feet above our heads.

I was told that in flight we would have no difficulty reaching them, although this was clearly something I would have to take on trust.

The controls themselves were many, and when I saw them, and thought about the bulk of the craft they directed, it was daunting to recall that until this day the most elaborate vehicle I had ever driven was a pony and trap!

The men explained everything in great detail, but I grasped little of what was said. In this, I felt Edwina's interpretations were unreliable, and even when I was confident she was conveying the meaning of their words accurately, I had difficulty with the concept described.

For example, I was shown a large glass panel – which was currently blank – and told that in flight there would be displayed upon it a picture of what was directly in front of the ship. This I could grasp, as it seemed to be common with the smaller projectile. However, there was a subtle refinement here. I was told repeatedly of a "target", and this was talked of in conjunction with a series of metal knobs protruding from a place below the screen. Furthermore, I was told that target was applied when using the green-tipped lever which, I already knew from my earlier flight, released a blast of green fire from the nose.

I decided that much of what puzzled me now would become clear by experimentation in flight.

The explanations went on until my mind was spinning. At last I had a broad idea of what was to happen – the actual firing of the cannon, for instance, would be controlled from a building outside the ship – and further, I knew roughly how much I could manoeuvre the craft while in flight.

My guides told me that the monsters were not planning their

first launch for another four days. We should therefore have plenty of time to make our escape before the monsters were ready.

I said that I would be happy to leave as soon as possible, for now the means was open to us I had no desire to stay on Mars a moment longer than necessary.

III

Amelia and I passed that night in one of the city dormitories. It had again been difficult for us to say much to each other, for Edwina was always in attendance, but when at last we took to a hammock we were able to talk quietly.

We lay in each other's arms; this was the one burden of our legendary roles that I found easiest to fulfil.

'Have you inspected the craft?' Amelia said.

'Yes. I think there will be no problem. The area is crowded with monsters, but they are all occupied with their preparations.'

I told her what I had seen: the number of projectiles ready to be fired at Earth, the arrangements within the craft.

'Then how many of the creatures are planning to invade?' Amelia said.

'The projectile we will be going in carries five of the brutes. I could not count the other projectiles ... certainly there were several hundred.'

Amelia lay in silence for a while, but then she said: 'I wonder, Edward ... if the revolution is now necessary. If this is to be the scale of the migration, then how many monsters will be left on Mars? Could the plan be for a total exodus?'

'That had crossed my mind too.'

'I saw this as a moment of unpreparedness, but how ironical it would be if in a few days' time there would be no monsters left to overthrow!'

'And the adversary would be on Earth,' I said. 'Do you not see how urgent it is that we fly to Earth before the monsters?'

A little later, Amelia said: 'The revolution is to start tomorrow.'

'Could the Martians not wait?'

'No ... the firing of our craft is to be the signal for action.'

'But could we not deter them? If they would only wait ...'

'You have not seen all their preparations, Edward. The excitement of the people is irrepressible. I have lit a gunpowder trail, and the explosion is no more than a few hours away.'

We said no more after this, but I for one could hardly sleep. I was wondering if this was indeed to be our last night on this unhappy world, or whether we should ever be free of it.

IV

We had gone to bed in a mood of worried calm, but when we awoke it was to a very different situation.

What awakened us was a sound which sent chills of fear down my spine: the howling of the monsters' sirens, and the reverberations of distant explosions. My first thought, prompted by experience, was that there had been another invasion, but then, as we jumped from the hammock and saw that the dormitory was deserted, we realized that the fighting must be between opposing forces within the city. The Martians had not waited!

A battle-machine strode past the building, and we felt the walls tremble with the vibration of its passage.

Edwina, who until this moment had been hiding beside the door, rushed over to us when she saw we were awake.

'Where are the others?' Amelia said immediately.

'They went in the night.'

'Why were we not told?'

'They said you were now only wanting to fly in the machine.'

'Who started this?' I said, indicating the bedlam beyond the building.

'It began in the night, when the others left.'

And we had slept through this noise and confusion? It seemed hardly likely. I went to the door and peered into the street. The battle-machine had gone its way, and its armoured platform could be seen above some near-by buildings. Some distance from me I could see a column of black smoke rising, and over to my left there was a smaller fire. In the distance there was another explosion, although I could not see any smoke, and in a moment I heard two battle-machines braying in response.

I went back to Amelia.

'We had better get to the cannon-site,' I said. 'It might still be possible to take the projectile.'

She nodded, and went to where our erstwhile friends had laid out two of the black uniforms for us. When we had put these on, and were preparing to leave, Edwina looked at us uncertainly.

'Are you coming with us?' I said, brusquely. I had been growing tired of her fluting voice and the unreliability of her translations. I wondered how much of our information had been misrepresented by her.

She said: 'You would like me to come, Amelia?'

Now Amelia looked doubtful, and said to me: 'What do you think?'

'Will we need her?'

'Only if we have something to say.'

I considered for a few seconds. Much as I distrusted her, she was our only contact with the people here, and she had at least stayed behind when the others left.

I said: 'She can come with us as far as the cannon-site.'

With that, and pausing only to collect Amelia's hand-bag, we set off at once.

As we hurried across the city it became obvious that although the Martians had started their revolution, damage was as yet minor, and confined to a few areas. The streets were not empty of people, nor yet were they crowded. Several Martians gathered together in small groups, watched over by the battle-machines, and in the distance we heard many sirens. Somewhere near the centre of the city we came across evidence of more direct revolt: several of the battle-machines had been somehow overturned, and lay helplessly across the streets; these provided effective barricades, for once set on its side a tower could not by itself stand up again, and so blocked the passage of the ground vehicles.

When we came to the place where the electrical force-screen was extended towards the cannon-site, we found that the monsters and their machines were much in evidence. Several ground vehicles, and five battle-machines, stood thickly together, their heat-cannons raised.

We paused at this sight, not sure whether to go on. There were no Martian humans to be seen, although we noticed that several charred bodies had been swept roughly into a heap at the base of one of the buildings. Clearly there had been fighting here, and the monsters retained their supremacy. To approach now would bring almost certain death.

Standing there, undecided, I sensed the urgency of reaching the projectile before the trouble worsened.

'We had better wait,' Amelia said.

'I think we should go on,' I said quietly. 'We will not be stopped wearing these uniforms.'

'What about Edwina?'

'She will have to stay here.'

However, in spite of my apparent resolution I was not confident. As we watched, one of the battle-machines moved off to the side, its heat-cannon pivoting menacingly. With its dangling metal arms it reached into one of the near-by buildings, apparently feeling for anyone hiding within. After a few moments it moved off again, this time striding at a faster pace.

Then Amelia said: 'Over there, Edward!'

A Martian was signalling to us from one of the other buildings, waving his long arms. Casting a watchful glance at the machines, we hurried over to him and at once he and Edwina exchanged several words. I recognized him as one of the men we had met the day before.

Eventually, Edwina said: 'He says that only drivers of the flying war-machines can go further. The two who showed you yesterday are waiting for you.'

Something about the way she said this aroused a faint suspicion, but for want of further evidence I could not say why.

'Are you to come with us?' said Amelia.

'No. I stay to fight.'

'Then where are the others?' I said.

'At the flying war-machine.'

I took Amelia to one side. 'What shall we do?'

'We must go on. If the revolution causes any more trouble, we might not be able to leave.'

'How do we know we are not walking into a trap?' I said.

'But who would lay it? If we cannot trust the people, then we are lost.'

'That is precisely my worry,' I said.

The man who had signalled to us had already disappeared into the building, and Edwina seemed to be on the point of running in after him. I looked over my shoulder at the monsters' machines, but there appeared to have been no movement.

Amelia said: 'Good-bye, Edwina.'

She raised her hand, spreading her fingers, then the Martian girl did the same.

'Good-bye, Amelia,' she said, then turned her back and walked through the doorway.

'That was a cool farewell,' I said. 'Considering you are the leader of the revolution.'

'I don't understand, Edward.'

'Neither do I. I think we must get to the projectile without further delay.'

V

We approached the battle-machines with considerable trepidation, fearing the worst with every step. But we went unmolested, and soon we had passed beneath the high platforms and were walking up the extension towards the cannon-site.

A deep mistrust of the situation was growing in me, and I was dreading the fact that soon we should have to pass beneath the scrutiny of the monsters who guarded the entrance. My feeling of unease was increased when, a few minutes later, we heard more explosions from the city, and saw several of the battle-machines dashing about the streets with their cannons flaring.

'I wonder,' I said, 'if our part in the revolt is now suspected. Your young friend was remarkably reluctant to be with us.'

'She does not have one of these uniforms.'

'That's true,' I said, but I was still not at ease.

The entrance to the cannon-site was nearly upon us, and the great sheds were looming up.

At the last moment, when we were no more than five yards from the monsters' observation-seats, we saw one of the two young Martians I'd been with the previous day. We went directly to him. There was an empty vehicle by the roadway, and we went around the back of it with him.

Once away from the sight of the monster-creatures at the gate, he launched into a most expressive foray of sibilance and expository gestures.

'What's he saying?' I said to Amelia.

'I haven't the faintest notion.'

We waited until he had finished, and then he stared at us as if awaiting a response. He was about to start his tirade again, when Amelia indicated the cannon-site.

'May we go in?' she said, evidently working on the assumption that if he could speak his language to us, we could speak ours to him, but assisting him by pointing towards the site.

His reply was not understood.

'Do you think he said yes?' I said.

'There is only one way to tell.'

Amelia raised her hand to him, then walked towards the entrance. I followed, and we both glanced back to see if this action provoked a negative response. He appeared to be making no move to stop us, but raised his hand in greeting, and so we walked on.

Now determined to see this through, we were past the monsters' observation panels almost before we realized it. However, a few paces further on a screech from one of the positions chilled our blood. We had been spotted.

We both halted, and at once I found I was trembling. Amelia had paled.

The screech came again, and was then repeated.

'Edward... we must walk on!'

'But we have been challenged!' I cried.

'We do not know what for. We can only walk on.'

So, expecting at best another bestial screech, or at worst to be smitten by the heat-beam, we stepped on towards the snow-cannon.

Miraculously, there was no further challenge.

VI

We were now almost running, for our objective was in sight. We passed through the ranks of waiting projectiles, and headed for the breech of the mighty cannon. Amelia, whose first visit to the site this was, could hardly believe what she saw.

'There are so many!' she said, gasping with the exertion of hurrying up the gradient of the mountain slope.

'It is to be a full-scale invasion,' I said. 'We cannot allow these monsters to attack Earth.'

During my visit the day before, the activities of the monsters had been confined to the area where the machines were assembled, and this store of gleaming projectiles had been left unattended. Now, though, there were the monsters and their vehicles all about. We hurried on, unchallenged.

There was no sign of any humans, although I had been told that by the time we entered the projectile our friends would be in charge of the device which fired the cannon. I hoped that word of our arrival had been passed, for I did not wish to wait too long inside the projectile itself.

The companionway was still in place, and I led Amelia up it to the entrance to the inner chamber. Such was our haste that when one of the monster-creatures by the base of the companionway uttered a series of modulated screeches, we paid no attention to it. We were now so close to our objective, so near to the instrument of our return to Earth, that we felt nothing could bar our way.

I stood back to allow Amelia to go first, but she pointed out that it would be sensible for me to lead. This I did, heading down that dark, frigid tunnel through the breech-block, away from the wan sunlight of Mars.

The hatch of the ship was open, and this time Amelia did go in before me. She stepped down the ramp into the heart of the projectile, while I attended to closing the hatch as I'd been shown. Now we were inside, away from the noises and enigmas of the Martian civilization, I suddenly felt very calm and purposeful.

This spacious interior, quiet, dimly lit, quite empty, was another world from that city and its beleaguered peoples; this craft, product of the most ruthless intellect in the Universe, was our salvation and home.

Once it would have been in the van of a terrible invasion of Earth; now, in the safe charge of Amelia and myself, it could become our world's salvation. It was a prize of war, a war of which even now the peoples of Earth were quite unsuspecting.

I checked the hatch once more, making certain that it was quite secure, then took Amelia in my arms and kissed her lightly.

She said: 'The craft is awfully big, Edward. Are you sure you know what to do?'

'Leave it to me.'

For once my confidence was not assumed. Once before I had made a reckless act to avert an evil destiny, and now again I saw destiny as being in my own hands. So much depended on my skills and actions, and the responsibility of my home world's future lay on my shoulders. It could not be that I should fail!

I led Amelia up the sloping floor of the cabin, and showed her the pressure tubes that would support and protect us during the firing of the cannon. I judged it best that we should enter them at once, for we had no way of telling when our friends outside would fire the craft. In the confused situation, events were unpredictable.

Amelia stepped into her own tube, and I watched as the eerie substance folded itself about her.

'Can you breathe?' I said to her.

'Yes.' Her voice was muffled, but quite audible. 'How do I climb out of this? I feel I am imprisoned.'

'You simply step forward,' I said. 'It will not resist unless we are under acceleration.'

Inside her transparent tube Amelia smiled to show she understood, and so I moved back to my own tube. Here I squeezed past the controls which were placed within easy reach, then felt the soft fabric closing in on me. When my body was contained I allowed myself to relax, and waited for the launch to begin.

A long time passed. There was nothing to do but stare across the few feet that separated us, and watch Amelia and smile to her. We could hear each other if we spoke, but the effort was considerable.

The first hint of vibration, when it came, was so minute as to be attributable to the imagination, but it was followed a few moments later by another. Then there came a sudden jolt, and I felt the folds of fabric tightening about my body.

'We are moving, Amelia!' I shouted, but needlessly, for there was no mistaking what was happening.

After the first concussion there followed several more, of increasing severity, but after a while the motion became smooth and the acceleration steady. The fabric tube was clutching me like a giant hand, but even so I could feel the pressure of our speed against me, far greater than I had experienced on the smaller craft. Furthermore, the period of acceleration was much longer, presumably because of the immense length of the barrel. There was now a noise, the like of which was quite unprecedented: a great rushing and roaring, as the enormous craft shot through its tube of ice.

Just as the acceleration was reaching the point where I felt I could no longer stand it, even inside the protective grasp of the tube, I saw that Amelia's eyes had closed and that inside her tube she appeared to have fallen unconscious. I shouted out to her, but in the din of our firing there was no hope that she would hear me. The pressure and noise were each now intolerable, and I felt a lightness in my brain and a darkness occluding my sight. As my vision failed, and the roaring became a dull muttering in the background, the pressure abruptly ceased.

The folds of the fabric loosened, and I stumbled forward out of the tube. Amelia, similarly released, fell unconscious to the metal floor. I leant over her, slapping her cheeks gently ... and it was not for several moments that I realized that at last we had been flung headlong into the ether of space.

SEVENTEEN

A Homeward Quest

•

I

So began the voyage which, in optimism, I had expected to take but a day or two, but which in actuality took nearer sixty days, as near as we could tell. They were two long months; for short periods it was an exciting experience, at other times it became terrifying, but for most of the sixty days it was a journey of the most maddening dullness.

I will not, then, delay this narrative with an account of our daily lives, but indicate those events which most exercised us at the time.

Thinking back over the experience, I recall the flight with mixed feelings. It was not an enjoyable journey in any sense of the word, but it was not without its better sides.

One of these was that Amelia and I were alone together in an environment which provided privacy, intimacy and a certain security, even if it was not the most usual of situations. It is not germane to this narrative to describe what occurred between us – even in these modern times, I feel I should not breach the trusts which we then established – but it would be true to say that I came to know her, and she to know me, in ways and to depths I had never before suspected were possible.

Moreover, the length of the journey itself had a purgatory effect on our outlooks. We had indeed become tainted by Mars, and even I, less involved than Amelia, had felt a conflict of loyalties as we blasted away from the revolution-torn city. But, surrounded as we were by a Martian artifact, and kept alive by Martian food and Martian air, as the days passed and Earth grew nearer, the conflicts faded and we became of single purpose once more. The invasion the monsters schemed was all too real; if we could not help avert such an invasion then we could never again call ourselves human.

But already my synopsis of this incredible journey through space is once more taking my narrative ahead of its natural order.

I have mentioned that certain incidents during the voyage were exciting or terrifying, and the first of these occurred shortly after we were released from the pressure-tubes, and found ourselves in command of a space ironclad.

II

When I had revived Amelia from her faint, and ensured that neither she nor I had suffered any ill-effects during the rigours of the blast, I went first to the controls to see where we were headed. Such was the ferocity of our firing that I was sure we were about to hurtle into Earth at any moment!

I turned the knob that illuminated the main panel – as my guides had shown me – but to my disappointment nothing could be seen except for a few faint points of light. These, I later realized, were stars. After experimenting for several minutes, and achieving no more than marginally increasing the brilliance of the picture, I turned my attention to one of the smaller panels. This displayed the view behind the craft.

Here the picture was more satisfactory, for it showed a view of the world we had just left. So close to Mars were we still that it filled the entire panel: a chiaroscuro of light and shadow, mottled yellows and reds and browns. When my eyes adjusted to the scale of what I was seeing I found I could pick out certain features of the landscape, the most prominent of which was the immense volcano, standing out from the deserts like a malignant carbuncle. Bulging around its summit was a gigantic white cloud; at first I took this to be the volcano's own discharge, but later I thought that this must be the cloud of water-vapour that had thrust us on our way.

The city we had left was invisible – it lay presumably beneath the spreading white cloud – and there were few features I could definitely identify. The canals were clearly visible, or at least they became visible by virtue of the banks of weed that proliferated alongside them.

I stared at the view for some time, realizing that for all the force of our departure we had neither travelled very far nor were now moving with much velocity. Indeed, the only apparent movement was the image of the land itself, which was rotating slowly in the panel.

While I was watching this, Amelia called out to me: 'Edward, shall we have some food?'

I turned away from the panel, and said: 'Yes, I'm hun—'

I did not complete my sentence, for Amelia was nowhere in sight.

'I'm down here, Edward.'

I stared down the sloping floor of the compartment, but there was no sign of her. Then I heard her laughing, and looked up in the direction of the sound. Amelia was there ... upside-down on the ceiling!

'What are you doing?' I shouted, aghast. 'You'll fall and hurt yourself!'

'Don't be silly. It's perfectly safe. Come down here and you'll see for yourself.'

To demonstrate, she executed a little jump ... and landed, feet first, on the ceiling.

'I cannot go down if you are above me,' I said pedantically.

'It is you who is above me,' she said. Then, surprising me, she walked across the ceiling, down the curving wall, and was soon by my side. 'Come with me, and I'll show you.'

She took my hand, and I went with her. I trod carefully at first, bracing myself against falling, but the gradient did not increase, and after a few moments I glanced back at my controls and saw to my surprise that they now seemed to be against the wall. We walked on, soon coming to the place where the food had been stored, and where Amelia had been. Now when I looked back at the controls they appeared to be on the ceiling above us.

During the course of our voyage, we grew used to this effect created by the spinning of the ship about its axis, but it was a novel experience. Until this moment we had taken it for granted, so accustomed were we to the lightness of the Martian gravity, and the craft was being rotated so as to simulate this.

(Later in the voyage, I found a way of increasing the rate of spin, with the intention of readying our bodies for the greater weight of Earth.)

For the first few days this phenomenon was a considerable novelty to us. The shape of the compartment itself lent peculiar effects. As one moved further up the sloping floor (or ceiling) towards the nose of the craft, so one approached the central axis of the ship and apparent gravity was less. Amelia and I often passed the time by exercising in this strange ambience: by going to the apex of the compartment and kicking oneself away, one could float across much of the space before drifting gently to the floor.

Still, those first two hours after the firing of the cannon were placid enough, and we ate a little of the Martian food, blissfully unaware of what was in store for us.

III

When I returned to the controls, the view in the rearward-facing panel showed that the horizon of Mars had appeared. This was the first direct evidence I had that the planet was receding from us ... or, to be more accurate, that we were receding from it. The forward panel still showed its uninformative display of stars. I had, naturally enough, expected to see our homeworld looming before us. My guides on Mars had informed me that the firing of the cannon would direct the craft towards Earth, but that I should not be able to see it for some time, so there was no immediate concern.

It did seem strange to me, though, that Earth should not be directly ahead of us.

I decided that as there would be neither night nor day on the craft, we should have to establish a ship time. My watch was still working, and I took it out. As near as I could estimate it, the snow-cannon had been fired at the height of the Martian day, and that we had been in flight for about two hours. Accordingly, I set my watch at two o'clock, and thenceforward my watch became the ship's chronometer.

With this done, and with Amelia content to investigate what provisions had been made for our sojourn in the craft, I decided to explore the rest of the ship.

So it was that I discovered we were not alone ...

I was moving along one of the passages that ran through the double hull when I passed the hatchway that led to the compartment designed to hold the slaves. I afforded it the merest glance, but then stopped in horror! The hatch had been crudely sealed from the outside, welded closed so that the door was unopenable, either from within or without. I pressed my ear to it, and listened.

I could hear nothing: if anyone was inside they were very still. There was the faintest sound of movement, but this could well have come from Amelia's activities in the forward compartment.

I stood by that hatch for many minutes, full of forebodings and indecision. I had no evidence that anyone was within ... but why should that hatch have been sealed, when only the day before I and the others had passed freely through it?

Could it be that this projectile carried a cargo of human food ...?

If so, just what was in the main hold ...?

Stricken with an awful presentiment, I hastened to the hatch that led to the hold where the monsters' machines had been stowed. This too had been welded, and I stood before it, my heart thudding. Unlike the other hatch, this was equipped with a sliding metal plate, of the sort that is installed in the doors of prison-cells.

I moved it to one side, a fraction of an inch at a time, terrified of making a noise and so drawing attention to myself.

At last it had been opened sufficiently for me to place my eye against it, and I did this, peering into the dimly lit interior.

My worst fears were instantly confirmed: there, not a dozen feet from the hatch, was the oblate body of one of the monsters. It lay before one of the protective tubes, evidently having been released from it after the launch.

I jumped back at once, fearful of being noticed. In the confined space of the passage I waved my arms in despair, cursing silently, dreading the significance of this discovery.

Eventually, I summoned enough courage to return to my peep-hole, and looked again at the monster that was there.

It was lying so that it presented one side of its body and most of its nasty face towards me. It had not noticed me, and indeed it had not moved an inch since I had first looked. Then I recalled what my guides had said ... that the monsters took a sleeping-draught for the duration of the flight.

This monster's tentacles were folded, and although its eyes were open the flaccid white lids drooped over the pale eyeballs. In sleep it lost none of its beastliness, yet it was now vulnerable. I did not have the steel of rage in me that I had had before, but I knew that were the door not unopenable I would once again have been able to slay the being.

Reassured that I would not rouse the brute, I slid the plate right open, and looked along as much of the length of the hold I could. There were three other monsters in view, each one similarly unconscious. There was probably the fifth somewhere in the hold, but there was so much equipment lying about that I could not see it.

So we had not after all stolen the projectile. The craft we commanded was leading the monsters' invasion of Earth!

Was *this* what the Martians had been trying to tell us before we left? Was *this* what Edwina had been keeping back from us?

IV

I decided to say nothing of this to Amelia, remembering her loyalties to the Martian people. If she knew the monsters were aboard, she would realize that they had brought their food with them, and it would become her major preoccupation. I did not care for the knowledge myself – it was unpleasant to realize that beyond the metal wall at the rear of our compartment were imprisoned several men and women who, when needed, would sacrifice themselves to the monsters – but it would not divert my attention from the major tasks.

So, although Amelia remarked on my pallor when I returned, I said nothing of what I had seen. I slept uneasily that night, and once when I wakened I fancied I could hear a low crooning coming from the next compartment.

The following day, our second in space, an event occurred that made it difficult to keep my discovery to myself. On the day after that, and in subsequent days, there were further incidents that made it impossible.

It happened like this:

I had been experimenting with the panel that displayed the view before the ship, trying to understand the device whose nearest translation had been target. I had found that certain knobs could cause an illuminated grid-pattern to be projected over the picture. This was certainly in accord with target, for at the centre of the grid was a circle containing two crossed lines. However, beyond this I had not learned anything.

I turned my attention to the rearward panel.

In this, the view of Mars had changed somewhat while we slept. The reddish planet was now sufficiently far away for most of it to be seen as a disk in the panel, though still, because of the spinning of our craft, appearing to revolve. We were on the sunward side of the planet – which was itself reassuring, since Earth lies to the sunward of Mars – and the visible area was roughly the shape that one sees on Earth a day or two before a full moon. The planet was turning on its own axis, of course, and during the morning I had seen the great protuberance of the volcano appear.

Then, just as my watch declared the time to be nearly midday, an enormous white cloud appeared near the summit of the volcano.

I called Amelia to the controls, and showed her what I had seen.

She stared at it in silence for several minutes, then said softly: 'Edward, I think a second projectile has been launched.'

I nodded dumbly, for she had only confirmed my own fears.

All that afternoon we watched the rearward panel, and saw the cloud drifting slowly across the face of the world. Of the projectile itself we could see no sign, but both of us knew we were no longer alone in space.

On the third day, a third projectile was fired, and Amelia said: 'We are part of an invasion of Earth.'

'No,' I said, grimly lying to her. 'I believe we will have twenty-four hours in which to alert the authorities on Earth.'

But on the fourth day another projectile was hurled into space behind us, and like each of the three before it, the moment of firing was almost exactly at midday.

Amelia said, with unassailable logic: 'They are conforming to a regular pattern, and our craft was the first piece in that pattern. Edward, I maintain that we are a part of the invasion.'

It was then that my secret could no longer be maintained. I took her into the passages that ran the length of the ship, and showed her what I had seen through the sliding metal panel. The monsters had not moved, still slumbering peacefully while their flight to Earth continued. Amelia took her turn at the hole in silence.

'When we arrive on Earth,' she said, 'we will be obliged to act quickly. We must escape from the projectile at the earliest possible moment.'

'Unless we can destroy them before we land,' I said.

'Is there any way?'

'I have been trying to think. There is no way we can enter the hold.' I showed her how the hatch had been fused. 'We could possibly devise some way of cutting off their supply of air.'

'Or introducing to it some poison.'

I seized on this solution eagerly, for since I had made my discovery my fears had been growing about what these creatures could do on Earth. It was unimaginable that they could be allowed to do their Devil's work! I had no idea how the air was circulated through the ship, but as my command of the controls was increasing so was my confidence, and I felt that this should not be impossible to solve.

I had said nothing to Amelia of the slaves in their compartment – for I was by now convinced that there were many aboard – but I had done her an injustice when anticipating her reaction.

That evening, Amelia said: 'Where are the Martian slaves, Edward?'

Her question was so forthright that I did not know what to say.

'Are they in the compartment behind ours?' she went on.

'Yes,' I said. 'But it has been sealed.'

'So there is no possibility of releasing them?'

'None that I know of,' I said.

We were both silent after this exchange, because the awfulness of the wretches' prospects was unthinkable. Some time later, when I was on my own, I went to their hatch and tried again to see if it could be opened, but it was hopeless. As far as I can recall, neither Amelia nor I ever referred directly to the slaves again. For this, I at least was grateful.

V

On the fifth day of our voyage a fifth projectile was fired. By this time, Mars was distant on our rearwards panel, but we had little difficulty in seeing the cloud of white vapour.

On the sixth day I discovered a control attached to the screens which could enhance and enlarge the images. When midday came around we were able to see, in relatively clear detail, the firing of the sixth cylinder.

Four more days passed and on each of them the mighty snow-cannon was fired, but on the eleventh day the volcano passed across the visible portion of Mars, and no white cloud appeared. We watched until the volcano had passed beyond the terminator, but as far as we could tell no projectile was fired that day.

Nor was there on the day following. Indeed, after the tenth projectile no more were fired at all. Remembering those hundreds of gleaming craft lying at the base of the mountain, we could not believe that the monsters would call off their plans with so comparatively few missiles en route for the target. This did seem to be the case, though, for as the days passed we never abandoned our watch of the red planet but not once again did we see any sign of the cannon being fired.

Of course, we occupied much time in speculating as to why this should be so.

I advanced the theory that this was the monsters' plan: that an advance guard of ten projectiles would invade and occupy an area of Earth, for after all they would have an armoury of at least fifty battle-machines with which to do this. For this reason I felt our watch should be maintained, arguing that more projectiles would soon be following.

Amelia was of a different mind. She saw the surcease in terms of a victory for the Martian humans' revolution, that the people had broken through the monsters' defences and taken control.

In either event we had no way of verifying anything other than what we saw. The migration had effectively finished with ten projectiles, at least for the time being.

By this time we were many days into our voyage, and Mars itself was a small, glowing body many millions of miles behind us. Our focus of interest was moving from this, for now, in the forwards panel, we could see our homeworld looming towards us: a tiny crescent of light, so indescribably lovely and still.

VI

As the weeks passed I became more at home with the controls, feeling that I understood the function of most. I had even come to understand the device the Martians had called the target, and had realized that it was possibly the most important of all the controls.

I had learned to use this when viewing Earth through the forwards panel. It had been Amelia who had first pointed out our world: a clearly defined brilliance near the edge of the panel. Of course, we were both much affected by the sight, and the knowledge that every day carried us thousands of miles nearer to it was a source of steadily growing excitement. But as one day followed another, the image of our world slipped nearer and nearer to the edge of the display, until we realized that it could not be long before it vanished from our sight altogether. I adjusted the controls of the panel equipment to no avail.

Then, in desperation, Amelia suggested that I should turn on the illuminated grid that was projected across the panel. As I did this I saw that a second, more ghostly grid lay behind it. Unlike the main one, this had its central circle fixed on the image of our world. It was most uncanny ... as if the device had a mind of its own.

At the same moment as the second grid appeared, several lights flashed on beneath the image. We could not understand their meaning, naturally enough, but the fact that my action had produced a response was significant in itself.

Amelia said: 'I think it means we must steer the craft.'

'But it was aimed accurately from Mars.'

'Even so ... it seems to me that we are no longer flying towards Earth.'

We argued a little longer, but at last I could no longer avoid the fact that the time had come for me to demonstrate my prowess as a driver. With Amelia's encouragement I settled myself before the main driving lever, gripped it in both my hands, and moved it experimentally to one side.

Several things happened at once.

The first was that a great noise and vibration echoed through the projectile. Another was that both Amelia and I were thrown to one side. And in addition everything in our compartment that was not secured flew willy-nilly about our heads.

When we had recovered ourselves we discovered that my action had had an undesired effect. That is to say, Earth had disappeared from the panel altogether! Determined to right this at once, I moved the lever in the opposite direction, having first ensured that we were both braced. This time, the ship moved sharply the other way, and although there was much noise and rattling of our possessions, I succeeded in returning Earth to our sight.

It took several more adjustments to the controls before I managed to place the image of Earth in the small central circle of the main grid. As I did this, the display of lights went out, and I felt that our craft was now set firmly on an Earthbound course.

In fact, I discovered that the projectile was wont to drift constantly from its path, and every day I had to make more corrections.

By this process of trials and error, I understood at last how the system of grids was intended to be used. The main, brighter grid indicated the actual destination of the craft, while the less brilliant, moving grid showed the intended destination. As this was always locked on the image of Earth, we were never in doubt as to the monsters' plans.

Such moments of diversion, however, were the exception rather than the rule. Our days in the craft were dull and repetitive, and we soon adopted routines. We slept for as many hours as possible, and dawdled over our meals. We would take exercise by walking about the circumference of the hull, and when it came to attending to the controls would divert more energy and time than was actually necessary. Sometimes we became fractious, and then we would separate and stay at different parts of the compartment.

During one of these periods I returned to the problem of how to deal with the unwelcome occupants of the main hold.

Interfering with the monsters' air-supply seemed to be the logical way of killing them, and in lieu of any substance which I knew to be poisonous to them, suffocation was the obvious expedient. With this in mind I spent the best part of one day exploring the various machines which were built into the hull.

I discovered much about the operation of the craft – for example, I found the location of the quasi-photographic instruments which delivered the pictures to our viewing panels, and I learnt that the craft's directional changes were effected by means of steam expelled from a central heat-source, and ducted through the outer hull by means of an intricate system of pipes – but came no nearer to finding a solution. As far as I could tell, the air inside the craft was circulated from one unit, and that it served all parts of the ship simultaneously. In other words, to suffocate the monsters we should have to suffocate too.

VII

The nearer we came to Earth the more we were obliged to make corrections to our course. Twice or three times a day I would consult the forwards panel, and adjust the controls to bring the two grids once more into alignment. Earth was now large and clear in the picture, and Amelia and I would stand before it, watching our homeworld in silence. It glowed a brilliant blue and white, unspeakably beautiful. Sometimes we could see the moon beside it, showing, like Earth, as a slender and delicate crescent.

This was a sight which should have brought joy to our hearts, but whenever I stood at Amelia's side and stared at this vision of celestial loveliness, I felt a tremendous sadness inside me. And whenever I operated the controls to bring us more accurately towards our destination, I felt stirrings of guilt and shame.

At first I could not understand this, and said nothing to Amelia. But as the days passed, and our world sped ever nearer, I identified my misgivings, and at last was able to speak of them to Amelia. Then it was that I found she too had been experiencing the same.

I said: 'In a day or two we shall be landing on Earth. I am minded to aim the craft towards the deepest ocean, and be done with it.'

'If you did, I would not try to stop you,' she said.

'We cannot inflict these creatures on our world,' I went on. 'We cannot shoulder that responsibility. If just one man or woman should die by these creatures' machinations, then neither you nor I could ever face ourselves again.'

Amelia said: 'But if we could escape the craft quickly enough to alert the authorities ...'

'That is a chance we cannot take. We do not know our way out of this ship, and if the monsters are out before us then we would be too late. My dearest, we have to face up to the fact that you and I must be prepared to sacrifice ourselves.'

While we had been talking, I had turned on the control that produced the two grids across the panel. The secondary grid, showing our intended destination, lay over northern Europe. We could not see the precise place, for this part of the globe was obscured by white cloud. In England the day would be grey; perhaps it was raining.

'Is there nothing we can do?' Amelia said.

I stared gloomily at the screen. 'Our actions are proscribed. As we have replaced the men who would have crewed this ship, we can only do what they would have done. That is to say, to bring the craft manually to the place already selected by the monsters. If we follow the plan, we bring the craft down in the centre of the grid. Our only choice is whether or not we do that. I can allow the craft to pass by Earth entirely, or I can head the craft to a place where its occupants can do no damage.'

'You spoke of landing us in an ocean. Were you serious?'

'It is one course open to us,' I said. 'Although you and I would surely die, we would effectively prevent the monsters from escaping.'

'I don't want to die,' Amelia said, holding me tightly.

'Nor I. But do we have the right to inflict these monsters on our people?'

It was an agonizing subject, and neither of us knew the answers to the questions we raised. We stared at the image of our world for a few more minutes, then went to take a meal. Later, we were drawn again to the panels, over-awed by the responsibilities that had been thrust upon us.

On Earth, the clouds had moved away to the east, and we saw the shape of the British Isles lying in the blue seas. The central circle of the grid lay directly over England.

Amelia said, her voice strained: 'Edward, we have the greatest army on Earth. Can we not trust them to deal with this menace?'

'They would be taken unawares. The responsibility is ours, Amelia, and we must not avoid it. I am prepared to die to save my world. Can I ask the same of you?'

It was a moment charged with emotion, and I found myself trembling.

Then Amelia glanced at the rearward panel, which, though dark, was an insistent reminder of the nine projectiles that followed us.

'Would false heroics save the world from those too?' she said.

VIII

So it was that I continued to correct our course, and brought the main grid to bear on the green islands we loved so dearly.

We were about to go to sleep that night when a noise I had hoped never to hear again emanated from a metal grille in the bulkhead: it was the braying, screeching call of the monsters. One has often heard the idiom that one's blood runs cold; in that moment I understood the truth of the cliché.

I left the hammock directly, and hurried through the passages to the sealed door of the monsters' hold.

As soon as I slid back the metal plate I saw that the accursed beings were conscious. There were two directly in front of me, crawling awkwardly on their tentacles. I was satisfied to see that in the increased gravity (I had long since changed the spin of the ship in an attempt to approximate the gravity of Earth) their movements were more ponderous and ungainly. That was a hopeful sign, when all else seemed bleak, for with any luck they would find their extra weight on Earth a considerable disadvantage.

Amelia had followed me, and when I moved back from the door she too peered through the tiny window. I saw her shudder, and then she drew back.

'Is there nothing we can do to destroy them?' she said.

I looked at her, my expression perhaps revealing the unhappiness I felt.

'I think not,' I said.

When we returned to our compartment we discovered that one or more of the monsters was still trying to communicate with us. The braying echoed through the metal room.

'What do you think it is saying?' Amelia said.

'How can we tell?'

'But suppose we are to obey its instructions?'

'We have nothing to fear from them,' I said. 'They can reach us no more than we can reach them.'

Even so, the hideous screeching was unpleasant to hear, and when it eventually stopped some fifteen minutes later we were both relieved. We returned to the hammock, and a few minutes later we were asleep.

We were awakened some time later – a glance at my watch revealed that we had slept for about four and a half hours – by a renewed outburst of the monsters' screeching.

We lay still, hoping that it would eventually stop again, but after five minutes neither of us could bear it. I left the hammock and went to the controls.

Earth loomed large in the forwards panel. I checked the positioning of the grid system, and noticed at once that something was amiss. While we had slept our course had wandered yet again: although the fainter grid was still firmly over the British Isles, the main grid had wandered far over to the east, revealing that we were now destined to land somewhere in the Baltic Sea.

I called Amelia over, and showed her this.

'Can you correct it?' she said.

'I think so.'

Meanwhile, the braying of the monsters continued.

We braced ourselves as usual, and I swung the lever to correct the course. I achieved a minor correction, but for all my efforts I saw we were going to miss our target by hundreds of miles. Even as we watched I noticed that the brighter grid was drifting slowly towards the east.

Then Amelia pointed out that a green light was glowing, one that had never before shone. It was beside the one control I had not so far touched: the lever which I knew released the blast of green fire from the nose.

Instinctively, I understood that our journey was approaching its end, and unthinkingly I applied pressure to the lever.

The projectile's response to this action was so violent and sudden that we were both catapulted forward from the controls. Amelia landed awkwardly, and I sprawled helplessly across her. Meanwhile our few possessions, and the pieces of food we had left about the compartment, were sent flying in all directions.

I was relatively unhurt by the accident, but Amelia had caught her head against a protruding piece of metal, and blood flowed freely down her face. She was barely conscious, and in obvious agony, and I bent anxiously over her.

She was holding her head in her hands, but she reached towards me and pushed me weakly away.

'I ... I'm all right, Edward,' she said. 'Please ... I feel a little sick. Leave me. It is not serious ...'

'Dearest, let me see what has happened!' I cried.

Both her eyes were closed, and she had gone awfully pale, but she repeated that she was not badly hurt.

'You must attend to driving this craft,' she said.

I hesitated for a few more seconds, but she pushed me away again, and so I returned to the controls. I was certain that I had not lost consciousness for even a moment, but it now seemed that our destination was much nearer. However, the centre of the main grid had moved so that it lay somewhere in the North Sea, indicating that the green fire had altered our course drastically. The eastwards drift, however, continued.

I went back to Amelia, and helped her to her feet. She had recovered her poise slightly, but blood continued to flow.

'My bag,' she said. 'There is a towel inside it.'

I looked around but could see her bag nowhere. It had evidently been thrown by the first concussion, and now lay somewhere in the compartment. Out of the corner of my eye I saw the green light still glowing, and a certainty that the grid was moving relentlessly on towards the east made me feel I should be at the controls.

'I'll find it,' Amelia said. She held the sleeve of her black uniform over the wound, trying to staunch the blood. Her movements were clumsy, and she was not articulating clearly.

I stared at her in worried desperation for a moment, then realized what we must do.

'No,' I said firmly. 'I'll find it for you. You must get into the pressure-tube, otherwise you will be killed. We will be landing at any moment!'

I took her by the arm and propelled her gently to the flexible tube, which had hung unused for much of the flight. I took off the tunic of my uniform, and gave it to her as a temporary bandage. She held it to her face, and as she went into the tube the fabric closed about her. I entered my own, and laid my hand on the extended controls inside. As I did so, I felt the fabric tightening about my body. I glanced at Amelia to ensure that she was firmly held, then applied pressure to the green lever.

Watching the panel through the folds of fabric I saw the image become entirely obscured by a blaze of green, I allowed the fire to blast for several seconds, then released the lever.

The image in the panel cleared, and I saw that the grid had moved back to the west once again. It now lay directly across England, and we were dead on course.

However, the eastwards drift continued, and as I watched the two grids moved out of alignment. The shape of the British Isles was almost obscured by the night terminator, and I knew that in England some people would be seeing a sunset, little realizing what was to descend into their midst during the night.

While we were both still safe inside the pressure-tubes I decided to fire the engine again, and so over-compensate for the continual drifting. This time I allowed the green flame to burn for fifteen seconds, and when I looked again at the panel I saw that I had succeeded in shifting the centre of the bright grid to a point in the Atlantic several hundred miles to the west of Land's End.

Time for this kind of visual confirmation was short: in a few minutes Britain would have disappeared beyond the night terminator.

I released myself from the tube, and went to see Amelia.

'How do you feel?' I said.

She made to step forward from the constraint of the tube, but I held her back.

'I'll find your bag. Are you any better?'

She nodded, and I saw that the bleeding had virtually ceased. She looked a dreadful sight, for her hair had matted over the wound and there were smears of blood all over her face and chest.

I hastened about the compartment in search of the bag. I found it at last – it had lodged directly above the controls – and took it to her. Amelia reached through the tube and fumbled inside the bag until she found several pieces of white linen, folded neatly together.

While she pressed one of the pieces of the absorbent material to her wound, and dabbed off most of the blood, I wondered why she had never mentioned the existence of these towels before.

'I shall be all right now, Edward,' she said indistinctly from within. 'It is just a cut. You must concentrate on landing this hateful machine.'

I stared at her for a few seconds, seeing that she was crying. I realized that our journey was ending none too soon and that she, no less than I, could think of no happier moment than that in which we left this compartment.

I returned to my pressure-tube, and laid my hand on the lever.

IX

As the British Isles were now invisible in the night portion of the world, I had no other guide than the two grids. So long as I kept them in alignment then I knew that I was on course. This was not as simple as it may sound, for the degree of drift was increasing with every minute. The process was complicated by the fact that whenever 1 turned on the engine, the panel was deluged in green light, effectively blinding me. Only when I turned off the engine could I see what my last measure had achieved.

I established a routine of trial and error: first I would examine the panel to see how much drift had occurred, then fire the braking engine for a period. When I turned off the engine, I would look again at the panel and make a further estimate of the drift. Sometimes I would have estimated accurately, but usually I had either over- or under-compensated.

Each time I fired the engine it was for a longer period, and so I fell into a system whereby I counted slowly under my breath. Soon each blast – which I discovered could be made more or less intense by the degree of pressure on the lever – was lasting for a count of one hundred and more. The mental torment was tremendous, for the concentration it demanded was total; additionally, each time the engine was fired the physical pressures on us were almost intolerable. Around us, the temperature inside the compartment was rising. The air ducted down through the tubes remained cool, but I could feel the fabric itself becoming hot.

In the few brief moments between the firings of the engine, when the constraint of the tubes relaxed a little, Amelia and I managed to exchange a few words. She told me that the blood had stopped flowing, but that she had a vile headache and felt faint and sick.

Then at last the drifting of the two grids became so rapid that I dared not slacken my attention at all. The instant I turned off the engines the grids bounced apart, and I pressed the lever down and held it in place.

Now given its full throat, the braking engine set up a noise of such immensity that I felt the projectile itself must certainly break into pieces. The entire craft shuddered and rattled, and where my feet touched the metal floor I could feel an intolerable heat. Around us, the pressure-tubes gripped so tightly we could hardly breathe. I could not move even the tiniest muscle, and had no notion of how Amelia was faring. I could feel the tremendous power of the engine as if it were a solid object against which we were ramming, for even in spite of the restraining tubes, I felt myself being pushed forward against the braking. So, in this bedlam of noise and heat and pressure, the projectile blazed across the night sky of England like a green comet.

The end of our voyage, when it came, was abrupt and violent.

There was an almighty explosion outside the craft, accompanied by a stunning impact and concussion. Then, in the sudden silence that immediately followed, we fell forward from the relaxing pressure-tubes, into the blistering heat of the compartment.

We had arrived on Earth, but we were indeed in a sorry state.

EIGHTEEN

Inside the Pit

•

I

We lay unconscious in the compartment for nine hours, unaware, for the most part, of the terrible disorder our landing had thrown us into. Perhaps while we lay in this coma of exhaustion we were spared the worst effects of the experience, but what we endured was unpleasant enough.

The craft had not landed at an angle best suited to our convenience; because of the craft's axial spin the actual position in relation to the ground had been a matter of chance, and that chance had left both the pressure-tubes and our hammock suspended on what now became the walls. Moreover, the craft had collided with the ground at a sharp angle, so that the force of gravity tumbled us into the nose of the projectile.

That gravity itself felt immense. My attempts to approximate Earth's gravity by spinning the craft more quickly had been too conservative by far. After several months on Mars, and in the projectile, our normal weights felt intolerable.

As I have described, Amelia injured herself shortly before we started our landing, and this new fall had reopened the wound, and blood poured from her face more profusely than before. In addition, I had hit my head as we fell from the pressure-tubes.

Finally, and most unbearable of all, the interior of the craft was overwhelmingly hot and humid. Perhaps it had been the exhaust of the green fire that slowed our flight, or the friction of the Earth's atmosphere, or most probably a combination of the two, but the metal of the hull and the air it contained, and everything within were heated to an insupportable level.

This was the degree of disorder in which we lay unconscious, and this was the kind of squalor to which I awoke.

II

My first action was to turn to Amelia, who lay in a huddle across me. The bleeding from her injury had stopped of its own accord, but she was in a dreadful state; her face, hair and clothes were sticky with congealing blood. So still was she, and so quiet her breathing, that at first I was convinced she had died, and only when in a panic I shook her by the shoulders and slapped her face did she rouse.

We were lying in a shallow pool of water, which had gathered on the floor under the spray from a fractured pipe. This pool was very warm, for it had taken heat from the metal hull of the projectile, but the spray was as yet cool. I found Amelia's bag, and took from it two of her towels. These I soaked in the spray, and washed her face and hands, dabbing gently at the open wound. As far as I could see, there was no fracture of her cranium, but the flesh of her forehead, just below her hairline, was torn and bruised.

She said nothing while I washed her, and seemed not to be in pain. She flinched only when I cleaned the wound.

'I must get you to a more comfortable position,' I said, gently.

She simply took my hand, and squeezed it affectionately.

'Can you talk?' I said.

She nodded, then said: 'Edward, I love you.'

I kissed her, and she held me fondly against her. In spite of our dire circumstances I felt as if I had been relieved of a great weight; the tensions of the flight had dissipated.

'Do you feel well enough to move?' I said.

'I think so. I am a little unsteady.'

'I will support you,' I said.

I stood up first, feeling giddy, but I was able to balance myself by holding on to a part of the broken controls which now overhung us, and by extending a hand I helped Amelia to her feet. She was more shaken than I, so I put one arm around her waist. We moved further up the sloping floor of the projectile to a place where, although the gradient was steeper, at least there was somewhere dry and smooth to sit.

It was then that I took out my watch, and discovered that nine hours had passed since we crash-landed. What had the monsters done in the time we lay unconscious?!

III

Feeling very sorry for ourselves, we sat and rested for several more minutes, but I was obsessed by a sense of urgency. We could not delay leaving the projectile any longer than absolutely necessary. For all we knew, the monsters might even now be marching from their hold and launching their invasion.

Immediate concerns were still to be considered, though. One was the enervating heat in which we were sitting. The very floor on which we rested was almost hotter than we could bear, and all around us the metal plates radiated suffocating warmth. The air was moist and sticky, and every breath we took seemed devoid of oxygen. Much of the food that had spilled was slowly rotting, and the stench was sickening.

I had already loosened my clothes, but as the heat showed no sign of abating it seemed wise to undress. Once Amelia had recovered her wits I suggested this, then helped her off with the black uniform. Underneath she still wore the ragged garment I had seen her in at the slave-camp. It was unrecognizable as the crisp white chemise it had once been.

I was better off, for beneath my uniform I still wore my combination underwear which, in spite of my various adventures, was not at all unpresentable.

After some consideration we agreed it would be better if I explored the present situation alone. We had no idea how active were the monsters, assuming that they had not been killed by the concussion, and that it would be safer if I were by myself. So, having made absolutely sure that Amelia was comfortable, I let myself out of the compartment and set about the climb through the passages that ran through the hull.

It will be recalled that the projectile was very long: it was certainly not much less than three hundred feet from stem to stern. During our flight through space, movement about the craft had been relatively simple, because the axial rotation provided one with an artificial floor. Now, however, the craft had buried itself in the soil of Earth, and seemed to be standing on its nose, so that I was forced to climb at a very steep angle. In the heat, which was, if anything, greater in this part of the hull, the only advantage I had was that I knew my way about.

In due course I came to the hatch that led into the slaves' compartment. Here I paused to listen, but all was silent within. I climbed on after catching my breath, and eventually arrived at the hatch to the main hold.

I slid open the metal plate with some trepidation, knowing that the monsters were certainly awake and alert, but my caution was in vain. There was no sign of the beasts within my view, but I knew they were present for I could hear the sound of their horrid, braying voices. Indeed, this noise was quite remarkable in its intensity, and I gathered that much was being discussed between the nauseous beings.

At last I moved on, climbing beyond the door to the very stern of the craft itself. Here I had hoped to find some way by which Amelia and I might leave the ship surreptitiously. (I knew that if all else failed I could operate the green blast in the way I had done in the smaller projectile, and so shift it from its landing-place, but it was crucial that the monsters should not suspect that we were not their regular crew.)

Unfortunately, my way was barred. This was the very end of the craft: the massive hatch by which the monsters themselves would exit. The fact that it was still closed was in itself hopeful: if we could not leave by this way, then at least the monsters too were confined within.

Here I rested again, before making my descent. For a few moments I speculated about where I had landed the craft. If we had fallen in the centre of a city the violence of our landing would certainly have caused untold damage; this again would be a matter for chance, and here chance would be on our side. Much of England is sparsely built upon, and it was more than likely we would have found open countryside. I could do no more than hope; I had enough on my conscience.

I could still hear the monsters beyond the inner hull wall, addressing each other in their disagreeable braying voices, and occasionally I could hear the sinister sound of metal being moved. In moments of silence, though, I fancied I could hear other noises, emanating from beyond the hull.

Our spectacular arrival would almost certainly have brought crowds to the projectile, and as I stood precariously just inside the main rear hatch, my fevered imagination summoned the notion that just a few yards from where I was there would be scores, perhaps hundreds, of people clustered about.

It was a poignant thought, for of all things I hungered to be reunited with my own kind.

A little later, when I thought more calmly,! realized that any crowd that might have gathered would be in dire danger from these monsters. How much more grimly optimistic it was to think that the monsters would emerge to a ring of rifle-barrels!

Even so, as I waited there I felt sure I could hear human voices outside the projectile, and I almost wept to think of them there.

At long last, realizing that there was nothing to be done for the moment, I went back the way I had come and returned to Amelia.

IV

A long time passed, in which there seemed to be no movement either by the monsters within the ship, or by the men whom I now presumed were outside. Every two or three hours I would ascend again through the passages, but the hatch remained firmly closed.

The conditions inside our compartment continued to deteriorate, although there was a slight drop in the temperature. The lights were still on, and air was circulating, but the food was decomposing quickly and the smell was abominable. Furthermore, water was still pouring in from the fractured pipe, and the lower parts of the compartment were deeply flooded.

We stayed quiet, not knowing if the monsters could hear us, and dreading the consequences if they should. However, they seemed busied about their own menacing affairs, for there was no decline in their noise whenever I listened by their hatch.

Hungry, tired, hot and frightened, we huddled together on the metal floor of the projectile, waiting for a chance to escape.

We must have dozed for a while, for I awoke suddenly with a sense that there was a different quality to our surroundings. I glanced at my watch – which in lieu of a pocket in my combinations I had attached by its chain to a buttonhole – and saw that nearly twenty hours had elapsed since our arrival.

I woke Amelia, whose head rested on my shoulder.

'What is it?' she said.

'What can you smell?'

She sniffed exaggeratedly, wrinkling her nose.

'Something is burning,' I said.

'Yes,' Amelia said, then cried it aloud: 'Yes! I can smell wood-smoke!'

We were overcome with excitement and emotion, for no more homely smell could be imagined.

'The hatch,' I said urgently. 'It's open at last!'

Amelia was already on her feet. 'Come on, Edward! Before it's too late!'

I took her hand-bag, and led her up the sloping floor to the passage. I allowed her to go first, reasoning that I would then be below her if she fell. We climbed slowly, weakened by our ordeal ... but we were climbing for the last time, out of the hell of the Martian projectile, towards our freedom.

V

Sensing danger, we stopped a few yards short of the end of the passage, and stared up at the sky.

It was a deep blue; it was not at all like the Martian sky, but a cool and tranquil blue, the sort that one rejoices to see at the end of a hot summer's day. There were wisps of cirrus cloud, high and peaceful, still touched with the red of sunset. Lower down, though, thick clouds of smoke rolled by, heady with the smell of burning vegetation.

'Shall we go on?' Amelia said, whispering.

'I feel uneasy,' I said. 'I had expected there would be many people about. It's too quiet.'

Then, belying my words, there was a resounding clatter of metal, and I saw a brilliant flash of green.

'Are the monsters out already?' said Amelia.

'I shall have to look. Stay here, and don't make a sound.'

'You aren't leaving me?' There was an edge to her voice, making her words sound tense and brittle.

'I'm just going to the end,' I said. 'We must see what is happening.'

'Be careful, Edward. Don't be noticed.'

I passed her the hand-bag, then crawled on up. I was in a turmoil of sensations, some of them internal ones, like fright and trepidation, but others were external. I knew that I was breathing the air of Earth, smelling the soil of England.

At last I came to the lip, and lay low against the metal floor. I pulled myself forward until just my eyes peered out into the evening light. There, in the vast pit thrown up by our violent landing, I saw a sight that filled me with dread and terror.

Immediately beneath the circular end of the projectile was the discarded hatch. This was a huge disk of metal, some eighty feet in diameter. It had once been the very bulkhead which had withstood the blast of our launch, but now, unscrewed from within, and dropped to the sandy floor, it lay, its use finished.

Beyond it, the Martian monsters had already started their work of assembling their devilish machinery.

All five of the brutes were out of the craft, and they worked in a frenzy of activity. Two of them were painstakingly attaching a leg to one of the battle-machines, which squatted a short distance from where I lay. I saw that it was not yet ready for use, for its other two legs were telescoped so that the platform was no more than a few feet from the ground. Two other monsters worked beside the platform, but each of these was inside a small legged vehicle, with mechanical arms supporting the bulk of the tripod while shorter extensions hammered at the metal plates. With every blow there was a bright flash of green light, and an eerie smoke, yellow and green combined, drifted away on the breeze.

The fifth monster was taking no part in this activity.

It squatted on the flat surface of the discarded hatch, just a few feet from me. Here a heat-cannon had been mounted in a metal structure so that its barrel pointed directly upwards. Above the support was a long, telescopic mounting, at the top of which was a parabolic mirror some two feet in diameter. This was presently being rotated by the monster, which pressed one of its bland, saucer-like eyes to a sighting instrument. Even as I watched, the monster jerked spasmically in hatred, and a pale, deathly beam – clearly visible in Earth's denser air – swept out over the rim of the pit.

In the distance I heard a confusion of shouts, and heard the crackle of burning timber and vegetation.

I ducked down for a few seconds, unable to participate in even this passive way; I felt that by inaction I became a party to slaughter.

That this was not the first time the beam had been used was amply evidenced, for when I looked again across the pit I noticed that along one edge were the charred bodies of several people. I did not know why the people had been by the pit when the monsters struck, but it seemed certain that now the monsters were keeping further intruders away while the machines were assembled.

The parabolic mirror continued to rotate above the rim of the pit, but while I watched the heat-beam was not used again.

I turned my attention to the monsters themselves. I saw, with horror, that the increased gravity of Earth had wrought gross distortions to their appearance. I have already noted how soft were the bodies of these execrable beings; with the increased pressure on them, the bladder-like bodies became distended and flattened. The one nearest to me seemed to have grown by about fifty percent, which is to say it was now six or seven feet long. Its tentacles were no longer, but they too were being flattened by the pressure and seemed more than ever snake-like. The face too had altered. Although the eyes – always the most prominent feature – remained unmarked, the beak-like mouth had developed a noticeable V-shape, and the creatures' breathing was more laboured. A viscous saliva dribbled continually from their mouths.

I had never been able to see these monsters with feelings less than loathing, and seeing them in this new aspect I could hardly control myself. I allowed myself to slip back from my vantage-point, and lay trembling for several minutes.

When I had recovered my composure, I crawled back to where Amelia was waiting, and in a hoarse whisper managed to relate what I had seen.

'I must see for myself,' Amelia said, preparing to make her own way to the end of the passage.

'No,' I said, holding her arm. 'It's too dangerous. If you were seen—'

'Then the same will happen to me that would have happened to you.' Amelia freed herself from me, and climbed slowly up the steep passageway. I watched in agonized silence as she reached the end, and peered out into the pit.

She was there for several minutes, but at last she returned safely. Her face was pale.

She said: 'Edward, once they have assembled that machine there will be no stopping them.'

'They have four more waiting to be assembled,' I said.

'We must somehow alert the authorities.'

'But we cannot move from here! You have seen the slaughter in the pit. Once we show ourselves we will be as good as dead.'

'We have to do something.'

I thought for a few minutes. Obviously, the police and Army could not be unaware that the arrival of this projectile presented a terrible threat. What we needed to do now was not alert the authorities, but to apprise them of the extent of the threat. They could have no notion that another nine projectiles were flying towards Earth at this very moment.

I was trying to stay calm. I could not see that the Army would be helpless against these monsters. Any mortal being that could die by the knife could be disposed of as easily with bullets or shells. The heat-beam was a terrifying and deadly weapon, but it did not make the Martians invulnerable. Further weighing against the invaders was the fact of our Earthly gravity. The battle-machines were all-powerful in the light gravity and thin air of Mars; would they be so agile or dangerous here on Earth?

A little later I crawled again to the end of the passage, hoping that under the cover of darkness Amelia and I would be able to slip away.

Night had indeed fallen, and any moonlight there might have been was obscured by the thick clouds of smoke that drifted from the burning heath, but the Martians worked on through the night, with great floodlamps surrounding the machines. The first battle-machine was evidently completed, for it stood, on its telescoped legs, at the far end of the pit. Meanwhile, the components of a second were being taken from the hold.

I stayed at the vantage-point for a long time, and after a while Amelia joined me. The Martian monsters did not so much as look our way even once, and so we were able to watch their preparations undisturbed.

The monsters paused in their work only once. That was when, in the darkest part of the night, and exactly twenty-four hours after our own arrival, a second projectile roared overhead in a blaze of brilliant green. It landed with a shattering explosion no more than two miles away.

At this, Amelia took my hand, and I held her head against my chest while she sobbed quietly.

VI

For the rest of that night and for most of the next day we were forced to stay in hiding inside the projectile. Sometimes we dozed, sometimes we crawled to the end of the passage to see if escape was possible, but for most of the time we crouched silently and fearfully in an uncomfortable corner of the passage.

It was unpleasant to realize that events were already beyond our control. We had been reduced to spectators, privy to the war-preparations of an implacable enemy. Moreover, we were much exercised by the knowledge that we sat in some corner of England, surrounded by familiar sights, people, language and customs, and yet were obliged by circumstances to huddle inside an artifact alien to our world.

Some time after midday, the first sign that the military forces were responding came in the form of distant sounds of artillery. The shells exploded a mile or two away, and we understood at once what must be happening. Clearly, the Army was shelling the second projectile before its grisly occupants could escape.

The Martians we were watching responded to this challenge at once. At the first sounds of the explosions, one of the monsters went to the battle-machine first assembled and climbed into it.

The machine set off at once, its legs groaning under the strain of the extra gravity and emitting several flashes of green from the joints. I noticed that the platform was not raised to its full height, but crawled along just above the ground like an iron tortoise.

We knew that if the second pit was being shelled then ours would be too, and so Amelia and I returned to the deeper recesses of the projectile, hoping that the hull would be strong enough to withstand explosions. The distant shelling continued for about half an hour, but eventually halted.

There followed a long period of silence, and we judged it safe to return to the end of the passage to see what the Martians were now doing.

Their frenzied activity continued. The battle-machine that had left the pit had not returned, but of the remaining four, three were standing by ready for use, and the last was being assembled. We watched this for about an hour, and just as we were about to return to our hiding-place to take a rest, there came a flurry of explosions all about the pit. It was our turn to be shelled!

Once again the Martians responded instantly. Three of the monstrous brutes hurried to the completed battle-machines – their bodies were already adapting to the stresses of our world! – and mounted the platforms. The fourth, sitting inside one of the assembly vehicles, continued stoically with its work on the last battle-machine.

Meanwhile, the shells continued to fall with varying degrees of accuracy; none fell directly into the pit, but some were close enough to send grit and sand flying about.

With their Martian drivers aboard, the three battle-machines came dramatically to life. With appalling speed the platforms were raised to their full one hundred feet height, the legs struck out up the sides of the pit, and wheeling around, the deadly devices went their separate ways, the heat-cannons already raised for action. In less than thirty seconds of the first shells exploding around us, the three battle-machines had gone: one towards the south, one to the north-west, and the last in the direction of the second projectile.

The last Martian monster worked hurriedly on its own tripod; this creature alone now stood between us and freedom.

A shell exploded nearby: the closest yet. The blast scorched our faces, and we fell back into the passage.

When I could again summon enough courage to look out I saw that the Martian continued its work, untroubled by the shelling. It was certainly the behaviour of a soldier under fire; it knew that it risked death but was prepared to confront it, while it readied its own counterattack.

The shelling lasted for ten minutes and in all that time no hits were scored. Then, with great suddenness, the firing halted and we guessed that the Martians had silenced the emplacement.

In the uncanny silence that followed, the Martian continued its work. At last it was finished. The hideous creature climbed into its platform, extended the legs to their full height, then turned the craft southwards and was soon lost to sight.

Without further delay we took the opportunity so presented to us. I jumped down to the sandy soil, landing awkwardly and heavily, then held out my arms to catch Amelia as she jumped.

We looked neither to right nor left, but scrambled up the loose soil of the pit walls, and hurried away in the direction no machine had so far travelled: towards the north. It was a hot, sultry evening, with dark banks of cloud building up in the west. A storm was brewing, but that was not the reason no bird sang, no animal moved. The heath was dead: it was blackened with fire, littered with the wreckage of vehicles and the corpses of both horse and man.

NINETEEN

How We Fell In With The Philosopher

•

I

On Mars I had dreamed of greenery and wild flowers; here on the blighted heath we saw only charred and smouldering grasses, with blackness spreading in every direction. On Mars I had hungered for the sights and sounds of my fellow Earthmen; here there was no one, only the corpses of those unfortunates who had fallen foul of the heat-beam. On Mars I had gasped in the tenuous atmosphere, yearning for the sweet air of Earth; here the odour of fire and death dried our throats and choked our lungs.

Mars was desolation and war, and just as Amelia and I had been touched by it when there, so Earth now felt the first tendrils of the Martian canker.

II

Behind us, to the south, there was a small town on a hill, and already the battle-machines had attacked it. A huge pall of smoke hung over the town, adding to the piling storm-clouds above, and through the still evening air we could hear the sounds of explosions and screams.

To the west we saw the brazen cowl of one of the machines,

turning from side lo side as its great engine bore it striding through distant, burning trees. Thunder rumbled, and there was no sign of the Army.

We hastened away, but we were both weak from our ordeal inside the projectile, we had had nothing to eat, and had hardly slept, for two days. Consequently our progress was slow in spite of the urgency of our escape. I stumbled twice, and we were both afflicted with painful stitches in our sides.

Blindly we ran, dreading that the Martians would see us and deal to us the summary execution they had dealt to others. But it was not mere instinct for self-preservation that urged us on our way; although we did not wish to die, we both realized that only we knew the full scale of the threat that was before the world.

At last we came to the edge of the common, and the ground fell down to where a small brook ran through trees. The top branches had been blackened by the sweep of the beam, but below was moist grass and a flower or two.

Sobbing with fear and exhaustion, we fell by the water and scooped up handfuls and drank noisily and deeply. To our palates long jaded by the bitter, metallic waters of Mars, this stream was pure indeed!

While we had been running frantically across the common, the evening had turned to night, speeded by the storm-clouds that were gathering. Now the rumbles of thunder were louder and came more often, and sheet-lightning flickered. It could not be long before the storm broke about us. We should be moving on as soon as possible: our vague plan to alert the authorities was all we lived for, even though we knew that there could be few people who did not realize that some mighty destructive force had erupted on to the land.

We lay low by the stream for about ten minutes. I placed my arm around Amelia's shoulders, and held her to me protectively, but we did not speak. I think we were both too overawed by the immensity of the damage to find words to express our feelings. This was England, the country we loved, and this was what we had brought to it!

When we stood up we saw that the fires caused by the Martians were burning still, and to the west we saw new flames. Where were the defences of our people? The first projectile had landed nearly two days ago; surely by now the whole area would be ringed by guns?

We did not have long to wait for an answer to that, and for a few hours it afforded us a certain reassurance.

III

The storm broke a few moments after we left our temporary refuge. Quite suddenly we were deluged with rain, of an intensity that took us completely by surprise. Within seconds we were both drenched to the skin.

I was all for taking shelter until the cloudburst had passed, but Amelia let go of my hand, and danced away from me. I saw her lit by the distant flames, the glow of red touching her. The rain was plastering her long hair about her face, and the bedraggled chemise clung wetly to her skin. She held up her palms to the downpour, and swept back the hair from her face. Her mouth was open, and I heard her laughing aloud. Then she turned about, stamping and splashing in the puddles; she took my hand, and whirled me gaily. In a moment I caught the joyous, sensuous mood from her, and together in that dark countryside we sang and laughed hysterically, totally abandoning ourselves to the thrill of the rain.

The cloudburst eased, and as the thunder and lightning intensified we sobered. I kissed Amelia fondly and briefly, and we walked on with our arms about each other.

A few minutes later we crossed a road, but there was no traffic of any kind, and shortly after this we approached more woodland. Behind us, now two miles or more away, we could see the town burning on the hill, the flames not doused by the rain.

Just as we walked beneath the first of the trees, Amelia suddenly pointed to the right. There, lined up under the cover of the woodland, was a small artillery battery, the barrels of the ordnance poking out through the camouflage of bushes and shrubs.

We had been noticed by the soldiers at the same moment – for the lightning still flickered with disconcerting brilliance – and an officer dressed in a long cape, gleaming in the rain, came over to us.

I went to him immediately. I could not see his face in the darkness, for his cap was pulled well down against the rain. Two gunners stood a short distance behind him, sparing us little attention, for they were staring back the way we had come.

'Are you in command here?' I said.

'Yes, sir. Have you come from Woking?'

'Is that the town on the hill?'

He confirmed this. 'Nasty business there I believe, sir. A lot of civilian casualties.'

'Do you know what you are up against?' I said.

'I've heard the rumours.'

'It is no ordinary enemy,' I said, raising my voice a little. 'You must destroy their pit immediately.'

'I have my orders, sir,' the officer said, and just at that moment there was a brilliant flash of lightning, repeated three times, and I saw his face for the first time. He was a man in his mid-twenties, and the clean, regular lines of his face were so unexpectedly human that for a moment I was dumbfounded. In that same illuminating flash he must have seen Amelia and me too, and noticed our untidy state. He went on: 'The men have heard rumours that these are men from Mars.'

'Not men,' Amelia said, stepping forward. 'Evil, destructive monsters.'

'Have you seen them, sir?' the officer said to me.

'I have more than seen them!' I cried over the rumbling of thunder. 'We came with them from Mars!'

The officer turned away at once, and signed to the two gunners. They came over directly.

'These two civilians,' he said. 'See them to the Chertsey Road, and report back.'

'You must listen to me!' I cried to the officer. 'These monsters must be killed at the first opportunity!'

'My orders are quite explicit, sir,' the officer said, preparing to turn away. 'The Cardigan is the finest regiment of horse-artillery in the British Army, a fact which even you, in your present deranged state, must admit.'

I stepped forward angrily, but I was caught by one of the soldiers. I struggled, and shouted: 'We are not deranged! You must shell their pit at once!'

The officer looked at me sympathetically for a moment or two – evidently assuming that I had seen my house and property destroyed, and was thus temporarily demented – then turned away and splashed across the muddy ground towards a row of tents.

The gunner holding me said: 'C'mon, sir. Ain't no place for civvies.'

I saw that the other soldier was holding Amelia by the arm, and I shouted at him to leave her go. This he did, so I took her arm myself and allowed the soldiers to lead us past the horse-lines – where the poor animals bucked and whinnied, their coats slick with rain – and into the heart of the wood. We walked for several minutes, during which we learned that the detachment had ridden down from Aldershot Barracks that afternoon, but no more information, then came to a road.

Here the soldiers pointed the way to Chertsey, then headed back to their emplacement.

I said to Amelia: 'They can have no idea of what they are facing.'

She was more philosophical than I. 'But they are alert to the danger, Edward. We cannot tell them what to do. The Martians will be contained on the common.'

'There are eight more projectiles to land!' I said.

'Then they will have to deal with them one by one.' She took my hand affectionately, and we started to walk up the road towards Chertsey. 'I think we must be careful how we tell people of our adventures.'

I took this as a mild rebuke, so I said defensively: 'The time was wrong. He thought I was mad.'

'Then we must be more calm.'

I said: 'There is already word about that the projectiles are from Mars. How could they have known?'

'I do not know. But I am sure of one thing, and it is a matter of importance to us both. We know where we are, Edward. We have landed in Surrey.'

'I wish I had thrown us into the sea.'

'If we are going to Chertsey,' Amelia said, not at all affected by my pessimism, 'then we are not a dozen miles from Sir William's house in Richmond!'

IV

As we entered Chertsey it was clear that the town had been evacuated. The first sign we saw of this was as we passed the station, and noticed that the metal gates had been drawn across the passenger entrance. Beyond them, a chalked sign declared that the train service had been suspended until further notice.

Further on into the town, walking through unlighted roads, we saw not a single lamp in any of the houses, nor anyone about the streets. We walked as far as the River Thames, but all we could see here were several boats and dinghies bobbing at their moorings.

The thunderstorm had passed, although it continued to rain, and we were both chilled through.

'We must find somewhere to rest,' I said. 'We are both done for.'

Amelia nodded wearily, and held a little tighter to my arm. I was glad for her sake that there was no one about to see us: our abrupt return to civilization served to remind me that Amelia, in her torn and wet chemise, was as good as unclothed, and I was little better dressed.

Amelia made an instant decision. 'We must break into one of the houses. We cannot sleep in the open.'

'But the Martians – '

'We can leave those to the Army. My dearest, we must rest.'

There were several houses backing on to the river, but as we moved from one to the other we realized that the evacuation must have been orderly and without panic, for each was securely shuttered and locked.

At last we came to a house, in a road only a short distance from the river, where a window came free as I pushed at it. I climbed inside at once, then went through and opened the door for Amelia. She came in, shivering, and I warmed her with my own body.

'Take off your chemise,' I said. 'I will find you some clothes.'

I left her sitting in the scullery, for the range had been alight during the day, and there it was still warm. I went through the rooms upstairs, but found to my dismay that all the clothes-cupboards had been emptied, even in the servants' quarters. However, I did find several blankets and towels, and took them downstairs. Here I stripped off my combinations, and placed them with Amelia's tattered chemise over the bar at the front of the range. While I had been upstairs I had discovered that the water in the tank was still hot, and while we huddled in our blankets beside the range I told Amelia she might have a bath.

Her response to this news was of such innocent and uninhibited delight that I did not add that there was probably only enough hot water for one.

While I had searched for clothes, Amelia had not herself been idle. She had discovered some food in the pantry, and although it was all cold it tasted wonderful. I think I shall never forget that first meal we ate after our return: salted beef, cheese, tomatoes and a lettuce taken from the garden. We were even able to drink some wine with it, for the house had a modest cellar.

We dared not light any of the lamps for the houses around us were darkened, and if any of the Martians should happen by they would immediately see us. Even so, I searched the house for some kind of newspaper or magazine, hoping to learn from it what had been known of the projectiles before the Martians broke free of the pit. However, the house had been effectively cleared of all but what we found around us, and we remained unenlightened on this score.

At last Amelia said she would take her bath, and a little later I heard the sound of the water being run. Then she returned.

She said: 'We are accustomed to sharing most things, Edward, and I think you are as dirty as I.'

And so it was that while we lay together in the steaming water, genuinely relaxing for the first time since our escape, we saw the green glare of the third projectile as it fell to the ground several miles to the south.

V

So exhausted were we that in the morning we slept on far beyond any reasonable hour; it was, considering the emergency, an undesirable thing to do, but our encounter with the artillery the evening before had reassured us, and our fatigued bodies craved for rest. Indeed, when I awoke my first thoughts were not at all of the Martians. I had, the evening before, set my watch by the clock in the drawing-room, and as soon as I was awake I looked at it, and discovered that it was a quarter to eleven. Amelia was still asleep beside me, and as I gently touched her to awaken her I was smitten with the first feelings of unease about the casual way we were behaving together. It had been as a natural result of our confinement together on Mars that we had started acting as man and wife, and much as it was of great pleasure to me – and, I knew, to Amelia too – the very familiarity of our surroundings, the pleasant villa in the quiet riverside town, reminded me that we were now back in our own society. Soon we would reach a place where the awful impact of the Martians was not yet felt, and then it would be incumbent upon us to observe the social customs of our country. What had passed between us before we fell asleep became improper in our present surroundings.

Beyond the house the countryside was silent. I heard birds singing, and on the river the noise of the boats knocking together at their moorings ... but there were no wheels, no footsteps, no hooves clattering on the metalled roads.

'Amelia,' I said softly. 'We must be on our way if we wish to reach Richmond.'

She awoke then, and for a few seconds we embraced fondly.

She said: 'Edward ... what is that noise?'

We lay still, and then I too heard what had attracted her attention. It was akin to a large weight being dragged ... we heard bushes and trees rustling, gravel being ground, and above all a grating of metal upon metal.

For an instant I froze in terror, then broke free of the paralysis and bounded out of bed. I rushed across the room, and threw open the curtains incautiously. As the sunlight burst in I saw that directly outside our window was one of the jointed metal legs of a battle-machine! As I stared at it in horror, there was a gusting of green smoke at the joints, and the elevated engine propelled it on beyond the house.

Amelia had seen it too, and she sat up in the bed, clutching the sheets about her body.

I hurried back to her, appalled by the amount of time we had wasted. 'We must leave at once.'

'With that outside the house?' Amelia said. 'Where has it gone?'

She scrambled out of the bed, and together we went quietly across the top floor of the house to a room on the other side. This was a child's bedroom, for the floor was littered with toys. Peering through the half-drawn curtains, we looked across in the direction of the river.

There were three battle-machines in sight. Their platforms were not raised to their full height, nor were their heat-cannons visible. Instead, what seemed to be an immense metal net had been attached to the rear of each platform, and into these nets were being placed the inert bodies of human beings who had been electrocuted by the dangling, metal tentacles. In the net of the battle-machine nearest us there were already seven or eight people, lying in a tangled heap where they had been dropped.

As we stared in dismay at the sight, we saw the metal tentacles of one of the more distant machines insinuate itself into a house ... and after about thirty seconds withdrew, clutching the unconscious body of a little girl.

Amelia covered her face with her hands, and turned away.

I stayed at the window for another ten minutes, immobilized by the fear of being noticed, and by the equal horror of what I was witnessing. Soon, a fourth machine appeared, and that too bore its share of human spoils. Behind me, Amelia lay on the child's bed, sobbing quietly.

'Where is the Army?' I said softly, repeating the words again and again. It was unthinkable that these atrocities should go unchallenged. Had the battery we had seen the night before allowed the monsters to pass undamaged? Or had a brief engagement already been fought, out of which the monsters had emerged unscathed?

Fortunately for Amelia and myself, the Martians' foraging expedition seemed to be at its end, for the battle-machines stood about, their drivers in apparent consultation. At length, one of the legged ground vehicles appeared, and in a short space of time the unconscious bodies were transferred to this.

Sensing that there was to be a new development, I asked Amelia to go downstairs and collect our clothes. This she did, returning almost at once. As soon as I had put on mine, I left Amelia on guard at the window, then went from one room to the next, looking to see if there were any more of the battle-machines in the vicinity. There was only one other in sight, and that was about a mile away, to the south-east.

I heard Amelia calling me, and I hurried back to her. She pointed wordlessly: the four battle-machines were turning away from us, striding slowly towards the west. Their platforms were still low, their heat-cannons as yet unraised.

'This is our chance,' I said. 'We can take a boat and head for Richmond.'

'But is it safe?'

'No safer than at any other time. It's a chance we must take. We will keep a constant watch, and at the first sign of the Martians we'll take refuge by the bank.'

Amelia looked doubtful, but put forward no other objection.

There was a trace of conformity still within us, in spite of the terrible anarchy around us, and we did not leave the house until Amelia had penned a brief note to the owner, apologizing for breaking in and promising to pay in due course for the food we had consumed.

VI

The storms of the day before had passed, and the morning was sunny, hot and still. We wasted no time in getting down to the riverside, and walked out on one of the wooden jetties to where several rowing-boats were moored, I selected what seemed to me to be a solid boat, and yet one not too heavy. I helped Amelia into it, then climbed in after her and cast off at once.

There was no sign of any of the battle-machines, but even so I rowed close to the northern bank, for here weeping willows grew beside the river and their branches overhung in many places.

We had been rowing for no more than two minutes when to our alarm there came a burst of artillery-fire from close at hand. At once I stopped rowing, and looked all about.

'Get down, Amelia!' I shouted, for I had seen over the roofs of Chertsey the four battle-machines returning. Now the glittering Titans were at their full height, and their heat-cannons were raised. The shells of the artillery exploded in the air about them, but no damage was inflicted that I could see.

Amelia had thrown herself forward across the planks at the bottom of the boat, and she crawled towards where I was sitting. She held on to my legs, clutching me as if this alone would turn the Martians away. We watched as the battle-machines abruptly altered their course, and headed towards the artillery emplacement on the northern bank opposite Chertsey. The speed of the machines was prodigious. As they reached the river's edge they did not hesitate, but plunged in, throwing up an immense spray. All the time their heat-beams were flashing forward, and in a moment we heard no more firing from our men.

In the same instant, Amelia pointed towards the east. Here, near where Weybridge was situated, the fifth battle-machine – the one I had seen earlier from the house – was charging at full spate towards the river. It had attracted the attentions of more artillery placed by Shepperton, and as it charged its gleaming platform was surrounded with fireballs from the exploding shells. None of these hit home, though, and we saw the Martian's heat-cannon swinging from side to side. The beam fell across Weybridge, and instantly sections of the town burst into flame. Weybridge itself, though, was not the machine's chosen target, for it too continued until it reached the river, and waded in at a furious speed.

Then came a moment of short-lived triumph for the Army. One of the artillery shells found its target, and with a shocking violence the platform exploded into fragments. With scarcely a pause, and as if possessed of a life of its own, the battle-machine staggered on, careening and swaying. After a few seconds it collided with the tower of a church near Shepperton, and fell back into the river. As the heat-cannon made contact with the water its furnace exploded, sending up an enormous cloud of spray and steam.

All this had taken place in less than a minute, the very speed at which the Martians were capable of making war being a decisive factor in their supremacy.

Before we had time to recover our senses, the four battle-machines which had silenced the Chertsey battery went to aid their fallen comrade. The first we knew of this was when we heard a great hissing and splashing, and glancing upstream we saw the four mighty machines racing through the water towards us. We had no time to think of hiding or escaping; indeed, so stricken with terror were we that the Martians were on us before we could react. To our own good luck, the monsters had no thought or time for us, for they were engaged in a greater war. Almost before they were beyond us, the heat-cannons were spraying their deadly beams, and once more the deep, staccato voice of the artillery by Shepperton spoke its ineffectual reply.

Then came a sight I have no wish ever to witness again. The deliberation and malice of the Martian invaders was never realized in a more conclusive fashion.

One machine went towards the artillery at Shepperton, and, ignoring the shells which burst about its head, calmly silenced the guns with a long sweep of its beam. Another, standing beside it, set about the systematic destruction of Shepperton itself. The other two battle-machines, standing in the confusion of islands where the Wey meets the Thames, dealt death upon Weybridge. Without compunction, both man and his effects were blasted and razed, and across the green Surrey meadows we heard one detonation after another, and the clamour of voices raised in the terror that precedes a violent death.

When the Martians had finished their evil work the land became silent again ... but there was no stillness about. Weybridge burned, and Shepperton burned. Steam from the river mingled with smoke from the towns, joining in a great column that poured into the cloudless sky.

The Martians, unchallenged once more, folded away their cannons, and congregated at the bend of the river where the first battle-machine had fallen. As the platforms rotated to and fro, the bright sunlight reflected from the burnished cowls.

VII

During all this Amelia and I had been so taken with the events about us that we failed to notice that our boat continued to drift with the stream. Amelia still crouched at the bottom of the boat, but I had shipped my oars and sat on the wooden seat.

I looked at Amelia, and with my voice reflecting in its hoarseness the terror I felt, I said: 'If this is a measure of their power, the Martians will conquer the world!'

'We cannot sit by and allow that to happen.'

'What do you propose we do?'

'We must get to Richmond,' she said. 'Sir William will be better placed to know.'

'Then we must row on,' I said.

In my terrible confusion I had overlooked the fact that four battle-machines stood between us and Richmond at that very moment, and so I took the oars and placed them in the water again. I took just one stroke, when behind me I heard a tremendous splashing of water, and Amelia screamed,

'They're coming this way!'

I released the oars at once, and they slipped into the water.

'Lie still!' I cried to Amelia. Putting my own words into effect, I threw myself backwards, lying at an awkward and painful angle across the wooden seat. Behind me I heard the tumultuous splashing of the battle-machines as they hurtled up-river. We were now drifting almost in the centre of the stream, and so lay directly in their path!

The four were advancing abreast of one another, and lying as I was I could see them upside-down. The wreckage of the battle-machine struck by the shell had been retrieved by the others, and now, carried between them, was being taken back the way they had come. I saw for an instant the torn and blasted metal that had been the platform, and saw too that there was gore and blood about much of it. I derived no satisfaction from the death of one monster-creature, for what was this to the spiteful destruction of two towns and the murder of countless people?

If the monsters had chosen to slay us then we would have had no chance of survival, yet once again we were spared by their preoccupations. Their victory over the two hapless towns was emphatic, and such stray survivors as ourselves were of no consequence. They closed on us with breathtaking speed, almost obscured by the clouds of spray thrown up by their churning legs. One of these sliced into the water not three yards from our little boat, and we were instantly deluged. The boat rocked and yawed, taking in water in such copious quantities that I felt we must surely sink.

Then, in a few seconds, the tripods were gone, leaving us waterlogged and unsteady on the troubled river.

VIII

It took us several minutes of paddling to retrieve our oars, and to bale out the water to make the boat manoeuvrable again. By then the Martian battle-machines had vanished towards the south, presumably heading for their pit on the common by Woking.

Considerably shaken by the prolonged incident I set myself to rowing, and in a few minutes we were passing the blasted remains of Weybridge.

If survivors there were, we saw none about. A ferry had been plying as the Martians struck, and we saw its upturned and blackened hull awash in the river. On the towpath lay scores, perhaps hundreds, of charred bodies of those who had suffered directly under the heat-beam. The town itself was well ablaze, with few if any buildings left untouched by the murderous attack. It was like a scene from a nightmare, for when a town burns in silence, unattended, it is no less than a funeral pyre.

There were many bodies in the water, presumably of those people who had thought that there lay refuge. Here the Martians, with their magnificent and wicked cunning, had turned their heat-beams on the river itself, so raising its temperature to that of boiling. As we rowed through, the water was still steaming and bubbling, and when Amelia tested it with her hand she snatched it away. Many of the bodies which floated here revealed by the brilliant redness of their skins that the people had been, quite literally, boiled to death. Fortunately for our sensibilities, the steam had the effect of obscuring our surroundings, and so, as we passed through the carnage, we were spared the sight of much of it.

It was with considerable relief that we turned the bend in the river, but our agonies were not at an end, for now we could see what damage had been inflicted on Shepperton. At Amelia's urging I rowed more quickly, and in a few minutes I had taken us beyond the worst.

Once we had turned another bend I slackened off a little, for I was rapidly tiring. We were both in a terrible state as a result of what we had seen, and so I pulled into the bank. We climbed to the shore and sat down in a heady state of shock. What passed between us then I will not relate, but our agonizing was much coloured by our acceptance of complicity in this devastation.

By the time we had recovered our wits, two hours had passed, and our resolve to play a more active role in fighting these monsters had hardened. So it was with renewed sense of urgency that we returned to the boat. Sir William Reynolds, if he were not already engaged in the problem, would be able to propose some more subtle solution than the Army had so far devised.

By now there was only the occasional piece of floating wreckage to remind us of what we had seen, but the memories were clear enough. From the moment of the Martians' onslaught we had seen no one alive, and even now the only apparent movement was the smoke.

The rest had restored my strength, and I returned to the rowing with great vigour, taking long, easy strokes.

In spite of everything we had experienced, the day was all that I had hungered for while on Mars. The breeze was soft, and the sun was warm. The green trees and grasses of the banks were a joy to the eye, and we saw and heard many birds and insects. All this, and the pleasant regularity of my rowing, served to order my thoughts.

Would the Martians, now they had demonstrated their supremacy, be satisfied to consolidate their position? If so, how much time would this give our military forces to essay new tactics? Indeed, what was the strength of our forces? Apart from the three artillery batteries we had seen and heard, the Army was nowhere evident.

Beyond this, I felt that we needed to adjust to our actual circumstances. In some ways, Amelia and I had been living still to the routines we had established inside the projectile, which is to say that our lives were patterned by the dominance of the Martians. Now, though, we were in our own land, one where places had names we could recognize, and where there were days and weeks by which one ordered one's life. We had established whereabouts in England we had landed, and we could see that England was enjoying a summer of splendid weather, even if other climates were foreboding, but we did not know which day of the week this was, nor even in which month we were.

It was on such matters, admittedly rather trivial, that I was dwelling as I brought our boat around the bend in the river that lies just above the bridge at Walton-on-Thames. Here it was that we saw the first living person that day: a young man, wearing a dark jacket. He sat in the reeds by the edge of the water, staring despondently across the river.

I pointed him out to Amelia, and at once altered course and headed towards him.

As we came closer I could see that he was a man of the cloth. He seemed very youthful, for his figure was slight and his head was topped with a mass of flaxen curls. Then we saw that lying on the ground beside him was the body of another man. He was more stoutly built, and his body – which from the waist up was naked – was covered with the filth of the river.

Still dwelling on my rather trivial thoughts of the moments before, I called out to the curate as soon as we were within hailing distance.

'Sir,' I shouted, 'what day is this?'

The curate stared back at us, then stood up unsteadily. I could see he had been severely shocked by his experiences for his hands were never still, fretting with the torn front of his jacket. His gaze was vacant and uncertain as he answered me.

'It is the Day of Judgement, my children.'

Amelia had been staring at the man lying beside the curate, and she asked: 'Father, is that man alive?'

No answer was forthcoming, for the curate had turned distractedly away from us. He made as if to move off, but then turned back and looked down at us.

'Do you need any help, Father?' Amelia said.

'Who can offer help when it is God's wrath vented upon us?'

'Edward... row in to the shore.'

I said: 'But what can we do to help?'

Nevertheless, I plied the oars and in a moment we had scrambled ashore. The curate watched as we knelt beside the prostrate man. We saw at once that he was not dead, nor even unconscious, but was turning restlessly as if in a delirium.

'Water ... have you any water?' he said, his lips parched. I saw that his skin had a slightly reddened cast to it, as if he too had been caught when the Martians boiled the river.

'Have you not given him any water?' I said to the curate.

'He keeps asking for it, but we are beside a river of blood.'

I glanced at Amelia, and saw by her expression that my own opinion of the poor, distracted curate was confirmed.

'Amelia,' I said quietly, 'see if you can find something to bring water in.'

I returned my attention to the delirious man, and in desperation I slapped him lightly about his face. This seemed to break through the delirium for he sat up at once, shaking his head.

Amelia had found a bottle by the river's edge, and she brought this and gave it to the man. He raised it thankfully to his lips, and drank deeply. I noticed that he was now in command of his senses, and he was looking shrewdly at the young curate.

The curate saw how we were helping the man, and this seemed to disconcert him. He gazed across the meadows in the direction of the distant, shattered tower of Shepperton Church.

He said: 'What does it mean? All our work is undone! It is the vengeance of God, for he hath taken away the children. The burning smoke goeth up for ever ...'

With this cryptic incantation, he strode off determinedly through the long grass, and was soon out of our sight.

The man coughed a few times, and said: 'I cannot thank you enough. I thought I must surely die.'

'Was the curate your companion?' I said.

He shook his head weakly. 'I have never before laid eyes on him.'

'Are you well enough to move?' said Amelia.

'I believe so. I am not hurt, but I have had a narrow escape.'

'Were you in Weybridge?' I said.

'I was in the thick of it. Those Martians have no mercy, no compunction – '

'How do you know they are from Mars?' I said, greatly interested by this, as I had been at hearing of the soldiers' rumours.

'It is well known. The firing of their projectiles was observed in many telescopes. Indeed, I was fortunate to observe one such myself, in the instrument at Ottershaw.'

'You are an astronomer?' said Amelia.

'That I am not, but I am acquainted with many scientists. My own calling is a more philosophical nature.' He paused then, and glanced down at himself, and was at once overcome with embarrassment. 'My dear lady,' he said to Amelia, 'I must apologize for my state of undress.'

'We are no better garbed ourselves,' she replied, with considerable accuracy.

'You too have come from the thick of the fighting?'

'In a sense,' I said. 'Sir, I hope you will join us. We have a boat, and we are headed for Richmond. There I think we may find safety.'

'Thank you,' said the man. 'But I must go my own way. I was trying to make for Leatherhead, for that is where I have left my wife.'

I thought quickly, trying to visualize the geography of the land. Leatherhead was many miles to the south of us.

The man went on: 'You see, I am a resident of Woking, and before the Martians attacked I managed to take my wife to safety. Since then, because I was obliged to return to Woking, I have been trying to join her. But I have found, to my cost, that the land between here and Leatherhead is overrun with the brutes.'

'Then as your wife is safe,' Amelia said, 'would it not be wise to fall in with us until the Army deals with this menace?'

The man was clearly tempted, for we were not many miles distant from Richmond. He hesitated for a few seconds more, then nodded.

'If you are rowing, you will need an extra pair of arms,' he said. 'I shall be happy to oblige. But first, because I am in such a state of untidiness, I should like to wash myself.'

He went down to the water's edge, and with his hands washed off much of the traces of the smoke and grime which so disfigured him. Then, when he had swept back his hair, he held out his hand and assisted Amelia as she climbed back into the boat.

TWENTY

Rowing Down The River

•

I

That our new friend was a man of gentle manners was affirmed the moment we entered the boat. He would not hear of my rowing until he had served a turn at the oars, and insisted that I sit with Amelia in the rear of the boat.

'We must have our wits about us,' he said, 'in case those devils return. We will take turns at the oars, and all keep our eyes open.'

I had been feeling for some time that the Martians' apparent inactivity must be temporary, and it was reassuring to know that my suspicions were shared. This could only be a lull in their campaign, and as such we must take the maximum advantage of it.

In accordance with our plan I kept a careful watch for sight of the tripods (although all seemed presently quiet), but Amelia's attention was elsewhere. Indeed, she was staring at our new friend with quite improper attention.

At length she said: 'Sir, may I enquire if you have ever visited Reynolds House in Richmond?'

The gentleman looked at her in manifest surprise, but immediately said: 'I have indeed, but not for many years.'

'Then you would know Sir William Reynolds?'

'We were never the closest of friends, for I fear he was not one for intimate friendships, but we were members of the same club in St James's and were occasionally wont to exchange confidences.'

Amelia was frowning in concentration. 'I believe we have met before.'

Our friend paused with the oars clear of the water.

'By Jove!' he cried. 'Are you not Sir William's former amanuensis?'

'Yes, I am. And you, sir, I think your name is Mr Wells.'

'That is my name,' he said gravely. 'And if I am not mistaken, I do believe you are Miss Fitzgibbon.'

Amelia instantly confirmed this. 'What a remarkable coincidence!'

Mr Wells politely asked me my name, and I introduced myself. I reached over to shake his hand, and he leaned forward over the oars.

'Pleased to meet you, Turnbull,' he said.

Just then the sunlight fell on his face in such a way that his eyes revealed themselves to be a startling blue; in his tired and worried face they shone like optimistic beacons, and I felt myself warming to him.

Amelia was still animated in her excitement.

'It is to Reynolds House that we are going now,' she said. 'We feel Sir William is one of the few men who can confront this menace.'

Mr Wells frowned, and returned to his rowing.

After a moment, he said: 'I take it you have not seen Sir William for some time?'

Amelia glanced at me, and I knew she was uncertain how to reply.

I said for her: 'Not since May of 1893, sir.'

'That is the last time I, or anyone else, saw him. Surely if you were in his employ, you know about this?'

Amelia said: 'I ceased to work for him in that May. Are you saying that he subsequently died?'

I knew that this last was a wild guess, but Mr Wells promptly corrected it.

'I think Sir William is not dead,' he said. 'He went into futurity on that infernal Time Machine of his, and although he returned once he has not been seen since his second journey.'

'You know this for certain?' Amelia said.

'I was honoured to be the author of his memoirs,' said Mr Wells, 'for he dictated them to me himself.'

II

As we rowed along, Mr Wells told us what was known of Sir William's fate. At the same time it was interesting to realize that some of our earlier surmises had not been inaccurate.

It seemed that after the Time Machine had deposited us so abruptly in the weed-bank, it had returned unscathed to Richmond. Mr Wells could not have known of our mishap, of course, but his account of Sir William's subsequent experiments made no mention of the fact that the Machine had been missing for even a short period.

Sir William, according to Mr Wells, had been more adventurous than even we had been, taking the Time Machine into a far-distant future. Here Sir William had seen many strange sights (Mr Wells promised to let us have a copy of his account, for he said the story would take too long to recount at the moment), and although he had returned to tell his tale, he had later departed a second time for futurity. On that occasion he had never returned.

Imagining that Sir William had suffered a similar mishap with the Machine as us, I said: 'The Time Machine came back empty, sir?'

'Neither the Machine nor Sir William have been seen again.'

'Then there is no way we can reach him?'

'Not without a second Time Machine,' said Mr Wells.

By now we were passing Walton-on-Thames, and there was much activity within the town. We saw several fire-engines rattling along the riverside road in the direction of Weybridge, the horses' hooves throwing up white dust-clouds. An orderly, but hurried, evacuation was taking place, with many hundreds of people walking or riding along the road towards London. The river itself was congested, with several boats ferrying people across to the Sunbury side, and we were obliged to steer carefully between them. Along the northern bank we saw much evidence of military activity, with scores of soldiers marching towards the west. In the meadows to the east of Halliford we saw more artillery being readied.

This distraction brought to an end our conversation about Sir William, and by the time we had passed Walton we sat in silence. Mr Wells was seeming to tire at the oars, so I changed places with him.

Once more occupied with the regular physical task of rowing, I found my thoughts returning to the orderly procession they had enjoyed shortly before we met Mr Wells and the curate.

Until this moment I had not tried to understand why we were so determined to reach Sir William's house. Mr Wells's mention of the Time Machine, though, had focused my thoughts directly on the reason: in some instinctive way it had occurred to me that the Machine itself might be used against Martians. It was, after all, the instrument by which we had first reached Mars, and its weird movements through the attenuated dimensions of Space and Time were certainly unequalled by anything the Martians commanded.

However, if the Time Machine were no longer available, then any such idea had to be abandoned. We were pressing on to Richmond, though, for Sir William's house, lying in its secluded position just behind the ridge of the Hill, would be a safer sanctuary than most from the Martians.

Facing Amelia as I was, I noticed that she too seemed lost in thought, and I wondered if she had been coming to the same conclusion.

At last, not wishing to ignore Mr Wells, I said: 'Sir, do you know what preparations the Army is making?'

'Only what we have seen today. They were taken quite unawares. Even from the early moments of the invasion, no one in authority was prepared to take the situation seriously.'

'You speak as if you are critical.'

'I am,' said Mr Wells. 'The fact that the Martians were sending an invasion-fleet has been known for several weeks. As I told you, the firing of their projectiles was observed by many scientists.

Any number of warnings was issued, both in scientific papers and in the popular press, yet even when the first cylinder landed the authorities were slow to move.'

Amelia said: 'You mean that the warnings were not taken seriously?'

'They were dismissed as sensation-mongering, even after there had been several deaths. The first cylinder landed not a mile from my house. It came down at about midnight on the 19th. I myself visited it during the morning, along with a crowd of others, and although it was clear from the outset that something was inside, the press would not publish more than a few inches about it. This I can attest to myself, because in addition to my literary activities I occasionally contribute scientific pieces to the press, and the papers are noted for their caution with all scientific matters. Even yesterday, they were treating this incursion with levity. As for the Army ... they did not turn out until nearly twenty-four hours after the arrival of the projectile, and by then the monsters were out and well established.'

'In the Army's defence,' I said, still feeling that it had been incumbent upon myself to alert the authorities, 'such an invasion is unprecedented.'

'Maybe so,' Mr Wells said. 'But the second cylinder had landed before a single shot was fired by our side. How many more landings are needed before the threat is understood?'

'I think they are alert to the danger now,' I said, nodding towards yet another artillery emplacement on the banks of the river. One of the gunners was hailing us, but I rowed on without answering. It was now well into the afternoon, and there were about four more hours until sunset.

Amelia said: 'You say that you visited the pit. Did you see the adversary?'

'That I did,' said Mr Wells, and I noticed then that his hands were trembling. 'Those monsters are unspeakable!'

I realized that Amelia was about to talk of our adventures on Mars, so I frowned at her, warning her to silence. For the moment at least, I felt we should not reveal our role in the invasion.

Instead, I said to Mr Wells: 'You are clearly shaken by your experiences.'

'I have been face to face with Death. Twice I have escaped with my life, but only by the greatest good fortune.' He shook his head. 'These Martians will go on and conquer the world. They are indestructible.'

'They are mortal, sir,' I said. 'They can be killed as easily as other vermin.'

'That has not been the experience so far. By what evidence do you say that?'

I thought of the screams of the dying monster inside the platform, and the ghastly eructation of gases. And then, remembering the warning I had signalled to Amelia only a few seconds before, I said: 'There was one killed at Weybridge.'

'A chance artillery shell. We cannot depend on chance to rid the world of this menace.'

III

Mr Wells took the oars again when we reached Hampton Court, as I was tiring. We were now only a short distance from Richmond, but here the river swings to the south, before turning a second time to flow northwards, and so we still had a considerable distance before us. For a while we debated whether to abandon the boat and complete our journey on foot, but we could see that the roads were crowded with the traffic of those escaping towards London. On the river we had our way almost to ourselves. The afternoon was warm and tranquil, the sky a radiant blue.

Here, by Hampton Court Palace, we saw a curious sight. We were now a sufficient distance from the effects of the Martians' destruction for the immediate dangers to seem diminished, yet still near enough for evacuations to be taking place. As a consequence, there was a conflict of moods. The local people, from Thames Ditton, Molesey and Surbiton, were abandoning their houses, and under the guidance of the overworked police and fire-brigades, were leaving for London.

However, the Palace grounds are a favourite resort for excursionist Londoners, and on this fine summer's afternoon the riverside paths were well thronged with people enjoying the sunshine. They could not be unaware of the noise and bustle around them, but they seemed determined not to let such activities affect their picnics.

Thames Ditton Station, which is on the south bank opposite the Palace, was crowded, and people were queuing up along the pavement outside, waiting for a chance to board a train. Even so, each train that arrived from London brought with it a few more late-afternoon excursionists.

How many of those blazered young men, or those young ladies with silken parasols, were ever to see their homes again? Perhaps to them, in their unguarded innocence, we three in our rowing-boat presented a strange sight: Amelia and I, still wearing our much begrimed underwear, and Mr Wells, naked but for his trousers. I think the day was unusual enough for our appearance to pass unremarked upon.

IV

It was as we were rowing towards Kingston-upon-Thames that we first heard the artillery, and at once we were on our guard. Mr Wells rowed more vigorously, and Amelia and I turned in our seats, looking westwards for a first sight of the deadly tripods.

For the moment there was no sign of them, but the distant artillery muttered endlessly. Once I saw a heliograph flickering on the hills beyond Esher, and ahead of us we saw a signal-rocket burst bright red at the peak of its smoky trail, but in our immediate vicinity, at least, the guns remained silent.

At Kingston we changed hands once more, and I braced myself for the final effort towards Richmond. We were all restless, eager for this long journey to be over. As Mr Wells settled himself in the prow of the boat, he remarked on the unseemly noise of the evacuees crossing Kingston Bridge. There were no excursionists to be seen here; I think that at last the danger had been brought home to everyone.

A few minutes after we left Kingston, Amelia pointed ahead.

'Richmond Park, Edward! We're nearly there.'

I glanced briefly over my shoulder, and saw the splendid rise of ground. It was not unexpected that there, on the crest of the hill and black against the sky, I saw the protruding muzzles of the artillery.

The Martians were expected, and this time they would meet their match.

Reassured, I rowed on, trying to ignore the tiredness in my arms and back.

A mile north of Kingston, the Thames, in its meandering way, swings to the north-west, and so the rise of Richmond Park moved further away to our right. Now, temporarily, we were moving towards the Martians once more, and as if this were significant, we heard a renewed volley from the distant artillery. This was echoed a few moments later by the guns laid in Bushy Park, and then too we heard the first shots from Richmond Park. All three of us craned our necks, but there was still no sign of the Martians. It was most unnerving to know that they were in our vicinity, yet invisible to us.

We passed Twickenham, and saw no signs of evacuation; perhaps the town had been emptied already, or else the people were lying low, hoping the Martians would not come their way.

Then, heading directly east again as the river turned towards Richmond, Amelia shouted that she had seen some smoke. We looked to the south-west, and saw, rising from the direction of Molesey, a column of black smoke. The artillery was speaking continuously. The Martians, moving quickly through the Surrey countryside, were difficult targets, and the towns they approached were laid helplessly before them.

Smoke rose from Kingston, and from Surbiton, and from Esher. Then, too, from Twickenham ... and at last we could see one of the Martian marauders. It was stalking quickly through the streets of Twickenham, not one mile from where we presently were. We could see its heat-beam, swinging indiscriminately, and we could see the ineffectual air-burst of the artillery-shells, never exploding less than a hundred feet from the predatory engine.

A second Martian tripod appeared, this one striking northwards towards Hounslow. Then a third: away to the south of burning Kingston.

'Edward, dear... hurry! They are almost upon us!'

'I am doing my best!' I cried, wondering if we should now head for the bank.

Mr Wells clambered towards me from the prow, and placed himself on the seat beside me. He took the right-hand oar from me, and in a moment we had established a fast rhythm.

Fortunately, the Martians seemed to be paying no attention to the river for the moment. The towns were their main objectives, and the lines of artillery. In the repeated explosions near at hand, I realized that the deeper sounds of the more distant batteries had long been silenced.

Then came what was perhaps the most disturbing noise of all. The Martian driving the tripod by Kingston uttered a note ... and it drifted towards us, distorted by the breeze. The Martian in Twickenham took it up, and soon we heard others from various directions. Here on Earth the note was deeper in timbre, and seemed more prolonged ... but there could be no mistaking the sinister braying siren of the Martians calling for food.

V

At last the tree-lined slope of Richmond Hill was before us, and as we rowed frantically around the bend past the green meadows we saw the white, wooden building of Messum's boat-house. I remembered the day I had called on Sir William, and how I had strolled along the riverside walk past the boat-house ... but then there had been promenading crowds. Now we were apparently alone, all but for the rampaging battle-machines and the answering artillery.

I pointed out the jetty to Mr Wells, and we rowed energetically towards it. At long last we heard the scraping of the wooden hull against the hard stone, and without further ceremony I held out my hand to help Amelia ashore. I waited until Mr Wells had stepped down, and then I too followed. Behind us, the little boat bobbed away, drifting with the current of the river.

Both Mr Wells and I were exhausted from our long ordeal, but even so were prepared for the last part of our effort: the climb up the side of the Hill towards Sir William's house. Accordingly, we hastened away from the jetty, but Amelia held back. As soon as we realized she was not following, we turned and waited for her.

Amelia had not been at her most talkative for the last hour, but now said: 'Mr Wells, you told us earlier that you went to the Martians' pit in Woking. What day was that?'

'It was the Friday morning,' Mr Wells said.

Looking across the river towards Twickenham I saw that the brazen cowl of the nearest battle-machine was turned our way. Artillery shells burst around it.

I said, with great anxiety: 'Amelia ... we can talk later! We must get under cover!'

'Edward, this is important!' Then to Mr Wells: 'And that was the 19th, you say?'

'No, the Thursday was the 19th. It came down at about midnight.'

'And today we have seen excursionists ... so this is Sunday ... Mr Wells, this is 1903, is it not?'

He looked a little puzzled, but confirmed this.

Amelia turned to me, and seized my hand. 'Edward! Today is the 22nd! This is the day in 1903 to which we came! The Time Machine will be in the laboratory!'

With that she turned abruptly away from me, and ran quickly up through the trees.

At once I ran after her, shouting to her to come back!

VI

Amelia, rested and agile, scrambled without difficulty up the side of the Hill; I was more tired, and although I used every remaining scrap of energy I could do no more than maintain my distance behind her. Below us, by the river, I heard the sound of the Martian's braying siren, answered at once by another. Somewhere behind us, Mr Wells followed. Ahead of me, from a point on the ridge, I heard the sound of a man's voice shouting an order ... and then there came the detonation of the artillery-pieces mounted on the Hill. Smoke poured down from them through the trees. More shots followed, from positions all along the ridge. The noise was deafening, and the acrid cordite fumes burned in my throat.

Ahead of me, showing through the trees, I could see the towers of Reynolds House.

'Amelia!' I shouted again over the noise. 'My dearest, come back! It is not safe!'

'The Time Machine! We can find the Time Machine!'

I could see her ahead of me, brushing without regard for herself through the tangle of bushes and undergrowth towards the house.

'No!' I screamed after her, in utter desperation. 'Amelia!'

Through the multitude of intervening events, across the seeming years and the millions of miles ... a stark memory of our first journey to 1903.

I remembered the artillery shots, the smoke, the alien sirens, the woman running across the lawn, the face at the window, and then the consuming fire ...

Destiny!

I hurled myself after her, and saw her reach the edge of the overgrown lawn.

Amelia started to run across to the glass wall of the laboratory: a lithe, distant figure, already beyond any help, already doomed by the destiny I had not after all averted ...

As I also reached the lawn, too breathless to shout again, I saw her come to the glass and stop by it, pressing her face against the panes.

I stumbled across the lawn ... and then I was behind her, and near enough to see beyond her, into the dim interior of the laboratory.

There, set beside one of the many benches, was placed a crude mechanical device, and upon it sat two youthful figures.

One was a young man, a straw boater set at a jaunty angle on his head ... and the other was a pretty girl holding herself to him.

The young man was staring at us, his eyes wide with surprise.

I reached out my hand to take Amelia, just as the young man within raised his own, as if to ward off the horror of what he too was seeing.

Behind us there was a scream from the Martian's siren, and the brazen cowl of the battle-machine appeared over the trees. I threw myself against Amelia, and dashed her to the ground. In the same instant the heat-beam was turned upon us, and a line of fire raced across the lawn and struck the house.

TWENTY-ONE

Under Siege

•

I

I had intended to throw myself across Amelia, so protecting her with my own body, but in my haste I succeeded only in throwing us both to the ground. The explosion that followed therefore afflicted us both to an equal degree. There was one mighty blast, which hurled us bodily across the garden, and this was followed by a series of smaller explosions of varying severity. We tumbled helplessly through the long grass, and when at last we stopped there was a rain of burning timber and broken masonry, crashing to the soil about us.

In the interval that followed I heard the braying of the Martian as it turned away from us, its hatred satisfied.

Then, although we heard further concussions in the near distance, it was as if a stillness had fallen. There was a moment when I could hear an animal squealing in pain, but a revolver fired and even that stopped.

Amelia lay in the grass about ten feet from me, and as soon as I had recovered my senses I crawled hastily towards her. There was a sudden pain in my back, and at once I realized my combinations were on fire. I rolled over, and although the burning pain increased momentarily, I succeeded in extinguishing the smouldering fabric. I hurried over to Amelia, and saw that her clothes too had been ignited. I beat out the tiny flames with my hands, and at once I heard her moan.

'Is that you, Edward ...?' she said indistinctly.

'Are you hurt?'

She shook her head, and as I tried to turn her over she climbed painfully to her feet of her own accord. She stood before me, looking very groggy.

'By Jove! That was close!'

It was Mr Wells. He came towards us from the bushes at the side of the lawn, apparently unharmed but, like us, shocked at the ferocity of the attack.

'Miss Fitzgibbon, are you injured?' he said solicitously.

'I think not.' She shook her head sharply. 'I have become a little deaf.'

'That is the blast,' I said, for my own ears were buzzing Just then we heard shouting beside the house, and we all turned in that direction.

A group of soldiers had appeared, all looking rather dazed An officer was trying to organize them, and after a few moments of confusion they stepped forward to the blazing house and attempted to beat out the flames with sacking.

'We had better help them,' I said to Mr Wells, and at once we set off across the lawn.

As we came around the corner of the building we met a scene of great destruction. Here the Army had mounted one of its artillery-pieces, and it was clearly at this that the Martian had fired Its aim had been deadly accurate, for there remained just twisted and melted metal scattered about a large crater. There was almost nothing recognizable of the gun, bar one of its huge spoked wheels, which now lay about fifty yards to one side.

Further back, several horses had been tethered by one of the outhouses in the garden, and we were distressed to see that some of these had been killed; the remainder had been efficiently quieted by their handlers, who had placed blinds over their heads.

We went directly to the subaltern in charge.

'May we offer our help?' Mr Wells said.

'Is this your house, sir?'

Amelia answered. 'No, I live here.'

'But the house is empty.'

'We have been abroad.' She glanced at the soldiers beating ineffectually at the flames. 'There is a garden hose in that shed.'

At once the officer ordered two of the men to find the hose, and in a few moments it had been brought out and connected to a standing tap against the side of the house. Fortunately, the pressure was high and a jet of water issued at once.

We stood well back, seeing that the men had evidently been trained well, and that the firefighting was conducted intelligently and efficiently. The jet of water was played on the more ferocious concentrations of fire, while the other men continued to beat with the sacking.

The officer supervised the effort with a minimum of orders, and when he stepped back as the flames were brought under control, I went over to him.

'Have you lost any men?' I said.

'Fortunately, sir, no. We had been ordered to move back just before the attack, and so were able to take cover in time.' He indicated several deep trenches dug across the lawn; they crossed the place where (so long ago!) I had sipped iced lemonade with Amelia. 'If we'd been manning the piece ...'

I nodded. 'Were you billeted here?'

'Yes, sir. We've caused no damage, I think you'll find. Just as soon as we've retrieved our equipment, we will have to withdraw.'

I understood that saving the house itself was not their main concern. It was lucky indeed that they needed to save their own possessions, otherwise we should have had great difficulty dousing the fire on our own.

Within a quarter of an hour the flames were out; it was the servants' wing which had been hit, and two of the rooms on the ground floor were uninhabitable, and the six gunners who had been billeted there lost all their equipment. On the floor above, the major damage was caused by smoke and the explosion.

Of the rest of the house, the rooms on the side furthest from the exploding gun were least damaged: Sir William's former smoking-room, for instance, had not even one broken window.

Throughout the rest of the house there was a varying amount of damage, mostly breakages caused by the explosion, and every pane of glass in the walls of the laboratory had been shattered. In the grounds there was a certain amount of grass and shrubbery on fire, but the gunners soon dealt with this.

Once the fire had been put out, the artillerymen took what they had retrieved of their equipment, loaded up an ammunition truck, and prepared to withdraw. Through all this we could hear the sounds of the battle continuing in the distance, and the subaltern told us he was anxious to join his unit in Richmond. He apologized for the damage caused when his gun had been destroyed, and we thanked him for his help in extinguishing the fire ... then the troop of men rode away, down the Hill towards the town.

II

Mr Wells said that he was going to see where the Martians now were, and stepped out across the lawn towards the edge of the ridge. I followed Amelia into the house, and when we were inside I took her in my arms and held her tightly, her face nestling against the side of mine.

For several minutes we said nothing, but then at last she held back a little, and we looked lovingly into each other's eyes. That momentary vision of our past selves had been a salutary shock; Amelia, with her face bruised and scarred, and her chemise torn and scorched, bore almost no resemblance to the rather prim and elegantly clad young woman I had glimpsed on the Time Machine. And I knew, by the way in which she was looking at me, that a similar transformation had come over my appearance.

She said: 'When we were on the Time Machine you saw the Martian. You knew all along.'

'I only saw you,' I said. 'I thought I saw you dying.'

'Is that why you took the Machine?'

'I don't know. I was desperate ... I loved you even then ...'

She held me again, and her lips pressed briefly against my neck.

I heard her say, in words so soft they were almost inaudible: 'I understand now, Edward.'

III

Mr Wells brought the sombre news that he had counted six of the monstrous tripods in the valley below, and that the fighting continued.

'They are all over the place,' he said, 'and as far as I could see there's almost no resistance from our men. There are three machines within a mile of this house, but they are staying in the valley. I think we shall be safe if we lie low here for a while.'

'What are the Martians doing?' I said.

'The heat-beam is still in use. It seemed as if the whole Thames Valley is on fire. There is smoke everywhere, and it is of amazing intensity. The whole of Twickenham has vanished under a mountain of smoke. Black, thick smoke, like tar, but not rising. It is shaped like an immense dome.'

'It will be dispersed by the wind,' Amelia said.

'The wind is up,' said Mr Wells, 'but the smoke stays above the town. I cannot account for it.'

It seemed to be a minor enigma, and so we paid little attention to it; it was enough to know that the Martians were still hostile and about.

All three of us were faint from hunger, and the preparation of a meal became a necessity. It was clear that Sir William's house had not been occupied for years, and so we held out no hope of finding any food in the pantry. We did discover that the artillerymen had left some of their rations behind – some tins of meat and a little stale bread – but it was hardly enough for one meal.

Mr Wells and I agreed to visit the houses nearest to us, and see if we could borrow some food from there. Amelia decided to stay behind; she wanted to explore the house and see how much of it would be habitable.

Mr Wells and I were away for an hour. During this time we

discovered that we were alone on Richmond Hill. The other inhabitants had presumably been evacuated when the soldiers arrived, and it was evident that their departure had been hasty. Few of the houses were locked, and in most we found considerable quantities of food. By the time we were ready to return, we had with us a sackful of food – consisting of a good variety of meats, vegetables and fruit – which should certainly be enough to sustain us for many days In addition we found several bottles of wine, and a pipe and some tobacco for Mr Wells.

Before returning to the house, Mr Wells suggested that we once more survey the valley, it was suspiciously quiet below, to a degree that was making us most uneasy.

We left the sack inside the house we had last visited, and went forward cautiously to the edge of the ridge There, concealing ourselves amongst the trees, we were afforded an uninterrupted view to north and west To our left we could see up the Thames Valley at least as far as Windsor Castle, and before us we could see the villages of Chiswick and Brentford. Immediately below us was Richmond itself

The sun was setting a deep-orange ball of fire touching the horizon. Silhouetted against it was one of the Martian battle-machines It was not moving now, and even from this distance of three miles or so we could see that the metal-mesh net at the back of the platform had been filled with bodies.

The black kopje of smoke still obscured Twickenham; another lay heavily over Hounslow Richmond appeared still, although several buildings were on fire.

I said: 'They cannot be stopped. They will rule the entire world.'

Mr Wells was silent, although his breathing was irregular and heavy. Glancing at his face I saw that his bright-blue eyes were moist Then he said 'You opine that they are mortal, Turnbull, but we must now accept that we cannot resist them.'

At that moment, as if defying his words, a solitary gun placed on the riverside walk by Richmond Bridge fired a shot. Moments later the shell burst in the air several hundred feet away from the distant battle-machine.

The Martian's response was instant. It whirled round and strode in our direction, causing Mr Wells and me to step back into the trees. We saw the Martian extend a broad tube from its platform, and a few seconds later something was fired from this. A large cylinder flew through the air, tumbling erratically and reflecting the orange brilliance of the sun It described a high arc, and fell crashing somewhere into the streets of Richmond town Moments later there was an incontinent release of blackness, and within sixty seconds Richmond had vanished under another of the mysterious static domes of black smoke.

The gun by the river, lost in the blackness, did not speak again

We waited and watched until the sun went down, but heard no more shots fired by the Army. The Martians, arrogant in their total victory, went about their macabre business of seeking out the human survivors, and placing such unfortunates in their swelling nets.

Much sobered, Mr Wells and I retrieved our sack of food and returned to Reynolds House

We were greeted by an Amelia transformed.

'Edward!' she called as soon as we walked through the broken door of the house. 'Edward, my clothes are still here!'

And dancing into our sight came a girl of the most extraordinary beauty. She wore a pale-yellow dress and buttoned boots, her hair was brushed and shaped about her face, the wound which had so disfigured her was concealed by the artistic application of maquillage. And, as she seized my hand gaily, and exclaimed happily over the amount of food we had gathered, I sensed once more that gentle fragrance of perfume, redolent of herbs.

For no reason I could understand, I turned away from her and found myself weeping.

IV

The house had evidently been closed after Sir William's final departure on the Time Machine, for although everything was intact and in its place (excepting those items damaged or destroyed in the explosion and fire), the furniture had been covered with dust-sheets, and valuable articles had been locked away in cupboards. Mr Wells and I visited Sir William's dressing-room, and there found sufficient clothing to dress ourselves decently.

A little later, smelling slightly of moth-balls, we went through the house while Amelia prepared a meal. We discovered that the servants had confined their cleaning to the domestic areas of the house, for the laboratory was as cluttered with pieces of engineering machinery as before. Everything here was filthy dirty, though, and much littered with broken glass. The reciprocating engine which generated electricity was in its place, although we dared not turn it on for fear of attracting the Martians' attention.

We ate our meal in a ground-floor room furthest away from the valley, and sat by candlelight with the curtains closed. All was silent outside the house, but none of us could feel at ease knowing dial at any moment the Martians might come by.

Afterwards, with our stomachs satisfactorily filled and our minds pleasantly relaxed by a bottle of wine, we talked again of the totality of the Martians' victory.

'Their aim is quite clearly to take London,' said Mr Wells. 'If they do not do so during this night, then there can be nothing to stop them in the morning.'

'But if they control London, they would control the whole country!' I said.

'That is what I fear. Of course, by now the threat is understood, and I dare say that even as we speak the garrisons in the north are travelling down. Whether they would fare any better than the unfortunates we saw in action today is a matter for conjecture. But the British Army is not slow to learn by its errors, so maybe we shall see some victories. What we do not know, of course, is what these monsters seek to gain.'

'They wish to enslave us,' I said. 'They cannot survive unless they drink human blood.'

Mr Wells glanced at me sharply. 'Why do you say that, Turnbull?'

I was dumbfounded. We had all seen the gathering of the people by the Martians, but only Amelia and I, with our privy knowledge, could know what was to happen to them.

Amelia said: 'I think we must tell Mr Wells what we know, Edward.'

'Do you have a specialist knowledge of these monsters?' said Mr Wells.

'We were . . in the pit at Woking,' I said.

'I too was there, but I saw no blood-drinking. This is an astonishing revelation, and, if I may say so, more than a little sensational I take it you are speaking with authority?'

'The authority of experience,' said Amelia 'We have been to Mars, Mr Wells, although I cannot expect you to believe us.'

Much to my surprise, our new friend did not seem at all perturbed by this announcement

'I have long suspected that the other planets of our Solar System can support life,' he said. 'It does not seem improbable to me that one day we shall visit those worlds. When we have conquered the drag of gravity we shall travel to the moon as easily as we can now travel to Birmingham.' He stared intently at us both 'Yet you say you have already been to Mars?'

I nodded. 'We were experimenting with Sir William's Time Machine, and we set the controls incorrectly.'

'But as I understood it, Sir William intended to travel in time only.'

In a few words, Amelia explained how I had loosened the nickel rod which until then prevented movement through the Spatial Dimension. From this, the rest of our story followed naturally, and for the next hour we recounted most of our adventures. At last we came to the description of how we had returned to Earth.

Mr Wells was silent for a long time. He had helped himself lo some brandy which we had found in the smoking-room, and for many minutes he cradled this in his hands.

Then at last he said 'If you are not inventing every word of this, all I can say is that it is a most extraordinary tale.'

'We are not proud of what we have done,' I said.

Mr Wells waved his hand dismissively. 'You should not blame

yourselves inordinately. Others would have done as you have, and although there has been much loss of life and damage to property, you could not have anticipated the power of these creatures.'

He asked us several questions about our story, and we answered them as accurately as we could.

At length, he said: 'It seems to me that your experience is itself the most useful weapon we have against these creatures. In any war, one's tactics are best planned by anticipating the enemy. Why we have not been able to contain this menace is because their motives have been so uncertain. We three are now custodians of intelligence. If we cannot assist the authorities, we must take some action of our own.'

'I had been thinking along those lines myself,' I said. 'Our first intention was to contact Sir William, for it had occurred to me that the Time Machine itself would be a powerful weapon against these beings.'

'In what way could it be used?'

'No creature, however powerful or ruthless, can defend itself against an invisible foe.'

Mr Wells nodded his understanding, but said: 'Unfortunately, we find neither Sir William nor his Machine.'

'I know, sir,' I said glumly.

It was getting late, and soon we discontinued our conversation, for we were all exhausted. The silence beyond the house was still absolute, but we felt we could not sleep easy in uncertainty. With this in mind, we crept out of the house before preparing for bed, and walked softly across the lawn to the edge of the ridge.

We looked down across the Thames Valley and saw the burning desolation below. In every direction, and as far as we could see, the night land was sparked with the glow of burning buildings. The sky above us was clear, and the stars shone brightly.

Amelia took my hand and said: 'It is like Mars, Edward. They are turning our world into theirs.'

'We cannot let them go on with this,' I said. 'We must find a way to fight them.'

Just then, Mr Wells pointed towards the west, and we all saw a brilliant green point of light. It grew brighter as we watched it, and within a few seconds we had all recognized it as a fourth projectile. It became blindingly bright, and for a terrible moment we were convinced it was coming directly towards us, but then at last it abruptly lost height. It fell with a dazzling explosion of green light some three miles to the south-west of us, and seconds later we heard the blast of its landing.

Slowly, the green glare faded, until all was dark once more.

Mr Wells said: 'There are six more of those projectiles to come.'

'There is no hope for us,' said Amelia.

'We must never lose hope.'

I said: 'We are impotent against these monsters.'

'We must build a second Time Machine,' said Mr Wells.

'But that would be impossible,' Amelia said. 'Only Sir William knows how to construct the device.'

'He explained the principle to me in detail,' said Mr Wells.

'To you, and to many others, but only in the most vague terms. Even I, who sometimes worked with him in the laboratory, have only a general understanding of its mechanism.'

'Then we can succeed!' said Mr Wells. 'You have helped to build the Machine, and I have helped design it.'

We both looked at him curiously then. The flames from below lent an eerie cast to his features.

'You helped design the Time Machine?' I said, incredulously.

'In a sense, for he often showed me his blueprints and I made several suggestions which he incorporated. If the drawings are still available, it would not take me long to familiarize myself with them. I expect the drawings are still in his safe in the laboratory.'

Amelia said: 'That is where he always kept them.'

'Then we could not get at them!' I cried. 'Sir William is no longer here!'

'We will blast the safe open, if we need to,' Mr Wells said, apparently determined to carry through his brave claim.

'There is no need for that,' said Amelia. 'I have some spare keys in my suite.'

Suddenly, Mr Wells extended his hand to me, and I took it

uncertainly, not sure what our compact was to be. He placed his other hand on my shoulder and gripped it warmly.

'Turnbull,' he said, gravely. 'You and I, and Miss Fitzgibbon too, will combine to defeat this enemy. We will become the unsuspected and invisible foe. We will fight this threat to all that is decent by descending on it and destroying it in a way it could never have anticipated. Tomorrow we shall set to and build a new Time Machine, and with it we will go out and stop this unstoppable menace!'

And then, with the excitement of having formed a positive plan, we complimented ourselves, and laughed aloud, and shouted defiance across the blighted valley. The night was silent, and the air was tainted with smoke and death, but revenge is the most satisfactory of human impulses, and as we returned to the house we were most uncommonly expectant of an immediate victory.

TWENTY-TWO

The Space Machine

•

I

Mr Wells and I each took one of the guest-rooms that night, while Amelia slept in her private suite (it was the first time for weeks that I had slept alone, and I tossed restlessly for hours), and in the morning we came down to breakfast still exercised by the zeal of vengeance.

Breakfast itself was a considerable luxury for Amelia and myself, for we were able to cook bacon and eggs on a ring in the kitchen (we judged it ill-advised to light the range).

Afterwards, we went directly to the laboratory and opened Sir William's safe. There, rolled untidily together, were the drawings he had made of his Time Machine.

We found a clear space on one of the benches and spread them out. At once my spirits fell, because Sir William – for all his inventive genius – had not been the most methodical of men. There was hardly one sheet that made immediate sense, for there was a multitude of corrections, erasures and marginal sketches, and on most sheets original designs had been overdrawn with subsequent versions.

Mr Wells maintained his optimistic tone of the night before, but I sensed that some of his previous confidence was lacking.

Amelia said: 'Of course, before we start work we must be sure that the necessary materials are to hand.'

Looking around at the dirty chaos of the laboratory I saw that although it was well littered with many electrical components and rods and bars of metals – as well as pieces of the crystalline substance scattered almost everywhere – it would take a diligent search to establish if we had enough to construct an entire Machine.

Mr Wells had carried some of the plans to the daylight, and was examining them minutely.

'I shall need several hours,' he said. 'Some of this is familiar, but I cannot say for certain ...'

I did not wish to infect him with my faintheartedness, so in the spirit of seeming to be of help – yet ensuring I was out of the way – I offered to search the grounds for more useful components. Amelia merely nodded, for she was already busily searching the drawer of one of the benches, and Mr Wells was absorbed with the plans, so I left the laboratory and went out of the house

I walked first to the ridge.

It was a fine summer's day, and the sun shone brightly over the ravaged countryside. Most of the fires had burnt themselves out during the night, but the inky depths of the black vapours which covered Twickenham, Hounslow and Richmond were still impenetrable. The dome-shapes had flattened considerably, and long tendrils of the black stuff were spreading through the streets which had at first escaped being smothered.

Of the Martian invaders themselves there was no sign. Only to the south-west, in Bushy Park, did I see clouds of green smoke rising, and I guessed that it was there the fourth projectile had landed.

I turned away from the scene, and walked past the house to the other side, where the grounds opened out on to Richmond Park. Here the view was uninterrupted across to Wimbledon, and but for the total absence of any people, the Park was exactly as it had been on that first day I called at Reynolds House.

When I returned to the house I immediately discovered a problem of pressing urgency, although it was not one which in any way threatened our safety. Beside the outhouse, where the gunners' horses had been tethered, I came across the corpses of the four animals that had been killed when the Martian attacked. During the summer night the flesh had started to decompose, and the raw wounds were crawling with flies and an unhealthy stench filled the air.

I could not possibly move the carcasses, and burning them was out of the question, so the only alternative was to bury them. Fortunately, the soldiers' trenches had been dug very recently, and there was much fresh, upturned soil about.

I found a shovel and wheelbarrow, and began the unpleasant and lengthy chore of covering the rotting bodies. In two hours I had completed the task, and the horses were safely buried. The work was not without its unexpected benefit, though, for during it I discovered that in their haste the soldiers had left behind them several pieces of equipment in the trenches. One of these was a rifle and many rounds of ammunition... but more promisingly, I discovered two wooden crates, inside each of which were twenty-five hand-grenades.

With great care I carried these to the house, and stored them safely in the woodshed. I then returned to the laboratory to see how the other two were faring.

II

The fifth projectile fell in Barnes that night, about three miles to the north-east of the house On the night following, the sixth projectile fell on Wimbledon Common.

Every day, at frequent intervals, we would walk out to the ridge and search for sign of the Martians. During the evening of the day we started work on the new Machine, we saw five of the glittering tripods marching together, heading towards London. Their heat-cannons were sheathed, and they strode with the confidence of the victor who has nothing to fear. These five must have been the occupants of the Bushy Park projectile, who were going up to join the others which even now, we assumed, were rampaging through London.

There were marked changes taking place in the Thames Valley, and they were not ones we cared for. The clouds of black vapour were swept away by the Martians: for one whole day two battle-machines worked at clearing the muck, using an immense tube which sent forth a fierce jet of steam. This soon swept away the vapour, leaving a black, muddy liquid which flowed into the river. But the river itself was slowly changing.

The Martians had brought with them seeds of the ubiquitous red weed, and were deliberately sowing them along the banks. One day we saw a dozen or so of the legged ground vehicles, scurrying along the riverside walks and throwing up clouds of tiny seeds. In no time at all the alien vegetables were growing and spreading. Compared with the Spartan conditions under which it survived on Mars, the weed must have found the rich soil and moist atmosphere of England like a well fertilized hothouse. Within a week of our return to Reynolds House, the whole length of the river visible to us was choked with the lurid weed, and soon it was spreading to the waterside meadows. On sunny mornings, the creaking of its prodigious growth was so loud that, high and set back from the river as the house was, we could hear the sinister noise when we were inside with the doors and windows closed. It was a constant background to our secret work, and while we could hear it we were always upset by it. The weed was even taking hold on the dry, wooded slopes below the house, and as it encroached the trees turned brown, although it was still the height of summer.

How long would it be before the captive humans were set to cutting back the weed?

III

On the day after the tenth projectile landed – this, like the three that had directly preceded it, had fallen somewhere in central London – Mr Wells summoned me to the laboratory and announced that he had at last made a substantial advance.

Order had been restored in the laboratory. It had been thoroughly cleaned and tidied, and Amelia had draped huge velvet curtains over all the window-panes, so that work could continue after nightfall. Mr Wells had been in the laboratory from the moment he had left his bed, and the air was pleasantly smoked from his pipe.

'It was the circuitry of the crystals that was baffling me,' he said, stretching back comfortably in one of the chairs he had brought from the smoking-room. 'You see, there is something about their chemical constituency that provides a direct current of electricity. The problem has been not to produce this effect, but to harness it to produce the attenuation field. Let me show you what I mean.'

He and Amelia had constructed a tiny apparatus on the bench. It consisted of a small wheel resting on a metal strip. Two tiny pieces of the crystalline substance had been attached to either side of the wheel. Mr Wells had connected various pieces of wire to the crystals, and the bare ends of these were resting on the surface of the bench.

'If I now connect together those wires I have here, you will see what happens.' Mr Wells took more pieces of wire and laid them across the various bare ends. As the last contact was made we all saw clearly that the little wheel had started to rotate slowly. 'You see, with this circuit the crystals provide a motive force.'

'Just like the bicycles!' I said.

Mr Wells did not know what I was talking about, but Amelia nodded vigorously.

'That's right,' she said. 'But there are more crystals used on the bicycles, for there is a greater weight to pull.'

Mr Wells disconnected the apparatus, because as the wheel turned it was tangling the wires which were connected to it.

'Now, however,' he said, 'if I complete the circuit in a different way ...' He bent closely over his work, peering first at the plans, then at the apparatus. 'Watch this carefully, for I suspect we will see something dramatic.'

We both stood by his shoulder, and watched as he connected first one wire then another. Soon only one remained bare.

'Now!'

Mr Wells touched the last wires together, and in that instant the whole apparatus – wheel, crystals and wires – vanished from our sight.

'It works!' I cried in delight, and Mr Wells beamed up at me.

'That is how we enter the attenuated dimension,' he said. 'As you know, as soon as the crystals are connected, the entire piece becomes attenuated. By connecting the device that way, I tapped the power that resides in the dimension, and my little experiment is now lost to us forever.'

'Where is it, though?' I said.

'I cannot say for certain, as it was a test-piece only. It is certainly moving in Space, at a very slow speed, and will continue to do so for ever. It is of no importance to us, for the secret of travel through the attenuated dimension is how we may control it. That is my next task.'

'Then how long will it be before we can build a new Machine?' I said.

'It will be several days more, I think.'

'We must be quick,' I said. 'With every day that passes the monsters tighten their hold on our world.'

'I am working as fast as I am able,' Mr Wells said without rancour, and then I noticed how his eyes showed dark circles around them. He had often been working in the laboratory long after Amelia and I had taken to our beds. 'We shall need a frame in which the mechanism can be carried, and one large enough to carry passengers. I believe Miss Fitzgibbon has already had an idea about this, and if you and she were to concentrate on this now, our work will end soon enough.'

'But a new Machine will be possible?' I said.

'I see no reason why it should not,' said Mr Wells. 'Now we have no desire to travel to futurity, our Machine need not be nearly so complicated as Sir William's.'

IV

Eight more days passed with agonizing slowness, but at last we saw the Space Machine taking shape.

Amelia's plan had been to use the frame of a bed as a base for the Machine, as this would provide the necessary sturdiness and space for the passengers. Accordingly, we searched the damaged servants' wing, and found an iron bedstead some five feet wide. Although it was coated with grime after the fire, it took less than an hour to clean it up. We carried it to the laboratory, and under Mr Wells's guidance began to connect to it the various pieces he produced. Much of this comprised the crystalline substance, in such quantities that it was soon clear that we would need every piece we could lay our hands on. When Mr Wells saw how quickly our reserves of the mysterious substance were being used up he expressed his doubts, but we pressed on nonetheless.

Knowing that we intended to travel in this Machine ourselves, we left enough room for somewhere to sit, and with this in mind I fitted out one end of the bedstead with cushions.

While our secret work continued in the laboratory, the Martians themselves were not idle.

Our hopes that military reinforcements would be able to deal with the incursion had been without foundation, for whenever we saw one of the battle-machines or legged vehicles in the valley below, it strode unchallenged and arrogant. The Martians were apparently consolidating their gains, for we saw much equipment being transferred from the various landing-pits in Surrey to London, and on many occasions we saw groups of captive people either being herded by or driven in one of the logged ground vehicles. The slavery had begun, and all that we had ever feared for Earth was coming to pass.

Meanwhile, the scarlet weed continued to flourish: the Thames Valley was an expanse of garish red, and scarcely a tree was left alive on the side of Richmond Hill. Already, shoots of the weeds were starting to encroach on the lawn of the house, and I made it my daily duty to cut it back. Where the lawn met the weeds was a muddy and slippery morass.

V

'I have done all I can,' said Mr Wells, as we stood before the outlandish contraption that once had been a bed. 'We need many more crystals, but I have used all we could find.' Nowhere in any of Sir William's drawings had there been so much as a single clue as to the constituency of the crystals. Therefore, unable to manufacture any more, Mr Wells had had to use those that Sir William had left behind. We had emptied the laboratory, and dismantled the four adapted bicycles which still stood in the outhouse, but even so Mr Wells declared that we needed at least twice as much crystalline substance as we had. He explained that the velocity of the Machine depended on the power the crystals produced.

'We have reached the most critical moment,' Mr Wells went on. 'The Machine, as it stands, is simply a collection of circuitry and metal. As you know, once it is activated it must stay permanently attenuated, and so I have had to incorporate an equivalent of Sir William's temporal fly-wheel. Once the Machine is in operation, that wheel must always turn so that it is not lost to us.'

He was indicating our makeshift installation, which was the wheel of the artillery piece blown off in the explosion. We had mounted this transversely on the front of the bedstead.

Mr Wells took a small, leather-bound notebook from his breast pocket, and glanced at a list of handwritten instructions he had compiled himself. He passed this to Amelia, and as she called them out one by one, he inspected various critical parts of the Space Machine's engine. At last he declared himself satisfied.

'We must now trust to our work,' he said softly, returning the notebook to his pocket. Without ceremony he placed one stout piece of wire against the iron frame of the bedstead, and turned a screw to hold it m place. Even before he had finished, Amelia and I noticed that the artillery wheel was turning slowly.

We stood back, hardly daring to hope that our work had been successful.

'Turnbull, kindly place your hand against the frame.'

'Will I receive an electrical shock?' I said, wondering why he did not do this himself.

'I should not think so. There is nothing to be afraid of.'

I extended my hand cautiously, then, catching Amelia's eye and seeing that she was smiling a little, I reached out resolutely and grasped the metal frame. As my fingers made contact the entire contraption shuddered visibly and audibly, just as had Sir William's Time Machine; the solid iron bedstead became as lissom as a young tree.

Amelia stretched out her hand, and then so did Mr Wells. We laughed aloud.

'You've done it, Mr Wells!' I said. 'We have built a Space Machine!'

'Yes, but we have not tested it yet. We must see if it can be safely driven.'

'Then let us do it at once!'

VI

Mr Wells mounted the Space Machine, and, sitting comfortably on the cushions, braced himself against the controls. By working a combination of levers he managed to shift the Machine first forwards and backwards, then to each side. Finally, he took the unwieldy Machine and drove it all around the laboratory.

None of this was seen by Amelia and myself. We have only Mr Wells's word that he tested the Machine this way... for as soon as he touched the levers he and the Machine instantly became invisible, reappearing only when the Machine was turned off.

'You cannot hear me when I speak to you?' he said, after his tour of the laboratory.

'We can neither hear nor see you,' said Amelia. 'Did you call to us?'

'Once or twice,' Mr Wells said, smiling. 'Turnbull, how does your foot feel?'

'My foot, sir?'

'I regret I inadvertently passed through it on my journey. You would not pull it out of the way when I called to you.'

I flexed my toes inside the boots I had borrowed from Sir William's dressing-room, but there seemed to be nothing wrong.

'Come, Turnbull, we must try this further. Miss Fitzgibbon, would you kindly ascend to the next floor? We shall try to follow you in the Machine. Perhaps if you would wait inside the bedroom I am using . . .?'

Amelia nodded, then left the laboratory. In a moment we heard her running up the stairs.

'Step aboard, Mr Turnbull. Now we shall see what this Machine can do!'

Almost before I had clambered on to the cushions beside Mr Wells, he had pushed one of the levers and we were moving forward. Around us, silence had fallen abruptly, and the distant clamouring of the weed-banks was absent.

'Let us see if we can fly,' said Mr Wells. His voice sounded flat and deep against the attenuated quiet. He tugged a second lever and at once we lifted smartly towards the ceiling. I raised my hands to ward off the blow ... but as we reached the wood and jagged glass of the laboratory roof we passed right through! For a moment I had the queer experience of finding just my head out in the open, but then the bulk of the Space Machine had thrust me through, and it was as if we were hovering in the air above the conservatory-like building. Mr Wells turned one of the horizontally mounted levers, and we moved at quite prodigious speed through the brick wall of the upper storey of the main house. We found ourselves hovering above a landing. Chuckling to himself, Mr Wells guided the Machine towards his guest-room, and plunged us headlong through the closed door.

Amelia was waiting within, standing by the window.

'Here we are!' I called as soon as I saw her. 'It flies too!'

Amelia showed no sign of awareness.

'She cannot hear us,' Mr Wells reminded me. 'Now . . . I must see if I can settle us on the floor.'

We were hovering some eighteen inches above the carpet, and Mr Wells made fine adjustments to his controls. Meanwhile Amelia had left the window and was looking curiously around, evidently waiting for us to materialize. I amused myself first by blowing a kiss to her, then by pulling a face, but she responded to neither.

Suddenly, Mr Wells released his levers, and we dropped with a bump to the floor. Amelia started in surprise.

'There you are!' she said. 'I wondered how you would appear.'

'Allow us to take you downstairs,' said Mr Wells, gallantly. 'Climb aboard, my dear, and let us make a tour of the house.'

So, for the next half-hour, we experimented with the Space Machine, and Mr Wells grew accustomed to making it manoeuvre exactly as he wished. Soon he could make it turn, soar, halt, as if he had been at its controls all his life. At first, Amelia and I clung nervously to the bedstead, for it seemed to turn with reckless velocity, but gradually we too saw that for all its makeshift appearance, the Space Machine was every bit as scientific as its original.

We left the house just once, and toured the garden. Here Mr Wells tried to increase our forward speed, but to our disappointment we found that for all its other qualities, the Space Machine could travel no faster than the approximate speed of a running man.

'It is the shortage of crystals,' said Mr Wells, as we soared through the upper branches of a walnut tree 'If we had more of those, there would be no limit to our velocity.'

'Never mind,' said Amelia. 'We have no use for great speed. Invisibility is our prime advantage.'

I was staring out past the house to the overgrown redness of the valley. It was the constant reminder of the urgency of our efforts.

'Mr Wells,' I said quietly. 'We have our Space Machine. Now is the time to put it to use.'

TWENTY-THREE

An Invisible Nemesis

•

I

When we had landed the Space Machine, and I had loaded several of the hand-grenades on to it, Mr Wells was worried about the time we had left to us.

'The sun will be setting in two hours,' he said. 'I should not care to drive the Machine in darkness.'

'But, sir, we can come to no harm in the attenuation.'

'I know, but we must at some time return to the house and leave the attenuated dimension. When we do that, we must be absolutely certain there are no Martians around. How terrible it would be if we returned to the house in the night, and discovered that the Martians were waiting for us!'

'We have been here for more than two weeks,' I said, 'and no Martian has so much as glanced our way.'

Mr Wells had to agree with this, but he said: 'I think we must not lose sight of the seriousness of our task, Turnbull. Because we have been confined so long in Richmond, we have no knowledge of the extent of the Martians' success. Certainly they have subdued all the land we can see from here; in all probability they are now the lords of the entire country. For all we know, their domain might be worldwide. If we are, as we suspect, in command of the one weapon they cannot resist, we cannot afford to lose that advantage by taking unnecessary risks. We have a tremendous responsibility thrust upon us.'

'Mr Wells is right, Edward,' said Amelia. 'Our revenge on the Martians is late, but it is all we have.'

'Very well,' I said. 'But we must try at least one sortie today. We do not yet know if our scheme will work.'

So at last we mounted the Space Machine, and sat with suppressed excitement as Mr Wells guided us away from the house, above the obscene red tangle of weeds, and out towards the heart of the Thames Valley.

As soon as we were under way, I saw some of the wisdom of the others' words. Our search for Martian targets was to be unguided, for we had no idea where the evil brutes currently were. We could search all day for just one, and in the boundless scale of the Martians' intrusion we might never find our goal.

We flew for about half an hour, circling over the river, looking this way and that for some sign of the invaders, but without success.

At last Amelia suggested a plan which presented logic and simplicity. We knew, she said, where the projectiles had fallen, and further, we knew that the Martians used the pits as their headquarters. Surely, if we were seeking the monsters, the pits would be the most sensible places to look first.

Mr Wells agreed with this, and we turned directly for the nearest of the pits. This was the one in Bushy Park, where the fourth projectile had fallen. Suddenly, as I realized we were at last on the right track, I felt my heart pounding with excitement.

The valley was a dreadful sight: the red weed was growing rampantly over almost every physical protuberance, houses included. The landscape seemed from this height to be like a huge undulating field of red grass bent double by heavy rain. In places, the weeds had actually altered the course of the river, and wherever there was low-lying ground stagnant lakes had formed.

The pit had been made in the north-eastern corner of Bushy Park, and was difficult to distinguish by virtue of the fact that it, no less than anywhere else, was heavily overgrown with weed. At last we noticed the cavernous mouth of the projectile itself, and Mr Wells brought the Space Machine down to hover a few feet from the entrance. All was dark within, and there was no sign of either the Martians or their machines.

We were about to move away, when Amelia suddenly pointed into the heart of the projectile.

'Edward, look... it is one of the people!'

Her move had startled me, but I looked in the direction she was indicating. Sure enough, lying a few feet inside the hold was a human figure. I thought for a moment that this must be one of the hapless victims snatched by the Martians ... but then I saw that the body was that of a very tall man, and that he was wearing a black uniform. His skin was a mottled red, and his face, which was turned towards us, was ugly and distorted.

We stared in silence at this dead Martian human. It was perhaps even more of a shock to see one of our erstwhile allies in this place than it would have been to see one of the monsters.

We explained to Mr Wells that the man was probably one of the humans coerced into driving the projectile, and he looked at the dead Martian with great interest.

'The strain of our gravity must have been too much for his heart,' said Mr Wells.

'That has not upset the monsters' plans,' Amelia said.

'Those beasts are without hearts,' said Mr Wells, but I supposed that he was speaking figuratively.

We recalled that another cylinder had fallen near Wimbledon, and so we turned the Space Machine away from the pathetic figure of the dead Martian human, and set off eastwards at once. From Bushy Park to Wimbledon is a distance of some five miles, and so even at our maximum speed the flight took nearly an hour. During this time we were appalled to see that even parts of Richmond Park were showing signs of the red weed.

Mr Wells had been casting several glances over his shoulder to see how long there was until sunset, and was clearly still unhappy with this expedition so soon before nightfall. I resolved that if the Martian pit at Wimbledon was also empty, then it would be I who proposed an immediate return to Reynolds House. The satisfaction of taking positive action at last had excited my nerve, though, and

I would be sorry not to make at least one kill before returning.

Then at last we had our chance. Amelia suddenly cried out, and pointed towards the south. There, striding slowly from the direction of Maiden, came a battle-machine.

We were at that moment travelling at a height approximately equal to that of the platform, and it was an instinct we all shared that the beast inside must have seen us, so deliberately did it march in our direction.

Mr Wells uttered a few reassuring words, and raised the Space Machine to a new height and bearing, one which would take us circling around the tripodal engine.

I reached forward with shaking hands, and took hold of one of the hand-grenades.

Amelia said: 'Have you ever handled one of those before, Edward?'

'No,' I said. 'But I know what to do.'

'Please be careful.'

We were less than half a mile from the Titan, and still we headed in towards it from an oblique angle.

'Where do you want me to place the Machine?' said Mr Wells, concentrating fiercely on his controls.

'Somewhat above the platform,' I said. 'Approach from the side, because I do not wish to pass directly in front.'

'The monster cannot see us,' said Amelia.

'No,' I said, remembering that ferocious visage. 'But we might see it.'

I found myself trembling anew as we approached. The thought of what was squatting so loathsomely inside that metal edifice was enough to reawaken all the fears and angers I had suffered on Mars, but I forced myself to be calm.

'Can you maintain the Machine at a steady speed above the platform?' I asked Mr Wells.

'I'll do what I can, Turnbull.'

His cautious words gave no indication of the ease with which he brought our flying bed-frame to a point almost exactly above the platform. I leaned over the side of our Space Machine, while

Amelia held my free hand, and I stared down at the roof of the platform.

There were numerous apertures here – some of which were large enough for me to make out the glistening body of the monster – and the grenade lodged in any one of them would probably do what was necessary. In the end I chose a large port just beside where the heat-cannon would emerge, reasoning that somewhere near there must be the incredible furnace which produced the heat. If that were fractured, then what damage the grenade did not inflict would be completed by the subsequent explosive release of energy.

'I see my target,' I shouted to Mr Wells. 'I will call out as soon as I have released the grenade, and at that moment we must move away as far as possible.'

Mr Wells confirmed that he understood, and so I sat up straight for a moment, and eased the restraining pin from the detonating arm. While Amelia supported me once more, I leaned over and held the grenade above the platform.

'Ready, Mr Wells...?' I called. '*Now*!'

At the selfsame instant that I let go the grenade, Mr Wells took the Space Machine in a fast climbing arc away from the battle-machine. I stared back, anxious to see the effect of my attack.

A few seconds later, there was an explosion below and slightly behind the Martian tripod.

I stared in amazement. The grenade had fallen through the metal bulk of the platform and exploded harmlessly!

I said: 'I didn't expect that to happen ...'

'My dear,' said Amelia. 'I think the grenade was still attenuated.'

Below us, the Martian strode on, oblivious of the deadly attack it had just survived.

II

I was seething with disappointment as we returned safely to the house. By then the sun had set, and a long, glowing evening lay across the transformed valley. As the other two went to their rooms to dress for dinner, I paced to and fro in the laboratory, determined that our vengeance should not be snatched away from us.

I ate with the others, but kept my silence throughout the meal. Amelia and Mr Wells, sensing my distemper, talked a little of the success of our building the Space Machine, but the abortive attack was carefully avoided.

Later, Amelia said she was going to the kitchen to bake some bread, and so Mr Wells and I repaired to the smoking-room. With the curtains carefully drawn, and sitting by the light of one candle only, we talked of general matters until Mr Wells considered it safe to discuss other tactics.

'The difficulty is twofold,' he said. 'Clearly, we must not be attenuated when we place the explosive, otherwise the grenade has no effect, and yet we must be attenuated during the explosion, otherwise we shall be affected by the blast.'

'But if we turn off the Space Machine, the Martian will observe us,' I said.

'That is why I say it will be difficult. We have both seen how fast those brutes react to any threat.'

'We could land the Space Machine on the roof of the tripod itself.'

Mr Wells shook his head slowly. 'I admire your inventiveness, Turnbull, but it would not be practicable. I had great difficulty even keeping abreast of the engine. To essay a landing on a moving object would be extremely hazardous.'

We both recognized the urgency of finding a solution. For an hour or more we argued our ideas back and forth, but we arrived at nothing satisfactory. In the end, we went to the drawing-room where Amelia was waiting for us, and presented the problem to her.

She thought for a while, then said: 'I see no difficulty. We have plenty of grenades, and can therefore afford a few misses. All we should do is hover above our target, although at a somewhat greater height than today. Mr Wells then switches off the attenuation field, and while we fall through the air Edward can lob a grenade at the Martian. By the time the bomb explodes, we should be safely back inside the attenuated dimension, and it will not matter how close we are to the explosion.'

I stared at Mr Wells, then at Amelia, considering the implications of such a hair-raising scheme.

'It sounds awfully dangerous,' I said in the end.

'We can strap ourselves to the Space Machine,' Amelia said. 'We need not fall out.'

'But even so ...'

'Do you have an alternative plan?' she said.

III

The following morning we made our preparations, and were ready to set out at an early hour.

I must confess to considerable trepidation at the whole enterprise, and I think Mr Wells shared some of my misgivings. Only Amelia seemed confident of the plan, to the extent that she offered to take on the task of aiming the hand-grenades herself. Naturally, I would hear nothing of this, but she remained the only one of the three of us who exuded optimism and confidence that morning. Indeed, she had been up since first light and made us all sandwiches, so that we need not feel constrained to return to the house for lunch. Additionally, she had fixed some straps – which she had made from leather trouser-belts – across the bedstead's cushions to hold us in place.

Just as we were about to leave, Amelia walked abruptly from the laboratory, and Mr Wells and I stared after her. She returned in a few moments, this time carrying a large suitcase.

I looked at it with interest, not recognizing it at first for what it was.

Amelia set it down on the floor, and opened the lid. Inside, wrapped carefully in tissue-paper, were the three pairs of goggles I had brought with me the day I came to see Sir William!

She passed one pair to me, smiling a little. Mr Wells took his at once.

'Capital notion, Miss Fitzgibbon,' he said. 'Our eyes will need protection if we are to fall through the air.'

Amelia put hers on before we left, and I helped her with the clasp, making sure that it did not get caught in her hair. She settled the goggles on her brow.

'Now we are better equipped for our outing,' she said, and went towards the Space Machine.

I followed, holding my goggles in my hand, and trying not to dwell on my memories.

IV

We were in for a day of remarkably good hunting. Within a few minutes of sailing out over the Thames, Amelia let forth a cry, and pointed to the west. There, walking slowly through the streets of Twickenham, was a Martian battle-machine. It had its metal arms dangling, and it was moving from house to house, evidently seeking human survivors. By the emptiness of the mesh net that hung behind the platform we judged that its pickings had been poor. It seemed incredible to us that there should still be any survivors at all in these ravaged towns, although our own survival was a clue to the fact that several people must still be clinging to life in the cellars and basements of the houses.

We circled warily around the evil machine, once again experiencing that unease we had felt the day before.

'Take the Space Machine higher, if you will,' Amelia said to Mr Wells. 'We must judge our approach carefully.'

I took a hand-grenade, and held it in readiness. The battle-machine had paused momentarily, reaching through the upper window of a house with one of its long, articulate arms.

Mr Wells brought the Space Machine to a halt, some fifty feet above the platform.

Amelia pulled her goggles down over her eyes, and advised us to do the same. Mr Wells and I fixed our goggles in place, and checked the position of the Martian. It was quite motionless, but for the reaching of its metal arms.

'I'm ready, sir,' I said, and slid the pin from the striking lever.

'Very well,' said Mr Wells. 'I am turning off the attenuation ... now!'

As he spoke we all experienced an unpleasant lurching sensation, our stomachs seemed to turn a somersault, and the air rushed past us. At the behest of gravity we plunged towards the Martian machine. In the same instant I hurled the grenade desperately down at the Martian.

'Bombs away!' I shouted.

Then there was a second lurch, and our fall was arrested. Mr Wells manipulated his levers, and we soared away to one side in the dead silence of that weird dimension.

Looking back at the Martian we waited for the explosion ... and seconds later it came. My aim had been accurate, and a ball of smoke and fire blossomed silently on the roof of the battle-machine.

The monster-creature inside the platform, taken by surprise, reacted with astonishing alacrity. The tower leaped back from the house, and in the same moment we saw the barrel of the heat-cannon snapping into position. The cowl of the platform swung round as the monster sought its attacker. As the smoke of the grenade drifted away we saw that the explosion had blown a jagged hole in the roof, and the engine inside must have been damaged. The battle-machine's movements were not as smooth or as fast as some we had seen, and a dense green smoke was pouring from within.

The heat-beam flared into action, swinging erratically in all directions. The battle-machine took three steps forward, hesitated, then staggered back again. The heat-beam flashed across several of the near-by houses, causing the roofs to burst into flame.

Then, in a ball of brilliant-green fire, the whole hideous platform exploded. Our bomb had ruptured the furnace inside.

To us, sitting inside the silence and safety of attenuation, the destruction of the Martian was a soundless, mysterious event. We saw the fragments of the destructive engine flying in all directions, saw one of the huge legs cartwheeling away, saw the bulk of the shattered platform fall in a hundred pieces across the rooftops of Twickenham.

Curiously enough, I was not elated by this sight, and this sentiment was shared by the other two. Amelia stared quietly across at the twisted metal that once had been an engine of war, and Mr Wells merely said: 'I see another.'

Towards the south, striding in the direction of Molesey, was a second battle-machine.

Mr Wells swung his levers, and soon we were speeding towards our next target.

V

By midday we had accounted for a total of four Martians: three of these were in their tripods, and one was in the control cabin of one of the legged vehicles. Each attack was conducted without danger to ourselves, and each time the chosen monster had been taken by surprise. Our activities were not going unnoticed, however, for the legged vehicle had been speeding towards the destroyed tripod in Twickenham when we spotted it. We realized from this that the Martians must have had some kind of intricate signalling system between themselves – Mr Wells hypothesized that it was a telepathic communication, although Amelia and I, having seen the sophisticated science on Mars, suspected that it would be a technical device – for our vengeful activities seemed to have provoked a good deal of movement on the Martians' behalf. As we flew to and fro across the valley, we saw several tripods approaching from the direction of London, and we knew that we would not run short of targets that day.

With the killing of the fourth Martian, though, Amelia suggested we rest and eat the sandwiches we had brought. As she said this we were still hovering about the battle-machine we had just attacked.

The killing of this monster had been an odd affair. We had

found the battle-machine standing alone on the edge of Richmond Park, facing towards the south-west. Its three legs had been drawn together, and its metal arms were furled, and at first we suspected that the machine was unoccupied. Moving in for the kill, though, we had passed in front of the multi-faceted ports and for a moment we had glimpsed those saucer-eyes staring balefully out across Kingston.

We had taken our time with this attack, and with my increasing experience I was able to lob the grenade into the platform with great accuracy. When the bomb went off it had exploded inside the cabin occupied by the monster, blasting open several metal plates and presumably destroying the monster outright, but the furnace itself had not been ruptured. The tower still stood, leaning slightly to one side and with green smoke pouring from within, but substantially intact.

Mr Wells took the Space Machine a decent distance away from the battle-machine, and settled it near the ground. By consensus we agreed to stay inside the attenuation, for the green smoke was making us nervous that the furnace might yet explode of its own accord.

So, overshadowed by the damaged Titan, we quickly ate what must have been one of the strangest picnic lunches ever taken in the rolling countryside of the Park.

We were about to set off again when Mr Wells drew our attention to the fact that another battle-machine had appeared. This was hurrying towards us, evidently coming to investigate the work we had done on its colleague.

We were safe enough, but agreed to take the Space Machine into the air, and so be ready for a quick foray.

Our confidence was increasing; with four kills behind us we were establishing a deadly routine. Now, as we rose above the Park, and saw the approaching battle-machine, we could not help but see that its heat-cannon was raised and its articulate arms were poised to strike. Clearly its monstrous driver knew that someone or something had attacked successfully, and was determined to defend itself.

We stayed at a safe distance, and watched as the newcomer went to the tower and closely inspected the damage.

I said: 'Mr Wells, shall we bomb it now?'

Mr Wells stayed silent, his brow furrowed over the top of his goggles.

'The creature is very alert,' he said. 'We cannot risk a chance shot from the heat-cannon.'

'Then let us seek another target,' I said.

Nevertheless, we stayed on watch for several minutes, hoping the Martian would relax its guard long enough to allow us to attack. However, even as the creature inside carried out a cautious examination of the damage, the heat-cannon turned menacingly above the roof and the tentacular metal arms flexed nervously.

With some reluctance we turned away at last, and headed back towards the west. As we flew, Amelia and I cast several backward glances, still wary of what the second Martian would do. Thus it was that we saw, when we were less than half a mile away, that our grenade had, after all, weakened the casing of the furnace. We saw an immense, billowing explosion of green … and the second battle-machine staggered backwards and crashed in a tangle of metal to the floor of the Park.

That was how, by a stroke of good fortune, we slaughtered our fifth Martian monster.

VI

Considerably cheered by this accidental success we continued our quest, although it was now with a bravura tempered by caution. As Mr Wells pointed out, it was not the Martian machines we had to destroy, but the monster-creatures themselves. A battle-machine was agile and well-armed, and although its destruction certainly killed its driver, the legged ground vehicles were easier targets because the driver was not enclosed above.

So it was that we agreed to concentrate on the smaller vehicles.

That afternoon was one of almost unqualified success. Only

once did we fail to kill a Martian with our first strike and that was when I, in my haste, neglected to pull the pin from the grenade. However, on our second pass the monster was effectively and spectacularly destroyed.

When we returned to Reynolds House in the evening, we had accounted for a total of eleven of the Martian brutes. This, if our estimate that each projectile carried five monsters was correct, accounted for more than one-fifth of their total army!

It was with considerable optimism that we retired to bed that night.

The following day we loaded our Space Machine with more grenades, and set off again.

To our consternation we discovered that the Martians had learned by our ventures of the day before. Now no legged ground vehicle moved unless it was accompanied by a battle-machine, but so assured of our impregnability were we that we resolved that this presented us with two targets instead of one!

Accordingly, we prepared our attack with great precision, swooped down from above, and were rewarded with the sight of the battle-machine being blown to smithereens! From there, it was but a simple task to chase and destroy the legged ground vehicle.

Later that day we disposed of two more in the same way, but that was our total score for the day. (One legged vehicle was allowed to pass unharmed, for it was carrying a score or more of human captives.) Four was not as healthy a tally as eleven, but even so we considered we had done well, and so once more retired in a state of elation.

The next day was one with no success at all, for we saw no Martians about. We ranged, in our search, even as far as the fire-blackened heath at Woking, but here simply found the pit and its projectile empty both of Martians and their devices.

At the sight of the ruined town on the hill, Amelia and I noticed that Mr Wells grew wistful, and we recalled how he had been so abruptly separated from his wife.

'Sir, would you like us to fly to Leatherhead?' I said.

He shook his head forcefully. 'I wish I could allow myself the indulgence, but our business is with the Martians. My wife will be well; it is obvious that the invaders moved to the northeast from here. There will be time enough for reunion.'

I admired the resolution in his voice, but later that evening Amelia told me that she had noticed a tear running down Mr Wells's cheek. Perhaps, she said, Mr Wells suspected that his wife had already been killed, and that he was not yet ready to face up to this.

For this reason, as well as for our lack of success, we were in no great spirits that night, and so we retired early.

The next day we were luckier: two Martians succumbed to our grenades. This was the odd fact though: both the battle-machines stood, like the one we had found near Kingston, alone and still, the three legs drawn together. There was no attempt at self-defence; one stood with its heat-cannon pointing stiffly towards the sky, the other had not even raised its. Of course, as we were attacking battle-machines we swooped with great care, but we all agreed that our kills were suspiciously easy.

Then came another day with no more Martians seen at all, and on that evening Mr Wells pronounced a verdict.

'We must,' he said, 'turn our attention at last to London. We have so far been snipers against the straggling flanks of a mighty army. Now we must confront the concentrated strength of that army, and fight it to the death.'

Brave words indeed, but ones which did not reflect the suspicion which, I afterwards discovered, had been growing in us all for the last three days.

TWENTY-FOUR

Of Science And Conscience

•

I

The day following Mr Wells's stern pronouncement, we stowed the remainder of our hand-grenades aboard the Space Machine, and set off at a moderate speed towards London We kept our eyes open for a sign of the battle-machines, but there was none about

We flew first over Richmond town, and saw the dark residue of the black smoke that had suffocated its streets Only by the river, where the red weed grew in mountainous tangling clumps, was there relief from the sight of the black, sooty powder that covered everything North of Richmond was Kew Gardens, and here, although the Pagoda still stood, most of the priceless plantations of tropical plants had succumbed to the vile weed

We headed more directly towards London then, flying over Mortlake Not far from the brewery, in the centre of an estate of modern villas, one of the projectiles had landed, and here it had caused untold damage with the force of its explosive landing I saw that Mr Wells was regarding the scene thoughtfully, so I suggested to him that we might fly a little closer Accordingly he brought the Space Machine down in a gentle approach, and for a few minutes we hovered above the terrible desolation.

In the centre of the pit was, of course, the empty shell of the projectile. What was much more interesting was the evidence that, for some time at least, this place had been a centre of the Martians' activity. There were no battle-machines in sight, but standing beside the gaping mouth of the projectile were two of the legged ground vehicles, and sprawled untidily behind them was one of the spiderlike handling-machines. Its many metal tentacles were folded, and the normal brilliant sheen of the polished surfaces had started to corrode in the oxygen-rich air.

I was all for landing the Space Machine and exploring on foot, so quiet was the scene, but neither Amelia nor Mr Wells considered it safe. Instead, we allowed the Machine to drift slowly about the pit, while we sat in silence. We were daunted and impressed by what we saw the pit itself had been re-fashioned, so that the earth thrown up by the impact had been built into high ramparts, and the floor had been levelled to facilitate the machines' movements One end of the pit had been reworked to provide a sloping ramp for the ground vehicles.

Suddenly, Amelia gasped, and covered her mouth with her hand.

'Oh, Edward ...' she said, and turned her face away

I saw what she had noticed. Dwarfed by the looming bulk of the projectile, and nestling in its shadow, was one of the killing cubicles. Lying all about, some half-buried, were the bodies of human beings. Mr Wells had seen the shocking sight in the same instant, and without further ado he sent the Space Machine soaring away from that place of hell ... but not before we had realized that lying in the shadow of the projectile were perhaps a hundred or more of the corpses.

We flew on, heading in an easterly direction, and in almost no time we were over the grey, mean streets of Wandsworth. Mr Wells slowed our passage, and set the Machine to hover.

He shook his head.

' I had no idea of the scale of their murders,' he said.

'We had allowed ourselves to neglect the fact,' I said 'Each monster requires the blood of a human being every day. The longer the Martians are allowed to stay alive the longer that slaughter will continue.'

Amelia said nothing, clutching my hand.

'We cannot delay,' said Mr Wells. 'We must continue bombing until every one is dead.'

'But where are the Martians?' I said. 'I assumed London would be teeming with them.'

We looked in every direction, but apart from isolated pillars of smoke, where buildings yet burned, there was not a single sign of the invaders.

'We must search them out,' said Mr Wells. 'However long it takes.'

'Are they still in London?' said Amelia. 'How do we know that they have not finished their work here, and are not even now destroying other cities?'

Neither I nor Mr Wells knew the answer to that.

'All we can do,' I said, 'is to search for them and kill them. If London has been abandoned by them, we will have to go in pursuit. I see no alternative.'

Mr Wells had been staring down disparagingly at the streets of Wandsworth; that most ugly of London suburbs had, unaccountably, been spared by the Martians, although like everywhere else it was deserted. He moved the controlling levers decisively, and set our course again for the heart of London.

II

Of all the Thames bridges we saw, Westminster was the one least overgrown with the red weed, and so Mr Wells took us down and we landed in the centre of the roadway. No Martian could approach us without walking out across the bridge, and that would give us enough warning so that we could start the Space Machine and escape.

For the last hour we had flown over the southern suburbs of the city. The extent of the desolation was almost beyond words. Where the Martians had not attacked with their heat-beams they had smothered with their black smoke, and where neither had been brought to bear the red weed had sprung willingly from the river to choke and tangle.

We had seen nobody at all, the only movement had been that

of a hungry dog, hopping with one leg broken through the streets of Lambeth.

Much debris floated in the river, and we saw many small boats overturned. In the Pool of London we had seen a score of corpses, caught by some freak of the tide, bobbing whitely by the entrance to Surrey Docks.

Then we had set our course by the landmarks we knew, and come to Westminster Bridge. We had seen the Tower of London, with its stout walls unscathed by the Martians, but its green swards had become a jungle of Martian weed. Tower Bridge too, its roadway left open, had long strands of weed cobwebbing its graceful lines. We had seen the high dome of St Paul's, and noticed how it stood undamaged above the lower buildings of the City; our mood changed as we passed beyond it and saw that on its western side a gaping hole had been made.

So at last we landed on Westminster Bridge, well depressed by what we had seen. Mr Wells turned off the attenuation, and ut once we breathed the air of London, and heard its sounds.

We smelt . . .

We smelt the residue of smoke; the bitter, metallic tang of the weed, the sweetness of putrefaction; the cool salty airs of the river; the heady odour of the macadamed roadway, simmering in the summer's sunshine.

We heard . . .

A great silence overwhelmed London. There was the flow of the river below the bridge, and an occasional creak from the weed which still grew prolifically by the parapet. But there was no clatter of hooves, no grind of wheels, no cries or calls of people, nor sound of footfall.

Directly before us stood the Palace of Westminster, topped by the tower of Big Ben, unharmed. The clock had stopped at seventeen minutes past two.

We pushed back our goggles, and stepped down from the Space Machine. I went with Amelia to stand by the side of the bridge, staring up the river. Mr Wells walked off alone, looking in a brooding fashion at the mountainous piles of weed that had submerged the Victoria Embankment. He had been silent and thoughtful as we toured the deathful city, and now as he stood by himself, staring down at the sluggishly flowing river, I saw that his shoulders were slumped and his expression was pensive.

Amelia too was staring at our friend, but then she slipped her hand into mine and for a moment rested her cheek against my shoulder.

'Edward, this is terrible! I had no idea that things were so bad.'

I stared gloomily at the view, trying to find something about it that would indicate some optimistic development, but the emptiness and stillness were total. I had never before seen the skies above London so free of soot, but that was hardly recompense for this utter destruction of the greatest city in the world.

'Soon everywhere will be like this,' Amelia said. 'We were wrong to think we could tackle the Martians, even though we have killed a few. What I find hardest to accept is that all this is our doing, Edward. We brought this menace to the world.'

'No,' I said instantly. 'We are not to blame.'

I felt her stiffen. 'We can't absolve ourselves of this.'

I said: 'The Martians would have invaded Earth whether we took a part or not. We saw their preparations. If there is any consolation to be found, then it is that only ten projectiles made it to Earth. Your revolution prevented the monsters from carrying out their plans to the full. What we see is bad enough, but think how much worse it might have been.'

'I suppose so.'

She fell silent for a few seconds, but then went on: 'Edward, we must return to Mars. While there is any chance that the monsters rule that world, Earthmen can never relax their guard. We have the Space Machine to take us, for if one can be built so hastily in the urgent circumstances in which we worked, another more powerful Machine can be built, one that would carry a thousand armed men. I promised the people of Mars that I would return, and now we must.'

I listened to her words carefully, and realized that the passions that had driven her on Mars had been replaced by wisdom and understanding.

'We will go back to Mars one day,' I said. 'There is no alternative.'

We had both forgotten Mr Wells's presence while we spoke, but now he turned from his position and walked slowly back towards us. I saw that in the few minutes he had been by himself a fundamental change had come over his bearing. The weight of defeat had been removed from his shoulders, and his eyes were gleaming once more.

'You two look most uncommonly miserable!' he cried. 'There is no cause for that. Our work is over. The Martians have not left ... they are still in London, and the battle is won!'

III

Amelia and I stared uncomprehendingly at Mr Wells after he had made this unexpected statement. He moved towards the Space Machine, and placing one foot on the iron frame he turned to face us, clasping his jacket lapels in his fists. He cleared his throat.

'This has been a war of worlds,' said Mr Wells, speaking calmly and in a clear, ringing voice. 'Where we have been mistaken is to treat it as a war of intelligences. We have seen the invaders' monstrous appearance, but persuaded by their qualities of cunning, valour and intelligence have thought of them as men. So we have fought them as if they were men, and we have not done well. Our Army was overrun, and our houses were burnt and crushed. However, the Martians' domain on Earth is a small one. I dare say when the recovery is made we shall discover that no more than a few hundred square miles of territory have been conquered. Even so, small as has been the battleground, this has been a war between worlds, and when the Martians came to Earth so rudely they did not realize what they were taking on.'

'Sir,' I said, 'if you are speaking of allies, we have seen none. No armies have come to our assistance, unless they too were instantly overcome.'

Mr Wells gestured impatiently. 'I am not speaking of armies, Turnbull, although they will come in good time, as will the grain-ships and the goods-trains. No, our true allies are all about us, invisible, just as we in our Machine were invisible!'

I glanced upwards reflexively, almost expecting a second Space Machine to appear from the sky.

'Look at the weeds, Turnbull!' Mr Wells pointed to the stems that grew a few feet from where we stood. 'See how the leaves are blighted? See how the stems are splitting even as they grow? While mankind has been concerned with the terrible intelligence of the monsters, these plants have been waging their own battles. Our soil will not feed them with the minerals they require, and our bees will not pollinate their flowers. These weeds are dying, Turnbull. In the same way, the Martian monsters will die even if they have not done so already. The Martian effort is at an end, because intelligence is no match for nature. As the humans on Mars tampered with nature to make the monsters, and thereby provoked Nemesis, so the monsters sought to tamper with life on Earth, and they too have destroyed themselves.'

'Then where are the monsters now?' said Amelia.

'We shall find them soon enough,' Mr Wells said, 'but that will come in time. Our problem is no longer how to confront this menace, but how to enjoy the spoils of victory. We have the products of the Martian intelligence all about us, and these will be eagerly taken by our scientists. I suspect that the peaceful days of the past will never entirely return, for these battle-machines and walking vehicles are likely to bring fundamental changes to the way of life of everyone in the world. We stand in the early years of a new century, and it is one which will see many changes. At the heart of those changes will be a new battle: one between Science and Conscience. This is the battle the Martians lost, and it is one we must now fight!'

IV

Mr Wells lapsed into silence, his breathing heavy, and Amelia and I stood nervously before him.

At length he moved from his position, and lowered his fists. He cleared his throat again.

'I think this is no time for speech-making,' he said, apparently disconcerted at the way his eloquence had silenced us. ' To see this through, we must find the Martians. Later, I will contact my publisher and see if he would be interested in an edition of my thoughts on this topic.'

I looked around at the silent city. 'You cannot believe, sir, that after this the life of London will return to normal?'

'Not to normal, Turnbull. This war is not an ending, but a beginning! The people who fled will return; our institutions will re-establish themselves. Even the fabric of the city is, for I he most part, intact, and can be quickly rebuilt. The work of rebuilding will not end with structural repairs, for the Martian intrusion has itself served to heighten our own intelligence. As I have said, that presents its own dangers, but we will deal with those as the need arises.'

Amelia had been staring across the rooftops throughout our exchange, and now she pointed towards the north-west.

'Look, Edward, Mr Wells! I think there are some birds there!'

We looked in the direction she was indicating, and saw a flight of large birds, black against the brilliant sky, whirling and diving. They seemed to be a long way away.

'Let us investigate this,' said Mr Wells, adjusting the goggles over his eyes once more.

We went back to the Space Machine, and just as we were about to step aboard we heard an intrusive sound. It was one so familiar to us that we all reacted in the same moment: it was braying call of a Martian, its siren voice echoing from the faces of the buildings that fronted the river. But this was no war-try, nor call of the hunt. Instead it was coloured by pain and fear, an alien lament across a broken city.

The call was two notes, one following the other, endlessly repeated. 'Ulla, ulla, ulla, ulla ...'

V

We saw the first battle-machine in Regent's Park, standing alone. I reached immediately for a hand-grenade, but Mr Wells restrained me.

'No need for that, Turnbull,' he said.

He brought the Space Machine in close to the platform, and we saw the cluster of crows that surrounded it. The birds had found a way into the platform, and now they pecked and snatched at the flesh of the Martian within.

Its eyes gazed blankly at us through one of the ports at the front. The gaze was as baleful as ever, but where once it had been cold and malicious, now it was the fixed glare of death.

There was a second battle-machine at the foot of Primrose Hill, and here the birds had finished their work. Splashings of dried blood and discarded flesh lay on the grass a hundred feet beneath the platform.

So we came to the great pit that the Martians had built at the top of Primrose Hill. This, the largest of all, had become the centre of their operations against London. The earthworks covered the entire crest of the Hill, and ran down the far side. At the heart of them lay the projectile that had first landed here, but the fact that the pit had been subsequently enlarged and fortified was everywhere evident.

Here was the Martians' arsenal. Here had been brought their battle-machines, and the spiderlike handling-machines. And here, scattered all about, were the bodies of the dead Martians. Some were sprawled in the mouth of the projectile, some simply lay on the ground. Others, in a last valiant effort to confront the invisible foe, were inside the many battle-machines that stood all about.

Mr Wells landed the Space Machine a short distance away from the pit, and turned off the attenuation. He had landed upwind of the pit, so we were spared the worst effects of the terrible stench that emanated from the creatures.

With the attenuation off we could once more hear the cry of the dying Martian. It came from one of the battle-machines standing beside the pit. The cry was faltering now, and very weak We saw that the crows were in attendance, and even as we stepped out of the Space Machine the last call of pain was stilled.

'Mr Wells,' I said. 'It is just as you were saying. The Martians seemed to have been afflicted with some disease, from drinking the red blood of Englishmen!'

I realized that Mr Wells was paying no attention either to me or Amelia, and that he was staring out across London, seeing the immense stillness of the city with tear-filled eyes. We stood beside him, overwhelmed by the sight of the abandoned city, and still nervous of the alien towers that stood around us.

Mr Wells mopped his eyes with his kerchief, then wandered away from us towards the Martian whose call we had heard.

Amelia and I stood by our Space Machine, and watched him as he carefully skirted the rim of the pit, then stood beneath the battle-machine, staring up at the glittering engine above. I saw him fumble in a pocket, and produce the leather-bound note-hook he had been using in the laboratory. He wrote something inside this, then returned it to his pocket.

He was by the battle-machine for several minutes, but at last he returned to us He seemed to have recovered from his moment of emotion, and walked briskly and directly towards us.

'There is something I have never said to you before,' he said, addressing us both. 'I believe you saved my life, the day you found me by the river with the curate. I have never thanked you enough.'

I said: 'You built the Space Machine, Mr Wells. Nothing that we have accomplished would have been possible without that.'

He dismissed this remark with a wave of his hand.

'Miss Fitzgibbon,' he said. 'Will you excuse me if I leave on my own?'

'You are not going, Mr Wells?'

'I have much to do We will meet again, never fear. I shall tall on you at Richmond at the earliest opportunity.'

'But sir,' I said. 'Where are you going?'

'I think I must find my way to Leatherhead, Mr Turnbull. I was on a journey to find my wife when you met me, and now I must complete that journey. Whether she is dead or alive is something that is only my concern.'

'But we could take you to Leatherhead in the Space Machine,' said Amelia.

'There will be no need for that. I can find my way.'

He extended his hand to me, and I took it uncertainly. Mr Wells's grip was firm, but I did not understand why he should leave us so unexpectedly. When he released my hand he turned to Amelia, and she embraced him warmly.

He nodded to me, then turned away and walked down the side of the Hill.

Somewhere behind us there came a sudden sound: it was a high-pitched shrieking, not at all unlike the Martians' sirens. I jumped in alarm, and looked all about me ... but there was no movement from any of the Martian devices. Amelia, standing beside me, had also reacted to the sound, but her attention was taken up with Mr Wells's actions.

The gentleman in question had gone no more than a few yards, and, disregarding the shriek, was looking through the notebook. I saw him take two or three of the pages, then rip them out. He screwed them up in his hand, and tossed them amongst the debris of the Martians' presence. He glanced back at us, and saw we were both watching him.

After a moment he climbed back to where we stood.

'There's just one other thing, Turnbull,' he said. 'I have treated the account of your adventures on Mars with great seriousness, improbable as your story sometimes seemed.'

'But Mr Wells – '

He raised his hand to silence me. 'It would not be right to dismiss your account as total fabrication, but you would be hard put to substantiate what you told me.'

I was astounded to hear my friend say such things! His implication was no less than that Amelia and I were not telling the truth! I stepped forward angrily ... but then I felt a gentle touch on my arm.

I looked at Amelia, and saw that she was smiling.

'Edward, there is no need for this,' she said.

I saw that Mr Wells was smiling too, and that there was something of a gleam in his eye.

'We all have our tales to tell, Mr Turnbull,' he said. 'Good day to you.'

With that, he turned away and strode determinedly down the Hill, replacing the notebook in his breast-pocket.

'Mr Wells is behaving very strangely,' I said. 'He has come with us to this cataclysm, when suddenly he abandons us just when we most need him. Now he is casting doubt on—'

I was interrupted by a repetition of the shrieking sound we had heard a minute or so earlier. It was much closer now, and both Amelia and I realized simultaneously what it was.

We turned and stared down the Hill, towards the north-eastern side, where the railway-line runs towards Euston. A moment later we saw the train moving slowly over the rusting lines, throwing up huge white clouds of steam. The driver blew the whistle for the third time, and the shriek reverberated round the whole city below. As if in answer there came a second sound. A bell began to toll in a church by St John's Wood. Startled, the crows left their macabre pickings and flapped noisily into the sky.

Amelia and I leapt up and down at the crest of Primrose Hill, waving our kerchiefs to the passengers. As the train moved slowly out of sight, I took Amelia into my arms. I kissed her passionately, and, with a joyous sense of reawakening hope, we sat down on the bedstead to wait for the first people to arrive.

BRINGING NEWS FROM OUR WORLDS TO YOURS . . .

Want your news daily?

The Gollancz blog has instant updates on the hottest SF and Fantasy books.

Prefer your updates monthly?

Sign up for our in-depth newsletter.

www.gollancz.co.uk

Classic SF as you've never read it before.

Visit the SF Gateway to find out more!

www.sfgateway.com